Praise for *Jasper Jo*

'If we see a more entertaining, more heartf _____ ....
literature in the next twelve months, it will be a rare year indeed . . .
With this singular novel Silvey confirms his place as a young writer
to watch. In all important respects *Jasper Jones* is an Australian
To Kill a Mockingbird.' Michael Williams, *The Monthly*

'*Jasper Jones* confronts inhumanity and racism, as the stories of
Mark Twain and Harper Lee did. Silvey's voice is distinctive: astute,
witty, angry, understanding and self-assured.' *Weekend Australian*

'A finely crafted novel that deals with friendship, racism and social
ostracism . . . Saluting *To Kill a Mockingbird* and *The Adventures
of Huckleberry Finn*, Silvey movingly explores the stifling secrets
that lurk behind the most ordinary of facades.' *Marie Claire*

'Impossible to put down . . . There's tension, injustice, young love,
hypocrisy . . . and, above all, the certainty that Silvey has planted
himself in the landscape as one of our finest storytellers.' *Australian
Women's Weekly*

'Terrific . . . this is an enthralling novel that invites comparison with
Mark Twain and isn't found wanting. Silvey is able to switch the
mood from the tragic to the hilarious in an instant.' *Mail on Sunday*

'A richly rewarding exploration of truth and lies by a masterful
storyteller.' *Kirkus Reviews* (starred)

'*Jasper Jones* is a riveting tale, studded with laugh-out-loud and
life-affirming moments yet underpinned by a clear-eyed examination
of human weaknesses and misdemeanours.' *Adelaide Advertiser*

'Huckleberry Finn meets Atticus Finch in a WA country town in the 60s. It's genius. In the spirit of a classic, and written from the perspective of thirteen-year-old Charlie Bucktin, Silvey captures perfectly the personal questioning and coming-of-age issues of a boy on the cusp of growing up, and sets them against much bigger ethical and moral issues—racism, war and prejudice.' *West Australian*

'An engaging historical portrait of an ambitious, intelligent boy labouring—often amusingly—under the parochialism of an isolated town.' *The Age*

'Such is the skill of storytelling—especially the wonderful dialogue— that it quickly hooked me . . . it's the way it captures so many new emotions that won me over. There are parts where you'll laugh out loud, others where you'll reach for tissues. This is a very special book, and deserves to be read widely.' *Good Reading*

'Another beautifully constructed book with a page-turning narrative and outrageously good dialogue . . . I have no doubt this novel will further cement Craig's place at the forefront of the next generation of Australian novelists.' Wendy Were, Artistic Director and Chief Executive, Sydney Writers' Festival

'An engrossing and immediate page-turner that evokes an influential literary history while producing an original and rewarding narrative in its own right.' *Readings Monthly*

'*Catcher in the Rye* meets *To Kill a Mockingbird* in a novel that confronts racism, injustice, friendship and the tenderness of first love—as seen by bookish, guileless, thirteen-year-old Charlie Bucktin, led astray by the intriguing, dangerous eponymous outcast, Jasper Jones.' *Easy Living*

Craig Silvey is an author and screenwriter from Fremantle, Western Australia.

His critically acclaimed debut novel, *Rhubarb*, was published in 2004. His bestselling second novel, *Jasper Jones*, was released in 2009 and is considered a modern Australian classic. Published in over a dozen territories, *Jasper Jones* has won plaudits in three continents, including an International Dublin Literary Award shortlisting, a Michael J. Printz Award Honor, and a Miles Franklin Literary Award shortlisting. *Jasper Jones* was the Australian Book Industry Awards Book of the Year for 2010.

Honeybee is his third novel.

CRAIG SILVEY

HONEYBEE

ALLEN&UNWIN

SYDNEY • MELBOURNE • AUCKLAND • LONDON

First published in 2020

 Department of **Local Government, Sport and Cultural Industries** GOVERNMENT OF WESTERN AUSTRALIA   This project has been assisted by the Department of Local Government, Sport and Cultural Industries.

Line on p. 63 from the Looney Tunes cartoon 'Rabbit of Seville' (1950) reproduced with permission of Warner Bros. Entertainment Inc.
Line on p. 350 from *Cat on a Hot Tin Roof* by Tennessee Williams. Copyright © 1954, 1955, 1982, 1983 by the University of the South. Reprinted with permission of Georges Borchardt, Inc., on behalf of the Tennessee Williams estate.

Every effort has been made to trace the holders of copyright material. If you have any information concerning copyright material in this book please contact the publishers at the address below.

Allen & Unwin
83 Alexander Street
Crows Nest NSW 2065
Australia
Phone: (61 2) 8425 0100
Email: info@allenandunwin.com
Web: www.allenandunwin.com

 NATIONAL LIBRARY OF AUSTRALIA   A catalogue record for this book is available from the National Library of Australia

ISBN 978 1 76087 722 4

Set in 12/18.7 pt Simoncini Garamond by Bookhouse, Sydney
Printed and bound in Australia by Griffin Press, part of Ovato

10 9 8 7

For Them On The Bridge

The End

I wasn't cold, but I was shivering when I walked onto the Clayton Road overpass. I wasn't scared either, even when I climbed over the rail. I didn't really feel much of anything.

It was late at night and it was quiet. No cars went past.

I looked at the road below. It was a long way down. I focused on the spot where I would probably land, between the white line and the brown gravel. I wondered if it would hurt or if I would die straight away. Then I wondered who would find me. Maybe it would be a truck driver or a shift worker. I felt bad for them.

I must have been thinking about things for a while, because when I looked across to my right, I saw a man down the other end of the overpass.

He was smoking a cigarette. I could see the orange end glowing in the dark. I got nervous. He was probably walking his dog or something. I didn't want him to come closer. I closed my eyes and let go of the rail, but then I realised it would be awful if he saw me do it. I decided to wait.

I looked back at the man from under my hoodie and I noticed something that I hadn't seen at first. He was on the other side of the rail too.

I wasn't sure what to do. I knew I should call out or say something, but I didn't have the courage. He ashed his cigarette and flicked it. I watched it spin in the air and hit the road below.

When I looked back up, the man was staring at me. I turned away. I felt like I had been caught out.

I heard his footsteps walking towards me. He didn't rush. I shuffled across and kept my head down. I thought about falling then and there, but my mind got really crowded and I froze.

I flinched when I heard his voice.

'I'm not here to talk you out of it.'

I was still looking down.

'Don't come any closer,' I said.

'Righto.'

I guessed he was a couple of metres away.

'Just stay there.'

'I understand.'

He was calm. I sneaked a look at him. He was old. He had a short grey beard and he wore a dark wool jumper and grey pants. He leaned on the rail and looked down at the road. He didn't say anything else.

I edged further away from him. He didn't move, but it felt like he was following me. I couldn't stop shaking. My teeth were clacking together. My head was still throbbing from before, and there was a high-pitched ringing sound in my ears. I felt so panicked and dizzy that my mind floated outside my body, and I could see myself from above. Everything went still and nothing mattered. It was peaceful and silent up there. I watched myself lean forwards.

And that's when I dropped.

For a moment I had no weight, then suddenly I stopped. The man had caught me by the arm. I wriggled and kicked and pulled.

'*Don't!* Let me go! Let me *go*! Don't! Let me go!'

I tried to tear his fingers off me, but his grip was too strong.

Then I looked down and it all felt real and I got scared. I stopped fighting and I held on.

'Don't let me go! *Don't let me go!*'

The man grunted and lifted me over the rail. He wrapped his arms tightly around me.

'It's alright, it's alright. I got you.'

He started coughing badly, still holding me. He couldn't get any air in. He let go and bent over and wheezed. I rubbed his back, but he waved me away.

Finally, he stopped. He straightened and spat over the edge. Then he put his hand on my shoulder, and we sat down together with our backs against the rail.

'I'm Sam,' I said.

'Vic.'

We were quiet for a while.

'How come you're up here?' I asked.

Vic didn't answer.

'I mean, why were *you* going to do it?'

He sighed.

'The dog died.'

I thought about it.

'You must have really loved your dog.'

He shook his head.

'I hated the little prick.'

That confused me.

'What kind of dog was it?'

'Small and loud.'

'Did you leave a note?'

He shook his head.

'How come?' I asked.

He shrugged.

It went quiet again. Then Vic slowly got to his feet, using the rail for support.

'Well, mate, I don't think it's our night, do you?'

Vic held out his hand but I didn't take it. He looked at me closely. He must have thought I looked strange, with all the make-up and the blood on my face and my patchy hair, but he didn't show it. He just looked tired. I pulled my hood back over.

'Come on,' he said.

I didn't want to go. I shook my head. Vic leaned down and gently pulled me to my feet.

'You spoiled my last smoke,' he said. 'So we're even.'

~

Vic led me to his old Kingswood station wagon. It was brown with racks on the roof. He opened the door. It was unlocked and the keys were still in the ignition.

'Weren't you worried somebody would steal it?' I asked.

'Wouldn't have been much use to me anymore, would it?'

Vic started the car.

'Get in. I'll give you a lift home.'

I hesitated, but Vic looked impatient, so I got in. His car smelled like dust and oil and stale pine air-freshener. I could tell he had looked after it, though. None of the upholstery was ripped or split. It felt cosy.

'Can we drive around for a while first?' I asked.

'What do you mean drive around? Where?'

'I don't know.'

'I'm not a taxi.'

Vic put the car in reverse.

'Where am I headed?'

'Can you take me to the city?'

Vic didn't seem too happy about that, but he didn't say no.

Vic focused on the road while I looked through the window at houses and parks and vacant blocks and industrial buildings with barbed-wire fences around them. Then we turned onto the freeway, and I stared out at the river.

When we reached the city, I asked Vic to drop me off at the train station.

He pulled over into an empty bus bay. He looked lost in his own thoughts.

I wasn't ready to get out. I wanted to say something meaningful, but I was too shy, so I just thanked him. Vic gave me a nod.

I got out of the car and Vic drove off. I walked around for a couple of hours. The city was quiet. I passed some boys sitting on milk crates down an alley listening to music on their phones. They called out to me but I ignored them. I walked around Northbridge. All the bars and clubs were shut. I heard reggae music coming from a backpacker hostel. I saw two homeless men yelling and pushing each other.

I was getting tired, but I wasn't going to sleep out there on the street.

After a while, I noticed a car driving slowly behind me. I could see its headlights, but I didn't want to turn around in case it was the police. I kept walking. The car drove up alongside me. It was a black Audi. The passenger-side window slid down and a man with thinning brown hair ducked his head so he could see me.

'You okay?'

I didn't answer.

'You got somewhere to go?'

I ignored him and kept walking with my head down.

He followed me all the way down the block.

'Listen, you need some help? I can get you some money.'

All I had in my pocket was my phone. I stopped and looked into the car. The man wore a blue button-up shirt and a jacket. He looked really concerned.

'You shouldn't be out here so late,' he said.

I shrugged.

'Why don't you get in? I can drop you off wherever you need to be.'

I shook my head and stepped back. He leaned across and pushed the door open.

'It's smart to be careful. There are some creeps around. Come on. You had a rough night?'

My feet were so sore and my head was still throbbing and I was really tired. I just wanted to sit down and rest. I got in. The car smelled like cologne. The man looked at me and smiled.

'I'm Neil,' he said.

I didn't say anything.

He talked a lot while he drove, but I wasn't listening. The car was so quiet that I fell asleep. When I woke up we were in Kings Park, surrounded by trees. He had stopped at a lookout. I could see the city through the windscreen.

Neil took his seatbelt off and shifted around in his seat. It was dark, but his face was lit by the dashboard.

'So what's going on with you?'

'Nothing,' I said.

'Why are you out on your own so late?'

I shrugged.

'How old are you?'

'Fourteen.'

He raised his eyebrows and nodded slowly. He was looking at me strangely. He reached across and pulled my hoodie back to see my face. He brushed his hand against the cut on my jaw, but I turned away.

'What happened to you?'

'Nothing.'

He rubbed my shoulder. He kept looking at me.

'You're so beautiful, you know that?'

I stared straight ahead.

'I want to help you out. I'm going to give you two hundred dollars, okay?'

I nodded. I was so tired.

He showed me the money in his leather wallet. Two green notes.

'Would you like that?'

I shrugged.

'Do you think you should give me something too?'

'I don't have anything.'

'Of course you do,' he said. He rubbed my shoulder some more, then he slid his hand down my chest and onto my lap. I didn't move. He started squeezing me. The leather seats creaked as he dipped his head down. He tugged at my pants. I could feel his stubble. Then it felt wet and warm and weird.

I looked around the car. There was a football club logo on his keyring and a packet of mints in a cup holder. My mind went outside my body again. I wasn't really anywhere. I could see all the lights in the city buildings. I thought about the people who had to work in those offices at this hour. They were probably the cleaners. The lights went blurry, and I must have fallen asleep again, because I flinched when Neil shifted back suddenly. He was touching himself. His face was red and he was breathing quickly.

'You don't like it?'

'Not really. Sorry.'

I buttoned up my jeans and looked out the window. He stopped touching himself.

'Get out.'

'What?'

'Get the fuck out of my car. Think I'm paying for this shit?'

He zipped his pants and tucked his shirt in, then he started the car. The radio came on. The song playing was 'Summer Rain'. He put his wallet back in his pocket.

'Go! Now! Get the fuck out.'

'Okay. I'm sorry.'

I got out. The second I shut the door, he reversed and then drove away fast.

I walked down a dark road until I found a lawned area with a view of the city. I sat down on a bench.

I didn't feel that bad about the money, because I had stolen a watch from the centre console. I took it out of my pocket. It was heavy and it had a French name that I couldn't make out. I put it on and it slid down my arm. I had never worn a watch before.

I fell asleep on the bench and I was woken by sprinklers. I got up quickly and ran. I sat on some concrete steps near the War Memorial and watched the sun rise over the hills. It was pretty nice.

I decided to give myself one last day.

~

I checked the time on the watch because my phone was out of battery. It was six forty-three.

There was a cafe nearby but it was closed. I found a tap on the side of the building and tried to scrub the make-up off my face. It wasn't until I ran my wet hands through my hair that I remembered it wasn't long anymore. The water made the cuts on my scalp sting, and short strands of hair came away in my fingers.

I walked towards the city. I passed people doing tai chi and exercise boot camps. I stopped to pat a dog that sniffed my feet. The owner didn't notice me, she just tugged the lead and kept walking.

At the station, I hopped a train. The carriage was full of schoolkids in uniform. I pulled my hood over and put my head down. Every time I heard them laugh I worried that it was about me.

I got off at Cottesloe. I walked past big houses and across a golf course to the beach. I took my shoes off and walked along the sand until I found a quiet spot where nobody could see me. I took off my clothes down to my underwear and wrapped the watch and my phone inside my hoodie. Then I dived into the ocean. It was cold and rough. My cuts stung in the salty water. I grabbed handfuls of sand and scrubbed my body and face.

I looked at the horizon and thought about swimming towards it as far as I could go, until I was too tired to swim back.

I floated around for a while, then I got out and put on my clothes and walked up to a grassy bank. I lay down on a patch of grass and slept with the sun on my back.

∼

When I woke up it was afternoon and there were more people around. Someone was cooking on a barbecue nearby and the smell made me hungry. I saw a woman sunbaking on the beach in a white bikini and big sunglasses. She stood up and walked towards the water. She moved so confidently. I stared at her breasts and her hips and her thick legs and her oily brown skin. Then I got up and left.

I took the train to Fremantle. The markets were open, and I stole a red apple from a grocer while he was bagging nectarines for an old lady. I ate it under a tree in the park, and I threw the core to a bunch of seagulls and watched them fight for it.

Time always went slow with no money or anywhere to go. Sometimes I went to the library because it was a quiet place where nobody paid any attention to you. My favourite thing was to sneak into the movies. There were a few ways to get in without paying for a ticket. One was to find a ripped stub from the bins outside, then sneak into the bathroom. When I came out, I would hold up the ticket and walk straight towards the usher and pretend I was in a rush to get back to the movie. Or, if it was busy, I would slip in behind a big group.

Today there wasn't even anyone attending, so I walked straight through. The movie was just starting. It was a remake of *Beauty and the Beast*. The costumes were really nice. I felt bad for the Beast, who was lonely and trapped inside a hideous body. I was happy for him when the curse got lifted.

When it was over, I slipped across to another cinema and watched a sci-fi film that was halfway through. The best thing about that movie was the tub of popcorn I found in the back row.

The next movie was a historical romance. It was really boring, so I stopped paying attention. Instead, I thought about Vic. I pictured him back at the overpass, standing in the same place, having his last cigarette again, all on his own. I imagined him falling and hitting the road below, and the thought upset me so much that I gasped.

A lady sitting a couple of seats along gave me a sympathetic look. She thought I was reacting to the movie. She reached across and put her hand over mine, but I got up and left.

It was dark outside. I couldn't stop worrying about Vic. There was a bike rack around the side of the cinema entrance. I found a bike that was secured with a cable lock. I pulled my hood over my head and crouched down. The lock was old, and I worked it open in less than a minute.

I rode off fast. I went south along the coast, and then turned left and went through an industrial area where there weren't many cars. At one point a truck flashed its lights behind me because I was in the middle of the lane, and I cut back to the kerb. The driver yelled at me, but all I could think about was Vic.

I made it to the overpass. I dumped the bike and ran halfway across. First I checked the rails, and then I looked down. I couldn't see anything. My legs were burning and my heart was beating fast. I sat down with my back against the rails.

I was relieved Vic wasn't here, but part of me had wanted to see him again. I held the watch up close to my face and squinted. I decided to wait until midnight, and if Vic hadn't turned up by then, I would climb over to where I had been last night and fall.

≈

Somebody was shaking my shoulder. I panicked and pushed back, but the person held onto me.

'Hey, hey, ease up. Easy, it's alright.'

I opened my eyes. It was Vic. At first I thought I was dreaming, but it was really him.

'You're not going to do it, are you?' I asked.

'Eh? No, no. That's not why I'm here.'

I looked at my watch. It was half past twelve. I was upset with myself.

'Listen,' Vic said, 'you want to go for a drive?'

I did, but suddenly I felt wary about getting into his car.

'I don't know.'

Vic didn't mind. He sat next to me. His knees cracked when he lowered himself. We sat without talking for a really long time. I listened to him breathing. He had a really strong chemical smell, like burnt oil.

A ute came over the overpass and stopped halfway. The driver wound his window down.

'You two alright?'

'All good, thanks mate.'

The driver gave Vic a suspicious look before he drove away.

'How come you came back then?' I asked.

I had an idea why, I just wanted to hear him say it.

'Couldn't get to sleep,' Vic said. 'I was sitting in the car earlier and you came to mind. I thought about what my wife would have said about you. She would have given me an earful.'

'Why?'

'Because I didn't do enough to help. I didn't get you home safe. A man wants to pass with a peaceful mind.'

'My home isn't safe.'

Vic nodded slowly.

'Is your wife dead?' I asked.

Vic nodded again.

'What was her name?'

'Edie. Edith.'

'You must have loved her a lot.'

'Very much.'

'How did she die?'

Vic didn't answer, so we sat in silence again. I liked that he didn't ask me any questions.

'Vic?'

'Yeah?'

'I'd like to go for that drive.'

~

Vic's Kingswood was parked in the same place as the night before. All the windows were partly open, but the doors were locked this time.

When I got in the car, it had that same strong oil smell.

Vic started the engine.

'Where do you want to go?'

'I don't know. Anywhere.'

Vic pulled out and drove. There were no cars around.

'Why does it smell so bad in here?' I asked.

Vic didn't answer that question either.

I wound the window right down. Maybe he had spilled something. I looked around. On the back seat I saw a few metres of garden hose. One end had a big wad of electrical tape wrapped around it. I looked at Vic. I understood what he meant earlier when he said he was sitting in his car trying to get to sleep.

Vic didn't have much of an expression, but I knew he was sad and tired. My throat got tight.

'I'm sorry, Vic.'

Vic kept looking straight ahead.

'Me too mate.'

I brought my knees up to my chest and leaned against the door. I closed my eyes and felt the wind on my face.

Last Meal

I woke up in a strange place.

The first thing I noticed was how stale the room smelled. I sat up. I was in a big bed under a heavy homemade quilt. I looked around. One wall was taken up with a big wooden wardrobe. In the corner was a vanity table. I could see myself in the mirror. I was still wearing my clothes, but my shoes were on the floor next to the bed.

I got up and sat at the vanity table. There was perfume, make-up, a foundation brush, a bottle of Oil of Olay, a hairbrush and a jewellery box. Everything had dust on it. There was a wedding photo in a silver frame. I recognised Vic. He had big bushy sideburns and a nice smile. He wore a dark green suit. I guessed that it was Edie next to him. She was really pretty. She had rosy cheeks and thick curly hair, and she was a lot shorter than Vic.

I put on my shoes and slowly opened the door. It was quiet. I crept down the carpeted hallway. I had an awful thought that Vic had left me there all alone and I would find his body.

'Vic? *Vic?*'

I didn't hear anything back. There was no answer.

I checked the bathroom but he wasn't there. I looked inside the next room along, but there was only a small single bed and a pile of folded clothes.

I found my way to a little kitchen. It was empty. I called out again.

I found Vic standing outside in his backyard. He was wearing a pair of black shorts with dried paint all over them and a faded yellow polo shirt that was ripped at the hem.

'Good morning,' I said.

He turned around.

'Afternoon.'

'Really?'

He nodded.

I squinted in the sun. The garden was really nice. There were rosebushes and bottlebrush and grevilleas and potted chrysanthemums. The lawn was spongy and trimmed. I saw that Vic was standing over a neat square of dirt in the grass. He caught me looking at it.

'Quiet here without the cranky little bastard. Yapped at everything.'

'What was its name?'

'Misty.'

Vic rolled his eyes and smiled. I walked over to the grave, then I realised.

'Oh,' I said. 'It was your wife's dog.'

Vic nodded.

~

I was thirsty so Vic took me inside for some water. The tap made a groaning sound. The glass he handed me was tinted yellow and looked like it cost thirty dollars at a vintage store. I drank the whole thing.

'You don't have an Android charger, do you?'

Vic just gave me a confused look and shook his head.

I glanced around the kitchen. It didn't look like he used it very often.

'Do you have any bread or something?'

Vic opened some cupboards. All his food was tinned.

'Out of bread. I can do you some beans. Or . . . corned beef. Steak and onion stew. Spaghetti.'

'What do you usually eat?'

Vic shrugged and held up the can of beans.

'You don't really cook much, do you?'

'I heat the tin up on the stove here.'

'You cook them still in the can?'

'Yeah. I take the lid off first, otherwise they go bang. Only made that mistake once.'

I knew what I was going to do.

'What food do you like?' I asked.

'Not fussy.'

'But you must have a favourite.'

Vic shrugged, but I didn't want to give up.

'What if you were on death row and the guard came to ask what you wanted for your last meal,' I said. 'You could have anything. They could re-create any meal you'd ever had in your life.'

Vic thought about it.

'Any meal?'

'Any meal, exactly as it was.'

Vic put the can down.

'Edie's lamb roast. Do I get dessert?'

'Yes.'

'Then my mother's Christmas trifle for afters.'

Vic had a small smile, like he was remembering those meals.

~

I told Vic I was going for a walk.

He lived in a cul-de-sac that was all brick houses with neat front gardens. A couple of places had tall palm trees. One driveway had a boat that said *Liquid Asset* on the side.

A woman two houses down was standing at her letterbox and staring at me. She had big blonde hair which was dark at the roots. I put my head down and kept walking, but I could still feel her watching me.

'Why are you coming out of that house?' she asked.

I pulled my hood over and ignored her, which only made her more aggressive.

'Excuse me! Answer me when I talk to you, please! Who are you and why are you coming out of that house?'

She followed me for a couple of steps.

'What's your name young man?'

She stopped walking and I kept going. A few houses further down, there was a girl around my age walking home from school. She had thick shoulder-length curly black hair. She was short with brown skin and big dark eyes and a backpack that looked really big on her. She must have seen the woman harassing me, because she stopped and rolled her eyes.

'Hey, don't worry about her, she's, like, pathologically rude.'

I looked over my shoulder. The woman was still watching me.

'I don't think she likes me.'

'She doesn't like anybody. Like, she's always been a bit frosty, but ever since her husband went to prison she's been fucking tyrannical.'

'What did he do?'

'Oh my goodness, it's the *craziest* story. You wouldn't believe me if I told you.'

I raised my eyebrows.

'Are there any shops around here?'

She gave me directions and I thanked her. The girl seemed friendly. She said goodbye and went inside a red-brick house.

Fifteen minutes later I reached a shopping strip with a hairdresser, newsagent, chemist and a Foodland. I went into the supermarket and picked up a plastic basket. I looked around to get my bearings.

I saw a mother pushing a trolley with her daughter in the child seat. I thought about shopping with my mum, how each time was like a secret adventure. I gave the little girl a smile, and she waved back at me. Her mum gave me a dirty look and pushed the trolley away, and I remembered the mess I had left behind.

~

My mum was nineteen when I was born.

She didn't realise she was pregnant because she was living in her college dormitory and going out every night, so she just thought she was hungover a lot. It was a few months in before she knew. By then she had dropped out of all her classes. Her parents were strict and had high expectations, so she didn't tell them anything. When they found out, they were really angry.

They told her to get rid of me, but it was too late to do it legally. Her dad wanted to go to court and get permission, but my mum wouldn't do it. They told her she was throwing her life away. My mum cut off all contact with her family and never allowed any of them to meet me.

After that she was on her own. She didn't know who my dad was. She admitted to me that she didn't remember much about that time. I used to invent stories about who he might be and why he couldn't be with us. Sometimes I imagined him as a soldier or a musician or a pilot.

When I grew into my face a little more, my mum thought she recognised who he might be. She had met a man at a pool hall next to the Aberdeen Street Backpackers whose eyes had looked a bit like mine. She never knew his name, but she remembered he had an Irish accent. She only met him once and never saw him again. Sometimes I wished she hadn't told me, because I never thought about him being a pilot or a soldier again.

For a long time, it was just me and my mum. We moved a lot. It always seemed to be the same one-bedroom apartment, just in a different suburb. A few times the landlord changed the locks with all our things inside. My mum would call her friend Dave, who was a locksmith, and he would get us back in. Then she sent me outside to play for an hour while she said thank you to Dave.

We never had any money. One of my earliest memories was sitting in the child seat of a trolley, watching my mum slipping food into her handbag. I didn't understand what she was doing at the time, I just remember how tense she was.

When I got older, it became a game we played.

Sometimes I wore my empty school backpack. She would put some things in the trolley, and fill my bag up too. When we got near the cashier, I would have a big tantrum, screaming and kicking and knocking things off the shelves, then she scolded me and yanked me out of the store, apologising to everyone and leaving the trolley behind.

Sometimes it went the other way. She would fill my bag up, and put a couple of cheap items in the shopping basket. At the checkout, I would politely ask if I could have a chocolate bar, and she would count out her coins and say only if I gave the lady behind the counter a nice smile, which I did. Nobody ever suspected us. We never once got caught. In the car, she would tell me what a good job I'd done and I would feel proud.

Our gas or electricity got disconnected a lot. Once when we had no power, my mum pretended we were on a camping trip. We made a tent out of a bedsheet and we lit candles to be our campfire. We toasted bits of bread on the end of forks and imagined they were marshmallows. When it got late, my mum blew out the candles and howled like a wolf to scare me. I acted afraid because I wanted her to comfort me and tell me they weren't real.

She left me on my own all the time. After dinner she would get dressed up. My mum loved clothes and she owned lots of them. I would help her select an outfit. We went through her wardrobe together and laid out the ones we liked on the bed. She narrowed them down to the last two, then she held them both up and let me choose.

'Okay. The A-line or the slip dress?'

'The slip dress. With your black heels.'

She nodded.

'Thank you, Honeybee.'

Then she would put on make-up in the bathroom. I sat on the counter or the side of the bath and watched. I knew all the little rituals. The way she turned her face from side to side to check her bronzer, or how her tongue always touched the corner of her lips when she was concentrating on her eyeshadow highlights. She put her lipstick on last, then she rolled her lips together and pouted and put a tissue between them and pressed down. She gave the tissue to me because I thought they were pretty and I liked to collect them. I had a whole shoebox full of her kisses.

I always noticed the way she looked at herself when she was done. Sometimes she was proud, sometimes she was disappointed, but she winked at the mirror and said the same thing every time.

'That'll have to do, kid.'

She transformed into a different person in there. She wasn't my mum, she was Sarah, dressed up for a world that didn't include me.

She would promise to be back in a couple of hours, but she always came back late. I tried to wait up, but I usually fell asleep on the couch or the floor or on my mattress, and I woke up when I heard the key in the door.

It was hard to tell what her mood would be when she came home. Sometimes she said mean things. Other times she slurred and swayed and collapsed on her bed. I would take her shoes off and put a blanket over her. Sometimes she came home full of energy. She would put on music and start cleaning and dancing. Other times she saw me standing by the door and got upset, and she would hug me and cry and apologise.

She always came home by herself. I don't know if it was to spare me from meeting a stranger, or if she was ashamed to have them see me. But it meant I felt safe in our apartment, even though I was by myself a lot, because it was our own little world.

I liked the nights she didn't leave. Sometimes she played her guitar and sang me a lullaby. She made them up on the spot using the same three chords. If she couldn't think of a word to rhyme, she just invented one and we would both laugh.

When I was seven, she started reading me the *Harry Potter* books before I went to sleep. One night we couldn't bear to stop, so she kept going. She read so much that she almost lost her voice. She whispered the last chapter, and then she fell asleep with me.

We never got to the last book, though. I still don't know how it ends.

~

When I was eight, I woke up late one night to a strange clanging noise. I went to the bathroom and found my mum lying on the tiles. She must have just come home. She was vomiting and having a seizure. It looked like she was being electrocuted. Her heels were hitting the toilet. Her face was red. She had wet herself and her eyes were rolled back. I shook her, but she didn't respond to me. I took her phone out of her handbag and called 911, because that's what they did on television. I used toilet paper to wipe the vomit off her face and I held her hand. Her skin was cold. I had never been so scared.

Two paramedics knocked on the door and I let them in. They asked me questions that I couldn't answer. They carried her out to the ambulance and attached a clear bag with a thin tube to her arm. They let me ride with them. The sirens were on.

At the hospital, I wasn't allowed to follow her into the ward. I panicked and started to cry, so a nurse took me into a separate room. She gave me a hot chocolate and a biscuit and she stayed with me for a while. She asked if there was anyone who could come get me. I shook my head.

I stayed in the room all night. In the morning, I woke up to a lady standing over me. She looked just like my mum, but she was heavier and had brown hair. She said her name was Gabby.

'I'm your mum's sister. You're going to come live with me while she gets treatment.'

'I want to stay here with her.'

'She's not staying here.'

'Where is she going?'

'She's being taken to a clinic because she's an alcoholic. And if she doesn't do the work and get better, she won't be able to take care of you anymore.'

This made me really upset and afraid. I didn't want to leave the hospital with her. I grabbed onto the chair I was sitting on and wouldn't let go.

Gabby leaned in close. She smelled like toothpaste and perfume. She spoke so nobody else could hear.

'You're going to stop crying and you're going to come with me, is that clear?'

She led me outside to her car. She didn't let me see my mum first to say goodbye.

Gabby lived in Claremont with her husband Miles and their toddler, Patience. Gabby only spoke to me when she was being mean about my mum or telling me I needed a haircut.

My grandparents came over to meet me for the first time. They didn't hug me, and they asked me a lot of questions about my mum. They loved Patience, though. They blew raspberries on her stomach and clapped and laughed at everything she did.

I hated it there. I planned to run away, but I didn't have to, because a week later my mum came to get me. I ran to the door and clung to her legs. She had a big fight with Gabby in the front yard. All the neighbours came out of their houses to watch. Gabby told my mum she wouldn't allow their parents to keep funding her toxic lifestyle. My mum said it didn't matter what choices she made, everyone would always be critical of her. Then she accused Gabby of only caring about how much money she was going to inherit.

Gabby was furious. She told me I deserved a better mother, then she went inside and slammed the door.

My mum took my hand.

'Come on, Honeybee.'

We went back to the apartment. My mum tried to do better. She emptied all her wine and vodka bottles down the kitchen sink. She stayed home at night for a couple of weeks, but then she started going out more than before and leaving me alone in the apartment for longer.

My grandparents stopped sending money. I didn't even know they had been. We were really broke.

That's when I started stealing on my own.

~

I went up and down the aisles and filled the basket with food. I took my time and got all the ingredients I needed.

Most smaller supermarkets have a storage section where the night-fill staff wheel in boxes to restock the shelves. Usually it's only separated by plastic strips or a swing door. There are often stacks of boxes back there and a cool room and a break area. And there's always an exit.

Once I had everything I needed, that's where I went. I didn't rush. There was nobody back there. But when I went out the exit, I saw a man sitting on a milk crate and smoking a cigarette next to the door. He looked at my basket.

'The fuck are you doing?'

'Some lady just slipped over in the freezer section. She's screaming. I think she hit her head. I came back here to find someone.'

'Fuck.'

He got up quickly and pushed past me and went inside.

I stole his pack of cigarettes and his plastic lighter before I left. Since I ruined Vic's last smoke, I thought it was the least I could do. I kept the lighter for myself in case I needed it later.

I unpacked the basket in Vic's kitchen. I had a lamb shoulder, garlic, rosemary, potatoes, carrots, peas, chicken stock and oil. And I had all the ingredients for a trifle. They were easy to make. It was just flour and eggs and sugar for the sponge, some milk and vanilla to make a custard, and some cream to whip. I also got some gelatine and fresh strawberries to make a jelly.

Vic watched me get everything arranged on the bench.

'Bloody hell. How much I owe you?'

'Nothing.'

'Nonsense. How much?'

'Nothing.'

Vic noticed the plastic basket, then he realised.

'You shouldn't have done that.'

'I don't have any money.'

'You need money, you take it out of that biscuit tin.'

28

He pointed to a shortbread container next to his toaster.

'Okay.'

Vic wasn't mad. He sat down at the table.

'I got you some cigarettes too.'

Vic took the pack. He smiled to himself and shook his head.

I turned on the oven and opened it. There were actual spider webs inside. I cleaned them out and removed an oven tray that had rust and dust on it. There were cockroaches and mouse droppings inside the cupboards too.

'Am I allowed to clean your kitchen?' I asked.

'Fill your boots.'

I started with the lamb shoulder. I took a paring knife and stabbed small holes into the meat. I stuffed bits of garlic and rosemary into them. Vic frowned.

'You know what you're doin' there?'

I gave him a small smile, then I spoke in a high-pitched voice.

'We're roasting Last Meal Lamb, served with a selection of vegetables and a decadent trifle dessert, today . . . on *The French Chef*!'

Vic just looked confused.

∿

While I was staying at Gabby's house, she let me play with her iPad. I had never used one before, and I loved it too much to give it up, so when my mum and I were leaving, I stuffed it under my shirt.

When my mum left me on my own again, I watched YouTube to pass the time. I clicked on cartoons and funny pets and pranks and music videos and tutorials. It was addictive. One day I clicked on a lady who was doing a cooking segment. It must have been a long time ago because it was in black and white. Her name was Julia Child. She had a strange singsong voice, and I fell in love with her. She was tall and elegant and sweet. She was really comforting. I watched her over and over. Whenever I felt lonely and hungry I would watch an episode of *The French Chef* and I would pretend she was my grandmother and she was teaching me how to cook in our own kitchen. Sometimes I spoke to her out loud, like it was just us. I liked the way she made mistakes and threw things away and laughed about it. She said it was okay to fail, because it just made you do it better the next time. I watched every episode of every show she ever made. I liked her rituals too. Watching her sit down and tuck her napkin into her collar and pour a huge glass of wine at the end of every episode always made me smile.

I wanted to be just like her, so I started practising in the kitchen. I would explain what I was doing in her voice. I was nine years old and I knew how to sweat onions and celery and carrots for a mirepoix, I knew how to make a roux and a bearnaise, I knew what herbs to pair with any meat. I baked a lot of sweets, because the ingredients were easy to find and steal. I could make a butterscotch gateau or a crepe stack or a tarte Tatin.

I tried to cook something every single day, and I got better at it. I thought about food all the time, maybe because we never had any and getting the ingredients was so risky. For me, every meal was important, especially when I cooked for my mum. I felt nervous giving her a dish that I had prepared. I would watch her closely as she took her first bite. Sometimes she couldn't believe that I had made it.

I always imagined being a chef with my very own restaurant. I would never leave the kitchen, but I would have some way of looking out at the tables so I could see my customers enjoying my food. Maybe a two-way mirror or something, so they wouldn't ever have to see me.

~

I plated up Vic's meal so it looked really nice. The lamb came out just right. I laid it in front of him.

'*Bon appétit!*'

Vic dipped his head close to the plate and inhaled.

'Smells good. Thanks mate.'

I sat down too. I was hungry, but before I could eat I wanted to see Vic's reaction. He took a bite and chewed and nodded.

'Is it as good as Edith's?'

He thought about it.

'It's different. You do your own thing. I like the gravy.'

'It's called a velouté. It's one of the five French mother sauces.'

Vic raised his eyebrows and nodded, but I could tell he wasn't that interested.

'Was she a good cook?'

Vic nodded.

'I was spoiled for a long time. This reminds me how lucky I was.'

'I can teach you. It's not that hard.'

'Bit late in the day for new tricks.'

Vic ate slowly and he couldn't finish his plate. I worried that he didn't like it and was just being polite.

'Are you sure it was alright?'

'Saving myself for afters. I always like the leftovers better anyway.'

I cleared away Vic's plate, and I came back with two bowls and the trifle. Vic had helped by finding a bottle of brandy in the back of one of the cabinets in the lounge room. It was covered in dust. Vic said it was a wedding present that he and Edie had planned to drink on their fiftieth anniversary.

It made me sad, and I didn't want to open it. I asked Vic if he was sure. He said there was no sense letting good booze go to waste, and Edie would have wanted it to be drunk.

Vic's eyes went wide when he saw the trifle. The sponge came out perfectly, and I had soaked it in brandy. It was layered with strawberry jelly and vanilla custard and topped with whipped cream.

'Look at that!' He sounded impressed.

I served him up a big bowl and I watched him closely again as he took a spoonful. He closed his eyes when he tasted it.

'You know what? This might be better than my mother's.'

I got a tingly feeling on the back of my neck.

'Really?'

'It's very good, thank you.'

Vic ate another mouthful.

'It tastes like Christmas Day,' he said. 'My mother always put a lucky two-bob bit in the bottom of the dish.'

'A what?'

'Two-bob bit. A florin.'

'What's a florin?'

'Two shillings.'

'What?'

'It's a coin, in the old money. Like a ten-cent piece, but worth more. See, she would throw one in the trifle before she dished it out, and whoever got it in their bowl got to keep it.'

'And did you ever get it?'

'Not even once. One of my sisters got it every year, except the very last time my mother ever made a trifle. My old man was a glutton for sweets. Went at it like a pig at a trough. And one Christmas he swallowed the coin. It got stuck in his throat and he sat up like he'd been struck by lightning. I had never seen him scared before.'

'What did you do?'

'Me? I started screaming with my sisters.'

'Did he die?'

Vic shook his head.

'My mother was calm as you like. While the old man was lurching around, she got up, went to the kitchen, come back with a rolling pin and thumped him straight in the guts. The coin came out, hit the deck and rolled under the upright piano. My mother gave him a couple of extra whacks after it came out. Had them stored up, I reckon. And she never made a trifle again.'

He had a couple more bites then put his spoon down.

33

'I'm stuffed to the gills,' he said. 'Very nice though, mate. Thank you.'

Vic cleared away the bowls. He came back with the bottle of brandy and two old teacups. He poured some into both. I didn't want any, but I didn't want him to drink it alone. Vic smelled the brandy and swirled it around the cup. We clinked the teacups together.

'Happy anniversary,' I said.

Vic nodded, took a sip and gave me a smile that seemed sad.

'How long were you married for?'

'Thirty-seven years.'

'How many kids did you have?'

'None.'

'How come?'

Vic just poured himself another cup of brandy and stayed quiet. He drank the whole cup before he spoke again.

'She died six years ago. When you're a young bloke, you think about your life in terms of possibilities. The job you'll have, the man you'll be, places you'll go. But when you get older, the way you think changes. You think about the stuff you've done, how you've done it, where you've gone. But the most important thing is who you've shared it with.'

Vic poured himself another drink, then he started talking again.

'She was my best mate. And when she died, I died too. My life went with hers, because it was *our* life that mattered, not my own.'

34

My throat got really thick and fat, and I couldn't swallow. I sniffed and wiped my eyes with my sleeve.

'I promised myself that I'd stick around to look after the dog, because she spoiled that thing more than she spoiled me, same with all her dogs. Didn't realise the little bastard would make it to seventeen. Arthritis, blind as a bat, pissed everywhere, bad-tempered, stubborn as a donkey. But not a bad little mate in the end. You get used to things being around, I suppose.'

Vic's voice was really shaky. He shook his head quickly and blinked a few times and puffed out his cheeks.

'Anyway . . .' He shrugged. 'Now the dog's dead.'

I didn't know what to say. We sat there without talking for over an hour. We were alone with our own thoughts, the same as a couple of nights ago on the overpass. We still had all the same problems, but I felt safe sitting there with Vic, and I didn't want to die right then. I didn't want Vic to die either.

'I hope you don't think I meant this to be your actual last meal,' I said.

Vic smiled and shook his head. He looked really tired. Half the bottle of brandy was gone.

'Vic?'

'Yes mate?'

'Is it alright if I stay the night here again?'

Vic looked me in the eye.

'You can live here as long as you like. But you can't die here. Understood?'

I nodded.

I got up and cleaned the dishes and put everything away in the empty fridge. When I was finished, I saw that Vic was asleep at the table. I felt bad for keeping him up. I shook his shoulder and startled him.

'Sorry,' I said. 'I thought you would be more comfortable in bed.'

He got up slowly, using the table for balance. He nodded.

'You're a good kid. Thanks for dinner.'

He slowly shuffled towards the spare room with the small bed and the stack of clothes.

'I can sleep in there,' I said. 'You don't have to give up your room.'

'No, no. This is where I sleep. Night mate.'

'Goodnight, Vic.'

The Black Shadow

It was late when I finally slept. I had the same nightmare that I always did. I was stuck on a train going in the wrong direction and I was trying to stop it. I hit the emergency buttons and ran down the carriages, but nobody paid any attention to me. I tried to force the doors open but they wouldn't move, and the train kept going faster and faster, and got further away.

I woke up when I heard a noise. I opened my eyes and it was dark and I was sweating. I heard the noise again, and I recognised it. Vic was vomiting in the bathroom. I got up and walked quietly down the hall. When it was my mum, I always knew what to do. I would hold her hair back and get her some water and help her to bed. But this was different. The toilet door was closed and I could hear Vic heaving and groaning. I hoped it wasn't my cooking that made him sick. I sat by the door and waited, and when the toilet flushed I crept back to bed.

∿

In the morning I found Vic in his garage. It smelled like oil and it was full of tools and engine parts that Vic was sorting into boxes. His hands were black with grease.

'Did I make you sick?'

Vic flinched because I startled him.

'Eh?'

'I heard you throwing up last night.'

'Oh. No, no. Bit too much brandy, I reckon.'

I stepped into the garage.

'What are you doing?'

'Packing this stuff up. Otherwise someone'll just run through here and toss it all out. Might get some use this way.'

I walked up to a big object that was covered by a white sheet.

'What's under here?'

Vic stopped what he was doing and wiped his hands on a rag. He came over and removed the sheet. Underneath was a motorcycle. It was shiny and black with a silver engine.

'This is a 1953 Vincent Black Shadow,' he said. 'It was my old man's.'

Vic went over to a shelf and kneeled down to open an old toolbox. He pulled out a small black-and-white photo and showed it to me. A man and a boy were standing on either side of the motorbike.

'Is that you?'

Vic nodded.

'Taken the day he first rode it home.'

Vic's dad looked a lot like him. He had a handkerchief tied around his neck and his jacket had patches on the elbows. Both of them were squinting, and neither of them were smiling.

'Your dad doesn't look very happy.'

Vic laughed.

'That's because the old girl had just slammed the front door off its hinges. He knew how much shit he was in.'

'How come?'

'He'd gone out that morning to buy an automatic washing machine, and that's what he came back with.'

'Oh.'

Vic smiled and shook his head.

'She saved the whole year for that washing machine. She gave him the money in an envelope and made me go with him so he couldn't take a detour to the pub. Soon as we're out the door, he tells me we're going to the races at Ascot. He knew a groom who gave him the inside word on a three-year-old colt by the name of . . . what was it? Raconteur. That's right. He put every pound in that envelope on the nose and made me promise not to tell. It was the boldest thing I had ever seen. I was shaking as they went into the barriers. He picked me up and put me on his shoulders so I could see. We bellowed it home. Came in with daylight in between. He let me hold the collect. I'd never seen so much money. We could barely fit it in the envelope. And within the hour it was all gone. Spent it all on this motorcycle right here.'

'I can see why your mum was so angry.'

'Angry doesn't even touch the sides. She never washed his clothes again.'

'Good for her.'

Vic rubbed the motorcycle with the rag. He was really gentle with it.

'Made no difference to him. He loved this bike more than any of us. He'd take me out sometimes and open it up along the coast. Hundred mile an hour on a limestone track.'

'Were you scared?'

'Out of my skin. You'd never meet a man more accident prone than my father. He'd had more broken bones than a squashed snake, but he never got so much as a scratch on the Black Shadow. He was a different man when he rode it. I'd sit right here and close my eyes and hold on for dear life. He never took my sisters out on it. It was just for us. He took it apart to clean and repair it, showed me how the engine worked. That's what got me started on all this.'

I looked at all the machine parts lying around.

'Does it still go?'

'Like the clappers. Hasn't been really opened up on the road in maybe seven or eight years now, though. Tyres need a pump. Otherwise she's good as new. Edie loved it.' He pointed over my shoulder, and I turned to see two helmets hanging on the wall. One was matte black, the other was polished and lavender-coloured.

'Which one is yours?' I asked.

Vic laughed, which made me feel good. But then he started coughing again and he had to sit down on a paint tin. I put

40

the sheet back over the motorcycle, then I went over to him. I was worried. His face was really red and he couldn't get any air in. He stopped after a while and spat into his rag. I could see blood.

'Are you okay?'

'Yeah mate.'

'Do you want some water?'

Vic shook his head. I waited until he had his breath back.

'Vic, do you mind if I borrow some clothes? I've been wearing this for three days and I'm starting to smell bad.'

'Yeah, I've got some old duds in a chest of drawers in the bedroom. Help yourself.'

'Thanks. Can I have a shower too?'

'Of course.'

～

Vic's bathroom was dirty. I took the watch off and showered then went back to the bedroom wrapped in a crusty old towel that was hanging on a rack. I opened the chest of drawers. It was full of shorts and singlets and polo shirts. The bottom drawer had handkerchiefs and underwear and socks. I found one apricot-coloured handkerchief with lace edges that was stained with old brown blood.

It felt strange going through Vic's clothes. I chose a pair of black King Gee drawstring shorts and a white t-shirt with a sunset print. I laid them on the bed.

I knew I shouldn't, but before I put them on I slid open the door of the wardrobe. It was filled with Edie's clothes.

It was like I had found treasure. Her taste was amazing. My heart was pounding as I worked my way along the racks. I found a black sequinned halterneck dress, an emerald green jumpsuit, a royal blue silk gown, a navy floral pinafore dress. There was an embroidered stonewash denim jacket, a crimson wide-shouldered wool blazer with pearl buttons, a black leather skirt, high-waisted pants with wide black and white stripes, a lavender cardigan with deep pockets. In a box, covered in tissue paper, was her wedding dress. It was like she had kept every piece of clothing she had ever worn in her whole life. At the end of one of the racks I found a cute tartan baby-doll dress with a round white collar. I held it against my body. It looked like it would fit me perfectly. It was so pretty. I wanted to try it on, but I didn't.

In the drawers beneath I found tops and some nighties. There was a whole drawer full of knitwear. I pulled out an oversized mauve scoop neck jumper and laid it on the bed on top of Vic's clothes. In the bottom drawer there were leggings and tights and sweatbands and a stack of old aerobics videos. I matched the mauve jumper with a pair of black leggings and a pair of white Reebok sneakers with a pastel pink trim.

I stared at the outfit and chewed on my lower lip. I worried that it was too risky, but I tried it all on anyway. Everything fit perfectly, even the shoes. The clothes smelled musty, so I sprayed my wrists with some Elizabeth Arden perfume from the vanity table.

I sat down on the stool. It was hard to look at myself in the mirror. The cut on my jaw had a yellow bruise around it, and my skin looked blotchy. I opened a tub of foundation cream and spread some across my cheekbones and my sore jaw, but I still looked really ugly. None of that mattered anyway because I couldn't fix my hair. I barely even recognised myself.

~

My hair had always been long. By the time I was six, it had grown down to my waist. I liked brushing it and braiding it and swooshing it around. I thought it was beautiful. It was the only thing I loved about myself.

My mum didn't care, as long as I looked after it and let her trim my split ends. People always thought I was a little girl, and they would pull a strange face when my mum corrected them.

I knew most boys had short hair, but it wasn't until I started school that I felt ashamed of it. Boys pulled my ponytail and teased me and laughed. The girls looked at me like I was disgusting, and gossiped about me.

My first-grade teacher told my mum that I wasn't integrating or learning proper socialisation skills, and I would continue to be isolated until I got my hair cut. My mum enrolled me at a different school, but it wasn't any better. A boy called Danny Tarrant snuck up behind me during Silent Reading and cut off a chunk of my hair. I turned around and pushed him. He fell and the scissors sliced his hand open. There was blood and hair everywhere. I watched him scream and cry.

I was sent to the principal, who called my mum in to pick me up. They had a meeting in his office while I waited outside. When she came out she looked tired. She drove me straight to a shopping plaza and didn't say a word. She led me into a salon called Hair To Dye For. I knew I was in trouble, so I just hid behind her and tried to be invisible.

Then a hairdresser with bright red highlights came over and reached for my hand. Her name was Doreen.

My mum said we were just there to trim my hair, so I went with Doreen. I sat in the high chair and she fixed a big black smock over me and sprayed my hair with water. Then she showed me a scrapbook with different boy's hairstyles. I pushed it away and started to squirm. Doreen tried to calm me down by saying how handsome I was going to look, but that just made it worse. My mum came over and told me to behave. I felt trapped. I started crying and I begged my mum to let me leave. Everyone in the salon was staring at me. Doreen started combing my hair, but the moment she picked up the scissors I panicked. I slid off the chair and ran outside with the smock still on. I went through the car park and ran across the road without looking. I kept running until there were houses around, and I hid in a carport behind a wheelie bin. After a while, a nice old lady came out of the house and sat with me.

A little while later I heard my mum calling out. She was walking down the street with some other people from the shopping plaza. The old lady waved her over. I was frightened when my mum charged up the driveway, but she pulled me to my feet and gave me a big hug. She promised not to take me to a hairdresser again.

That night I agreed to let her cut my hair just past shoulder length, and she taught me how to tie a low braided bun so I might get teased less at school.

It had been a stressful day for her, so she went out that night. When she came home she could barely stand and she was angry. She started yelling at me. She told me she got fired because she had to leave her shift early to come to my school. She had no money because of me. No life because of me. She was alone because of me. She would never have anything because of me.

The next morning she didn't remember any of what she had said. But I never forgot it.

~

I got up from the vanity table and went to the garage to see if Vic wanted me to make him breakfast. He looked up and stopped what he was doing and stared at me. I took a step back because I knew I had made a mistake. He looked shocked.

'What are you doing?'

'I don't know. You said—'

'Why are you in those clothes? Are you trying to be funny? You think this is a joke? Take them off!'

His face was red and his eyes were glassy. I wanted to say sorry but no words came out.

'Take them off! Now!'

He slammed his hand down hard and loud on the workbench. My knees went weak and I collapsed in the doorway, but I quickly got back up and walked through the house and straight out the front door. My face was really hot and I felt sick in my stomach. I folded my arms and hunched over and put my head down and walked quickly down the street. Then I heard someone call out.

'Hey!'

I worried it was the mean lady, so I kept walking.

'*Hey!*'

It didn't sound like her. I stopped and looked around.

'Over here, dopey!'

I turned and saw the girl from the day before waving from a window of the red-brick house.

'Nice kicks!'

I didn't say anything.

'Hey, you want some brownies? I made like a whole tray. They kind of have the texture of wood, but they taste okay.'

I looked at the ground and shook my head.

'No. It's okay.'

But she insisted.

'Come on!' she said. 'I'll open the door.'

I hesitated. Then I slowly walked up to her house. The door opened and she smiled. She had dimples. She looked different out of her school uniform. Her hair was messy. She wore black jeans and a black t-shirt and her feet were bare.

'Come on, come in!' she said.

She turned off the television and picked up the tray of brownies, which were burned on top. She led me through the house like I had been going there for years. It was really clean and nice.

'I was just watching *Buffy*, even though I can essentially recite the whole thing. My parents aren't here. My mum is making my dad try Pilates because he will *not* shut the fuck up about his sore back. She's convinced it's because he has zero flexibility, which is true in every conceivable sense.'

I tried to keep up, but she spoke really fast.

Her room was a mess. The bed was unmade and her clothes and shoes were all over the floor. She had a shelf full of books, and rows of small fantasy figurines on display. Her desk was piled with textbooks.

There was a brass instrument open in a case. She caught me looking at it.

'It's a euphonium.'

I nodded slowly. She kicked the case closed and put on a strange accent.

'It's naht a tooba! It's naht!'

I must have looked confused.

'Schwarzenegger? No? Nobody ever laughs at that. I'm in the school band. My dad says the brass section suits me because I'm full of hot air, so, you know, lame jokes run in the family.'

She sat on her bed and patted a spot for me to sit on.

'My brother's home, but he's still asleep, which is his natural state. Oh! I'm Aggie! Sorry.'

She waved and shook my hand in an awkward way.

'Actually it's Agnes. I *know*. I have the world's ugliest name. Agnes Meemeduma. My mum's Scottish and my dad's Sri Lankan. Apparently my dad insisted that we all had to be burdened with his surname, so my mum was like, well, if you're

47

going to perpetuate the patriarchy, I'm choosing the first names of our children, which was just a sly excuse to double-fuck us by giving us the names of her grandparents. Why she would knowingly bring *Agnes* into a new millennium I can't tell you. Obviously everyone at school calls me Fagness and Faggie. So, it's been a dream run.'

She rolled her eyes and took a breath.

'Though when I'm annoying her she calls me the Ag Ness Monster, which is pretty cute. And to be fair to my dad, the alternative was *her* surname. I'm not even kidding, her maiden name is McNutt. Can you believe it? If my dad wasn't so obstinately fucking retrograde, we would have been the McNutts. I'll take the ethnic profiling, thanks. Oh my goodness, I do *not* shut up. I'm sorry. What's your name?'

'Sam. Watson.'

'See? That's a good, solid name. You can go anywhere with that name. You're very . . . *striking*, Sam Watson. Is that a weird thing to say? Do you want a brownie? I'm going to, like, plug my mouth with one.'

'I'm not very hungry.'

Aggie took a chunk of brownie and bit down hard on it with the side of her mouth. A piece broke off with a loud snap and she laughed.

'It's okay, my dad's a dentist. Like, for real.'

'So what's your brother's name?'

'Oh my God.' She crunched the brownie and talked with her mouth full. 'So this is where it's *so* unfair. His name is Dylan, which is an objectively stylish name, right? I tried to argue that

I should have been called Dylan, but he's three years older, so he got dibs. Anyway, he doesn't deserve it. I mean, I'm a genuine nerd, but he's on a whole different spectrum of social dysfunction. He leaves his room about as often as that fucking groundhog that forecasts the weather, and when he does he just grunts or tries to lecture someone about cryptocurrency.'

She stopped speaking for a moment to try another bite of brownie, but she thought better of it and started laughing again.

'I think you might have baked them too long,' I said.

She sighed.

'Nobody in this house can cook to save themselves. We're like a primitive tribe or something. Like, we all just huddle around the toaster and poke it with a stick. I really felt like brownies today.'

'I can make them for you.'

'Shut *up*. Seriously?'

I nodded. It felt good that she was impressed.

'Oh, wait. I think I used all the butter.'

'That's okay. There's other stuff you can use.'

'What do you mean? What kind of wizardry is that?'

I shrugged.

'If you made me brownies right now, I would literally die with gratitude.'

Aggie looked at me expectantly.

'Okay.'

She bounced off the bed and led me to the kitchen. The oven was still on, set at the highest temperature.

I turned it right down.

'Your oven was too hot.'

'It's weird. The recipe said three hundred and something, but our oven doesn't even go that high.'

'I think that's in Fahrenheit. The oven is Celsius.'

She blushed and covered her mouth with her hands.

'Oh my God, that is *genuinely* embarrassing. I feel this sudden need to credentialise and tell you that I'm the top of my year in physics and chem, but I actually think that makes it worse.'

'It's okay. I've made the same mistake before. The person who taught me to cook was American.'

'You're very forgiving, Sam Watson.'

I blushed and turned away and opened the pantry door. There was so much food in there. I was amazed. I found a jar of coconut oil.

'We can use this instead of butter.'

'Seriously? You really *are* a wizard.'

All the other ingredients were still on the kitchen bench. I measured the flour while Aggie scraped her brownies into the bin. Even though I was in a different house with somebody I didn't know, I felt calm.

'How would you like them to turn out?' I asked.

'Honestly, I'll be dazzled by anything that's not fossilised.'

'No, I mean do you want them chewy, or more like cake, or like fudge?'

'Wait, you can do that on purpose?'

'Sure.'

'Can I have fudgey?'

'Yeah. It's easy. You just need more egg.'

Aggie gasped and slapped her forehead with her palm. Then she walked to the fridge and took out a carton of eggs.

'I forgot to put these in.'

She groaned and knocked her head against my shoulder. It felt nice.

I pulled up my sleeves and mixed the batter. I spilled some on the bench and on my wrist.

'Hey, holy shit, nice watch,' Aggie said.

I just shrugged and poured the batter onto a greased tray. I put the tray in the oven and we went back to her room.

'So what's the deal with you and Vic? Is he your grandfather?'

I shook my head.

'Oh, so he's like a family friend or something?'

'Sort of.'

'Are you living with him?'

'Not anymore.'

'Oh. That's a shame. It was good you were there. I've never seen anyone visit him. He seems a bit lonely.'

'His wife passed away.'

'I know. It's so sad.'

'Do you know how she died?'

Aggie shook her head.

'All I know is that she went in her sleep. I think it might have been an aneurysm or something?'

Aggie started talking about something else, but I wasn't really listening. I kept thinking about Vic waking up and turning over to say good morning to Edie. I imagined him trying to wake her up, and realising that she had died right next to him. I almost started to cry, but then the oven timer went off.

Aggie bounced off the bed and clapped.

'Brownies!'

I followed her to the kitchen. I pulled the tray out of the oven and tested the brownies with a knife. They came out really well.

Aggie reached for the knife to cut into them.

'You have to leave them for another ten minutes at least,' I said.

'But they smell so *good*!'

'They still cook while they're cooling down. If you eat one now it'll be a bit underdone.'

'I'm learning so much. Can I enshrine your creation on Instagram?'

'Okay.'

Aggie took a photo with her phone.

'Hey, I'll tag you.'

'I don't have an account or anything,' I said.

'Seriously?'

I shrugged.

'Of course you don't,' she said. 'Because for you, baking brownies while looking ridiculously fashionable isn't some cynical excuse to draw attention to yourself on the internet, it's just who you are every damn day.'

'That's not it,' I said.

'It totally is. Anyway, I'm not as modest as you, so I'm going to show you off to my dozens of followers, half of which are seedy men from Mumbai. But if you ever want to see how famous you get, my Instagram is "memedoomer", except, like, *meem* is spelled like meme and *duma* is spelled like doom-er, because, as you know, I'm a very lame person. Can I eat it now? Please?'

I smiled.

'No, not yet.'

'Okay. How about just this piece that fell off?'

Aggie raised one eyebrow and cut a piece off the end. She blew on it and put it in her mouth and I got nervous.

Her eyes went wide as she chewed.

'Holy fucking *shit*! Sam! This tastes amazing! How did you do that?'

'They're pretty easy,' I said. I was relieved and happy that she liked them.

Aggie's brother walked into the kitchen. He was in his late teens and he looked like he had just woken up. He was tall and chubby and wore glasses. I stepped closer to Aggie as he opened the fridge door.

'This is my new friend Sam,' Aggie said. 'Look, he made brownies.'

'Hey,' he said without looking at me. He drank from a bottle of orange juice then walked back out.

'He has no interpersonal skills. I've diagnosed him with, like, six behavioural disorders, but he refuses to see anyone about them.'

'Shut the fuck up, Aggie,' he called out from another room.

'See?' Aggie laughed quietly, and I smiled because she had called me her friend. Nobody had ever said that about me before.

When they were cool, Aggie cut six brownies and put them on a plate. I started cleaning up, but Aggie made me stop. We went back to her room. I felt bad about leaving the kitchen a mess, but Aggie didn't seem worried.

'Hey, you know Mrs Boyd knocked on our door yesterday.'

'Mrs Boyd?'

'The woman who accosted you on the street. She came to warn my parents about this young troublemaker she saw coming out of Vic's place.'

'Really?'

Aggie laughed.

'I told you. She's a menace.'

'Do you think she'll call the police or something?'

'For what? Occupying space in the universe?'

'I don't know.'

'I doubt she wants anything to do with the police anyway.'

'Because of her husband?'

'Do you want to know why he went to jail?'

'Okay.'

Aggie sat forwards and dusted crumbs off her lap.

'You might have actually heard the story. It made the news everywhere. It's *crazy*. So, their house got burgled a few years ago while they were still home. I mean, it must have been genuinely frightening. Like, I'd feel sorry for her if she wasn't so irritating. Anyway, it essentially turned Mrs Boyd into a hyper-vigilant ball of paranoia. She got sensor lights and cameras installed everywhere, deadbolts and security windows, the whole thing. Then Mr Boyd goes a step further. I don't know if he was like, totally emasculated or just embarrassed by having his stuff taken and not being able to intervene, but he adopts this rescue dog called Marvin, which was a ridgeback or something and *insanely* aggressive. Marvin barked constantly, and they couldn't take him to the park because he tried to eat anything that moved. The only creature Marvin didn't want to straight up assassinate was Mr Boyd, so he had to take Marvin out for walks late at night while there was nobody else around. Anyway, late one night he's walking Marvin through the neighbourhood, like, six blocks away from here, and he hears a woman calling out in distress from inside a house. She's like, '*Stop, please, God no, stop, please!*' So Mr Boyd figures it's probably the same burglars from his place, right, and this time he's going to stop them. He tries the front door, but it's locked, so he opens the side gate and runs to the back of the house with Marvin. He shoulder-charges the back door and goes through the house. He bursts into a bedroom and finds an older woman tied to bed, her clothes all ripped, and there's an older man standing over her. So Mr Boyd pushes this guy, hard. And Marvin goes fucking crazy and starts attacking him, like, really savage. The woman on the bed starts screaming, and the man is begging for help, trying to fend off Marvin. Then Mr Boyd looks around and sees, like, these sex accessories or whatever on the bed and realises he has completely misinterpreted the situation and he's just barged in on a married couple who just like it spicy and are in the middle of some fetish roleplay. So he tears Marvin off this man, who is panicking so much that he can't breathe. The woman is still tied to the bed and she's, like, *shrieking*. Mr Boyd locks Marvin in a bathroom and calls an ambulance, and here's the thing: the man has a massive coronary infarction and dies on the way to the hospital. And even though Mr Boyd explained that he went in there to save this woman who he thought was being attacked, he's charged and convicted with trespass and manslaughter. Seriously. He got three years. Not only that, the woman sued him in a civil trial and got this huge payout.'

'When does he get out?'

'That's the other thing. He was released in like eighteen months, but he was a totally different person. He divorced Mrs Boyd and moved to Bali and now she's this bitter neighbourhood despot.'

'What happened to Marvin?'

'Good question. I assume they put him down. That's what they usually do when a dog attacks somebody, right?'

'I guess. I feel sad for him.'

'Marvin? Are you kidding? I don't. He was an arsehole.'

'It wasn't his fault. He was abandoned. He was probably scared and worried all the time, and that's why he was so aggressive. He didn't belong anywhere. I don't know. Maybe it was for the best that they killed him. He never really had much hope. Maybe Marvin felt relieved in the end. You know, because he didn't have to be afraid anymore.'

Aggie went quiet. She looked at me for a long time. I worried that I said the wrong thing. Then she nodded.

'I didn't think about it like that,' she said.

~

I stayed at Aggie's for hours, mostly listening to her talk. She was really smart. Late in the afternoon she plugged her phone in to charge, and I remembered that I left my phone at Vic's. I had to go back.

I told her I had to leave.

Aggie walked me to the door. Then she held her arms out and gave me a hug. I flinched at first, but she felt really warm and soft.

'Thanks for making me brownies, Sam Watson.'

'That's okay.'

'Come over again?'

'Sure.'

Aggie closed the door. I liked her.

I put my head down and walked fast past Mrs Boyd's house. At Vic's, I took a deep breath and knocked on the door, but he didn't answer. I knocked again. He probably didn't want to speak to me.

I went around the side and climbed onto a bin and looked through the garage window. The Kingswood was gone. I worried that he wasn't coming back and it was my fault.

I sat by the front door with my knees pulled up to my chest and made myself as small as I could. I waited until it started to get dark. Lights in the houses across the street turned on one by one. I looked at my watch. I thought about going back to the overpass.

Then, finally, Vic pulled up.

He got out of the car to open the garage door and he saw me. He put his hand on his chest.

'Jesus *wept*,' he said. 'Don't run off like that.'

'Vic, I'm really sorry. I just wanted to say that. I'm going to go and leave you alone. I just need to get my phone. But I wanted to tell you I was sorry as well.'

Vic sighed.

'It's alright mate. Come on inside.'

I followed him in. He hadn't even locked his front door.

Vic turned on the lights and pulled out a seat for me at the table. He looked really tired.

'Sit down,' he said.

'Do you want me to get changed first?'

'No mate. It's fine. Come on. Sit.'

I sat down and pulled my sleeves over my wrists.

Vic scratched his beard. He looked uncomfortable.

'I'm sorry I got worked up and gave you a fright,' he said. 'It was just a shock to me, seeing those clothes. I thought you were being funny, making a joke of her.'

'I wouldn't do that. I'm really sorry. I just didn't think. I won't wear them again, I promise.'

'No, no. Look, if that's what you want to wear, you can wear them.'

Vic looked at the mauve jumper.

'It's nice to see them out and about.'

'You really think so?'

'Yeah.'

'You don't think I'm . . .'

I went quiet.

Vic frowned and shook his head.

'Mate, you'll have to forgive me. I'm not very good at this. I was your age a long time ago. The world's very different now. But I know that Edie would love that you were giving her kit a run. She would've . . .'

Vic cleared his throat and tapped the table. Then he kept going.

'She would've enjoyed having you here. She missed having someone like you in her life. She'd be fussing all over you right now.'

'Really?'

'My wife used to see a sale rack and go weak at the knees. She bought more clothes than she had places to wear them.'

'Her wardrobe is really beautiful.'

'It's all lost on me, mate. Never had much of an eye for that sort of thing.'

'Vic, you really honestly wouldn't mind if I wore some of her other clothes? It's not going to upset you?'

'No.'

'Are you sure?'

'If you like them, you're welcome to them.'

My hands were shaking, and I put them under the table and squeezed them between my legs. I blushed.

'Thank you,' I said.

∼

Later, I got undressed in front of the vanity mirror.

I looked at my body. With short hair, my head looked smaller and my neck looked longer. There were bruises all over my body. Some were big and red and purple. The smaller ones were green and yellow. My skin was really pale. I hated how straight and bony my shoulders were. I hated my ribs. I hated my thin hips. I hated my arms and the veins that ran up my wrists. I hated my flat chest. I hated my cheekbones and I hated my jaw and I hated the lump in my throat. I hated my penis. I hated my legs and the thick brown hairs that grew from my thighs to my feet.

I looked away and folded my arms and sat on the bed and felt sick in my stomach. I realised I was in a strange house with a man I didn't know. Vic was nice to me, but I didn't know why. I felt lost. I thought about my mum and my chest seized up. It had only been a couple of days, but I missed her really badly. I wanted to call her, but I knew I had ruined everything and I couldn't go back. I was on my own and it was my fault and it made me feel small and afraid. It was hard to breathe and the room started to spin. I closed my eyes tight and dug my nails into my palms but it didn't work.

I got out the plastic lighter that I stole from behind the supermarket. I made a flame and kept it burning until the metal around it went black. Then I pressed it against my thigh. When I took it off a small strip of my skin tore away. I heated the metal again. The piece of skin smoked and smelled awful. I held the lighter down where I was bleeding and it made a small hiss. I closed my eyes again and I gritted my teeth and I started to feel better.

Venus and Mars

When I was really young I used to wear my mum's t-shirts with nothing else except underwear. They went all the way down to my knees. I liked the bright colours and patterns and all that soft fabric around me. I liked the way the neckline was so big that it exposed my shoulder. Sometimes I cinched the waist with a belt. My mum would dress me at the start of the day in fitted clothes she got from op shops, but I always took them off and went to her drawers. She had a royal blue crushed velvet t-shirt that I wore every chance I got.

My mum worried that I was just trying to mimic her, because our world was so small and I didn't have any other role models. She took me to the park sometimes and made me play with other boys. I was shy and I didn't care about trucks or dinosaurs or water pistols or ball games. But I tried hard because she told me that this was what boys liked to do.

I hated my school uniforms, which were always shorts and polo shirts. In my first year of school I took a pleated skirt out of the lost property box and put it on. My teacher made me take it off and told me that boys and girls had to have separate uniforms, like players on different teams.

When I was in year three, I was taken out of class by Mrs Barnes, the school counsellor. She took me to her office. She had sandy grey hair and was really thin and looked at me without blinking. I thought I was in trouble. She asked questions about my long hair, about why I had no friends, about my mum, about my dad, about things I liked and didn't like. Then she asked if I was a boy or a girl.

'I don't know,' I said. 'I'm just myself.'

She asked me again. It was a question other kids always asked when they were teasing me. I knew that being a girl was something weird and wrong and shameful.

I told her I was a boy.

She went out of the room for a while, and she came back with an envelope. She told me to give it to my mum when I got home. I opened it as soon as school ended. It said that I should see a psychologist. I ripped it into little pieces and threw it away.

I tried harder to fit in, but there wasn't a space for me. I didn't know how I was supposed to be. It was like I was born speaking a language that nobody else could understand, but I couldn't talk any other way. So I stopped speaking, and I learned how to be invisible.

One night a couple of months after speaking to Mrs Barnes, I was watching cartoons on the iPad I stole from Gabby. Bugs Bunny was being chased by a little bald man with a gun. To trick him, Bugs disguised himself as a woman in a green jumpsuit and red lipstick, and he danced and sang a little song. It gave me a strange queasiness in my stomach and I got tingles all down my neck. I watched it over and over.

My mum was out, so I went into her room and found a green summer dress. I had never put on a dress before. Then I went into the bathroom and tried on her red lipstick. I pressed my lips together with a tissue between them, just like she always did. I stared at myself. I had never felt pretty before, and I liked it.

I put on a pair of low black heels and spent the next few hours swooshing and dancing and singing that little song: 'Can't you see that I'm much sweeter? I'm your little senorita.'

My mum came home around midnight and caught me. She was really angry. She said she could hear me singing from the bottom steps of the apartment block. She grabbed me hard by the arm and marched me towards the bathroom. She smelled like licorice and cigarettes and perfume. When her heels fell off my feet she dragged me the rest of the way. She scrubbed at my lips and told me that if I ever wore her clothes or her make-up again she would leave me out on the street. Then she pulled the dress up over my head so fast that my arm got caught and the seam ripped. She yelled at me for a long time about how she had no privacy and nothing for herself and that I made everything difficult and I didn't respect the sacrifices she made.

I didn't dress up again for a few months after that, not even in my mum's t-shirts. I thought about it every day, though. I wanted to feel that way again, but I didn't want her to abandon me.

Then I found a communal laundry room in the apartment block. People would run a dryer cycle overnight and pick up their clothes in the morning. When my mum was out at night, I went down there and opened the dryer and stole anything that was small and looked nice. I took them back and put them on. Then I coloured my lips with red crayon and used an old watercolour set for eyeshadow. I played for a couple of hours, then I would hide the clothes in a garbage bag and wash my face.

I felt ashamed, because I knew it was wrong, but I couldn't stop. It was addictive. I started looking forward to my mum going out and leaving me by myself. When I dressed up, I felt relaxed and happy. It was like unclenching my fist. I didn't have to be Sam anymore. I liked looking at this new person in the mirror.

The more I enjoyed it, the worse I felt afterwards. I thought I was the only person in the world who did it. When I stuffed the clothes back in the garbage bag, I always told myself it was the last time, but the next chance I got, I dressed up again.

Then everything got really hard.

We had been living in an apartment block in Midland for about six months. A week after my eleventh birthday, I got home from school and my mum was stuffing all her clothes into suitcases and black plastic bags. She told me to hurry up and do the same, because our landlord was coming back with the police to evict us. I only had a few minutes. We threw all our clothes and anything valuable into my mum's Hyundai and drove away just as the police came around the corner. I was really upset that we had to leave all my kitchen utensils behind. Then I remembered that I left the shoebox full of tissue kisses under the bed. Then I remembered the most precious thing of all.

'Did you bring the honeybee?' I asked.

'What? No, I don't think so. Be quiet, I have to think.'

I begged her to go back, but she wouldn't. I was devastated. The honeybee was gone. I tried to cry as silently as I could.

We didn't have any money or anywhere to go. All her credit cards had been cancelled. We couldn't find a place to rent because we had been blacklisted. She was too proud to stay with her friends or at a refuge, so we lived in the car.

She told me we were on a camping trip, a real one this time. In the evenings we went to the beach and used the showers in the change rooms. Then we drove to the closest supermarket and crept around the back to go on a treasure hunt, which meant looking through the skip bins for food. A lot of it was still in plastic packaging and okay to eat.

Late at night we parked in quiet neighbourhoods near ovals or parks and locked the doors. We slept on the back seat and kept each other warm. My mum hummed songs and I pretended to fall asleep. I felt safe with her. We got caught a few times by security guards and had to move. It was cosy and fun at first, but I missed having a kitchen, and I really missed dressing up.

After a few days my mum started going to pubs at night. She left me in the car and told me she would be back in an hour. I would sit there until the pub closed and she came out.

Some nights she took me in with her. I sat on my own and watched horseracing on the television or rolled balls on the pool table. Sometimes someone who worked behind the bar would bring me a basket of chips or a side salad or a glass of Coke. At one pub I found a ten-dollar note under a table. I gave it to my mum at the bar. She was talking to a man in a pink collared shirt. When he saw me, he said he had to make a call and left. My mum put the ten-dollar note on the beer mat, and later I saw the barman take it. The man in the pink shirt never came back, but she was already talking to somebody else.

My mum was really beautiful. She had long blonde hair and a nice figure and high cheekbones. Wherever we went men looked at her. Sometimes they called out rude things, or they walked up and flirted. She was always gossiping or complaining about men on the phone with her friends, but she never introduced me to any of them.

We had been living in the car for almost three months and we both knew we couldn't do it for much longer. Then my mum met Steve, and everything changed really quickly.

I met Steve on the day we moved into his house in Scarborough. He had a square jaw and a big chest and a round gut and he was tall. He had faded tattoos down his left arm. He was ten years older than my mum.

My mum told me he was her friend, but I knew they were together. He grabbed her waist a lot, and he liked to put his arm around her shoulder and pull her close. She would smile and lean into him. They had only known each other for a few days.

66

Steve's house had two storeys and it was close to the beach. We had never lived anywhere like it. There was a boat on a trailer in the driveway. In the garage he had a late-model ute and a four-wheel drive and a jetski and a dirt bike. The lounge room had a huge couch and a big television. Upstairs, there was a whole room filled with electric guitars and amplifiers, and another room had an exercise bike and a set of dumbbells with dust on them.

Steve led me to a room with a new bed that hadn't been assembled yet and an empty wardrobe. It was my first ever bedroom. Steve asked what I thought, and I couldn't say anything because I was so shy and overwhelmed. Later, my mum pulled me aside and told me to be more grateful because Steve was saving us. When I thanked him, he said loudly that it was his pleasure. I think he liked that he was helping us out of a rough place. He talked about it all the time.

I heard them having sex a lot. The first time it happened I ran down the hall when I heard my mum crying out. I thought Steve was attacking her. I charged into their room and I saw my mum on her knees and Steve behind her. I ran up and pushed him and told him to stop. He shoved me away really hard, and I hit my head on the nightstand.

My mum picked me up and took me to my room. She calmed me down and told me Steve wasn't hurting her, and I should never enter their room without knocking again. I crept back down the hall after she left, and I heard her apologising to him.

My mum fell in love with him really quickly, and she wanted me to feel the same way. I told her I didn't like Steve and that

I wanted to go back to how things were. She slapped my face, which she had never done before, and told me I didn't know how lucky I was. I had never had a father figure, and now there was somebody who was prepared to help raise me. She wanted us to be a family.

Later, she told Steve what I had said about him, and that hurt more than the slap.

Steve tried to win me over. He bought me a computer. He picked me up from school and asked how my day was. He took me to the park and tried to teach me how to kick a football and play cricket, but I was bad at all of it. If my mum was there he would be patient and encouraging, but if it was just the two of us he was hard on me. He told me I was too soft because I had been spoiled my whole life and he was going to make a man out of me. He told me I needed to cut my hair and stand straight and toughen up. He made me try sit-ups and push-ups on the playground equipment.

One day at the park he asked me if I liked boys or girls. I didn't know what he meant, so I shrugged and said I didn't really like anyone. He pointed at a woman jogging past in tight-fitting activewear. She was really pretty. He asked me if I liked her body and I said yes. He smiled and told me I was a good boy.

He took us fishing on his boat. I hooked a skipjack one time and Steve crowded me and shouted and I panicked and lost the fish.

'Why did you stop reeling? I told you, pull up and reel down! It's easy!'

'I'm sorry.'

My mum was wearing a straw hat and drinking prosecco. She was nice about it.

'It's okay. You'll get the next one, Honeybee.'

Steve lost his temper.

'Stop treating him like a baby.'

'Excuse me?'

'Stop coddling him. He messed up. He needs to learn.'

'Don't tell me how to raise my son.'

Steve snatched the fishing rod out of my hand.

'My parents didn't raise a son, they raised a man. Calling him fucking Honeybee and protecting his feelings isn't going to help him grow up.'

'Well I've been doing this longer than you.'

'Fine. Keep wrapping him in cotton wool. I don't give a shit.'

Steve started the boat and took us back to shore and didn't speak to either of us for the rest of the day.

After that, she never called me Honeybee again.

I wanted to show Steve what I was good at, so I cooked dinner a few times. He never seemed impressed, and sometimes didn't finish what I had made. He didn't have much interest in nice food or spices. I only ever saw him eat burgers and pizza and pies and Chinese takeaway.

My mum stopped going out at night. She almost never left the house. She sat on the balcony and drank wine and smoked cigarettes and tanned her legs and read magazines and sketched pretty dresses in a notepad. She had hundreds of designs. She could draw really well, and she was really stylish and creative.

I wished that I could talk to her about clothes and tell her my secret.

She didn't see her friends anymore. Steve didn't like them. He told her she needed a fresh start and better guidance. He should be her inspiration, he said. He had come from nothing. His family were poor and lazy. His brother was in jail and he had cousins who were patched members of motorcycle gangs. His old friends were addicts and criminals and dealers and losers. He could have been trapped in that world, but he learned a trade and worked hard and now he was rich and successful. He had to leave his family and friends behind, because he knew they would drag him back down.

Steve was a boilermaker. He worked on location up in the mines. He would fly out for two weeks and then come home for one. I was always relieved when I saw him packing his bags. When he came home he was tired and moody for a couple of days. He sat on the couch and played *Call of Duty* and my mum would bring him beer and potato chips and crawl up beside him like a pet cat. She was a different person when Steve was home. She treated him like a king. It made me jealous. She cleaned all the time and did his laundry and agreed with everything he said.

Once I brought one of Steve's Gibson guitars downstairs so she could play and sing. She got embarrassed and said Steve was much better than her, which wasn't true. When she took the guitar back upstairs, Steve grabbed my arm hard and told me never to touch his things without his permission. He let me go when she came back down.

One night I heard her crying. I got out of bed and watched from the stairs. She was sitting at the table with Steve, holding a piece of paper. The police had come to the house and given her a court summons for default payments and unpaid fines. They warned her if she didn't attend she would be sent to jail. I almost ran to her when I heard her say that, but I knew I would be in trouble for listening.

Steve wanted to know about her debts. My mum was ashamed and she cried for a long time. Finally she admitted to all her unpaid rent and her credit card debts and her court fees and her fines for driving an unregistered car without a licence. She owed tens of thousands of dollars. She said she had ignored it because it was too stressful, and the problem had got worse.

Steve was annoyed that she hadn't told him. My mum said she was scared he would leave her. Steve put his hands on her shoulders. He was really calm. He told her he was an expert at personal finances, and he did all his own taxes. He knew all the tricks, and he would help her get through it. He offered to pay her outstanding fines, and after that she would have to apply for bankruptcy. He said the agency collectors would still chase her, but they were easy to ignore, and after three years all her debts would be erased. She wouldn't owe anything, except to him, but he would never hold it over her.

We had never needed help from anyone before. We had always found a way together. I wanted her to refuse, but she gave in. She cried and Steve put his arms around her. He was the most important person in her life now. I knew that she would never leave him.

I felt so alone. I watched Julia Child videos on my new computer and it made my chest settle down a bit. I pretended she was talking directly to me.

'One of the secrets of cooking is to learn to correct something if you can, and bear with it if you cannot,' she said.

'Okay,' I said. 'I'll try.'

I wanted to dress up. I missed it so much that I ached. It was like being really hungry or really cold: it was all I could think about. But I had left all my clothes behind at the apartment, and I couldn't risk it anyway. Instead, I looked at pictures of pretty dresses online and imagined I was wearing them. It wasn't the same.

～

I started at Ocean View High School. I mostly kept to myself. I ate lunch with some Sudanese kids who didn't mind me sitting with them. The first term wasn't so bad, but then some boys from the year above started coming for me.

I had never met them, but they all seemed to know my name. They teased me in the halls between classes. They started rumours about me. They punched me hard in the thighs and pushed me to the ground and spat on me and told me faggots belonged on their knees. One recess they pushed me into the toilets and pinned me down and kicked me and ripped my shorts off and threw them outside. They turned everyone against me. The Sudanese kids said I couldn't sit with them anymore.

I tried to ignore them, but that made it worse. I started hiding before and after school, and I stayed close to the teachers on lunchtime duty, but they always got to me. They would sneak up behind me and elbow me in the back of the head or pull my hair so hard I fell backwards. I started flinching a lot.

By the start of the second term they were branding me. They did it by heating the end of a cigarette lighter and pressing it against my arm or my leg or my neck. The skin would blister and scar.

I was really unhappy. I started dressing up again, late at night. I took my mum's skirts and dresses and stockings from the dirty clothes basket, then I locked my bedroom door and put Steve's dumbbells behind for extra security. I got dressed up and brushed my hair out and looked at myself in the mirror, and it was me who looked back. I would wear my mum's clothes for an hour or so before I got changed and put them back. I always felt guilty and disgusted with myself, but it was the only thing I had to look forward to.

Once I started again, I couldn't stop. I skipped school and went into the city to steal clothes. I hit cheap department stores and op shops. I was careful and patient. Most stores had undercover detectives and the staff knew what to look out for. I never took my bag with me, I never looked nervous, I never scouted the cameras, and I never got caught.

I was good at it. I had a few tricks that worked. Sometimes I would wait until a middle-aged lady approached the store, then I entered with her so the staff thought I was her son. If I was lucky she went to the women's clothing section and I would quickly look around, take something off the rack and stuff it under my hoodie. Then I walked out of the store with her.

Make-up was easy to lift because no one expected me to steal it. I would go into a chemist and say I wanted to buy my mum some lipstick for her birthday. The person behind the counter would show me where they kept the cosmetics. Sometimes they tried to help, but mostly they left me alone to look. Then I would drop something and stuff a bunch of samples in my pockets as I bent down to pick it up. When I left, I would thank the sales assistant and tell them I would be back when I got my pocket money.

I dressed up every night, and I did it for longer and longer. I didn't sleep much. I felt dazed during the day, then at home I came alive. I was two separate people. I walked around my room in a slip dress or a maxi or a playsuit and pretended I was a person that everybody liked. I whispered imaginary conversations. I moved and spoke differently and I wasn't afraid.

I still thought I was the only person in the world who behaved this way, but one night I got curious. I googled **do other boys dress up like girls?** and there were over a billion results. I thought it must be a mistake, so I clicked on a few of the sites that had come up. That's how I discovered drag.

It was like finding out there was a whole new nation of people who were just like me. I looked at thousands of photos. I dressed up and watched videos of lip syncs and dance performances at clubs. I watched every episode of *RuPaul's Drag Race*. It was all so big and loud and elegant and colourful. The queens were so beautiful and confident and funny. It wasn't anyone's secret.

I was relieved there were other people like me, but watching from my room in my stolen clothes and my messy make-up made me feel really far away and even more lonely.

I found an old documentary called *Paris is Burning* about the underground drag balls in New York City. One performer was called Venus Xtravaganza. She was small and pretty and softly spoken. She started dressing up when she was thirteen years old and she hid it from her family too. When they caught her, she ran away.

Watching her, my chest got tight and my throat swelled up so much I couldn't swallow. Then she said something that made me start shaking.

'I don't feel like there's anything mannish about me, except maybe what I might have between me down there, which is why I want my sex change, to make myself complete.'

I went back and listened to her say it again and again. I felt queasy and I couldn't breathe. In my head I didn't know what any of it meant, but in my heart I understood.

I typed: can a girl be born as a boy?

Everything made sense and nothing made sense at the same time. I read lots of articles and I filled out questionnaires and I was confused and I was certain. I didn't feel relieved to know. I felt scared. And I felt revolting. I didn't want to be this way. I didn't want to be mixed up. I just wanted to be normal. But I wasn't. I was all wrong, and I didn't know how to be right. Now I knew that you could change your body, like Venus had wanted, but I didn't know how or who to speak to.

I stopped reading about it. I ignored everything. I told myself that it wasn't true. I stopped dressing up. I threw out the clothes I had stolen. I stopped eating, and I didn't want to cook anymore. I stopped watching Julia Child.

My body was changing. I grew taller. Hair started growing in other places. There was no way to stop it. I started having the nightmare about being trapped on the train. I would wake up in the dark feeling like there was somebody sitting on my chest. It was hopeless.

I hated my body. I stole my mum's cigarette lighter and at night I would press the hot metal into my skin like the boys at school did. I burned myself in places nobody would see, under my armpits, between my legs, then on the skin of my penis. I would concentrate all my thoughts onto that small area, and it made everything else less noisy. I could get to sleep that way.

When I woke up in the morning I always had a couple of seconds of emptiness before I remembered who I was and what was wrong and I felt full of dread and shame. It was like I had done something terrible and I was in a lot of trouble, except the trouble never came. I was just stuck waiting to be punished.

It wasn't ever going to get better. Every single day I got further and further away from who I was. There was never going to be a happy ending.

There was no happy ending for Venus Xtravaganza. Before she got her chance to change, a man strangled her to death and left her body under a bed in a motel room, and nobody found her for days.

Stories

It was still strange waking up in Vic's bed. In the morning, I would lie there wondering if anyone was looking for me. It was the longest I had ever gone without seeing my mum. I thought about charging my phone, but I still couldn't do it.

Vic kept to himself. He was quiet except for the coughing. He pottered around packing up the garage or fixing parts of the house or napping. It was nice knowing that he was nearby.

In the afternoons I went to Aggie's house after she got home from school. I would bring food I had baked. I met her parents and they were really lovely. Her dad was short and balding and he smiled a lot. He wore dress shirts at home. Her mum was tall and loud and had curly red hair. I liked her Scottish accent and the way she said 'Meemadooma'.

One day I brought over a plate of madeleines and her mum answered the door.

'Oh my saints! Aren't you clever? They look incredible!'

She was always amazed by my cooking.

'They're madeleines.'

'For us?'

I nodded and gave her the plate.

She smelled them and her eyes went wide.

'May I have one now?'

I smiled and nodded again.

'Aggie's in her room.'

I walked down the hall and knocked softly on Aggie's door. I always felt a bit nervous before she opened it. I had never had a friend before, and I was never sure if Aggie would be happy to see me. But she smiled and hugged me.

'Samwise! Why do you smell like a vanilla bean?'

'I made you madeleines.'

'I don't even know what they are, but I want them in my face.'

'Your mum has them.'

'That's an unforced error. They may never come back. Anyway, I'm *so* glad you're here. I'm studying for a test on periodic trends and I'm retaining none of it.'

Aggie collapsed onto her bed. I sat at her desk. Her textbooks were open. It looked like another language. Aggie sat up.

'Oh, hey, has your mum sold your house yet? Do you know where you're going to live over here?'

Aggie had been asking a lot of questions about my family and where I came from. I was too scared to tell her the truth, so I made up a story about how my dad was high up in the navy and he was out at sea, and I said that my mum was a consultant, even though I didn't really know what that meant. We were from Sydney but we were moving to Perth because my mum had just got a big job working for the government. She was still over east because there was a problem selling our house, which meant we hadn't bought one here yet. I was staying with Vic, who was an old friend of my dad's. I hadn't enrolled in school because we didn't know which suburb we would be living in.

I felt bad about lying to Aggie, but I liked pretending that I was normal and that my family had money and impressive jobs.

'Mum thought there was a buyer,' I said, 'but it fell through, so I'll be at Vic's place for a little while longer.'

'Can I selfishly confess that I'm a bit happy about that, because it's very fun having you live a couple of houses down?'

That made me blush.

'You're not going to move too far away are you?' she asked.

I shrugged and changed the subject.

I picked up one of the figurines on her desk.

'What are all these?'

'That's a half-orc barbarian.'

'Okay.'

'They're for D&D.'

I nodded as if I understood, but she could tell that I didn't know what she was talking about.

'Dungeons and Dragons. It's a role-playing game.'

'What's that?'

'Do you *really* want to know?'

'Yes.'

Aggie took a deep breath.

'Alright, but it's going to require me to nerd out on you, so just stop me when you're bored. Or, like, just get up and leave, I won't be offended.'

'No, I want to know. You have so many of them.'

'I painted every single one too. That's why I kept them.'

'So is it like Monopoly or something?'

'Oh, my sweet child, *no*. It's like, more of an epic story that you participate in as a character that you create. You don't really win or lose, it's about being part of an adventure. So you might go on a dragon-slaying quest or a treasure hunt or whatever, and the story gets determined by the choices you and the other players make along the way. Plus some luck, because you have to roll a dice to, like, execute those choices. Are you still with me?'

'I think so.'

'So the game gets controlled by a Dungeon Master.'

I raised my eyebrows.

'I know, it sounds weird,' she said. 'But the Dungeon Master is like a cross between a narrator and God, because they describe the events of the story but they can also decide the outcome of the choices you make, depending on how successful your roll is.'

'Okay. I think I understand.'

'I used to play every Sunday with the same five boys. We met at the house of this guy Graham, who *insisted* on being the Dungeon Master. We were all, like, genuine enthusiasts, but Graham was *super* into it. He knew the handbook backwards. He spent all week preparing his own campaign for us to play.

He constructed stories and mazes and puzzles and riddles and drew up watercolour maps and, like, parchment messages with wax seals and stuff. It was pretty amazing.'

'That sounds fun.'

'Oh my goodness, Sam, *stop* being so polite.'

'I mean it! Was this orc your character?'

'No. *God*, no. Ew. I would never be associated with a half-orc. I played a Lawful Good Elf Wizard. She was obstinately righteous and eloquent and widely respected and admired for both her intelligence and her mellifluous brass horn playing. I don't know if that reminds you of anyone.'

'I think I can guess.'

'That's the thing about it. Your character can be like an extension of yourself. It can be an expression of who you really are, or the person you wish you *could* be if you had permission. Like, I know I'm unbearably obnoxious at home, but I'm actually pretty shy out there. I'm like the chubby quiet brown girl who is decent academically, but who never risks venturing an opinion. It's weird, because, like, in a world full of frost giants and dwarves and demons and spellcasting, my fantasies were really about being a confident, decisive person who had their shit together and was listened to.'

'I know what you mean.'

'Totally, right? And it was the same for the other nerds at our table. Except this one kid called Gabriel who played with us over one summer. His parents were Adventists or something. He was tiny, like, really thin and short and pale, bowl haircut, and clinically odd. He had been bullied at his school to the point where his parents removed him and homeschooled him. He was insanely book smart. He had a photographic memory, but zero social ability. Our table was literally his only regular interaction with people his own age. But instead of playing a big aggressive paladin or a barbarian like the other boys, Gabriel played a halfling monk with absurdly low stats whose backstory was that he'd been excommunicated from his religious order for apostasy.'

'I don't know what that means.'

'Oh. For not believing, basically. So Gabriel's character was this persecuted, lone wolf weakling with no armour or melee abilities, who refused to cast spells and who lost every single battle he was in. It's like, he wasn't playing to escape anything, he was reliving the shittiest parts of his life. That's how he dealt with it. Weird, right?'

'Yeah, but I kind of get it.'

'Gabriel used to borrow Graham's fantasy novels and sneak them home. But his parents must have found them, because they called Graham's parents and accused them of promoting the occult, and we never saw Gabriel again.'

'They never let him come back?'

'Nope. They were pretty zealous. Thing is, they didn't know the *half* of what we did in there. For eleven-year-olds, we were covering some pretty messed-up territory.'

'Like what?'

Aggie scrunched up her face.

'Let me think. Oh, okay, so I remember this one scenario that Graham invented. We came to the outskirts of a village that was being ravaged by a virulent flesh-eating plague. There we encountered a witch, who told us that she could concoct a healing potion which we could pour into the village aqueduct and save everyone. However, in order to make the potion, the witch required the beating heart of a single uncontaminated infant.'

'What did you do?'

'Oh my God, it was so awful. We spent an hour debating the right course of action. Is it the moral thing to sacrifice one innocent to save thousands of lives? And by what authority do we intervene and make that choice? I mean, what would *you* do?'

'I don't know. There doesn't seem to be a right answer. I guess you just do the thing that does the least wrong.'

'Exactly. That's what we concluded. In the end, we stole a baby and gave it to the witch to be sacrificed. But here's the thing: the witch tricked us. She made a potion like she promised, but she drank it all herself. It was an elixir that ensured her immortal youth. And everybody in the village died. How fucked up is that?'

'That's really dark. Did you kill the witch?'

'We didn't. She got away. It was actually genuinely upsetting, and I was really angry at Graham. When my turn came, I cast a spell of reincarnation, to see if I could bring the baby back to life in some form.'

'You could do that?'

'Yeah, well, I tried. I ended up rolling a critical fail though, which was catastrophically unhelpful. So Graham, as the Dungeon Master, brought the baby back to life, but it was reincarnated as an angry badger that was hell-bent on vengeance. So every other week there would be this surprise fucking badger attack we had to contend with.'

'I don't really blame the badger though.'

Aggie laughed.

'You have a point. Anyway, we had this amazing collective imagination. We built a whole world together and got totally lost in it. And then it all went gross.'

'Why? What happened?'

'Puberty.'

'How do you mean?'

'I mean their nefarious little dicks suddenly periscoped up from under the table and became five extra participants. Every campaign involved some big-titted succubus or a seductive priestess or a lonely water siren or a comely peasant girl or something equally lame. Worst of all, Graham kept putting my character in these creepy situations. Like, I'd be lashed to some torture device or imprisoned as a sex slave and would require their rescue. I don't know, the whole mood just changed, and it wasn't fun or clever or unpredictable anymore. It was just icky, so I stopped going, and I haven't played since.'

'Maybe they'll grow out of it.'

'I doubt it. That's the shitty thing about being a girl some-times. Things get contaminated. Like, this is going to sound ridiculous, but I would hate to be an objectively stunningly beautiful woman.'

'Really?'

'Seriously. It must fuck you up. You'd be constantly fending off romantic approaches and weird infatuations from men who want to win you like some sort of prize, and dealing with a whole bunch of envious bitchiness from women. Like, no wonder the pretty girls at my school are a bit guarded and hostile. I used to think they were really imperious and up themselves, but now I just feel sorry for them. It must be so isolating and exhausting. And it's so unfair, because there's literally no downside at all to being a conspicuously attractive boy, no offence. But doors just open for you. You're playing life on the lowest difficulty setting, Sam Watson. You're lucky.'

I sat there and nodded, but my heart was breaking, because I knew I could never tell Aggie the truth about myself.

There was a knock on the door. Mrs Meemeduma opened it. She was hiding something behind her back.

'What have you got?' Aggie asked.

Mrs Meemeduma showed us the empty plate that the madeleines had been on.

Aggie sat up, shocked.

'You *didn't.*'

Mrs Meemeduma nodded. Her face was red with embarrassment. Aggie was outraged.

'You ate them *all?* Just then?'

'They were so good! I couldn't help it.'

'Oh my *God!*'

Aggie threw a pillow at her, and I got anxious because I thought they were going to have a fight, but they both started laughing. Mrs Meemeduma gave me the plate back.

'I'm so sorry, Sam.'

'Why are you apologising to him? They were for me!'

CRAIG SILVEY

'It's okay,' I said. 'I can make more.'

'Agnes, you should marry this boy and make him my son.'

Aggie rolled her eyes.

'Oh my God, *out!*'

Mrs Meemeduma winked at me and closed the door.

'Let's just pretend that exchange never happened,' Aggie said.

I just smiled and blushed.

~

Every night I cooked one of Vic's favourite meals, like shepherd's pie or lamb casserole or apricot chicken. He never ate much, even though he said he liked what I made.

I got braver about what I wore inside the house. I would pick something from Edie's wardrobe and ask Vic if it was alright to wear it. He would look at the outfit and smile to himself, and then shrug and say I could wear whatever I liked. I started with jumpers and t-shirts over leggings, then I tried on her blouses, then I wore skirts over tights with camisoles or wrap tops, and finally I put on her dresses. I wore some make-up too. Not too noticeable, just some foundation with a bit of eyeshadow and dabs of lipstick.

Every time I put on a new outfit, I felt nervous walking down the hall, but Vic never got angry with me again. He didn't really react at all. But for me it was exciting for someone else to see me dressed up, to see me as I was.

After dinner I would ask Vic questions about his life.

He had left school early and started an apprenticeship as a mechanic at a shop owned by two brothers, Frankie and Dougie

Byrne. They paid him cash and offered extra if he helped bring in new customers on slow days. They did it by running scams, which they called setting traps.

I wanted to know how the traps worked, so Vic explained. Frankie and Dougie would send Vic out to the supermarket or a grocery store, and he would hide and wait for a wealthy-looking woman to park her car. Once she went inside, Vic snuck over and popped the hood of her car just enough to get his hands inside. He loosened the cable clamps from the terminal posts of the car battery, then he wiped his hands with a rag and waited for the woman to return.

If she knew anything about engines, she would open the hood and tighten the clamps and drive away. If she didn't, Vic approached and said his uncle had a shop around the corner who could probably fix it.

Dougie towed the car in, then Frankie looked over the engine and told the lady she needed a replacement battery, but all he did was wipe down the old one and put a new sticker on it. If it was a really slow week, Frankie squeezed them for a new alternator or a timing belt.

Vic said he felt so guilty that he resigned as soon as he got his apprenticeship. A few months later the shop burned down. Frankie and Dougie were arrested for starting the fire.

One night I asked Vic where he and Edie met.

He took a big breath, held it in, then sighed.

'Fremantle.'

I thought that was all he was going to say, but after a minute he kept going.

'I'd just finished my tour. Couple hundred of us army boys hitched a ride back with the RAN. We docked at the wharf and there was a good-sized crowd. Thousands down there. The boys thought they were there to cheer us in. We swaggered down the gangplank all smiles, straight into the gauntlet. They weren't there to welcome us; it was an anti-war demonstration. People yelling and screaming, pandemonium. Never seen anything like it. Mounted coppers beating them back, barricades, the whole works. I just kept my head down. But as soon as my boots hit the ground, some bastard threw a chunk of limestone and hit me square in the ear. Eighteen months dodging bullets, and I got hit the moment I set foot on home soil. I went down like a sack of spuds, and out the corner of my eye I saw someone break through the police line and take a run at me. So I held my hand out and gave them the don't argue. Then I hear a voice say, "Pull your head in. If you get blood over my new dress I'll give you a knock worth worrying about!"'

'Was it Edie?'

Vic nodded and smiled.

'I looked up and I saw the most beautiful girl I'd ever seen in my life. She put her handkerchief over my ear, and got me to my feet She pulled me through the crowd. People spitting on me, calling out. Terrible stuff. She walked me all the way to Fremantle Hospital. They put me on a gurney and started to wheel me away, but I hopped off and legged it after her. I tried to give her hanky back, which was a sorry-looking rag by that time. She looked at me like I was a lunatic and told me to keep it. I still have it too. I think she felt a bit sorry for me, because then she said, "If you survive the day, you can take me to the pictures and a sit-down meal." I was so giddy I didn't even feel the stitches.'

Vic pointed to his left ear, which had a purple scar and a little piece missing.

'I knew why they were protesting, and they were right. But they made us feel ashamed to come home. That was the worst thing. They were yelling at the wrong blokes. A lot of us had no choice. We were just boys. I reckon Edie saw that the moment I got hit. And you know, I'd go through it all again if it meant meeting her at the end of it.'

'You were in a war?'

'Vietnam. Drafted in sixty-eight.'

'What do you mean drafted?'

'National Service.'

Vic could see that I didn't know what that meant either.

'Used to be a birthday ballot. If you were a young man of a certain age born on a certain day, you got drafted into the military, did your training and all that, and some of those fellas were deployed.'

'What do you mean a ballot?'

'Like the lotto, but the prize is pretty ordinary.'

'What if you didn't want to go?'

'You served your time in jail.'

'Really?'

Vic nodded.

'But I wanted to go,' he said.

'How come?'

'Because I was young and stupid and I thought it was the right thing to do.'

'So one day you were a mechanic, and then you just had to stop everything and go kill people?'

'Not quite as simple as that, but that's what it boiled down to. First few months over there were the same as home, just with more humidity and artillery fire. They had me servicing vehicles at a support base. Other pogo duties too. Worked a mop, cleaned latrines, camp maintenance. Unloading ammunition crates and drums of herbicide. Foul-smelling stuff. Burned like hell if it got on your skin.'

'So did everybody over there have the same birthday?'

Vic raised his eyebrows and smiled.

'No, the ballot didn't quite work like that, mate.'

'Did you have to fight?'

Vic nodded.

'Six months in they sent me outside the wire. I joined up with an infantry battalion.'

'Were you scared?'

Vic took a deep breath and rubbed his face. He looked down at the table for a couple of minutes. I worried that I was asking too many questions. I was about to say sorry when he spoke.

'I never told Edie this. Early on, we were stationed at a base camp south of a village on an NVA supply route. One day we were out on patrol, just a half-platoon of us. Hot as hell. Thick jungle. Hard to breathe. I was right at the rear.'

Vic stopped. He tapped the table again and cleared his throat.

'Next up the line was a private by the name of Reuben Martin. City boy, from Melbourne; been with us maybe a month. Real jittery, size of a jockey, had Coke-bottle glasses that fogged up with the humidity. I had one eye on his helmet, the other in the trees. At one point he stopped cold, white as a sheet. Waved me up. Said he'd lost sight of the men in front, and he'd veered us further off course trying to link back. We were lost.'

Vic stopped talking. His hands were shaking. He swallowed hard and kept going with his story.

'I took us east down a ridge to try to intersect the platoon, old Reuben treading on my ankles. I halted at the base of the ridge. I could see movement through the leaves. I crouched down and looked down the sight of my SLR. Next to me, Reuben did the same. The NVA were always well camouflaged, see, and not always in uniform. Someone came into view. I saw black hair, a face. Then I heard a burst of fire. It was Reuben. I pushed his barrel down. Waited. No return fire. So I crept forwards. He was maybe twenty, twenty-five metres away, but it felt like it took ten minutes to reach him. But it wasn't a soldier—it was a young girl. About your age. Skinny as a rabbit, still holding on to a basket. She'd been shot in the chest, the leg and the shoulder. She was still alive. She was so scared she never made a sound. I picked her up and I told her she would be alright. I could feel the exit wound on her back, and I plugged my hand hard up against it. We had to get her back to camp for treatment. It was touch and go but we had to try. We doubled back. Made it a few hundred metres before our platoon commander appeared. They'd heard the gunshots. He had a med kit. I laid the girl down but she was already gone. Her eyes were still open and she still looked scared. All the things I've forgotten in my life, I wish I could forget that. But it's like it happened yesterday.'

'What did you do next?'

'We buried her. Right there.'

'And what happened to the man who shot her?'

Vic shook his head slowly.

'Nothing at all. Except he had to live with what he'd done for the rest of his life.'

We both went quiet. Vic's shoulders were hunched forwards. He blinked hard a couple of times, then he stood up.

'Time for bed,' he said.

~

That night I stared at the ceiling and I couldn't sleep. I kept thinking about how Vic had to stop his life and go to war. It was unfair that he didn't have a choice. It reminded me of the Dungeon Master in Aggie's game, the person who didn't play but decided the rules, then everything came down to a roll of the dice.

Vic said it was all worth it because he met Edie when he came home. It was really romantic. Then I remembered something. I got up and opened Vic's chest of drawers. I took out the lace-fringed apricot handkerchief with the bloodstains. I knew it must be the one she had given him the day they met. Vic had kept it all this time. It felt really precious, like a piece of history, like it belonged in a museum. I held it to my face, but I couldn't smell anything.

I folded it up, but I didn't want to put it back. I kept it in my hand and I lay down again. I felt sad, because Vic missed her so much. Then I felt jealous, because nobody would ever love me as much as Vic loved Edie. And I knew that I would go to war too if it meant coming home to someone.

~

The next day I was looking through Edie's wardrobe for something to wear, but there were a couple of suitcases in the way. I thought they were empty but they were really heavy. I dragged one out and opened it. Inside were stacks of notebooks with hard covers. They were Edie's diaries.

The oldest one went back to 1975. I opened it. I knew it was wrong to read something so private, but since I had been sleeping in her bed and wearing her clothes, I felt really close to Edie. I wanted to know more about her.

At first the entries were pretty short. She would write a few lines about what the weather was like, people she saw that day, food she ate, movies she watched, books she was reading, songs she liked on the radio. She added more detail as the year got going. She was worried about money, because she and Vic had just built the house. They had been trying to start a family, but she couldn't fall pregnant. Edie was jealous of her sisters and her friends, who were all having children at the same time. Some of the pages had photos slipped between them, so I could put faces to names. I saw pictures of parties and picnics, and Edie and Vic camping or painting the house.

I finished 1975 that night. The next day I started 1976. And every day after that I read more. I liked Edie's voice. I felt like she was speaking straight to me, the same as it was with Julia Child, except Edie was telling me her secrets and her most private thoughts. She was so tough and fearless, and she cared about so many people. She was always taking a pepper beef pie and a Swiss roll to her friend Irene who had broken her ankle, or watering the garden for her friends Judy and Pete who went to Kakadu on their honeymoon.

She was always busy. She worked so many different jobs. She was a cleaner. She worked at a nursery. She was a sales assistant in a gift store. She was a secretary for a trucking company. She worked behind the cosmetics counter at Myer. She was an aerobics instructor. She played tennis and golf and badminton. She belonged to a sewing circle and a book club. She was always trying new things. She never complained, and even when things were going bad, she would tell herself that a fix was around the bend. She was a very hopeful person. She had a habit of saying that she was 'in fine fettle'. I didn't know what it meant, but I liked to say it to myself.

The only time she was really upset was when she wrote about trying to have a baby. She felt like she had failed as a woman. Her body was betraying her, and she was letting everybody down, especially Vic. She never told anybody how she was feeling. She carried it all on her own. One day at work she got her period and she locked herself in a storeroom and cried for an hour. It made me cry too, because I knew how helpless and frustrated she felt.

It was heartbreaking. All she wanted was to have a son or a daughter to love. She visited doctors and had a lot of tests, but nobody could tell her what was wrong. Then a specialist did some tests on Vic. He wasn't in the clinic when all the results came back, so Edie was on her own when she learned that he was the reason they couldn't conceive. It wasn't her fault after all.

But when Edie got home she told Vic that his tests were clear. She didn't have the heart to tell him the truth. She was the only person who ever knew. Except now I did.

Edie was devastated that she and Vic wouldn't have children of their own, but she didn't give up hope. A few years later they applied to adopt, and they went through a whole process of interviews and assessments. But just when they were at the last stage, something bad happened with Vic's business, and they were suddenly in a lot of debt. They got knocked back.

Edie never wrote about having children again. Maybe she didn't want to talk about it anymore because it hurt too much. But even then, she had love to spare. She started part-time work in childcare, and she volunteered at Princess Margaret Children's Hospital one day a week.

One afternoon in 1985, Vic brought home a stray dog that had been hanging around his workshop. It was skinny and shy and they didn't know what breed he was. Edie loved him immediately. She called him Pirate because he had a black patch over his right eye. There was a polaroid photo of him and Edie.

She had permed hair and I recognised her knit jumper as the first one I had worn. They both looked really happy.

Edie rescued a lot of dogs from then on. At one point they had four at once. But she never adopted puppies, she only brought home older dogs, especially ones whose owners had died or couldn't care for them anymore. She thought they deserved to have a friend until the end.

Sometimes they got so sick and old that she had to arrange to put them down. The first time she did it was a Labrador called Sandy who had bowel problems and terrible arthritis.

Edie carried Sandy into the vet and laid her down on the table. She asked if she could stay with her, because it was important that Sandy didn't die alone and she didn't want her to feel scared. Edie smiled and scratched Sandy behind the ears, which made her tail wag. Edie told her that she was a good girl, that her pain was going to stop, and she had earned a big sleep. And when Sandy's tail stopped wagging and she stopped breathing, Edie hugged her and started crying so loudly that all the other dogs started barking and howling.

It never got any easier for Edie. She dreaded it, but she always went in with the old dogs and held them before they went to sleep.

I loved Edie. Not just because she was so kind and strong, but because she felt lost sometimes too. Her diaries were full of things she was unsure about, questions she was afraid to ask anybody, all of her worries and fears and doubts.

She wished Vic would talk to her more. He never talked about the war, or his business, or anything that was troubling him. She knew that he had awful thoughts swirling around in his head. She said it was like getting blood from a stone.

He had bad dreams sometimes. He woke up kicking his legs and shouting and covered in sweat. He wouldn't tell her about it. He just got out of bed and got dressed and went for a long ride on the Black Shadow.

It was strange, because Vic had told me things that he hadn't told Edie. I knew the secrets they kept from each other.

Edie's diaries made me realise life was made up of lots of small moments that you could control and a few big ones that you couldn't. For weeks at a time, Edie would write about how she wanted to learn French, or how she couldn't get her chrysanthemums to grow, or how the price of bananas was too high, or how her friend Caroline was having an affair with the maths teacher at her son's high school, or how she wanted to get her hair cut short. And then, without any warning, her brother fell asleep while he was driving and crashed into a tree and died.

The same thing happened to me with Edie.

It was the entry for 21 May 2011. Edie wrote about putting money aside to take a cruise down the Danube River. She wanted to surprise Vic with tickets. She wondered if she would leave Misty at a kennel or with friends. The next day she would see a travel agent, after her appointment with the physiotherapist, because her knee had been flaring up. Then she wrote that she was going to bed early, because she had a headache and her eyes felt tired.

I turned the page, and there was nothing there. I kept turning them, but they were all blank.

At first I was confused. I went back to the suitcase because there were still some journals in there, but they were all empty too. And then I realised, and I sat on the bed and looked at the two suitcases and I started to cry. She was gone. She didn't get to learn French. She didn't get to see the Danube River. She didn't get to say goodbye to anyone.

I crawled up into her spot on the bed, the place where she died, and I hoped that she didn't feel alone when she went. I hoped that she knew that Vic was next to her.

But I knew she didn't want to go yet. I wanted to trade places with her, so she could do all the things she wanted to do before she died, and Vic could share them with her. I lay there all night thinking about it.

And that's when I had my idea.

Internal Combustion

Vic wasn't really interested.

The next night I cooked him a sausage and bean cassoulet. Vic said it tasted really good, but he was eating less and less. He seemed quiet and far away, like he was focused on something else.

I knew it probably wasn't the right time, but I couldn't help asking. I had been thinking about it all day. I cleared away his plate and made him a cup of tea with one sugar and no milk. I was wearing a lime-green cotton dress with a Peter Pan collar. I sat down and smoothed the skirt out over my legs.

'What's something that you always wanted to do?' I asked. 'Like, something really fun or frightening or even dangerous?'

Vic didn't really give it much thought.

'I dunno mate.'

'Say there were no consequences, or no problems with money or what anybody thought, and you were allowed to do the one thing that you've always dreamed about doing, what would it be?'

Vic just shrugged. I tried again.

'I thought maybe we could each do something we always wanted to do before we . . . you know. And I thought maybe we could help each other do it together.'

Vic wasn't really listening. He closed his eyes and pinched the bridge of his nose and looked really pained and uncomfortable and tired and I realised it was a stupid idea and I lost hope in it.

~

After I finished reading Edie's diaries, I spent more time with Vic in the garage as he sorted through everything. It was comforting being around him. He worked slowly and carefully. I watched him take things apart and check them. Sometimes he fixed them or cleaned them, or threw them away.

One day he needed help shifting a big piece of machinery so he could work on it while he sat down. It was heavy and red. We put it down on a sheet of cardboard. I had black grease on my arms.

'What is it?' I asked.

'It's an old HR engine block.'

'How does it work?'

'The engine?'

'Yeah.'

'Internal combustion.'

'What's that?'

Vic looked up at me.

'You really wanna know?'

I never had any interest in cars, but I liked asking Vic questions, and I liked being shown things.

'Yeah, I do.'

'Grab that milk crate over there and come sit down. I'll teach you the same way my old man taught me.'

Over the next couple of days we took the engine apart, and Vic explained how it all worked. He had a really patient way of demonstrating what each part did. I found it hard at first, because there were so many things to remember. But once we removed the cylinder head and the manifolds, and Vic turned the flywheel by hand and pointed to where the fuel and air made a small explosion that pushed the piston down, and showed me how a tiny spark was the start of a chain of events that made the wheels go round, I finally understood. I was amazed. It was all so intricate. Vic popped the hood of the Kingswood and taught me how all the other parts worked together. Every little piece had something important to do.

Vic showed me all the things that were wrong with the HR engine. There was rust all over the block and the cylinder head cover. There was burned oil in the exhaust manifold. The valves needed refacing and the springs were tired and the piston rings were corroded. It needed new spark plugs and a timing belt and a head gasket.

'Mostly wear and tear and old age,' he said. 'It's had its run.'

'Will it still work though?'

Vic wiped it down with a rag.

'Not without a lot of coughing and sputtering. But if somebody wanted to do the work, it could still tick over alright.'

'We could fix it,' I said. 'You could teach me.'

Vic shook his head.

'No mate, this one's a bit too far gone.'

'But we know what's wrong with it.'

'It's not as easy as that. I'm not really set up for repair here, and parts for these old motors are hard to source. You've got to scour through wreckers' yards or look in the classifieds. Remember what this is?'

He picked up a part. I nodded.

'That's a carburettor. You said it's like the heart of the engine.'

'They don't make them anymore. Cars these days have fuel injection systems that go straight into the chamber. This one's cracked, see?'

'We could fix it,' I said. I didn't know why it was so important to me, but it was. Vic just shook his head.

'Sorry mate. Come on, help me put all these parts in that wood crate over there.'

I helped Vic pack everything away.

'How come you're keeping them then?'

'Some of it can be salvaged. Been meaning to sift through it for years.'

'Where did you get all this stuff?'

'I took it all from the shop.'

'The business you owned?'

'It was a partnership. V&R Auto Repair out near O'Connor. Creditors were coming to strip the workshop, so I grabbed as much gear as I could.'

'You mean you stole it?'

'Can't steal what's yours. The only thieves I ever met had white collars.'

'I know about creditors.'

'Is that so?'

'It means you were in a lot of debt.'

Vic seemed a bit annoyed. His face turned red and he started throwing parts into the crate without taking much care.

'I wasn't. The shop was. Let me give you a bit of advice. Never go into business with your mates.'

'Why?'

'Because if it all goes to shit, you lose more than money.'

'Is that what happened to you?'

Vic nodded and threw a handful of bolts into the crate.

'Was that with Ray and Denise?'

Vic stopped and looked at me.

'How do you know that?'

I felt caught out. I had read about them in Edie's diary. Vic and Ray had been close friends. There were photos of the two couples together. And then they suddenly disappeared and Edie never wrote about them again.

'I think you mentioned them before.'

Vic frowned.

'Oh. Did I?'

'Yeah. Was Ray the R in V&R?'

'That's right. We opened the shop in eighty-four. Built it from the ground up, just a box of tools between us, and got it humming. Few years in, we trained apprentices and had an extra mechanic four days a week. Ray dealt with the front of house, spoke to the customers, gave the quotes and did the inventory and orders. I was happier out the back. Always preferred the company of cars to people. They make a lot more sense, and when they fuck up on you, at least there's a good reason.'

'And you know what to do to fix it.'

Vic nodded.

'Denise did the bookkeeping. Insisted on her own office, of course. Aircon, too. Ray thought the sun shone out of her backside. Thought she was a bloody magician with money too, so he had her do all our accounting and tax stuff. Turned out he was right, except her trick was making it disappear.'

'Did she steal it?'

'Embezzled is the term you would use. You'd never meet a more impatient woman than Denise. Had to have everything right under her chin the moment she thought of it. Edie could never understand how those two were taking trips to Bali and Thailand and Mauritius and paying for two kids in private school while we were living hand to mouth, but neither of us ever suspected she had her fingers in the till.'

'Because they were your friends.'

Vic shrugged.

'We only found out when Ray wanted to move to Queensland and asked me to buy out his half of the shop at a good rate.

Me and Edie didn't have much in the way of savings, so I extended the loan on the house. It was only once they were gone that we found out why they were in such a rush to sell and skip out. To cover all the money she stole, she'd taken out a line of credit, then covered those payments with new loans. This was in the eighties, when interest was very dear. In the end, she ran out of lenders and the business was drowning. I'm guessing that's when she told Ray. But instead of coming clean, they took me for one last ride. Maybe he knew the whole time, who can say?'

'What did you do?'

'Not much I could do. She'd been stiffing our suppliers, so I couldn't get parts in. Nobody would deal with us. I laid off the mechanics and the apprentices. I tried to renegotiate my loan with Western Mutual, but they didn't give a rat's arse. I was just blood in the water. They tried to sell it from under me. When that fell through, they liquidated the assets. So I took what was mine before they could.'

'What about Denise? Did she ever get in trouble?'

'I met with a lawyer. Real old money type. What was his name . . . Edward Denley. He said we had a clear case, but I didn't have the money to risk. In the end, I didn't see the point.'

'But you worked so hard. It's not fair.'

'No. It's not.'

'Aren't you angry at them?'

'I was. For a long time. But I've come out the other end of that.'

'You forgave them?'

'I just let it go. I had to. At the end of the day, I know Ray was ashamed, and he pissed off over east because he couldn't face me. I can choose to ignore it, but they're the ones who have to live with what they did. But I will *never* forgive that smug prick manager at Western Mutual, because he just didn't care. I didn't exist to him. I was just a number on a page. I had to beg the man not to take my house, and I spent the rest of my working life putting money in his pocket to pay off that loan. Tell you what, you asked me what I always dreamed about doing? For many years, I thought about going back into that bank and taking back what they took from me.'

'You mean robbing it?'

He nodded.

'I wanted to clear his shop out like he did with mine.'

'Like with a gun and a mask?'

'I didn't put that much thought into it, mate. It was just a nice picture in my mind.'

I got excited.

'That's what we should do then.'

Vic smiled and shook his head.

'I'm serious,' I said. 'That's what we have to do.'

'No it's not.'

'It is. Vic, I can help you. I want to help you.'

Vic stared at me. Normally I would look away, but this time I held my ground.

'No,' he said. 'It's not happening.'

'But I can *do* it. I can help you do it. You can have the thing you always wanted.'

'No I *can't.*' Vic raised his voice. 'Anyway, there's no point now, is there? What do I need money for? I don't want to hear about it again. I shouldn't have told you.'

We put the rest of the engine in the wooden crate in silence. Then we washed the grease off our hands in a bucket of soapy water that smelled like oranges.

Vic handed me a dry rag.

'What about you?' he asked.

'What do you mean?'

'What is it *you* want to do?'

I dried my hands. I knew what it was, but I didn't know what Vic would think. I was nervous.

'I don't know,' I said.

'You sure?'

I shrugged and kept wiping my hands.

'I've always wanted to go out and see a drag show.'

Vic looked confused.

'Not what *I* want to do mate, what *you* want to do.'

Now I was confused.

'What?'

'It's nice you've taken a bit of interest here with the cars, but forget about me and what I like.'

'But that's what I want,' I said. 'I want to see a drag show.'

'You want to go to the speedway?'

I realised what he meant.

'No, not that. I mean like . . . don't worry about it.'

'No, no. What do you mean?'

'I mean a show with, you know, drag queens. At a bar.'

Vic widened his eyes.

'Oh. Righto. Okay.'

'Forget about it. It's stupid.'

I folded the rag and put it on the workbench. My hands were still dirty. I wanted to go into Vic's room and hide in Edie's wardrobe and curl up into a little ball. I knew it could never happen.

'No, look, if it's what you want to do.'

'What you mean?'

'We can do it.'

I looked up at Vic.

'Would you take me? I mean, would you come too?'

Vic nodded.

My heart started beating really fast.

'Would it be okay if I wore one of Edie's outfits?'

'Mate, you can wear what you like. But there's not much chance you'll squeeze me into one of them.'

I smiled.

'You don't have to dress up.'

'Good to hear.'

'You'd look cute in a jumpsuit though.'

'Is that right?'

'Yep. Some hoop earrings and a pair of heels too. You would fit right in.'

'My sisters used to dress me up for their tea parties. Put me in lipstick and hats and feather scarves. They had a fine time.'

'You didn't mind?'

He shrugged.

'Didn't think about it one way or the other, really. The old girl got a bit annoyed when I ran under the sprinklers in her silk nightie, but that was about it.'

'But you don't think I'm a freak or anything?'

'Mate, I think you're just *you*, and there's nothing the matter with that.'

I had to look away then, because nobody had ever said that to me, and I didn't think they ever would. I chewed the inside of my mouth so that I wouldn't cry.

'Thanks Vic.'

Vic just shrugged, like it was nothing.

'When can we go?' I asked.

'Whenever you like.'

'There's a bar in the city called The Gavel. They have drag nights on Fridays. But that's tomorrow.'

'Righto then.'

'Seriously?'

'It's what you want, isn't it?'

'Well, yes. I just never thought . . .' I couldn't finish the sentence. I felt scared and excited. 'It will probably start pretty late though.'

'I'll have a nap in the arvo.'

We started walking into the house, but then I had a thought and it stopped me.

'Oh. Wait. I won't be able to get in. I don't have an ID or anything.'

Vic put his hand on my back.

'We'll play it by ear. I'll try sort something out.'

Cinderella

On Friday I spent the whole afternoon trying to choose an outfit. I pulled out a gorgeous red chiffon bell-sleeve dress and a cute pearl-white flare dress with navy embroidering on the neckline and shoulders. I laid them both on the bed and stared at them but I couldn't decide. I went through Edie's wardrobe again, and right at the back I found a rose gold sequinned flapper dress. It was stunning.

I chose a pair of silver strappy heels and a little gold clutch to pair with the outfit. I didn't have anything to put inside, so I stuffed some tissues and lipstick in it.

My hair had grown back enough to comb and style. I made a little curl on my fringe in a twenties style. I clipped in a white barrette too, even though I didn't need to. I filed and shaped my nails and painted them silver.

It got dark outside. I forgot to make Vic's dinner.

I spent hours on my make-up. I couldn't get the contouring right, and I was shaking so much that I scraped my eye with a mascara wand. I chose some smoky grey eyeshadow, and Edie had a nude matt lipstick that went with the dress. I pressed my lips down on a tissue and looked at the kiss I had made. It made me miss my mum.

I went through Edie's jewellery boxes and found a necklace with a single pearl. I also clipped on some sparkly art deco earrings.

I stood up to see the whole ensemble in the mirror. I looked disgusting. I looked like a boy in a dress. I decided that I wasn't going to go. I was about to wipe the make-up off when there was a knock on the door.

It was Vic. He was wearing a pair of jeans and a belt and a clean tucked-in button-up shirt and a pair of polished brown leather shoes. He had brushed his hair and trimmed his beard.

He stepped back when he saw me and stared for a long time.

'You look beautiful, mate.'

I blushed and shook my head.

'No I don't. Let's just stay here.'

Vic shrugged.

'Well, it's up to you. But I found this. I don't know . . . it might work.'

He held out a little card. I looked at it. It was Edie's old driver's licence. It had her picture on it.

'What do you reckon, should we give it a crack?'

I looked at myself in the mirror again, turning my head from side to side. Then I winked.

'That'll have to do, kid.'

~

We drove around the city for a while. I knew what The Gavel looked like from the outside, but I didn't know the street name or anything. There was lots of traffic.

I sat low in the seat so nobody could see me. My heart was beating fast. I pinched and twisted the skin of my wrist, which made me feel a bit calmer.

'There it is,' I said and pointed. 'On the right.'

Vic pulled into a small, dark car park behind The Gavel. It was unpaved and there were potholes everywhere. Vic shut the engine off. I felt like throwing up. I wanted to go back to Vic's and make him a cup of tea and talk until he was tired.

Vic got out. I stayed in the car. I watched the side mirror to see if there was anybody walking past on the street. I didn't want to get any strange looks. This had all been a big mistake.

I heard my door open and I flinched.

Vic was holding his hand out.

'You'll be right.'

'I can't. I can't do it.'

Vic just stood there and patiently waited for me.

After a few minutes, I took a deep breath and got out. I was wobbly on my heels, but Vic held my arm. I hid behind him and tried to ignore all the cars going past. I stared at the ground as we walked around the corner. I could hear music and people talking inside.

I felt relieved when we reached the entrance, but then a

bouncer stepped in front of us. He was dressed all in black and he had a shaved head and a big chest.

I moved closer to Vic.

The bouncer put his hand on my shoulder. He looked impatient.

'Come on. ID,' he said.

My hands were shaking as I dug around in Edie's clutch.

'You know, I think I left it at the last bar we were at.'

The bouncer shrugged.

'I can't let you in.'

'We're just meeting a friend in here, and then we're heading somewhere else,' I said. 'Do you mind if we just go in and find them?'

'He can. You can't.'

I went through the purse again and took out Edie's licence. The moment I gave it to him I knew it wouldn't work.

The bouncer frowned. He looked at me, then back to Edie's photo. He turned it over. Then he looked at Vic. He squinted at the licence.

A group of people had started queuing behind us. I couldn't breathe. My face was really hot.

'This expired in 2010.'

I didn't say anything.

'Says you were born in 1949.'

I didn't say anything. I could hear the people behind me laughing. The bouncer was annoyed.

'Are you almost seventy years old?'

I didn't say anything.

The bouncer turned to Vic.

'*You* are.' Then he gave the licence back to me. 'But you look about twelve.'

'Listen,' said Vic, 'the kid just wants to see a show. We're not here to drink alcohol or anything of that nature. I'll make sure—'

The bouncer stepped really close to Vic.

'You're lucky I don't beat your fucking skull in. I thought I'd seen everything at this place.'

'I don't know what you're—'

'You don't know what, eh? You don't know what? You don't know you're a dog? You don't know you're a disgusting pedo fuck?'

The bouncer shoved Vic hard against the wall. He grabbed his collar and put his face right up close to Vic's.

'What? What are you gonna do? Don't like being faced with a real man, do you? Hey?'

'Stop!' I tried to pull his arm back, but he was too strong. Vic was wheezing and blinking hard.

'He can't breathe!' I shouted. 'Stop!'

Vic started coughing. A spray of spit and blood hit the bouncer's chin. He let Vic go and wiped his face. Then he saw the blood on his hand and he was furious. He pushed Vic to the ground.

'Stop! *Stop!* Please!' I shouted.

I put myself between him and Vic, and the people in the queue behind us held the bouncer back and told him to calm down.

'He just spat blood on me! You filthy cunt!'

Vic was still coughing and struggling to breathe. I helped him to his feet. It was hard to balance on my heels, and I slipped and scraped my knee. More people on the street stopped and stared at us. The bouncer was still yelling as we walked back to the car park.

I lowered Vic down and we both sat on the kerb next to the car. I took some tissues out of Edie's clutch and gave them to him. Vic wiped his mouth and got some air in.

I rubbed his back.

'I'm so sorry, Vic.'

My lips were twitching but I didn't want to cry. I felt awful. We should never have come.

'It's alright mate. I'm alright.'

A taxi pulled in and lit us up with its headlights. Somebody got out and the taxi drove away. I heard a dramatic gasp.

'Oh my stars, you are *adorable*! Look at that dress. I am pushed. *Pushed!*'

I looked up and saw a drag queen. She was tall and soft-looking. Her hair was blonde with old Hollywood curls and she wore a white glittery gown and a pair of sneakers. She was holding a big black bag. She walked up to us.

'What happened to you? Your knee's all banged up.'

'I slipped over.'

'Oh, petal. That's no good. What's your name?'

'Sam. This is Vic.'

'Well, Sam and Vic, *I* am Miss Fella Bitzgerald, and good

Lord, I want to pinch those peachy cheeks of yours. What are you two doing out here in a grubby car park?'

'The man at the door wouldn't let me in. He hurt Vic.'

Vic shook his head.

'I'm alright.'

'Ugh, that guy is such a meathead. Are you okay, sir?'

'I'm fine.'

Vic sounded a bit irritated. Fella Bitzgerald threw her hands in the air.

'Now you're all dressed up with nowhere to go!'

'It's okay,' I said.

'No! I won't have it! Have it I will *not*! Why don't you come with me and I'll sneak you in through the rear?' She smiled and winked. 'Don't fret, Daddy, I'm only playing.'

Fella Bitzgerald held out her hand to me. She seemed nice.

'Come on dear, I won't bite.'

'I don't know,' I said. 'I should go home with Vic. He's not feeling very good.'

Vic slowly got to his feet.

'No, no. You go inside. I'll sit in the car.'

He opened the door of the Kingswood and started coughing again. Fella Bitzgerald looked concerned. Her voice went serious.

'Goodness, that sounds rough, Vic. How persistent is your cough? Have you seen a GP? You might have an infection. What colour is your phlegm?'

Vic waved her off and shook his head. He cleared his throat and his cough settled down.

'I'm fine. You go in. Go on. I'll be right here.'

I touched Vic's arm.

'Don't wait outside. I'll get a taxi back or something. You should go lie down where you're comfortable.'

'Sure?'

I nodded.

Vic looked at Fella Bitzgerald, like he was making sure he could trust her.

'I'll take good care of your girl,' she said.

I had been called a girl so many times, but never like that before. She made it seem so normal. I liked her already.

Vic took all the money out of his pocket and gave it to me.

'You have a good time.'

'Are you sure?'

'Go on. Take it.'

I took the money and I felt overwhelmed. I hugged Vic.

'Thank you,' I said.

He nodded and slowly got into the car. I watched him drive away and I felt sad for him. Then Fella Bitzgerald hooked her arm through mine.

'You want to have some fun?'

'Okay,' I said.

She led me to a door next to a skip bin full of boxes and bottles. She pressed an intercom button and said, *'Babooshka, bitches!'* and a moment later the door buzzed and she pulled it open.

I followed her through a dark area stacked with drink crates and down a hallway which smelled like old cigarettes and perfume. We came to a dressing room full of drag queens getting ready. Some weren't in their outfits yet; others were putting on their final touches. One whole wall was mirrored and had vanity lights and a table running all the way down. There were a couple of clothes racks and a pedestal fan blowing. The room was loud and busy.

Fella Bitzgerald stepped in and clapped her hands. I stayed back in the hall.

'Hello treasures! Look what I've got!'

She waved me into the room. All the queens stopped what they were doing and turned to look at me.

'I found this little urchin outside in the bushes with a man and she's all done grazed her knee.'

Fella Bitzgerald gave me a cheeky smile. She introduced me to everybody.

'Now, this here is Blanche Boudoir, this is Delta Goodhand, Pip Smears, Luna Moons, Slim Busty, and this creaky old broad is the Duchess. Girls, this is Sam. Wait. No. We need to do a little better than that. You're in the sisterhood now, sweetie. What should we call you?'

I didn't even think. I just blurted it out.

'Honeybee,' I said. 'Call me Honeybee.'

They all clapped and I did a shy little curtsy.

'Honeybee! Welcome to the hive, sugar. Come on in.'

The girls all spoke over each other really fast.

'Such a baby fish!' said Luna Moons.

'A fishlet!' said Blanche Boudoir.

'A little Ann Chovy,' said Slim Busty.

'We found Nemo!' said Pip Smears.

Delta Goodhand got up and held me by the shoulders then bent down to give me air kisses on each cheek. She was tall in her heels and was wearing a glittery gold bodysuit. She hadn't fit her wig yet.

'Girl, you are a young Audrey Hepburn,' she said. 'Those big eyes!'

'No!' said the Duchess. 'Look at that pixie face and tell me she's not serving Mia Farrow in *Rosemary's Baby* in our presence.'

'When you're right, you're right,' Delta agreed.

'Your dress is gorgeous,' said Blanche Boudoir. 'And look at that skin! I want to tear it off and wear you like a jacket.'

'Put the lotion back in the basket, Buffalo Bill-anche!' said Fella Bitzgerald, and everybody laughed. She led me towards an empty chair at one end of the long table.

'Have a seat here before they devour you. And let's get you a bandaid for that knee. Don't worry, nobody will even notice it; they'll be too busy gawking at the rest of you.'

I squeezed past Slim Busty, who was pulling a pair of pantyhose over foam padding on her thighs. I sat down. Fella Bitzgerald took a small leather satchel out of her big bag. She ripped open a sachet and dabbed my knee gently with a swab. I winced.

'Sorry to sting you, Honeybee. But don't worry, I'm a registered nurse.'

'That's not the only register she's on,' said Luna Moons.

Fella Bitzgerald put a big square bandaid over my knee.

'All better!' she said, and smiled.

Someone behind me yelled out.

'Motherfucking mother-*tucker*!'

It was Pip Smears. She was bent over forwards.

'This cheap-arse boat tape isn't sticking! Fuck!'

Blanche Boudoir stood up.

'Let me help you, girl,' she said.

'No! I'm fine. It just won't fucking stick.'

'Come on, calm down. I got you. Just trust me. They call me Friar Tuck, girl. They call me the Bush Tucker Man. Now, put your eggs in the nest and let's get this thing tucked away.'

I blushed and watched out of the corner of my eye. Pip squatted, then Blanche got behind her and reached between her legs.

'Sweet Jesus of Nazareth! Of course you can't tuck this in! It's like I'm shaking hands with an eight-year-old boy!'

All the queens were howling with laughter. I laughed too.

'Seriously!' Blanche said. 'I'm going to have to staple this thing to your shoulderblades!'

'Is it sticking down?' Pip asked.

'You're swampy as a mangrove back here, doll. That's the problem. Throw me those tissues; let's give this pip a smear.'

'Turn that fan up!' Pip complained. 'It's too hot in here.'

'That's for *damn* sure,' said Luna.

'Okay, now some fresh tape. *Et voila!*'

Blanche stood up, and Pip straightened. Everybody clapped.

Luna Moons took a big gulp of her margarita and fanned herself with her hands. Delta raised her eyebrows.

'Thirsty?'

'Oh, you don't know the *half*. It's been so long I've started seeing subliminal penises.'

'*Please*.'

'I'm telling you. Yesterday I was babysitting my niece—'

'Stop right there!' the Duchess called out.

'Hush up, you old bag! I was babysitting my niece, and all she wants to do is watch *Peppa Pig*, because that show is like crack to them. And I found myself just staring at the screen for an hour, and I'll tell you why: it's because Peppa Pig's big pink face is the exact shape of a cock and balls.'

'Shut your whore mouth,' said Delta.

'I'm telling you, it's the truth.'

'You've lost your marbles, girl.'

Slim Busty looked it up on her phone.

'Holy shit, you're right.'

She showed everybody a photo and they laughed as soon as they saw it. Even Delta had to admit there was a resemblance.

'Peppa the motherfucking *Dick*-Pig. Who knew?'

'I told you: it's that damn homosexual agenda,' said Luna. 'Subconsciously training young minds to covet the penis. It's a gay-spiracy.'

'The only sensible conclusion,' said Pip.

'Ugh!' the Duchess called out. She slapped her hands down on the dressing table. 'This look is *not* working. I look like Pennywise the fucking clown.'

'Sweetie, please, go easy on yourself, that's *simply* not true,' said Fella Bitzgerald. 'You're actually serving John Wayne Gacy at a children's birthday party.'

The queens howled.

'Shade!'

The Duchess pointed a finger at Fella Bitzgerald.

'Don't come for me, Argentina!'

Pip Smears was now wearing a beautiful sapphire gown with peacock feathers flaring out from the shoulders. She slowly spread her hands out wide.

'*Send in . . .*'

Everybody stopped and joined in, even the Duchess.

'*. . . the clowns.*'

A man suddenly appeared in the doorway. He wore jeans and a white shirt and he had a lanyard around his neck. I ducked down behind Fella Bitzgerald so he couldn't see me.

'Fifteen minutes, ladies. We've got three hens' parties out there, so it's gonna get rowdy.'

The man left.

'If any of those bitches touch my wig, they'll be rolling down the aisle in a wheelchair,' said Delta.

Luna Moons did some stretches.

'Blanche, what happened with that ginger trade hanging off you last week?'

'He got the full Rex Hunt, girl. Reeled him in, gave him a big wet kiss, and threw him back.'

'Good,' said Slim Busty. 'He had shifty little eyes. He looked sex-offendy.'

Luna Moons lowered herself slowly into a side split.

'Oof. He could roofie my cocktail any night of the week.'

'*Luna!*' said Fella Bitzgerald. 'Jesus, girl. That's a yellow card.'

'What? You know, just once I'd like to hear a positive drink-spiking story. Some nice boy who knocks you out gently, takes you home, cleans off your make-up, tucks you into bed, and when you wake up there's a tray of fresh muffins and he's cleaned the grout in your shower recess.'

'You are too much,' said Pip. 'Seek therapy.'

Fella Bitzgerald turned to me. I was still crouched down. My dress had slid back, and I saw her noticing the scars on my inner thigh. I covered them over with my dress and looked away.

'Come on up, Honeybee,' she said. 'Sit here. I've got something for you.'

I sat back down on the chair, and in the mirror I could see Fella Bitzgerald searching through her bag behind me. She pulled out a beautiful sandy-blonde wig. She gave it a couple of brushes, and then she fit it onto my head.

'How's that? Snug? Too tight?'

'No, it's good,' I said.

'It's better than good. You are *stunning*. Look at yourself. Look!'

She pointed at the mirror, and it made me smile and blush. She adjusted the wig and styled it. Then she knelt down and kept looking at me in the mirror. She spoke so only I could hear.

'This is your cape, okay? And you are a superhero. But the difference is, you're not playing a character when you wear it, you're letting your true self out, and fuck anybody who doesn't like it. This is your cape. It's yours to keep.'

'I can't take it,' I said.

'Sure you can.'

'I can't. It's yours.'

'No. It's *yours*. Now, shush. I need your help. Will you do something for me?'

She handed me a small bottle of liquid eyeliner.

'What's this for?'

Fella Bitzgerald pointed to her cheek.

'I want you to give me a beauty mark just here.'

I dabbed on a small dark dot.

'How do I look?' she asked. 'Am I bringing Marilyn?'

I nodded.

'You're really beautiful.'

'Oh stop it,' she said, then she whispered, '*Keep saying that!*'

The man with the lanyard came back and knocked on the doorframe.

'Five minutes. Let's head out.'

The queens began to move out of the room. I tapped Fella Bitzgerald on the elbow.

'What should I do?'

'Come with me, Honeybee, you'll be alright.'

I followed her down the hallway and through to an area beside the stage.

'You can watch from here, okay?'

I nodded and said thank you, but it didn't come out loud enough for her to hear. I peeked around the corner and saw the bar was packed.

'Okay, girls,' said Luna Moons. 'I'm going in!'

She stepped out onto the stage with a big smile and a margarita. She waved at the crowd and she didn't look nervous. She stood behind a microphone stand and blew kisses.

'Hello, hello, *hello*, ladies and gentle, *gentle* men! Are we ready to have some fun?'

The crowd cheered.

'Now, I've been told we've got some hens in the house tonight, yes?'

A few sections of the audience screamed.

'Welcome, you messy bitches. We're *so* happy you're here.'

She rolled her eyes to somebody in the front row, and the whole room laughed.

'Do we have a bride-to-be?'

A girl close to the stage whooped and called out.

'Oh, look at you. You've even got your sash and your tiara. Good for you! You go right ahead and remind everybody here that you're entitled to a legally recognised matrimonial service. You're like a ham sandwich in a synagogue, sweetie. But you *should* celebrate! It's your special day coming up, isn't it? It's every little girl's dream: fifty grand for a plate of chicken Kiev and some rambling speeches. Don't you worry about all that credit card debt, sweetie, because those memories are *priceless*. And you've got your bridesmaids and your girlfriends here. Ride or die, am I right, girls?'

A group of women screamed.

'Now, sweetie, let me tell you these girls are *not* bitching behind your back about your endless bullshit. They are *not* calling you an entitled cunt or a nauseating over-controlling nightmare. No they *aren't*. They *love* you. And it's your special day, and they want to *support* you. What's your name, hun?'

'Belinda!'

'Belinda. Of *course* it is. And how old are you, Belinda?'

'Twenty-four!'

'Twenty. Four.'

Luna Moons closed her eyes nodded slowly.

'Twenty-*four*. That's a perfectly acceptable age to be betrothed . . . in Elizabethan England. But it's fine, sweetie, because you've found the *one*. Love transcends age, and common sense, and financial security. You're a believer. That's what I like about you, B. You're *optimistic*. He's going to love you forever, isn't he? It's true love. You're soulmates. Two become one, sweetie. Well . . . *almost* one. We don't tell each other *everything*, do we? I mean, while he's ploughing away at you in standard missionary, or however you people do it, he's not going to admit that sometimes he closes his eyes and pretends he's fucking your maid of honour just so he can finish. It's true, it's true. And where *is* your maid of honour, is she here? Put your hand up, sweetie. Oh, yeah. He *definitely* is. She is *way* hotter than you, B. I'm sorry girl. But *he's* not going to tell you that, because he *loves* you. And this is *true* love, ladies and gentlemen. Enshrined under the laws of God.'

Everybody was laughing really hard, even the bride. The meaner Luna was, the sweeter she sounded.

'No, we don't tell each other everything. And it works both ways. You're not going to tell him how much of a greedy, indis-criminate cock-hound you were at university, are you? Those two guys you swallowed balls-deep in the bathroom at the Varga Lounge for a rail of coke? He doesn't need to know about that, sweetie, that's in the past. This is now. You've *changed*. It's your special day. And where is your man right now? I'm going to call him Darren. Where is Darren right now? At his bucks' night?'

'Yes!'

'You look a bit nervous about that, sweetie, but let me tell you, while you're here being roasted by a fat queen, your Darren is definitely *not* being motorboated by a sex worker. He's *not*. Don't even think that. She is *not* grinding away at the throbbing bulge in his lap while his hands explore her perfectly sculpted, limber body. And he's not staring into her vacant eyes and reconsidering his commitment to an arcane monogamous institution for the *rest of his living days*. He's *not*, sweetie. Strike that from your mind, because you know what? Your Darren's not like that. You are *more* than enough woman to capture a man's undivided sexual and spiritual attention for the next *fifty years*. And don't you ever even get suspicious. Not even when he suddenly takes up recreational beach swimming for no reason and dyes his hair chestnut brown and starts staying back at work late and then, one Wednesday night in June, you drive to Bayswater Settlements on Lawrence Street with a tray of homecooked enchiladas to surprise him with dinner because he's been working *so* hard and the two of you haven't been communicating and you walk into the break room and you discover that he's already eaten . . . out . . . his new receptionist, Raelene, who happens to volunteer as a beach lifeguard on weekends and is now being jackhammered against a table so passionately that neither of them even notice you come in, so you retreat without speaking to the car where your son is sitting in the passenger seat playing his Game Boy and you tell him that Daddy's not hungry and you both go home and eat your feelings and one day that child blossoms into a bitter, jaded drag queen.'

Luna Moons stepped back from the microphone and opened her eyes wide and blew out her cheeks while everybody laughed really loud. She shook her head quickly and then drank her whole margarita in one swallow. She paused until everybody stopped laughing and cheering.

'Wow,' she said. 'That got real. I just unloaded some stuff. Tonight's performance is brought to you by Daddy Issues, ladies and gentle men. Co-sponsored by self-sabotaged romantic relationships and a bottomless lust for positive reinforcement.'

Everybody laughed, then Luna Moons turned around and arched her back and slapped her own behind.

'What the fuck am I talking about, bottomless?'

The crowd whistled and cheered.

'Yeah, yeah, that's it! Nourish my famished ego! Feed me! Oh, that's the good stuff. Now, a round of applause for Belinda, ladies and gentlemen! Oh, she's in tears. Chin up, sweetie! You're gonna be just fine. Now! This next girl is a tribute to all the peacocks out there. I'm looking at you, sir. Put your hands together for Pip Smears!'

Pip Smears stepped out on stage and Lady Gaga's 'Telephone' started playing. Pip glided up and down the stage lip-syncing, and when the chorus hit, she jumped up and tossed her hair and waved her arms and cartwheeled. She finished the song with a death drop. It was incredible. I forgot myself and cheered and clapped for her.

Next up was Slim Busty, who was dressed all in black leather with a huge black wig. She ran out on stage and performed 'Bad Reputation' by Joan Jett. She sneered and pulled finger signs and shook her fists, and at one point she jumped straight into the crowd. They caught her and passed her across the room and carried her back onto the stage.

The Duchess came out next and did Björk's 'It's Oh So Quiet', which was really theatrical, then Delta Goodhand did 'Timebomb' by Kylie. After that Blanche Boudoir came out wearing a black sequinned dress and started performing the Gloria Gaynor version of 'I Want to Know What Love Is'. She bent over during the chorus, like she was truly in pain. She even cried and her mascara ran and she crouched down and went really still during the finale of the song. As she did, a guitar riff from a different song started playing over it, getting louder and louder, and Blanche started moving again, nodding her head up and down. Suddenly she leaped up onto her feet and tore away her black dress which revealed a red latex bodysuit underneath, and the song turned into 'This Is Love' by PJ Harvey. Blanche got really aggressive. She smeared her wet make-up all over her face and messed up her wig and paced up and down the stage and beat her chest with her fist. She was bold and fierce and I stepped right up close to the side of the stage because she was so powerful to watch.

Luna Moons burst out next, and she did Robyn's 'Call Your Girlfriend'. She skipped across the stage and got the whole crowd clapping. Everybody loved her. She danced really well.

Halfway through the song, Luna pretended to be exhausted. She puffed out her cheeks and put her hands on her hips and staggered to the side of the stage. Then she grabbed me by the hand and dragged me out in front of everyone. I panicked and shook my head and tried to pull away, but the other queens forced me onto the stage. Luna took me right into the centre and let me go. I was scared and alone. I stood completely still and looked out and all I could see was a bright light, but I could hear the crowd screaming and clapping along with the music. I blushed and shook my head and tried to make myself small. I could hear the crowd encouraging me, and I knew that I was disappointing everyone. A few metres away, Luna Moons was staggering around me and fanning herself. I didn't know what to do. I wanted to run off the stage, but I was frozen with fear.

Then Luna Moons sashayed towards me with a huge grin. She grabbed my hand again and, just as the chorus started, she held it straight up, like I'd just won a boxing match. The crowd went crazy and I felt electricity down my spine and I suddenly forgot to be afraid. I started singing with Luna Moons, and I danced with her too, like I did when I was alone in front of a mirror. It was so loud and so bright, I didn't really think about what I was doing, I just got swept up in it. I felt like I didn't have any weight at all. It was like being in a dream. I felt like

I was the honeybee again. I turned to the crowd and performed the song to them and I didn't feel alone anymore.

And then the song was over. The crowd screamed and whistled. Luna Moons wrapped me up in a big sweaty hug, and she held my hand up again for everyone to applaud. She waved to everyone and blew kisses, and I waved too as we ran to the side of the stage. Luna hugged me again, and I hugged her back.

'Was that fun?'

I couldn't speak, so I nodded.

The other queens hugged me too and said nice things. My heart was beating really fast. I was too shocked to understand what had just happened.

Fella Bitzgerald bent down and gave me a kiss on the cheek. I could hardly hear over the noise, but I thought I heard her say, '*I'm so proud of you!*' And then she walked out on stage.

A spotlight followed her as she walked over and stood behind the microphone. She put her finger to her lips and waited until everyone went silent. She was so graceful and elegant.

Then the music started up. It was a big band, lots of horns and strings. And then Fella Bitzgerald started actually singing into the microphone. Her voice was smoky and heartfelt. It was an old song called 'I'm Through with Love' that Marilyn Monroe sings in *Some Like It Hot*. It was beautiful. I had to blink a lot because my eyes were full of tears and I wanted to see her properly.

When the song finished, the crowd was quiet for a moment, then they cheered when Fella Bitzgerald did a deep bow. She suddenly straightened, and a voice came over the speakers.

'*Oh, you don't understand, Osgood! I'm a man!*'

Then Fella Bitzgerald ripped off her wig, revealing her short brown hair underneath, and another voice came over the speakers.

'*Well . . . nobody's perfect!*'

Then all the lights went out.

The audience went wild, and when the lights came back on, all the queens were back on stage, and 'Wannabe' by the Spice Girls started playing.

Suddenly someone grabbed my arm and I spun around. It was the bouncer from outside.

'How the fuck did you get in here?'

Before I could say anything, he dragged me away from the side of the stage. He was holding my arm so tight it hurt and it was hard to keep up in Edie's heels.

'Fella Bitzgerald! She let me in! She said it was okay. Fella Bitzgerald!'

I tried to pull away, but he was too strong. When we got to the back door, he opened it and pushed me out.

'I don't wanna see you here again. Stay the fuck away. You shouldn't be here.'

'Wait! Wait!'

He slammed the door shut.

I stood there in a daze. It had been so loud and bright and now I was outside in the dark and it was quiet. I remembered the intercom.

'Hello? Fella Bitzgerald? I'm out the back, I got thrown out. Is anyone there?'

I waited and tried a few more times, but nobody answered and the door stayed locked. I sat down on an old crate, and I realised Edie's clutch with all the money Vic had given me was still in the dressing room. I got up to try the intercom again, but then I started to worry that I might have got Fella Bitzgerald in trouble for letting me in, and maybe she was angry with me. I took a deep breath and pushed down the button.

'It's me again. Um, Sam. I just wanted to say that I'm really sorry if you're in trouble because of me. And I also wanted to say thank you for being so nice. You're all so talented. I really loved watching you. It was amazing. Anyway, so, that's all. I'm going to go now. I'm sorry. Bye.'

I sat down and hugged my knees and I thought about what I was going to do next. I didn't have any money to get a taxi back to Vic's house. I couldn't go anywhere. The thought of walking in the city while I was dressed up was so frightening that I started to shake. I didn't feel like a superhero.

I thought about stealing a car from the car park, but I didn't know how to connect the wires to make it start. I thought about breaking into somebody's house to steal some different clothes. I decided to risk heading to the station to catch a train back to Vic's.

I crept down the side of the building and looked towards the street. I waited for a loud group of girls in tight dresses to go past. I thought about walking close behind them to try to blend in, but I didn't want them to notice and call me out, so I went out alone. I kept my head down and walked quickly as I could. I made sure the wig hung over my face. I didn't look up to see if anyone was watching me. I tried to make myself invisible.

At one point, I stepped out to cross the road, and a car braked hard and honked. The lady driving yelled out at me.

'Watch where you're going, you silly bitch!'

It was a mean thing for her to say, but she actually gave me confidence because she didn't see me as a boy. I lifted my head and swept the hair back from my face. I thought about what Fella Bitzgerald said to me, and I started to walk the way I had always wanted. I realised it was the same as shoplifting. If I looked nervous or afraid, I would get caught. I had to act like I belonged.

I walked like I had somewhere to be. I swung my arms and let myself look around. I went past people getting late-night kebabs and people smoking outside a jazz club and drunk people trying to wave down a taxi at the corner of Weld Square. Nobody noticed me.

My mind went back to performing on stage with Luna Moons. It didn't seem real. I thought about all those people cheering and clapping, and it made me smile to myself. I couldn't wait to tell Vic. He had given me the thing I had always wanted. And I knew then that I was going to do the same for him.

Then I turned onto the James Street Mall, next to the museum. I saw two guys ahead of me smoking cigarettes on a bench. One was tall and fat and combed his short hair forwards with too much gel. The other was thin and short with pale skin and he wore a button-up black shirt that needed ironing.

'Hey gorgeous,' the thin one called out.

I looked down and didn't say anything.

He stood up and blocked my path.

'Hey, how's your night?' he said.

The big one got up too. I should have stepped around them and kept walking. I should have kept going past the art gallery and taken the pedestrian overpass to the station. But I got scared and I stopped. And then I turned around and I walked fast back the way I came.

They followed me.

'Hey, wait up. Where you going?' the thin one said.

'I don't think she likes you, man.'

I turned onto a darker, quieter road near a hostel. The thin one caught up and took hold of my wrist.

'Hey, hold up.'

I snatched my hand back and kept walking.

'I'm just being friendly. Where you headed? We'll walk you there. What's your name? Where are your friends?'

He put his arm around my shoulder. I ducked and stepped back. The strap on my left heel snapped and it slipped off.

'Don't touch me!'

He held his hands out while I kneeled to fix my shoe.

'Whoa, take it easy. I'm only playing. Here, let me help.'

He crouched down and put his hand on my ankle.

'Stop it! Leave me alone!'

I kicked my foot into the toe of the shoe and tried to walk away, but it slipped off again. The thin one was right next to me. I could smell cigarettes and cheap spray-on deodorant.

'There's no need to be like that. Just relax. I'm a nice guy. You want a smoke? What's your name?'

I bent over to take off my right heel, then I was going to run. But my hands were shaking so much I couldn't loosen the strap. The big one was standing close and watching me. He suddenly grabbed the thin one by the shoulder.

'Dude, dude. Stop. I think it's a dude.'

'What?'

'That's a *guy*.'

'Fuck are you talking about?'

I hooked my finger behind the strap and pulled at it, but I lost my balance and tipped onto the kerb.

'It's a fucking guy. Look!'

The big one pushed my wig back, then he started laughing.

'Holy shit! Fuck, man, you are *never* living this down!'

'Fuck off!'

The big one kept laughing.

'Oh my God! Dude. You were trying to tune a dude!'

'Shut the fuck up, cunt. No I wasn't.'

I tried to stand, but the thin one punched me hard in the face and stood over me.

'Fuck is wrong with you? Huh?'

He kicked me hard. Then he punched me again. I put my arms up to protect myself but I was too weak and dazed and he was too fast and angry. He spat on me.

'What the fuck are you doing? Hey? Fucking faggot. Why are you dressed like that?'

I didn't really feel him hitting me. It was his friend laughing that hurt.

The thin one put his hands around my neck and squeezed tight then dragged me across the pavement and slammed me against a low brick wall. The back of my head stung. I could see sparks in the corners of my eyes.

'Hey! Hey! *Hey!*' I heard someone call out. It was a man's voice. Loud and deep and powerful. I looked to my right. My vision was blurry, but I recognised Fella Bitzgerald. She was sprinting with her shoes in one hand and Edie's clutch in the other.

The big one grabbed his friend's shoulder and pulled him off me.

'Come on, let's go,' he said.

The thin one pushed him away. Then he reached down and ripped Edie's dress open. He tore a strip right down the centre. Sequins sprayed over the pavement, and I thought about Steve. Fella Bitzgerald was getting closer, calling out my name, warning them to stop, and I thought about my mum. Because this had happened before. And it would keep happening.

It would always be this way. So when the thin one balled up his fist and swung it towards me, I didn't feel scared. I knew what was coming and I didn't flinch, because I wanted it all to stop.

And then everything switched off.

Fracture

It all fell apart because of a holiday.

A few times a year, Steve would travel up the coast to Lancelin with his friends. They camped for three or four days and fished on his boat and went waterskiing and dived for crayfish. Sometimes they took their dirt bikes up to ride them on the dunes. My mum always wanted Steve to take me with him, but he never allowed it. He pretended to be sorry, and I pretended to be disappointed. He promised I could go when I was older.

When I turned thirteen, my mum got her way. I tried to get out of it, but she insisted. She said spending more time with Steve's friends would be good for me.

We drove up in his four-wheel drive with Steve's friends Rosso, Mick and Wayne, who also worked out on the mines. They wore singlets and thongs and sunglasses. They smoked cigarettes and drank cans of beer from an esky. Every fifteen minutes

Mick made everyone be quiet and turned up the radio so he could listen to a horse race he had money on.

I sat on my own, right up the back in the enclosed cab with all the bags and boxes and Rosso's grey staffy, Snags. He was less than a year old and he had sad blue eyes.

I didn't realise how far it was to Lancelin. We had been on the road for an hour, and I was uncomfortable because I had drunk a whole bottle of apple juice that Steve had bought me from a service station. I really needed to go. I didn't want to ask Steve to pull over because I knew he would be annoyed. He was already complaining about losing time because of the city traffic. He drove over the limit and overtook cars even though he had a trailer with the dirt bikes attached.

I tried to distract myself by squirming and pinching myself and biting the inside of my mouth and counting cars out the window, but nothing helped.

It got unbearable. It was almost leaking out of me. I stared at the empty bottle of apple juice and wished I hadn't drunk it all, but it gave me an idea. I unscrewed the lid. Then I moved forwards in the seat and slowly pulled down my shorts. I awkwardly poked my penis into the bottle and as soon as I did it all gushed out, so much that I thought they might hear, but nobody turned around.

For a second I felt relieved, then I saw that the bottle was almost full. I panicked and looked around for another bottle or a plastic bag, but there was no time.

I twisted in the seat just before the bottle overflowed and aimed at the floor. Snags looked at me strangely and sniffed at my urine and stepped in it. When I finished, there was a puddle soaking into the carpet next to Snags. I put the cap back on the bottle and pulled my shorts up and I felt queasy with dread.

I waited. A few minutes later, I saw Rosso and Wayne frown and look at each other in the back seat.

A little while after that, Steve screwed up his face.

'The fuck is that smell?'

'Mate, it smells like piss back here,' said Wayne.

Mick played around with the controls on the centre console.

'It might be your aircon,' he said. 'Gets mouldy in the vents and smells rotten. Maybe needs a clean out.'

'Bullshit,' said Steve. 'I had this serviced and detailed two months ago.'

Steve saw me in the rear-view mirror. He must have noticed how guilty I looked.

'What?' he said. 'Eh?'

I was too scared to say anything.

'What?' Steve said again.

I opened my mouth, but no words came out.

Rosso turned and looked at me. Then he poked his head over the back seat and saw the puddle.

'Oh fucking hell! *Fuck!*'

'What?' yelled Steve. He was barely looking at the road.

'Jesus Christ,' said Rosso.

'I've had enough of this,' said Steve. He pulled over and turned around in his seat.

I was shaking.

'Fuck,' said Rosso. 'I'm sorry mate. Snags has pissed all over the back here.'

He grabbed Snags by the collar and shook him.

'Bad boy! *Bad!* You little bugger!'

'Don't!' I said. 'It's not his fault!'

I thought Rosso would be angry with me, but he didn't even notice. He just shook his head and got out of the car. So did Steve. Wayne and Mick thought it was funny.

Steve opened the rear door.

'I told you not to bring your dog.'

'Sorry mate. Susie's out of town. He hasn't done this for a while. I'll put some towels down.'

Rosso ordered Snags out of the cab and wiped him down. Steve pulled some of the bags and boxes out of the way. He muttered to himself. Snags came over to sniff them and Steve slapped him hard on the nose and shoved him away. Rosso didn't see because he was laying a beach towel over the puddle.

Steve looked at me angrily.

'Why didn't you say anything? Eh?'

'It's not the boy's fault mate,' said Rosso. 'I'll give the carpet a shampoo later.'

We drove in silence the rest of the way. Steve was still annoyed when we got to the caravan park. I threw the apple juice bottle into a bin as soon as I could.

Once the tents were up, I helped Rosso clean out the car. I climbed inside and scrubbed the carpet and patted it dry with a fresh towel. He said I was a good kid, and bought me a mint-choc Cornetto from a vending machine.

At sunset, I prepared dinner over by the gas barbecues. I sliced tomato and lettuce and cheese. I toasted buns on the hotplate, then I sweated some onions and cooked beef patties on high heat and made burgers for everyone.

When they were finished, I cleaned up their plates. They called me the Camp Wife and told Steve I was very well behaved. He didn't say anything. I gave my burger to Snags because I still felt bad about him getting in trouble. He ate it in one bite.

I went to bed early and listened to them talk about the Eagles' midfield and brands of sonic fish-finders and subdivision applications and lifting the ban on professional cage fighting. Steve bragged about how attractive my mum was and showed them private photos on his phone. They drank a lot of beer and laughed really loudly. I didn't sleep at all.

The next morning I went with Steve to the ablution block on the far side of the caravan park. Change rooms always made me nervous, and I didn't want to stay in there very long. I kept my shorts on while I showered then dried off quickly and brushed my long hair. I cleaned my teeth so fast my gums bled.

I left Steve there and started walking back to the campsite down a thin sandy path. Suddenly I stopped. There was a grey snake coiled up a metre in front of me. I was so shocked I couldn't do anything but stare at it.

'What are you doing? Come on, hurry up.'

Steve was behind me. I didn't move. He gave me a nudge. I stumbled forwards and almost stepped on the snake. I yelled and threw my weight back. The snake lifted its head. Steve saw it and grabbed my shoulder. He pulled me back to the ablution block. I was upset.

'Why did you push me?'

Steve was annoyed that I was angry.

'I just saved your life! If it wasn't for me you would have got bit.'

'Because you *pushed* me!'

I had never spoken like that to him before. He narrowed his eyes. Then he grabbed me, picked me up and carried me over his shoulder, taking me a different way back to the campsite. I squirmed and kicked, but he was too strong.

When we got back to the campsite, he let me go. His whole mood changed.

'You alright, mate?' he asked. 'Eh?'

I couldn't understand why he was being so nice to me. Mick, Wayne and Rosso were drinking coffee and eating toast and cereal around the campfire.

'What happened?' Mick asked.

'Poor little bugger's a bit shaken up, I think. Almost stepped on a dugite outside the shower block. I grabbed him just in time.'

'Jesus,' Mick said, and whistled.

'Lucky you were there, eh?' said Wayne.

Steve puffed out his cheeks and raised his eyebrows.

'Close call. I better give these fellas the heads-up.'

I watched Steve walk to all the other tents around us to warn them about the snake. With each person he spoke to, the snake got bigger and more aggressive. He told them I was playing around and the snake struck out at me, but he snatched me out of the way and hit it with a lump of wood. He told them it slithered away but it was still alive. People shook his hand and patted his back. An old lady with permed hair came over and offered me a piece of watermelon and told me I was lucky my dad was so brave.

'I don't like watermelon,' I said, but that was a lie.

What I wanted to say was, 'He's not my dad.'

~

Later that morning we drove out to the dunes. They rolled their dirt bikes off the back of the trailer. I stayed in the car with Snags. Rosso told me not to let him out unless he was on the leash because he chased the bikes. They rode off.

Snags whined and climbed all over the car. I sat in the passenger side and watched them ride up and down the big white hills of sand in the distance.

They had been going for about an hour when I saw Steve going really fast towards one of the smaller dunes to jump off it. When he got to the top, his front wheel caught in the soft sand and he flipped over the handlebars. I didn't see him land.

Watching it through the windscreen, I didn't really feel anything. It was too far away to seem real. I still didn't think it was that bad when another rider went over there and started waving his arms. Then a few others rushed over. It was only when an ambulance came past me and headed across the flat sand that I knew it was serious. My first thought was that maybe he was dead.

I was worried about getting out because I had been told to look after Snags, but I left him in the car and walked over to where the ambulance had stopped. It was windy and the sand was hot and crunchy beneath my feet.

By the time I got there, the paramedics were carefully carrying Steve back over the dune. They had strapped him to a gurney, and he had a neck brace on. His eyes were open and his face was red and puffy and sweaty. They slid him into the ambulance and closed the doors. A dozen other riders were standing around watching.

After the ambulance drove away, Rosso put his hand on my back.

'You okay, sport?'

I nodded, because I really was fine. Rosso squeezed my shoulder.

'You're a tough kid.'

We went back to the campsite and quickly loaded everything up. Nobody talked much. I wondered if Steve was paralysed and if that meant my mum would have to care for him. She would never be able to leave him then. It would never be just the two of us again.

At the hospital we sat in the waiting area. After an hour or so, my mum arrived. She walked straight past me to speak to Wayne and Rosso and Mick. She was really upset, and it took them a while to calm her down. She folded her arms and shook her head, and Mick put his arms around her and patted her back.

A nurse came out and said Steve had asked to see me and my mum. It was strange that he asked to see me too. It made me worried and suspicious.

I followed my mum into the room. Steve was lying on a bed. He wasn't wearing the neck brace anymore. There was a thin tube going into his arm.

My mum rushed in and crouched by the bed. I could tell she wanted to hug him, but she knew she had to be gentle, so she just held his hand.

Steve ignored her. He waited until the nurse had left the room, then he looked straight at me.

'Did you talk to any of those paramedics?'

I shook my head.

'You tell anyone here at the hospital my name?'

I shook my head again.

'What about Rosso and the boys? They didn't fill out any forms or anything?'

I shrugged.

'I don't think so.'

'You don't think so or you don't know?'

Steve was really intense.

'I didn't see them fill out anything,' I said.

'You don't speak to anyone, is that clear? Not a word.'

'Okay,' I said.

'Steve, what's going on?' my mum asked. 'What did the doctor say? Are you going to be alright?'

Steve pushed himself up the bed, wincing with pain.

'Listen,' he said in a low voice. 'My name is John Smith, okay?'

My mum was getting worked up.

'What?'

'My name is John Smith.'

'No it's not.'

'Yes. It is. Listen to me. The doctor wants to schedule me for a CT scan right away. We have to leave now.'

'Why? What are you *talking* about? What have they given you?'

'Jesus fucking Christ, Sarah. Just do what I say. Go back out to the waiting room and tell the boys to leave. Tell Rosso to take the car and the bikes back to his place. Then I want you to find a wheelchair and bring it in here. We're going to put this blanket over me and we're leaving.'

'Steve, one of the nurses said you might have broken your back. I don't want to move you.'

Steve grabbed her wrist and held it tight. He was sweating.

'Just do it. Now.'

My mum gave in. As we left the room, she told me to find a wheelchair while she spoke to Rosso, Wayne and Mick. I walked up the corridor and peeked inside the rooms. I found one with a wheelchair. I crept inside. The lady on the bed was old and wrinkly. The television was playing *Deal Or No Deal*, but the lady was asleep. I slowly backed the chair out.

When I wheeled the chair into Steve's room my mum was already waiting. She helped Steve to sit up. He groaned with pain. Then he pulled the tube out of his arm and slowly slid off the bed. He was breathing really quickly and his face was red. My mum supported him.

'Help me,' she said.

We lowered Steve into the wheelchair. He was so heavy that it was hard to be gentle. He clenched his jaw and gripped the armrests.

'Blanket,' he said.

My mum took a blue blanket from the end of the bed and draped it over his lap.

'No, around my head. Cover me up.'

I knew my mum wanted to ask more questions, but she did what he said. She wheeled him out of the room and into the corridor. I walked ahead and scouted for nurses or staff, and I waved them forwards when it was clear. When we reached the corner before the main exit, my mum touched my shoulder and pointed at the lady behind the administration desk. I knew what to do.

I went up to the lady and told her I was looking for my mum and didn't know where to go. She asked for my mother's name and why she was at the hospital. I made up a name and a reason, and the lady typed on her computer. Behind me, my mum pushed Steve through the exit.

I told the lady I was going outside to call my dad. When I walked out, my mum was helping Steve into the front seat of a taxi. The driver was shaking his head and complaining about hospitals discharging people too early.

∼

When we got home, Steve couldn't walk up the stairs, so we helped him onto the couch. My mum prepared a heat pack, but Steve was in a bad mood and all he wanted was pain medication.

I found some Panadol and some anti-inflammatories in the bathroom cabinet, but Steve said they weren't strong enough. My mum raised her voice and told him he should have stayed at the hospital. Steve ignored her and told me to bring him his phone.

Half an hour later there was a knock at the door. I opened it, and there was a thin man in a navy blue polo shirt and grey track pants. He had small eyes and olive skin and he carried a backpack. Behind him in the driveway was a white van that said Kwik Traffik Courier Service on the side.

He looked over my shoulder.

'Steve here?'

I led him through to the lounge room. Steve smiled when he saw the man and introduced him as his friend Whippy. They had grown up together, but they hadn't seen each other in a long time.

Whippy shook my mum's hand, then raised his eyebrows at Steve.

'Family man these days. This why we don't see you anymore?'

Whippy sat down at the dining table and asked Steve about his injury. Then he searched through his bag and took out two boxes of pills. Steve told me to get his wallet and give Whippy all the money that was in there. He was forty dollars short, but Whippy didn't mind. He gave me the boxes. The name on the pack was Fentanyl.

'Go easy on them, hey,' said Whippy. 'They'll knock you the fuck out. Just take one for now and see how you go.'

I walked over to the couch and handed Steve the box.

He grabbed my arm before I could step away.

'Oi, you tell your mum I saved your life today?'

My mum looked at us.

'What?'

'Kid almost trod on a snake. I grabbed him up just in time.'

My mum put her hand over her mouth.

'Oh my God. Sam? Why can't you be more careful?'

'What kinda snake?' Whippy asked.

'Dugite. Huge bastard. Would have been all over.'

Whippy whistled through his teeth.

'Yeah, that would have done it.'

'Thank God you were there,' my mum said.

Steve winced and tried to sit up.

'Yeah, well, this is the fucking thanks I get.'

I wanted to tell them Steve had pushed me, but I knew they wouldn't believe me, so I didn't say anything. Whippy stood up. He pulled a little clear bag out of his pocket.

'You want some hydro?'

'Nah, cheers.'

'Sure?'

'Can't mate. I'm back on site in a few days and they're testing all the time now.'

'No problems. I'll leave you with that then. I got to get going, but we're due a catch-up, hey? Don't leave it another three years to call me. You know your brother's out?'

'Yeah.'

'You seen him yet?'

Steve shook his head.

Whippy shrugged and said goodbye then left. My mum walked him outside. When she came back, she looked angry.

'You are *not* going back to work in a few days.'

Steve didn't say anything. He opened the pack of pills.

'Steve, you can barely walk. You're not going back on site.'

'Yes I am.'

'Why? Just call and tell them you've hurt your back.'

'No.'

'Then *I'll* do it. You're not going. You can't.'

'Don't even think about it.'

Steve swallowed two small white pills. My mum sat on the coffee table.

'You can't go back to work; you're going to make it worse. Are you in denial or something? I don't get it.'

'Stop fuckin' nagging me, Sarah.'

'I'm trying to make you see sense. Do you see how crazy you're being right now? I mean, what's all this John Smith rubbish? Why am I sneaking you out of the hospital? Why are you inviting one of your old mates over instead of getting a prescription? You might need physical therapy. You might need a brace. We don't know until you've had all the tests.'

'And I will have them. Just not yet.'

'Why?'

'Just trust me. I'll handle it.'

My mum shook her head and put her hands over her face.

'Why are you being like this? It's so stupid!'

'Stupid am I? Is that what you reckon? Or do you think for a minute I might know what I'm doing? You think I've got this

152

far in life being a fucking idiot? Is it my stupidity that pulled you out of the gutter and put a roof over your son's head and sorted all *your* shit out?'

'I just want to know what's going on.'

Steve shook his head and sighed.

'You don't get it, do you? If I'm out of work with an injured back, I'm fucked. I've got no money coming in. And what are you gonna do then? Are you gonna earn my wage? Eh? Are *you* gonna pay *my* debts? Or are you gonna leave me for the next sucker with cash in his pocket?'

'Don't *say* that. I'm worried about you. You can't go back up there so soon. Not the way you are.'

'I won't be there long.'

'What do you mean?'

'I mean, if I play this right, I'll never have to work again.'

'How?'

'Jesus, Sarah, are you gonna make me spell this out? *I* didn't fuck my back up in Lancelin. Some bloke called John Smith did. But I *am* going to fuck my back up in a workshop in Karratha. Okay? Because if I'm on premises, they'll have to shell out. So you tell me. I'm either fucked financially, or I'm sitting on an early retirement.'

'What if you get caught?'

'I won't. It doesn't cost the company a cent. They handball all that shit to their insurance, and *they* foot the bill for my tests and rehab and compensation for lost work. If my back *is* broken, the payout could be millions.'

My mum thought about it, then she looked at Steve.

'What can I do to help?'

'Delete everything from today off your phone. Don't mention Lancelin to anybody.'

'What about Mick and Rosso and Wayne?'

'They'll be alright. They're good boys. They won't say anything.'

'How will you do it?'

'Dunno yet. I'll probably work through smoko or something, wait till the warehouse is cleared out, then I'll make it look like the scaffolding has buckled and tipped me off.'

'Are there cameras?'

'No, not where I'll be. It'll be easy.'

'Is there anyone you can trust on site to act as a witness? It would help with your claim. Maybe you could cut them in?'

Steve smiled. He looked a bit drowsy.

'Cut them in, eh? You've been watching too much TV. Just leave it to me. I'll sort it all out.'

'I know my way around. I'm not stupid either.'

'It's too risky to trust someone else. There won't be any problems. These companies get thousands of claims every year. Plus all the proof I need will be in the medical report. I've just got to get on the plane and walk in there looking alright.'

Steve squinted at the box of pills and read the label, then he smiled and closed his eyes.

'Fuck these are good.'

~

For the next three days, my mum looked after Steve. She brought him food and helped him shower and go to the toilet. Steve mostly slept and played video games. Rosso returned the car and the trailer. He was concerned that Steve was going back to work too soon, but Steve said he was feeling fine. He asked Rosso not to tell anyone about his accident because he was embarrassed about it.

By the time Steve left for the airport he could walk slowly, though he had to use his luggage like a walking stick. My mum was anxious after he was gone. She opened a bottle of wine and cleaned the whole house.

The next day she got a phone call from the warehouse foreman telling her Steve had suffered a bad accident and he was being medevaced to a hospital in Perth. My mum sounded shocked and worried on the phone. She even started crying. The moment she hung up she took a deep breath and closed her eyes and she looked relieved.

Steve was in hospital for a few days. He had all his scans and tests done and the doctors told him he had a compound fracture in his spine. A specialist looked at his X-rays and said if Steve rested his back and wore a special brace he would probably heal without needing surgery.

When Steve got home, he called a lawyer who specialised in workplace compensation and injury claims. He got the number from a television advertisement which promised a *No Win, No Fee* guarantee.

The lawyer visited. His name was Angelo DeAngelo. He wore a suit that was too small and his head was bald and shiny. He sat with Steve at the dining room table and went through his statements and financial paperwork. Steve said that his welding career was probably over, and he wanted to make sure Angelo would claim for future earnings. Steve also admitted he had fallen into a dark depression and his quality of life had suffered. Angelo DeAngelo nodded as he took notes.

'That's all good stuff,' he said. 'I'll book you a psych evaluation and submit that with our medical reports.'

Steve's claim was for two and a half million dollars. Angelo DeAngelo said it was unlikely the whole amount would be paid out, but it was good practice to aim high. Steve called the lawyer every second day for an update. Angelo would tell him the case was still pending, because a claim of that size invited extra scrutiny.

One afternoon an investigator from the insurance company came to the house. She was a young woman with a blonde ponytail and thick glasses. She carried a slim folder. She asked Steve a lot of questions about the accident and his injuries and she recorded his answers on her phone. She also wanted to know what Steve had been doing in the days before he had gone to work. Steve lied and said he had been at home. She asked if anyone could confirm his statements, so Steve had me and my mum answer some questions too. Steve stared at me while I spoke.

Steve spoke to Angelo DeAngelo after the investigator had left. He said Steve shouldn't have answered any of her questions without him there. Steve was annoyed and defensive and said he knew what he was doing.

Three weeks later, two different, older investigators showed up, a woman and a man. The man opened a briefcase full of thick folders. The lady did all the talking. She wasn't as cheerful as the last investigator. She told Steve they had reviewed his financial transactions for the week before his accident. They showed a purchase at a service station in Yanchep, which was where he had bought fuel and my apple juice. Later that day he had used the same credit card at a caravan park in Lancelin.

While she spoke, the man pushed documents with high-lighted parts across the table. Steve folded his arms and didn't look at them.

Then the lady mentioned a local dirt bike rider called Graeme Collins who had called an ambulance for a man who had crashed in the dunes the following day. Graeme had been sent the paramedic bill because the patient had left the hospital without giving his name or details. When the investigators met with Graeme, he identified Steve from a photograph. The attending paramedics and hospital staff had also recognised him, and they had all provided signed statements.

Steve looked down at all the papers in front of him for a long time. He read through them and cleared his throat a lot and tapped his finger on the table. My mum looked worried. The investigator asked Steve to confirm that he had an accident prior to the incident at work. Steve said he wasn't going to say any more until his lawyer was present.

~

Everything went bad really fast.

Steve's claim was denied and he was charged with insurance fraud. Angelo DeAngelo dropped him as a client. He also told Steve that he had breached their contract by knowingly making false statements, which meant he was liable for fees. Angelo DeAngelo sent Steve a bill for thirty-five thousand dollars.

Steve was fired. His boss called to tell him he would never be hired in the welding industry again, because he would personally contact any of his future employers to tell them what Steve had done.

The more things went wrong, the more Steve pretended everything was going the way he wanted. He contested the charges and he planned to represent himself in court.

Then one day Steve was supervising me as I washed his car, and Rosso pulled into the driveway. I could see Snags poking his nose through a gap in the back window. I went over to pat him. Rosso got out and handed Steve a piece of paper. Steve stood up from his deckchair.

'What's this?'

'I've been subpoenaed.'

'What for?'

'To appear as a witness at your trial.'

Steve looked at the document again.

'And what are you gonna say?'

'That's why I'm here. Mate, I can't risk it. I can't lie about all this. Me and Susie are trying for a baby, and I've just moved into the new house.'

Snags licked the soap off my hands. I could see Steve was getting angry.

'Then stay at home.'

'Steve, it's a subpoena. If I don't rock up, they'll just come and arrest me. I could get done for contempt of court.'

'So you'd rather just sell me out.'

'I'd rather not have anything to do with this shit.'

'So why are you getting involved? Stay the fuck out of it if you can't man up and do the right thing.'

'You don't get it. *They* came to *me*. Mick and Wayno got the call-up too.'

'And what are they gonna do?'

'I have no idea. You'll have to ask them.'

Steve raised his voice.

'So they'll be playing ball, but it won't mean shit, because you'll be backing up the bosses. You just need to shut your fucking mouth. It's simple. Anything they ask up there, your answer is *I don't remember*. And let me tell you this once: I can do a lot worse than a contempt of court charge.'

'Excuse me?'

'You heard what I said.'

Steve was standing over him, but Rosso didn't look scared.

'Mate, you've got to let this go. They've got you bang to rights.'

Steve grabbed Rosso by the throat and walked him back.

'They've got fuck all except for you. Keep your *fuckin'* mouth shut.'

Rosso slapped Steve's hand off his throat and pushed him hard in the chest. Steve staggered back and fell, but he snatched at Rosso's shirt and brought him down too. Steve was on his back. He got Rosso in a tight headlock and punched at his ribs.

My mum must have heard the shouting, because she ran outside.

'Stop! Steve! No! Stop it!'

She tried to pull them apart. Snags was barking and pawing at the window. Without thinking, I opened the car door. Snags leaped out and ran across the driveway. He bit Steve on the forearm and wouldn't let go, even after Rosso got free. Snags was snarling like a wild animal. There was blood on Steve's arm and neck. Steve tried to push Snags off.

'Get your fuckin' dog off me!'

His voice was high. He sounded afraid. Rosso was winded. He rolled onto his knees and tried to get his breath back.

My mum screamed and rushed forwards and kicked Snags hard in the ribs, but Snags just growled and held on tighter. She kicked him again and again, until Rosso got to his feet and grabbed Snags by the collar and forced his hand between the dog's jaw and Steve's arm. Snags finally let go. His fur was covered in blood. Rosso lifted him up and held him against his chest.

Steve tried to sit up. There were flaps of skin hanging from his arm and blood dripped onto the lawn. Snags kept barking and growling so Rosso held his mouth shut.

'Get the fuck off my property,' said Steve.

Rosso shook his head.

'You're a disgrace.'

He put Snags in the car and walked around to the driver's seat. Steve called out to him.

'I got security cameras set up out here. One phone call, I can have that dog killed. Keep that in mind.'

'Do what you want, mate. But I'm not lying for you.'

Rosso reversed out of the driveway and drove away fast.

My mum tried to help Steve stand, but he was too heavy and in too much pain. I walked over and held my hand out to help but Steve slapped it away.

'I saw what you fucking did,' he said.

～

Rosso didn't have to testify.

Steve was sent a brief of evidence. It was in a black binder that was an inch thick. He realised that he was going to lose, so he settled privately with the insurance company. They ordered him to pay two hundred thousand dollars. He had six months to raise the money, or they would take the case back to court. I was disappointed that Steve settled, because otherwise he might have been sent to prison. Then it would have been me and my mum again.

Steve blamed Rosso for everything falling apart. He talked about him all the time. He said that Rosso had always been jealous because Steve had more money and a bigger house and my mum was pretty and Rosso's wife was plain-looking.

He said Rosso must have called their boss and told him about the accident. He said one day he would get him back for what he had done.

Steve couldn't afford the physical therapy for his back. It was painful for him to walk or bend over, so he didn't move much. Whippy brought over more Fentanyl at least once a week. I could tell when Steve had run out. He went from being tired and quiet to bitter and short-tempered.

None of his friends came to see him. He called around looking for work, but nobody was hiring. Steve fell behind on his mortgage and his car and boat payments. He had credit card debts, and the insurance company fine, and Angelo DeAngelo's fee. All his medical bills had diverted back to him, and he had to pay for the medivac flight and the ambulance trip from Lancelin.

One night my mum suggested that he file for bankruptcy, just like he had told her to do. Steve grabbed her hair and wrenched her neck back and told her if she ever said that again she would be out on the street where she belonged. Then he let her go. I waited for my mum to take my hand and tell him we were leaving, but she just said she was sorry.

~

Within four months, Steve had sold everything. His guitars, his jetski, his boat, his ute, his dirt bike and most of his furniture. He sold the computer he bought me. And, finally, he sold the house.

We packed what was left and moved into a place in Hamilton Hill, near where Steve grew up. The house was owned by his cousin, Gavin, who was a lot older than Steve. Gavin was a member of the Devil's Army Motorcycle Club. He had short grey hair and a goatee and tanned leathery skin and he only wore black clothes.

Steve said the house was Gavin's investment property, but it didn't seem worth much. Half the houses in the cul-de-sac were empty. They all had weeds and cracked cement paving out the front, and they were divided by broken asbestos fences. Most of the front windows had bedsheets for curtains, and our place was no different. Steve said we would only be there for a few weeks while he got back on his feet.

I had my own room at least. Part of the wall was caved in and it smelled like cigarettes and old vomit. The carpet had dark patches and lumps of candle wax and bits of broken glass everywhere. I picked up all the shards I could find and put sheets of cardboard over the floor and then I laid towels over the top. My clothes were back in black plastic bags again. I still had my bed and my old iPad and my phone.

For the first two weeks we had no power or hot water. The kitchen was small and dirty and dark and there were ants everywhere. The oven didn't work and only one burner on the stove would ignite.

Nobody had lived there in over a year, but the door of the small storage cupboard in the hallway had a slide bolt and padlock that looked shiny and new. I asked Steve what was in there, and he told me to mind my own business.

Steve's old friends started visiting. One of them was his younger brother Mark. He was a foot shorter than Steve. He had tattoos down both his arms and across his chest, and he smoked all the time. Mark had just been in prison for grievous bodily harm. He had beaten someone up outside a nightclub because they had spoken to his girlfriend.

Steve had another old friend called Dane. He had big muscles and a buzz cut and he was in the army. He complained a lot about his ex-wife because while he was away on his last tour she had got an injunction from the family court to stop him from seeing his son. He said that even though Afghanistan was a shithole, at least women there knew how to respect men. He planned to take his son and move to Tasmania and go off grid. Both Steve and Mark said that they would help. Whippy was over all the time too. His real name was Ricky Wragg. He used to live across the road from Steve and Mark when they were growing up. Most days they all sat in the lounge room and smoked and drank and played video games and watched sport or action movies.

Steve had stopped taking Fentanyl by this time. He was still stiff and sore, but his back had healed enough for him to move around without the brace. He kept buying it from Whippy, though, because my mum had started taking it.

I don't know when or why she started, but she had it every day. Steve kept the pills in his pocket, so when she wanted more she had to ask him. Sometimes he refused. She would beg or complain or argue with him, but once Steve made up his mind, he never gave in. He told her she was weak and she needed him to be strong for her.

Sometimes my mum went to pubs and clubs with Steve and his friends, but she never left the house by herself anymore.

Some days she was full of energy and she would tell me she had a job interview or had applied to a design and dressmaking course, but she never went to them.

She bought a cheap second-hand sewing machine and some fabric and used it twice before putting it back in its box. I took it to my room and taught myself how to sew curtains and I hung them up. Then I made a pillowcase. Then one night I made a shift dress out of grey heather cotton. It didn't fit very well, but it felt light and soft. I hid it under my mattress.

I hated our new house. Being back in his old neighbourhood made Steve meaner and rougher. His temper was worse. I was tense all the time. He looked for any excuse to single me out. He blamed me for making a mess or leaving doors open or anything that annoyed him. Denying it made him angrier, so I just apologised and I started cleaning up after everyone.

Sometimes I would catch him staring at me. He wouldn't blink. It was like he could look straight through me, like he knew my secrets. If there was nobody else around he would shoulder bump me down the hallway or pin me against a wall and try to bait me.

'Stand up for yourself. Be a fuckin' man. Do you even know what that means? It means sorting your shit out and taking some fucking responsibility. All you do is fucking sulk about around here living off my good graces. All I fucking do is give. You're an ungrateful, lazy little cunt. Well you're not suckin' on my tit any longer. You need to grow the fuck up. No more moping around looking miserable. Buy your own food. Get your own shit. Get a fucking haircut. I'm sick of telling you.

I've given you enough. If you don't like it here, fuck off and find somewhere else to live. Then you'll see how hard life really is. You've got no idea. You think you're better than me, don't you? So prove it. Get your hands up, defend yourself. I might even fucking respect you. Come on.'

I would just look down and wait until he left me alone.

I hadn't enrolled at a new school since we moved and I had missed the first three terms of year nine. During the day I kicked around Fremantle or took the train into the city. At home I spent time in the backyard because Steve never went out there. There were three stray cats that I talked to. I stole tins of tuna for them. There was a tabby that had a scar across its mouth that sometimes left a dead mouse for me on our back step.

Mostly I stayed in my room. I didn't have a lock but I wedged a piece of wood under the door so I felt safe. I always had headphones on because Steve and his friends were so loud.

One night, Gavin came over while everyone else was out. He was with another man I had never seen before. Gavin unlocked the storage cupboard in the hallway. It was lined with shelves. I peeked through a gap in my bedroom door and watched him take out a shotgun and a pistol and a small canvas bag. He handed the shotgun to the other man then locked the door and they left. Four hours later he returned and put everything back in the cupboard.

I missed cooking, but the kitchen was terrible and I was never hungry anymore. Sometimes I went days without eating. I was getting really thin but I felt so heavy. I was really unhappy.

Food didn't taste the same. Colours weren't as bright. Sounds were dull and far away. Time went really slow. It was like I was fading into a ghost. There were only two things that made me feel better: burning myself with a lighter, and dressing up.

I was stealing clothes and cosmetics again, and I was taking stupid risks because I didn't care anymore if I got caught. I didn't have a mirror in my bedroom, so I used the camera on my iPad to apply my make-up. I didn't just pose for myself either. I started going on random webcam sites where strangers could see me.

I wore sunglasses and brushed my hair over my face. I was shy and nervous and I never spoke to anyone, I just wanted to see their reactions. It was usually older men. Some of them clocked me and laughed or frowned and left the chat session. Mostly they thought I was a girl and they would say flattering things. A lot of the time they would touch themselves. They told me I was attractive and asked me to pose for them, and sometimes I did. I turned around and bent over and blew them kisses. Sometimes I took my sunglasses off and showed my face. They would ask me to take my clothes off, but I never did that, even when they offered me money.

It made me feel even more dirty and ashamed, but it was an addiction. I hated myself afterwards, but like always, the next night I couldn't wait to do it again.

～

Steve paid his settlement fee after the sale of his house cleared, but he still owed money elsewhere and nobody would hire him.

He got a lot of calls from collection agencies. He would yell abuse and then hang up and block the number.

'Fucking parasites. They buy debt for cents on the dollar and think it's a licence to stalk you.'

Steve was on the couch complaining to Whippy, who was sitting on a beanbag and messaging on his phone.

'I don't know,' Whippy said. 'Maybe I should hire them to look after *my* shit.'

My mum was at the table smoking a cigarette.

'What do you mean?' she asked.

Whippy held up his phone.

'I mean like this fucking parrot right here. He's into me for, like, fifteen hundred and he's chasing two points for tonight, even though he can't even cover the rate, let alone the principal. It's getting to the stage where I won't sell on tick anymore.'

'You're an idiot for trusting them at all,' said Steve.

'Well I only offer credit for repeat customers, so I know who they are and where they live. Plus it's a twenty per cent mark-up on price, plus interest if they don't pay me back on time, so it's usually worth the risk. But chasing up these dickheads is the biggest pain in my arse. They ghost you for weeks, then it's every excuse under the sun when their other connect is dry and they're chasing again. I'm not gonna lie, I'd fucking love a collection agency to take care of it.'

My mum twisted around in her seat. She had a crafty look on her face.

'How much do they all owe?'

'I don't know. All up? I reckon I must have fifty grand out there.'

'*Fifty grand?*'

'Easy. Plus another ten I've lost on counterfeit scams and rip-offs that I never bothered about.'

My mum looked at Steve.

'*You* should do it.'

'Do what?'

'Collect his debts. Same as an agency.'

Steve scoffed and shook his head.

'I'm being serious,' my mum said. 'He's got their details. You've just got to go get it off them. They don't know who you are. It's not like they're going to the cops about money they owe *him*, are they? It's perfect. You'd be so good at it.'

Steve thought about it. Then he looked at Whippy and raised his eyebrows.

∾

My mum was right. Steve was good at it.

Whippy gave him a list of people who owed him money. The first thing Steve did was message them through an encrypted app requesting that they clear the debt. Most of them refused or ignored him, but Steve had a few different ways to get people to pay. He stalked them on social media and found out as much about them as he could. If he knew their address, he checked their mail and staked out their house like a private detective to see if they had security cameras or housemates. He harassed them with messages and added interest to the amount they owed. He gave them a deadline, and if they still didn't pay, then he did something to intimidate them.

If they had a car, he would stab their tyres. If the car was old enough, he got Mark to steal it, and offered to return it once the debt was cleared. He stole one lady's cat from her backyard and she paid within two hours. Sometimes he took photos of their parents' house or their kids' school and sent it to them. A couple of times Steve printed out flyers with the person's name and photograph saying they were on the sex offender registry and posted them in letterboxes all over their neighbourhood.

If they made excuses about not having the money, Steve sent them information on how to set up a short-term loan online. Some companies would approve loans in under an hour. Then he instructed them to go to a cash machine and leave the money under the doormat of one of the vacant houses across the street. He would wait and watch them from inside our lounge room.

If nothing else worked, he threatened people physically. Dane and Mark went with him for the fun of it. Dane called them recovery missions and treated them like an army operation.

They went at night. Before they left they sat around drinking rum and Coke and smoking from a glass pipe and listening to loud metal music. When it was time to go, they stood up and slapped each other and yelled. They took ski masks and a cricket bat. Sometimes Steve unlocked the storage cupboard and took one of the guns. Then the house would go quiet for a few hours. When they returned, they were either boastful or angry, depending on what had happened.

Usually they were out until late. But one night they came back in less than an hour. I didn't hear them because I was in my room with my headphones on. I was wearing a dark red slip dress and knee-high black stockings and I had applied cat-eye make-up and plum-coloured lipstick. I was showing myself on the webcam to a man from England. He was sitting on a brown couch and listening to music in the background.

I didn't hear Steve yelling at me from the hallway. He had forgotten to close the door to the storage cupboard before he left, and he was furious because he thought I had opened it.

I *did* hear him bang on my door. I flinched and then I froze. I pulled my headphones off. I told him to wait outside, I told him not to come in. He kept bashing at the door and trying to open it. The wooden wedge was coming loose, so I went over and tried to keep the door shut, but it burst open and Steve saw me. He stopped for a second. He looked confused.

'The fuck are you doing?'

'Nothing.'

I tried to close the door, but he blocked me.

'The fuck is this?'

'Nothing.'

'Doesn't fucking look like nothing.'

He stepped inside and I backed away.

'It's nothing. I'm sorry, I'm sorry, I'm sorry.'

He pushed me hard. I fell back. He closed the door behind him. Then he picked up the iPad.

'Who's this? What are you, a faggot?'

I shook my head.

Steve snapped the iPad in half and threw it aside.

'You're not a faggot?'

'No.'

'Then what are you?'

'Nothing.'

'You're nothing?'

'Yes. No.'

Steve leaned over me.

'What? Fucking speak up when I'm talking to you. Show me some fucking respect. So what are you? Are you a whore?'

'No.'

'Then why are you dressed like a whore?'

'I don't know.'

'What?'

'I don't know. I'm sorry.'

'You're sorry? So what are you? Are you a woman?'

'What? No. *No.* No.'

'Then what the fuck are you doing in these clothes? What's all this shit on your face? The fuck is wrong with you? Huh? Is this what you do in here? Why?'

'No. I don't know.'

'You dunno. You dunno. You're a fucking embarrassment. To me, to your mother, to yourself. You don't have an answer for me? Hey? What the *fuck* is wrong with you?'

I was shaking. I couldn't look at him.

'I don't know.'

Steve slapped me hard across the face.

'What?'

'I don't know.'

'I don't fucking know either.'

He slapped me again. Then he pushed me against the wall and held me there. I couldn't breathe. I was so scared I started to cry.

'What, you gonna fucking cry now? Be a *man*. I'm sick of dealing with your shit. You're a fucking disgrace. If you won't be a man, I'm going to make you one.'

He let me go and I dropped down and hugged my knees to my chest.

'Stand up,' he said.

I shook my head.

'Stand up.'

'No.'

'Get up. Stand up for yourself. Take a fucking swing at me. I know you want to. I know you fucking hate me. After all I've done for you. Do it. Have a swing.'

I just shook my head. He slapped me hard on the side of my head and for a few seconds I couldn't hear or see.

'Are you gonna do this again? Hey? Are you gonna dress like a woman?'

I shook my head.

Steve grabbed me by the neck and lifted me up and threw me on the mattress. I kicked my legs and tried to protect myself. Steve picked up the fabric shears next to the sewing machine.

'Come here.'

'No!'

'Fucking come here, *now*!'

He grabbed my ankle and pulled me towards him. He put his knee on my chest and pinned me to the bed and he hacked off chunks of my hair. Every time I put my hands up to stop him, he slapped me. The scissors cut into my scalp. My hair was everywhere, in my eyes and mouth. He turned me over onto my stomach and cut the rest of my hair and I just gave up and cried into the blanket.

When he was finished, he threw the shears across the room. Then he turned me back over and he ripped my dress right down the front and tore it off me. He did the same with the stockings. He spat on my face and used the stockings to wipe my make-up off.

'If I see you dressed like this again, I'll give you something to cry about. It's not happening again, is it? Hey? *Is it?* Answer me!'

He slapped me and shook me.

My mum ran into the room. She shrieked and started beating at Steve's back.

'Get off him! Get off! What are you doing?'

Steve pushed me away. My mum kneeled down and looked at my face.

'What have you done?'

'Well you're not fucking raising him, are you? Fuckin' junkie. What have *you* done? What hope has he got? He needs to learn. He's not right.'

I curled into a ball and shut my eyes and covered my ears so I couldn't hear them argue. Then Steve left and slammed the door behind him.

My mum touched me on the shoulder.

'Sam, I'm sorry.'

I pulled away from her.

'Leave me alone!'

And she did. She got up. I didn't want her to. I wanted her to hold me. I wanted her to say that she would never leave me alone, that she would always be there. I wanted her to tell me everything would be alright.

She looked down at me for a long time. For a moment I felt hopeful. Then she brushed away the strands of my hair that were stuck to her clothes. She sighed.

'He's trying to help you,' she said.

My chest squeezed so tight I couldn't breathe. She picked up the ripped slip dress and folded it up tight. She looked sad.

'I don't know why you do this. But maybe it needs to stop.'

She walked out, still holding the dress, and closed the door behind her.

And I knew nothing would ever be alright.

I waited for about fifteen minutes. Then I got up. I felt dizzy and my head was throbbing. I had to sit on the mattress to put my jeans on, because it was too hard to stand. Then I pulled on a hoodie and some shoes and put my phone in my pocket. I wanted to message my mum later to tell her that I was sorry, and to say goodbye. I opened the window. Then I climbed out.

And that's when I met Vic.

Pressure Cooker

I don't remember getting into the taxi, but I remember Fella Bitzgerald with me in the back seat. She held my eyelids open and asked what my name was and where I lived and how old I was. I didn't really know the answers, I just mumbled and watched the streetlights passing by through the window.

Then I remember feeling weightless. I had that sensation again, the one where I was above myself and looking down. Fella Bitzgerald carried me across the front yard of Vic's house. She knocked on the door. Vic didn't answer. She knocked again, loud and fast.

Someone shone a torch from behind us.

'What on earth is going on?'

It was Mrs Boyd. She was wearing a bathrobe and slippers.

'Does an older gentleman live here?' Fella Bitzgerald asked. 'I think his name was Vic.'

'Excuse me?'

'I got this address from a driver's licence, but it's expired.'

The front door opened and the outside light came on. When Vic saw me limp in Fella Bitzgerald's arms he was upset.

'No no no no! What has he done? He hasn't, has he? What's happened? *What has he done?* '

I wanted to speak, but I was too weak and tired and lost inside myself.

'He was assaulted in the street. After he left the club.'

'Jesus Christ.'

'Who are these people and what are they doing here?' Mrs Boyd called out.

'Go back to bed, Beverley, and mind your own bloody business!'

The torch went off. I had never heard Vic sound so angry. Vic put his hand gently under my chin.

'Sam? You hear me? You stay with me, alright? You be tough.' Then to Fella Bitzgerald he said, 'He needs an ambulance. We need a medic. Why didn't you take him to a hospital?'

Fella Bitzgerald was calm.

'Because it's Friday night and he'd be sitting in the waiting room in emergency for three hours before anyone came to look at him. It's alright. I'm a nurse. I can look after him.'

'Come on then, come inside. Quick.'

Vic turned on lights as he led Fella Bitzgerald down the hallway to the main bedroom. He waited at the door while Fella Bitzgerald laid me on the bed and the ripped dress fell open. She held my eyelids open again and looked straight at me. Then she gently took the wig off my head. The cap was soaked in blood. She turned to Vic.

'Do you have a first-aid kit?'

'Is he gonna be alright?' Vic sounded frantic.

Fella Bitzgerald stayed professional.

'He will be fine, but I need your help. I need a first-aid kit, if you have one, and some water and a towel please.'

Vic left. A few minutes later he came back with a tin the size of a lunchbox in one hand and a bowl of water in the other. He had a blue towel tucked under his arm. He stood at the doorway.

'Here you go.'

Fella Bitzgerald was kneeling down and examining the cut on the back of my head.

'Okay, can you open the kit and pass me a pair of scissors, please?'

Vic didn't move. He still couldn't bring himself to walk into his old bedroom. He looked down at me and he looked so hurt and scared that it made me wake up. I came right back. I knew how hard it must have been for him to see me lying on Edie's side of the bed, wearing her torn dress. But Fella Bitzgerald didn't know this. She was firm with him.

'Vic, come on. He needs sutures.'

Vic took a breath and stepped into the room. The tin was rattling in his hand. He gave Fella Bitzgerald the water and the towel, then he sat on the end of the bed. He opened the lid of the kit and got the scissors.

Fella Bitzgerald washed the cut on my head, and it stung. She dabbed it dry with the towel and trimmed away the hair around it. Then I could feel a strange tugging sensation on the back of my head. It was quiet in the room, except when Fella Bitzgerald asked Vic for tweezers or needles or thread or disinfectant from the first-aid kit. She described everything she was doing, and she told me I was brave and strong.

I could feel Vic's hand on my ankle. His skin was leathery and cool. When she was done, Fella Bitzgerald wrapped a bandage around my head and rolled me onto my back.

'These will have to come out in a few days. We're going to need to put some ice on your face to stop the swelling, okay?'

'Okay,' I whispered.

'You're with me?'

'Yes.'

'Can you follow my finger with your eyes?'

She moved her finger from side to side. I could see her knuckles were bruised and split.

'What's your name?' she asked.

'Sam.'

'And who is this?'

'It's Vic.'

'Good. You know, it's getting a bit old patching you up, kid.'

Fella Bitzgerald smiled, then she squeezed my arm.

'How do you feel?'

'I'm in fine fettle.'

I don't know why I said it. Maybe because I was still dazed. Or maybe because I wanted to be strong and hopeful like Edie. Or maybe because I didn't want Vic to worry about me. But the moment I said it, he let go of my ankle. He looked shocked and a bit confused. He looked around the room, behind him, up at the ceiling, like Edie was here with us. Then he put his hands over his face and he took a really sudden deep breath. Then he started to cry. He was quiet, but his shoulders were shaking and his face was red. I tried to sit up, but I was too dizzy and weak. I wanted to put my arms around him. I wanted to hold him.

'Don't cry,' I whispered. 'Don't cry, Vic!'

Fella Bitzgerald gently held me down, and she spoke softly in my ear.

'Shh. It's okay. I'll look after him. You rest. Call out if you need anything.'

She kneeled beside Vic and put her hand on his knee. She waited. She let him cry. When he slowed down, she unrolled the rest of the bandage so he could wipe his face and blow his nose.

'Why don't you come out with me?'

Fella Bitzgerald helped Vic to his feet and walked him out of the room. He looked really small and thin.

After a while Fella Bitzgerald returned with a pack of frozen peas wrapped in a tea towel. She sat on the bed and pressed it gently against the side of my face.

'Is Vic okay?'

She didn't answer my question.

'Are you feeling any dizziness? Are you nauseous?'

'I'm worried about Vic.'

'I know, sweetie. I know. But I'm worried about *you*. Listen, you're in a safe place now. I'm so sorry I didn't look after you well enough tonight. You should never have been put in a position where you were out walking by yourself.'

'It's not your fault. You've been really nice to me.'

Fella Bitzgerald held my hand.

'Look at me. You're not on your own, Sam. Whatever you're feeling, someone else has felt it. Whatever you're going through, someone else has gone through it. And if we haven't, we can do our best to understand.'

She let go of my hand. There was a piece of paper in my palm.

'That has my number written on it. My name is Peter. And I want you to know you can call me, any time of the day or night, for any reason at all. If you need someone to talk to, about anything, call. Because if you keep it all inside it's going to poison you. I'm here for you, okay?'

Fella Bitzgerald looked at me and curled my fingers around the piece of paper. She had big sad eyes.

'Sometimes the family we're born into don't support who we are. My parents are very devout JWs. They kicked me out when I was fifteen. I moved to the city and lived in a group home for two years. I got very good at fixing up cuts and bruises. It's why I became a nurse. But I've still got scars of my own. See? Right here.'

She pointed to a raised line next to her right eye, which was coated in foundation.

'And in here.'

She tapped her chest, just above her heart.

'And here.'

She showed me her left wrist, which had rows of old cutting marks.

'There would be more if I hadn't found my new family. You met some of them tonight. They're my sisters and my mothers. They would fight to the living end for me, and that helps to remind me that I matter. I'm worth something. A lot. And you matter too. You're strong. You're beautiful. And you've been formally adopted into the House of Bitzgerald, girl. Like it or lump it. And I'm here to tell you that you can heal. You can be who you want to be. And you've got a big, bold, meaningful life ahead of you.'

She kissed my hand, then she stood up.

'Goodnight. Get some sleep.'

She started to walk out.

'Peter?'

'Yes?'

'You've got a really nice singing voice.'

'Oh, I know, sweetie.'

She winked and turned out the light.

I slept through the next few days. I felt heavy and sore and I didn't want to do anything. I didn't shower or brush my teeth. I stayed in bed and flicked through Edie's diaries or some of the old *Women's Weekly* magazines that I found under the bed. They were full of knitwear patterns and bad recipes and pictures of people I didn't recognise. Edie had done all the crosswords and the word puzzles.

The only reason I got out of bed was to make sure Vic was okay and that he was eating. I didn't want to go outside, so

I cooked what was left in the house. I made a vegetable soup, and I made damper out of flour and water and milk. Neither of us ate much.

One afternoon I saw Aggie walking towards the front door in her school uniform. She knocked. I asked Vic to say that I was away visiting my mother for a few days. He didn't want to do that, so neither of us answered.

After a week, the swelling and the bruising on my face went down and the dizzy headaches stopped. The stitches on the back of my head were really itchy, and I asked Vic to remove them with tweezers and scissors. He had to wear Edie's reading glasses because he couldn't see very well. It hurt, but he got them out.

I found a drawer full of old DVDs under the television in the lounge room. There was an Alfred Hitchcock collection and a Marilyn Monroe box set and lots of old classic films. There were some Westerns that Edie had bought Vic for his birthday.

We started watching them at night, sitting on the couch with the lights out. Vic always started snoring within twenty minutes. Most nights I crawled over and leaned against him and put my head on his shoulder. He was warm and I liked the rhythm of his breathing. Sometimes he woke up, but he didn't mind me being there. He would pat my leg and slowly get up and go to bed, then I would curl into the spot he just left.

One night we were watching *Rear Window*. There was an actress called Grace Kelly in it. She was so elegant and beautiful and perfect that it just made me think about how ugly I was. I looked over at Vic. He was asleep. I wondered why he bothered with me, and why he let me stay with him. I touched the watch on my wrist and I thought about the man in the black Audi. Then I thought about all those old men on the webcam sites. I wondered if Vic looked at me the same way, but he was just too polite to say anything.

I shifted closer on the couch. I rested my hand on his stomach. I watched him sleep. I figured that I owed him, and it was the right thing to do because he was lonely and he had been kind to me. And if Vic did feel that way about me, at least I was worth something.

I was nervous. I lifted up his shirt, and I slid my hand under the elastic of his shorts. He was really hairy. I moved further down, and I curled my fingers around his penis. The skin was really soft and warm and loose. I gently squeezed.

Vic woke up. After a moment, he grabbed my wrist. I let him go. Then he took my hand out and held it. He looked me in the eye and he shook his head.

'Don't do that,' he said.

He didn't seem angry or upset with me. He stood up and left the room. I was really embarrassed.

Vic didn't say anything about it the next day. But we never watched any movies again after that.

~

I thought a lot about going back to the Clayton Road overpass. I thought about going to a train station and stepping onto the tracks. I thought about the knives in the kitchen drawer. I thought about ways to do it all the time. The only thing that stopped me was the promise I made to Vic, even though he didn't know about it. But I couldn't figure out how I was going to fulfil it.

So I went to see Aggie.

'Oh my *God*! Where have you *been*?'

She hugged me. She was warm and soft. I handed her the plate of butterfly cakes I had made and she dragged me inside.

Her mum and dad were in the living room. Mr Meemeduma was reading on a tablet. He looked at me over the top of his glasses and smiled and waved. Mrs Meemeduma was at the table marking schoolwork. She stood up and gave me a hug too.

'We've missed you!' she said.

'I was away visiting my mum.'

'Did she sell your house?' Aggie asked.

'There's a couple from overseas who want to buy it, I think.'

Aggie put the plate of cakes on the kitchen counter. She pointed at Mrs Meemeduma.

'Don't devour all of these! That goes for both of you.'

'Yes, daughter.' Mr Meemeduma laughed.

Aggie's room was even messier than usual. She had stacks of books and folders on her desk and her chair. She moved them so I could sit down, and she kicked her clothes under the bed.

'Sorry. My life is in a general state of disorder right now.'

'What's wrong?'

Aggie sat on her bed and sighed.

'I don't know. I met with this career counsellor a week ago because I've got to select subjects for next year, so I need to establish at least a vague notion of what I want to do with my life, but the truth is I have absolutely no idea. It's not that I have a lack of interests; I'm just, like, super fucking aware that it's one of the most critical decisions I'll ever make, and I'm *so* not ready to make it. I mean, how do you *know*? My mum is ridiculously supportive, you know, but she just speaks in fluent Inspirational Quotes, things like, 'Just follow your passions and you'll discover who you are,' which is lovely, of course, but totally unhelpful. And my dad is so sanguine and chill, and, like, rationally I'm aware that he'll be happy regardless of what I do, but he's also like this intimidating intellect. He literally reads books about quantum theory and macroeconomic trends and ornithology and fucking biodynamic agricultural practices for *fun*, and so, like, how do I pursue a vocation that actually earns his admiration, you know? And I *know* what you're thinking. *Oh, poor Aggie, she has too many career options!* I recognise this, hence my shame spiral. It's such a middle-class problem. Like, did I ever tell you how my dad became a dentist?'

'No.'

'So I once asked him why he chose to look at teeth all day and be a source of dread for most of the population, and he told me this incredible story. Wait, before I tell you, are you actually interested, or are you just being sweet?'

'No. I want to hear it.'

'Okay. So my dad grew up in Colombo, and his whole family lived in a two-bedroom apartment pretty much bordering a slum district. They shared a kitchen and a bathroom with all these other families. There was no money for school or anything. They stole electricity by running cables straight from a power line. When he was a kid, my dad worked out how to fix an old radio that he found, and he listened to it all the time. And because he's a savant, he learned how to speak English by listening to the BBC World Service and cricket commentary and syndicated *American Bandstand* episodes. He told me he used to think that Americans were crazy because all their songs used the word "baby". He was like, "Why are they singing all these songs about infants?" It must have been so confusing. Can you imagine how gross and peculiar popular music would be if we took the word "baby" literally in the lyrics? Like, I don't know, "Baby, I Need Your Loving".'

We both laughed. I thought of one.

'"Baby Got Back",' I said.

Aggie screamed with laughter. It made me feel good.

'Oh my fucking *God!* That's too much. My sides hurt. Okay. Anyway, so after he could speak it, he taught himself how to read and write in English too. He would take books home from the back of the city library, because sometimes they threw out these old obscure volumes.'

'He never went to school?'

'Nope. It's crazy. So when my dad was fourteen, he was working like ten hours a day at this industrial laundry. One night he gets home and his dad, my grandfather, is howling in pain. He's got a fever, headache, he's in and out of consciousness. But my dad is super calm. He kneels beside him, checks his temperature, and tries to work out what's wrong. He takes a look inside his mouth, and he sees that one of his lower teeth has this gnarly abscess, probably because he was addicted to betel nut. Anyway, my dad has this old nineteenth-century medical guidebook that he found at the back of the library, and he finds the right procedure and he turns to the page with diagrams and a method. Then he gets a pair of pliers and a peeling knife, and he literally performs a molar extraction on his own dad.'

'Seriously?'

'I honestly didn't believe it. But he still has the book. And his dad's blood is even on that page.'

'Whoa. Did it work?'

'His dad was fine in like two days, and chewing betel nut again like a fucking idiot. Not only that, he's bragging to everyone with ears that his son fixed his tooth. So two weeks later, some old guy turns up at their house with his cheek the size of a mango and he wants to see this miracle child dentist that everyone is talking about. And my dad pulled *his* tooth out and sent him on his way. So *more* people start to show up. Meanwhile, he's reading everything he can about dentistry, calling up actual dentists to get them to donate supplies. And a month later he's administering to six people a day and making enough money to provide for the whole family. Then this NGO hears about him, and they sponsor him to go study in the UK, and that's where he met my mum. Crazy. And literally the most impressive thing I have ever done is finish runner-up in a state spelling bee.'

'That's still impressive.'

'Want to know what word I got wrong?'

'What?'

'Periodontology.'

'I don't know what that means.'

'It's like the study of gum diseases and stuff. Like, of all the words to spell wrong, right? My dad thought it was hilarious, but I was devastated about losing.'

'But you came second.'

'I know, but, like, I've always had this anxiety about failing and not living up to the legacy of my parents. It would be so much easier if they were complete fuck-ups. You must feel the same way though sometimes?'

'How do you mean?'

'Well, your dad's like a vice-admiral and your mum is this super-connected consultant. Don't you feel like you've got all this pressure on you to be successful and influential and to live an important life?'

I shrugged.

'I don't really think about it.'

'See, that's because you're sensible and emotionally stable and I'm a neurotic mess. You've probably got everything worked out. Do you know who you want to be?'

Her question made me blush and look away. I wanted to tell her she was wrong about me. I wanted to confess that everything I had told her about my family had been a lie. The truth was right there in my chest. I took a deep breath.

'How would you rob a bank?' I asked.

Aggie laughed really loudly.

'Well, yeah, we've always got that up our sleeve. There's always armed robbery.'

'No. Seriously. How would you do it?'

'How would I rob a *bank*?'

'Yeah. Say you really had to, but you couldn't get caught.'

'Oh my God, *Sam*!'

Aggie stared at me for such a long time with her mouth open that it made me nervous.

'That's *such* a fucking good question,' she said.

All Aggie talked about for the next few days was how to rob a bank. She was obsessed. She said it was just like a role-playing game, but I think she wanted a distraction from her other problems.

We decided that going in with guns and balaclavas would never work. Aggie said we needed a more creative approach. We talked through a lot of ideas. One included dressing up and posing as cash-in-transit security guards and fooling the bank staff into giving us bags of money from the vault. Another was playing a long con by becoming an actual bank employee and clearing out all the till money without anyone knowing. We talked about breaching their security systems by hacking, but neither of us had any skills with computers.

Aggie read online that most suburban banks were accessible through the ceiling space, and she made up a plan to enter at night through the roof cavity and drop explosives to open the vault. We both agreed that was too complicated.

We talked about stealing a whole ATM. We watched security footage on YouTube of people chaining a cash machine to a big ute and ripping it out of a wall. It was the most promising idea so far, but Aggie still wasn't convinced.

Then one Friday afternoon, I came over with a plate of dark chocolate and cherry muffins. Aggie was at her desk with her laptop open.

'Holy shit, I've fucking got it!'

I sat on the bed. Aggie didn't even look at the muffins.

'Here's the thing. We've been going about this all wrong. We've been thinking all *Ocean's Eleven*, but it should be as simple as possible. It's not a heist, it's a *robbery*, right?'

'Right.'

'So I've been reading about all these successful bank robberies, and they all have one thing in common.'

'What?'

'It's just one person.'

'I like that.'

'Oh my God, I've read *way* too much about this, but I've worked it out. Do you want to hear my plan? It's diabolical and literally foolproof.'

My heart started beating fast.

'I really do.'

'Okay, so, here's how you do it. You just walk into the bank. You want to be smartly dressed, like you're some normal desk-job professional. But *some* kind of disguise is critical, obviously, because there are cameras everywhere; so you've got to obscure your face, but not in a way that draws any attention. Now, you're also carrying a bag, like a backpack or a gym bag.

Something unassuming, but it has to look like it's got some weight to it.'

'Why?'

'I'll get to that. It's genius, I promise. So you wait your turn, like you're there to make a deposit or whatever, but it's okay if you start to look a bit nervous at this point, because when it's your turn, you walk straight up to the teller. You don't say a word, you just slide a letter across the counter. You've written this letter on generic printer paper. And you wrote it out with your left hand, or you've copied a different style of handwriting so they can't do an accurate analysis.'

'What does it say?'

'Okay, so, bear with me, because it gets a *bit* complicated here. The letter says that you're just a courier who is being ordered against their will, because the author of the letter, who is the mastermind behind the robbery, is holding a member of your family hostage or something, and you've just been sent out to collect the money. Get it?'

I nodded.

'See, this scenario gives you plausible deniability if you get caught, right? I told you it's genius. Anyway, so the letter says that you, the courier, have a remotely controlled bomb in your bag, and it instructs the teller to give you all the cash in their drawer, but only the large denominations, because the twenties might have a tracer or a dye pack.'

'What's a dye pack?'

'They're *amazing*. Basically, they're these small explosives that they conceal in wads of cash, and they're designed to detonate once the thief is a certain radius from the bank. But it's not this huge atomic blast; what happens is the thief gets sprayed with a bright-coloured dye, so the police can identify them easily.'

'Seriously? They use them in banks here?'

'They seriously do. But they're mostly in the twenties, from what I read, so you have to *specifically* demand the hundreds and the fifties. The teller will just give you the money, too, because complying with demands is their standard procedure.'

'Really?'

'Yeah, well, think about it. These corporations are huge. It's going to cost them less for a single branch to give up a few thousand dollars than it would to refuse and have a customer get injured in a shootout or something. Even so, you want to maximise your chances of getting away safely. So once the teller gives you the money, what you need to do is put the backpack down and leave it in the bank. The letter will explain that if they press a panic button, or if they lock the doors or call the police, the bomb will be remotely triggered. Once the money is delivered safely to the mastermind, the bomb will be disarmed. That allows you to walk outside to your getaway car or whatever. Now, I *know* what you're going to ask me.'

'What am I going to ask?'

'You're going to ask, *Agnes, why would I be so fucking gormless as to leave a bag full of evidence for detectives to analyse?* to which I would reply, *Listen kid, when you've been in the game as long as I have, you pick up some tricks, so show me some goddamn respect.*'

'It's a good question.'

'Sure, for a rookie criminal like you. The reason it won't be an issue forensically is because protocol dictates that the area will be cleared and the bomb squad will be called, and they'll send in that little robot thing to remove the bag, then they take it out to a facility and do what's called a proactive detonation.'

'But it's not a real bomb, right?'

'No, fuck no. It's totally fake. But either way they blow it up as a precaution, and all they can do afterwards is sift through what's left. By that time, you're drinking Dom Pérignon and rubbing your face with Beluga caviar. The best part of the plan is that it sounds elaborate, but all you really need is a bag full of junk and a story. And, you know, *enormous* balls. But it's genius, right?'

I nodded.

'I think it might work,' I said.

～

That night I cooked Vic a chicken and chickpea tagine. I left the garlic out because it upset his stomach. I was still awkward around him because of what I did on the couch the other night, but he seemed to have forgotten about it. He seemed really far away. He moved slowly, and sometimes he had to hold on to the table or the wall to steady himself.

After I cleared the plates, I asked Vic if he wanted to take the Black Shadow for a ride next week. He thought about it and nodded. He said it was a nice idea.

I helped tune up the Black Shadow that weekend. Vic sat on a crate and showed me what to do. I drained the sump and replaced the engine oil. I adjusted the clutch cables and tightened bolts around the frame. I patched the back tyre and checked the globes in the brake lights and the headlamp. Vic showed me how to grease the chain, and gave me a rat-tailed rasp to sharpen the sprockets. He was in a happier mood while I was working on the Black Shadow. Sometimes he looked at me with a little smile.

On Sunday afternoon, we got it running and Vic took it for a test ride around the block. He said it was good as new. He told me I did really good work which made me smile.

When I wasn't working on the Black Shadow I was preparing for the robbery. I found a canvas duffel bag in the garage and shook all the spiders out of it, then I collected things to fill it with. I took an old pressure cooker from the back of a kitchen cupboard, and I grabbed a distributor cap and a timing belt and some loose wires from the garage. I strapped them to the pressure cooker with electrical tape to make it look like a fake bomb.

I trimmed Fella Bitzgerald's wig to shoulder length and cut a fringe into it. From Edie's wardrobe I chose a grey pantsuit and a black blouse and a pair of black ballet pumps. In a drawer of the vanity table I found a pair of rose-coloured sunglasses from the eighties that were so big and square that they covered half my face.

I tore blank pages from Edie's diaries to write the note. I wore dishwashing gloves so there wouldn't be fingerprints, and I wrote it with my left hand. I tried to remember all the details that Aggie told me. I messed it up dozens of times.

Everything was ready, except me. I was really anxious about it, but every time I thought of giving up, I remembered how unfair life had been for Vic. I wanted us to beat the bank before we left. I wanted us to outsmart them. I wanted to give Vic that bag of money and tell him that he got his revenge. I wanted to see him smile with surprise. I wanted to prove to him that I could do things. I wanted him to be proud of me.

The night before I didn't sleep at all. I stared at the ceiling and kept going through the plan in my mind. I imagined waiting in line and keeping my head down. I imagined stepping up to the teller and handing them the note. I imagined them reading it, then quickly stuffing money into a bag. Then I imagined leaving the bomb in the bank and walking out. I went over it again and again.

I started applying make-up as soon as the sun came up. I chose a heavy contour and a plump lip to disguise my face a bit more. I brushed the wig out and gave it plenty of volume.

I put on my outfit and fit my hair and finished with the sunglasses. I stared at myself in the mirror for a long time.

'That'll have to do, kid.'

~

Late in the morning, I walked into the garage and found Vic wheeling the Black Shadow out onto the driveway. I made sure there were no neighbours around, then I followed him outside. He was wearing dark blue jeans and black leather gloves and a brown leather jacket. He looked younger and stronger.

Vic turned and looked at me strangely.

'You sure you wanna wear that?'

I took a step back and looked down.

'What I mean is, it's better to wear a jacket and some thick strides in case we come off. You're gonna get cold too when we open her right up.'

'I'm going to wear this,' I said.

'Up to you.'

He pulled the bike onto its kickstand and went into the garage. He came back with the helmets and a pair of gloves for me.

'What's the bag for?'

'It's a surprise.'

'Do you need it? Looks heavy. Might throw your balance for your first time on the bike.'

'I need it.'

'Fair enough. You ready?'

I hesitated for a moment.

'Can we stop at the shops on Glenfield Road first?'

'If you want. She's not registered, so we've got to keep to the back streets anyway.'

Vic helped me put on Edie's helmet. He fixed the chinstrap and gave the top a slap. He kept looking at me.

'What?' I said.

Vic got serious for a moment.

'Listen, I want to have a word with you about some stuff tonight.'

'What kind of stuff?'

'I'll explain.'

'Do you want me to leave? Is it because of what happened on the couch?'

'No, no. It's not that. It's a . . . good thing. Don't worry. Come on, let's get going.'

Vic climbed on, and he waved me up. It was hard sitting with the bag on my back.

'You on? She's not a big bike, so you'll have to squeeze up. Pop your feet on these pegs here.'

Vic kickstarted the engine.

'Still got the same purr!' He smiled, then he reached for my hands and wrapped my arms around his waist.

'Hold on tight, okay?' he shouted.

'Okay.'

'Don't shift around too much. You'll be alright.'

We started moving. The street was empty. Even Mrs Boyd wasn't outside. I held on tight to Vic and pressed my head into his back. I closed my eyes and felt every little bump and turn as I was carried along. I was so nervous I could barely breathe.

I opened my eyes just as the shopping plaza came into view. I tapped Vic on the shoulder and yelled out for him to stop at the park down the road. He pulled in under the shade of a big tree. I stepped off the bike and my legs felt heavy. I was a bit queasy.

'You alright?' Vic asked.

I didn't say anything. I took off my helmet and looked across at the plaza. It had a newsagent, a health food store, a post office, a florist, a hairdresser, a small supermarket and a Western Mutual Bank branch.

'I'll be back in a few minutes,' I said.

Vic nodded. I stayed where I was for a moment. I tried to take a deep breath, but my chest was so tight I couldn't get anything into my lungs.

'Sure you're alright?' Vic said.

I wanted Vic to guess what I was about to do and stop me, but he didn't.

'I'm okay,' I said.

I walked across the road and stared straight ahead. It was terrifying being dressed up in public during the day. There were a lot of people around. I expected them to stop and stare at me, but nobody took any notice. I stopped outside the bank. I waited for the calm feeling I usually got when I was shoplifting or stealing, but all I felt was dread and fear. It made me even more nervous.

The sliding doors suddenly parted, and a customer stepped out. It was an older man wearing a neck brace, and he gave me a little smile as he went past. I didn't have a choice. I went inside while the doors were still open.

It was quiet in the bank. There were two tellers at the counter, and a lady waiting in line with a really thick folder. I stood behind her in the queue. My heart was beating really fast and I couldn't swallow. I glanced around to see if anyone was looking at me suspiciously, but everyone was busy.

The lady in front got called to the counter. Then the doors opened and an old woman came in on a mobility scooter. She rode right up behind me. Then a tradesman in a fluorescent work vest and navy shorts and big boots came in straight after.

I blinked really hard behind the glasses. Everything was tinted pink. I felt dizzy. It was hard to stay on my feet.

Then a teller became available. She was young and pale and chubby with dyed red hair. The badge on her lapel said *Suzanne*. She smiled at me.

'Next please.'

I didn't want to do it. I wanted to run away. But the old lady started rolling forwards on her scooter and Suzanne waved me over so I stepped out. I went to the counter.

'Welcome to Western Mutual, how can I help you?'

My hands were shaking. I reached inside my jacket for the note, but it wasn't in the pocket. I reached as deep as I could, then I tried the other side, but that pocket was empty too. I realised what I had done. I had forgotten the note. It was still on Edie's vanity table. I could feel sweat starting to drip from under the wig.

'How can I help you today?' Suzanne asked again, still smiling.

I froze. I didn't know what to do. The door to the bank opened and a young woman came in pushing a pram with twin toddlers. I could see the car park through the doors, and the park beyond. I wanted to run. Then the doors closed.

'Miss?'

I didn't want to speak, so I pinched my thumb and my finger together and made a gesture in the air like I wanted to write something. Suzanne did a slow nod.

'*Ohh*, okay, I understand.'

She turned to the teller on her right, who was still busy with the person with the thick file.

'Excuse me, Irene, you speak Auslan don't you?'

'No, that's Gwen. I think her nephew is deaf? The one who had the meningitis.'

'Where is she?'

'She's in with Paul.'

'Okay.'

Suzanne turned back to me and held her index finger up, then she spoke loud and slow.

'One moment, please.'

I made the writing gesture again, but Suzanne just spoke even louder.

'It's okay, I'm getting somebody who can help you!'

She went into a separate office. I felt like I was trapped in a bad dream and I couldn't wake up. Behind me, the old lady sighed impatiently. Suzanne came back with a woman wearing a cable knit sweater. A pair of reading glasses hung around her neck on a chain. Her name badge said *Gwen*.

She started using sign language to speak to me. I didn't know what any of it meant. I kept making the writing gesture. The doors to the bank opened again, and a middle-aged man speaking on his phone walked in and joined the queue. One of the twins in the pram started crying, and the mother bent over to comfort him.

Suzanne got me a pen and a sheet of paper to write on. I started writing with my left hand, but I still had gloves on and I was shaking and I couldn't write fast enough, so I swapped back over.

'What's going on?' the lady on the scooter asked.

'We'll be with you in a moment, ma'am,' Suzanne said.

'Can't the other girl open a window?'

'I'm not authorised for that, I'm afraid,' said Gwen.

'I just want to hand in a cheque.'

'I'll process that for you in a moment, ma'am. Thank you for your patience.'

I tried to remember all the details in the first note, but I was under so much pressure that my mind went blank. I panicked and wrote as much as I could.

> *There is a bomb in the bag.*
> *A man has my family hostage.*
> *He wants the large notes from the cash drawer.*
> *If I don't bring him the money he will kill my family and*
> *blow up the bomb remotely.*

I slid the note across the desk.

Gwen put on her glasses and read the note with Suzanne, who gasped and put her hand over her mouth and stared at me. Gwen frowned and read through the letter again. She looked at me over her glasses.

'Is this true?' she asked.

'They should put more staff on,' the old lady complained behind me.

Gwen raised her voice. She sounded mad.

'Is this true?'

I didn't say anything.

'Speak to me! Now!'

I nodded.

The tradesman in the queue stepped out.

'Everything alright?'

'I'm going to ask you to stand back please, sir. We have a situation.'

Gwen didn't take her eyes off me. Suzanne looked afraid.

'What kind of situation?' asked the mother.

The tradesman came closer.

'Is there a problem?'

I saw Suzanne's hand reach under the counter and I panicked. I snatched the note from Gwen and I backed away. I started to walk quickly towards the doors. Gwen called out.

'Come back here!'

'What's going on?' said the old lady.

I could feel everyone staring at me. The tradesman followed me. He reached out and grabbed the bag.

'Hey! Stop!'

I slipped my shoulders out of the straps and left him holding it. Then I ran out of the bank. I sprinted across the car park and back across the road to where Vic was waiting.

'Go, go, go!'

'What's the matter?'

'We need to go. We need to go *now*!'

I put the helmet on and climbed onto the bike and put my arms around Vic's waist. I looked back towards the bank, but nobody was chasing me.

Vic started the bike and we pulled away.

'Faster, faster!'

As we sped off I saw the mother with the pram and the old lady on the scooter coming out of the bank. The tradesman was already outside and waving at other shoppers, telling them to leave. I turned away and closed my eyes tight.

We rode for a while. I tried to focus on being swept along by the bike, but I got so anxious that I started beating on Vic's shoulder. He pulled over and I leaned over and vomited. It was yellow and slimy and it burned my throat.

'You alright?'

'Can we go home?'

'Bit bumpy is it? That's okay mate. It's not for everyone.'

I heard sirens in the distance, and I retched again. I didn't have anything left inside me. It was like I was turning myself inside out.

'I'll ride real slow. You'll be right.'

'No!' I said. 'Go fast. Please. Go fast.'

I fought my stomach all the way back. Every time Vic stopped at an intersection I hid my face and waited to be dragged off the back of the bike and pinned to the ground and handcuffed. I thought every driver in every car must know who I was.

When we got back to Vic's place, I jumped off the Black Shadow and quickly pulled up the garage door. Once Vic wheeled the bike inside, I slammed it down again. Vic took his helmet off and put the bike on its stand.

'What's going on? Where's your bag?'

'Vic, I did something really stupid.'

Vic took off his gloves and jacket.

'What?'

'I tried to take money from that bank.'

'What do you mean? How?'

'I told them I had a bomb.'

'You *what*?'

'In the bag. It wasn't real or anything.'

'Hold up a second, what are you saying to me? You just tried to rob that bank?'

'I wanted you to get your money back.'

He stared at me with his mouth open for a moment.

'What the *bloody* hell were you thinking?'

'It's what you wanted! It's the thing you dreamed about doing!'

'No! I *told* you I didn't want that!'

Vic's face was red and his voice was loud.

'I know! I know you did! But I wanted to show you I could do it. I wanted to help you like you helped me! But it didn't work. And now I'm in trouble and I ruined everything. We should have just gone for a ride, but I ruined that too. I know. I'm sorry.'

Vic took a deep breath and rubbed his forehead.

'It's *wrong*, mate. Stealing is *wrong*.'

I got really upset at that and suddenly I was shouting too.

'Well, *I'm* wrong! Okay? *I'm* all wrong! And I do wrong things!'

I ran into the house and went to the bathroom and locked the door. I wrenched off the wig and pulled off Edie's pantsuit and blouse and got in the shower and turned on the cold water. I scrubbed away the make-up and then I slid down the shower wall and put my head in my hands and retched again. After a while I started shivering.

I don't know how long I sat like that before Vic knocked on the door.

'Sam? *Sam!* What are you doing in there?'

I didn't want to answer him because I was so ashamed.

'Sam? Talk to me! Are you alright?'

I heard a loud bang, and I flinched. I looked up. There was another big crack. A chunk of the frame came loose and the door swung open.

Vic rushed in and grabbed me.

'Are you alright? What have you done?'

'Nothing. I'm okay. I'm sorry.'

Vic looked relieved. He turned the water off. He was soaking wet. He sat down with his back against the base cabinet and started coughing and wheezing. He didn't stop. I crawled towards him and rubbed his back. Vic blinked hard. His face was purple and his eyes were wide and he grabbed my arm. He had this awful wheeze and he couldn't breathe in. I was really scared. Finally his chest cleared. He kept holding my arm. He coughed up a wad of bloody phlegm, and he turned his face and it dribbled out of his mouth onto the bathroom floor. His eyes were red and watery and he sucked in air.

'I'm tired,' he said.

~

I helped Vic down the hall and onto his bed. Then I went to the kitchen to get him a glass of water. His eyes were closed by the time I got back. I kneeled down beside him.

'I'm sorry,' I whispered.

I was still wet from the shower. I went back to the bedroom. In a pile next to the chest of drawers, I found the jeans and the hoodie I was wearing when I first met Vic. I put them on. My phone was still in the pocket. I sat down and crossed my legs and faced the wall and put my head against it and closed my eyes. I was lost and alone and I hated myself. I knew the police were coming. I was scared, but I was also relieved.

I sat like that for a long time.

Then there was a knock on the front door.

I got to my feet and walked slowly down the hall. I paused outside Vic's room. I didn't want to wake him up to say goodbye. There was more knocking, fast and loud. I put my head down and went to the front door.

It was Aggie.

'Are you fucking kidding me?'

She was really angry.

'Was it you? It's all over the news. They're saying a woman attempted a fucking *bank robbery* today, four *fucking* kilometres away. Apparently she handed over a note saying she had a bomb and her family was being held hostage. Was it you? Because that would be quite a fucking coincidence if it wasn't!'

I looked at my feet.

'Answer me! Was it you?'

I lifted my head and tried to speak, but Aggie already knew.

'Holy fucking *shit*! What the fuck were you *thinking*? Why would you do something so . . . I mean . . . I can't fucking *believe* it! I can't fucking believe you would actually *do* this. You *used* me! I thought you were posing a hypothetical question, not looking for a co-conspirator in an *actual* fucking scheme to *actually* defraud an *actual* bank out of *actual* fucking money! I mean, are you fucking serious? How could you do that to me?'

'I'm sorry. I really am.'

'*Fuck*, Sam! I really liked you. Like, *really* liked you. My parents fucking *love* you. My mother's practically subsumed you into our family, to the extent that she literally wants you to come to Aberdeen with us for a family holiday to meet everyone.'

'I'm so sorry.'

'Like, I thought I had actually found a real friend. I felt like I could tell you anything. But now I don't even know who the fuck I'm looking at. I don't know you at all!'

'You *don't* know me.'

'No shit! The Sam I *thought* I knew wouldn't betray my confidence and put *my* whole future at risk to do something so fucking stupid. What's going to happen if they catch you? I could be an accessory, do you *understand* that? My fucking internet search history alone is totally inculpatory.'

'I would never tell them anything about you. I promise.'

'Oh, you *promise*, do you? And how much fucking value does that have? Am I supposed to just trust you? Like you're this stand-up guy who would look out for me?'

Aggie shook her head and I could see she was fighting back tears.

'What I don't understand is *why*. Why would some rich kid risk throwing his life away to rob a fucking bank? You're not some gentle, sweet-natured boy, are you? You're a fucking arrogant, entitled jerk who has never had the burden of experiencing consequences. You know that one of your parents will make a call and bail you the fuck out of whatever mess you're in. This is probably all some childish, attention-seeking, bullshit rebellion that they've had to indulge a hundred times before. But here's the thing, Sam. Here's the fucking thing. You're not just being careless with your own life, you're threatening *mine*. And I don't have the advantages you do. I'm trying to build something, and you might have just torn it all the fuck down. What if I do get implicated? How am I going to face my parents? How am I going to apply for internships or universities or jobs, or any of the things that normal people have to navigate? But none of that has occurred to you, has it? Because you don't actually give a shit about me or the trajectory of my life. If you did, you wouldn't have been so casual about deceiving me. Fuck you, you fucking arsehole. Don't ever come to my house again!'

I didn't have the chance to say anything, because Aggie walked away so fast. I wanted to go after her and tell her that I would never let her get into trouble, but it was too late, and everything she had said was right. I hadn't thought about her. And I had ruined the only friendship I ever had.

I closed the door and went back inside. Vic was awake now and sitting at the kitchen table. He was wearing an old blue singlet and shorts. He smoothed down his hair with his hands, but it poked straight back up again. He looked exhausted.

'Who was that?' he asked.

'It was Aggie. From a few houses down.'

Vic nodded.

'Sit down, mate. I need to talk to you about some stuff.'

I didn't move.

'I can't take any more, Vic. I can't do it. I'm sorry about what I did.'

'It's not about that. Listen. It's important. I'm going to make some arrangements for you.'

'What kind of arrangements? For me to go somewhere?'

Before Vic could answer, there was another knock on the door. I thought Aggie must have come back, so I went down the hall and opened it.

Standing outside were two police officers, a man and a woman.

'Sam Watson?' the lady asked.

I wanted to slam the door and hide, but instead I froze.

'I'm Constable Bowden, and this is Constable Russell. Could I ask you to come outside with me?'

I didn't move. I looked over my shoulder. I wanted to make sure Vic would be safe.

'He didn't know anything about it,' I said. 'It was all me.'

'Come on outside, Sam. It's alright.'

Constable Bowden led me out to a black sedan in the driveway. Next to it was a police wagon. The lights weren't on.

'Am I under arrest?' I asked.

Constable Bowden opened the door of the black car.

'Let's just get you in here for a moment.'

I sat inside and she closed the door. I watched her walk back to Constable Russell, and they both went into the house.

'He didn't do anything!' I yelled out.

I tried to open the door, but it was locked. The neighbours from across the road came out onto their lawn. I banged on the window to get their attention.

'Can you let me out, please? Hello? Can you open the door?'

They stared at me and didn't move. I broke the plastic door handle trying to get out.

After a few minutes, Vic came out. His hands were cuffed behind his back. He had his head down and he was being led by Constable Russell. I felt sick. I beat at the windows and screamed.

'It was me! It was *me*! He didn't know about any of it! He didn't know!'

Constable Bowden opened the back of the wagon and her partner pushed Vic inside then closed the door behind him.

'Please don't hurt him! Don't *hurt* him! He didn't know! He didn't *know*!'

They ignored me. Constable Russell got in the driver's seat of the wagon and Constable Bowden stood beside the car I was in. I put my head in my arms and I rocked back and forth. When I looked up again, the police wagon with Vic inside was reversing out. Then it drove away.

More neighbours had come out to watch. I saw Mrs Boyd speaking with a middle-aged couple outside her house. She was pointing towards me and nodding. Behind her I saw Mr and Mrs Meemeduma and Dylan standing on the kerb.

The only person I didn't see was Aggie.

Jail

They put me in a room that was bare apart from a table with two chairs on either side. There was a clock on the wall and a small camera attached to the ceiling in one corner. I knew I was in a lot of trouble, but all I cared about was Vic.

I sat there for a long time before the door opened and a man walked in. He wore a black polo shirt tucked into grey chinos. He carried a folder and a bottle of water. He had short hair and he smelled like cologne. He sat down and put the water in front of me.

'Sam, my name is Detective Buchanan.'

'Vic didn't have anything to do with it. It was all me. I planned the whole thing all on my own. Nobody else knew about it. Please let him go. *Please.*'

Detective Buchanan held his palms up.

'Okay, slow down. Listen, let's wind back, okay? Just help me catch up.'

'I didn't even get anything. Nobody got hurt. I didn't mean

212

to scare anybody. It was a stupid thing to do. I shouldn't have done it. But Vic honestly didn't know. Please don't arrest him.'

'Sam, calm down. *Sam.*'

I was shaking. Detective Buchanan bit the cap off a pen and opened his folder.

'Okay,' he said. 'Tell me about Vic.'

'I already told you, he didn't know anything about it.'

Detective Buchanan frowned and shook his head and wrote something down.

'Can you describe to me how you two met?'

'I don't want to say.'

'Was it online? Did he contact you on social media or anything like that?'

'No. Vic doesn't have a computer.'

'So he approached you on the street somewhere?'

'I don't want to say.'

'Okay.' Detective Buchanan nodded and wrote on his pad again. 'That's fine. So let's just say that after meeting and speaking with you, Vic invited you back to his house and encouraged you to stay with him—is that correct?'

'No. No, *I* asked if I could stay with him.'

'And how long ago was this?'

'I don't know. A few weeks.'

'A few *weeks*?'

'Yes.'

'You're sure about that?'

'Yes.'

He went quiet and scribbled on his pad again.

'I don't like it when you write things down,' I said.

'Sorry. It's a habit.'

He put the cap back on the pen. He watched me for a moment, and I looked away.

'Did Vic ask for anything in exchange for you living with him?'

'What do you mean?'

'Like rent money, or . . . some other kind of trade.'

'No. I cook him dinner though. And I clean the house. I try to look after him.'

'And how else does Vic want you to look after him?'

I was really confused.

'He doesn't want anything really. He's just nice to me, so I want to be nice back.'

'And how is Vic nice to you?'

'I don't know. He's just . . . nice. I can be myself around him.'

'Does he say nice things to you?'

I thought about it.

'Not really. Well, maybe, I guess. He told me I looked beautiful once. That meant a lot.'

Detective Buchanan leaned back and folded his arms.

'He said you were beautiful?'

'Yes.'

'Okay. And where do you sleep at Vic's place? Do you have your own room?'

'Yes. I sleep in his bedroom.'

Detective Buchanan nodded, then he leaned forwards.

'Sam, I'm going to ask you something quite personal, okay?'

'Okay?'

'Has Vic ever expressed himself physically?'

'What?'

'Has he ever touched you, or encouraged you to touch him?'

I blushed and shook my head.

'What? No. He never wanted anything like that. He's a nice man. He's the nicest man I have ever met. He just wanted to help me, and I ruined everything. I told you, Vic didn't have anything to do with it. Put me in jail. I don't care. But let him go home. He doesn't deserve any of this. He's a good person. I don't get why you're asking me all these questions.'

Detective Buchanan sighed and looked through some of the papers in his folder.

'Have you been in contact with your mother since you've been staying with Vic?'

'No.'

'You didn't reach out to anybody to tell them where you were? Not even your friends?'

I shrugged. Detective Buchanan tapped the pen against his knuckles.

'Sam, what's your relationship with your mother like? Can you tell me about that?'

I shrugged again.

'Did you leave your home residence on your own terms? Was there any reason for you to feel unsafe or threatened there?'

I shrugged and shook my head.

'I'm trying to help you, Sam. Okay? But you've got to be honest with me so I can coordinate with the right departments. Tell me what's been going on, mate.'

'Nothing.'

Detective Buchanan scratched his jaw.

'Are you familiar with a Beverley Boyd?'

'Not really.'

'Well, she has an interest in you. She's what you might call a particularly vigilant neighbour. She's contacted her local station on six separate occasions to report suspicions of an inappropriate relationship between a teenage boy and an older man at the address we found you at today.'

'There's nothing inappropriate about it.'

'Since she could provide no evidence of her claims, our local officers weren't inclined to follow up. She did also provide a first name and some photographs of you to the state missing persons centre but no report had been made.'

'She took photos of me?'

'Several. Now, this morning, your mother contacted the centre to report you missing. If it wasn't for Beverley Boyd, she wouldn't have been able to identify you from the database, and we wouldn't have been able to locate you so quickly.'

I shook my head. I hated Mrs Boyd. Detective Buchanan closed the folder.

'But there's something here that doesn't add up for me, Sam, and I need your help. According to your mother, you'd only been missing overnight, which we both know isn't true. And we both know she wasn't aware that you were staying at Vic's over the past few weeks. Do you see any reason why she would wait so long before making a report?'

'I don't know. I don't know about any of this. Why am I here? Why did you arrest Vic?'

'He's just answering some questions.'

'About what?'

'About your domestic situation and the nature of your relationship. It's why I need you to be completely honest with me, Sam. And before you reunite with your mother, I want to be sure that home is a safe place for you. Your welfare is the most important thing here, and I need you to understand that you've got options.'

'You don't want to ask me about anything else?'

'You tell me. What should I ask you about?'

I went quiet for a while, trying to get my head around everything. I figured he must be tricking me into talking about the bank. Maybe Vic had told them the truth already, and the detective wanted to catch me in a lie.

'Sam?'

'Where is my mum?'

'She's been contacted and was told to come to the station.'

'Is she here now?'

'I presume so.'

'Does she know I'm in trouble?'

'Sam, you're not in any trouble. You haven't done anything wrong.'

'What do you mean? Am I under arrest?'

'Of course not.'

My heart was pounding. Nothing made any sense. I looked up at him.

'Wait, can I go? Like, now?'

Detective Buchanan looked me in the eyes. Then he reached into his pocket.

'Sam, I'm going to give you my card. If you need to get in touch with me for any reason at all, this has my direct contact details. Here.'

I took it, but I didn't want it.

'Are you going to let Vic go too?' I asked.

Detective Buchanan stood up. He seemed disappointed in me.

'Come on,' he said. 'Let's get you home.'

~

My mum was sitting alone on a plastic chair in the administration area. She stood up when she saw me. She was thin and pale. Her hair was stringy and she was wearing one of Steve's t-shirts and a pair of leggings. She ran towards me and hugged me really tight and she wouldn't let me go.

'Oh my God! My boy! My little boy. Sam.'

She smelled different and she felt bony and small. She pulled away and put her hands on my cheeks and kissed my forehead and looked at me. She was crying. Her eyes were red with dark bags under them.

'We looked everywhere,' she said. 'We went everywhere. I thought you'd gone. I thought you'd left us. Don't ever do that again. Don't *ever* do that to me again.'

She held me close again and I held her back. I was feeling too many emotions at once. I was happy to see her because I loved her and she was my whole world, but I was angry with her for taking so long to try to find me. I felt embarrassed for causing all this to happen, and to have so many people looking at me. I was relieved that I was allowed to leave the police station, but I dreaded going back with her. I was still worried that someone would recognise me from the robbery, and I still felt guilty and ashamed and anxious about Vic and Aggie. I just wanted to sit in a small room on my own so I could breathe. Going to jail didn't seem that bad.

My mum put her arm around me and led me towards the automatic doors. It was dark outside.

'What happened to you? Where did you go? Who was that man you were with? Where did you live?'

Just as we were about to step outside, I heard coughing behind me. I knew exactly who it was.

I ran back through the waiting area and past the administration desk. I followed the sound down a hall and then into another corridor. I saw Vic. He was coughing into a tissue. There was a man standing beside him, but he didn't have handcuffs on anymore.

'Vic, I'm here,' I said.

I rubbed his back and helped him to a chair next to a water fountain. I kneeled down beside him. As Vic wheezed, I talked fast and low, so that only he could hear.

'I'm so sorry. I'm sorry they took you. It was all my fault. They don't know anything about today. I just want you to know that I didn't mean for any of this to happen.'

My mum came charging down the corridor. She grabbed my arm and dragged me away from Vic, then she slapped him hard across the face.

'You stay away from my son! Don't you come anywhere near him again, you filthy fucking dog!'

I put myself between them and held her back.

'No! Stop it! Stop! He's my friend!'

'No he's not, Sam!'

The man who had been escorting Vic stepped in to restrain my mum.

'That's enough,' he said.

I felt Vic take my hand and turned to him. He looked so frail and his eyes were watery.

'Go with her, mate. Go on.'

He squeezed my fingers.

Then he let me go.

∼

We took a taxi home. My mum sat with me in the back seat.

'Who is that old man?' she asked.

'Nobody.'

'Were you living with him?'

I shrugged.

'Did anything happen to you?'

I shook my head.

'Were you talking to him on the internet?'

'No.'

'I don't want you seeing him again. Ever.'

I didn't answer. My mum held my arm and snuggled into me.

'I've got you back. You're not leaving me again. I'm not letting you go. You're mine. You're my sweet boy.'

I just looked out the window at the power lines going past, like I had the first night I met Vic. I knew I probably wouldn't ever see him again, and I missed him already.

~

My mum got the taxi to pull over before it turned into our street. She paid the driver in cash. I got out and heard dogs barking. My mum held my hand as we walked down the street to our house.

'Is he still there?' I asked.

'Yes.' She squeezed my hand. 'He feels bad about what happened. He knows he lost his temper and he's going to try to be better. But he gets worked up sometimes because he cares about you so much. He's still learning how to be a parent. He's doing his best. And you've got to try to meet him in the middle. We can work it all out, okay? We're a family now.'

I didn't say anything.

From the street I saw the house. There was a new orange motorcycle under the carport. Inside, Steve was sitting on a beanbag playing *Grand Theft Auto*. He stood up and smiled when he saw me.

'Here he is.'

He walked over and put his hand on my shoulder. I tried not to flinch.

'We were so worried about you, mate. Your mum's been a complete wreck, do you know that? She's been up and down the city, day and night, talking to kids and shop owners and homeless people, showing them photos, the whole works. You scared the shit out of her. You get that? Hey?'

I frowned and looked down.

Steve pulled me roughly towards him and patted my back.

'But we got you back safe, that's what matters. And you're never gonna leave like that again, are you?'

He said it in a nice way, but it sounded like a threat.

I shook my head.

'Come on,' he said. 'Show you something.'

I followed him down the hall to my room. The cardboard and towels on the floor were gone and the carpet had been cleaned. There was a set of drawers to put my clothes in, and a small desk with a chair and a lamp. On the desk was a tablet to replace the one he broke.

'It's all yours,' he said.

'What do you say?' my mum asked.

I looked around the room. He said it was mine, but it felt like someone else lived here. I walked over and opened the drawers. None of my outfits or skirts or dresses were in there. They had thrown them out. The sewing machine was gone too. I went to the desk and picked up the tablet. They had scratched over the lens of the camera. There was a new lock on my bedroom window, and outside they had installed security bars.

'Thank you,' I said.

'Sorta my way of saying sorry,' Steve said. 'Let's put it behind us, hey?'

He held his hand out. I shook it firmly, like a man. I shook it like the person they wanted me to be. The person who belonged in this room. Because my mum was right. It had to stop. I was sick and I had to get better.

'It's okay,' I said. 'I deserved it.'

∼

The next day was hot and sunny. Late in the morning I went to the backyard to see if the cats were around, but everything had changed.

Half the yard was shaded by a khaki tarpaulin and underneath was a bunch of exercise equipment. There was a heavy bag hanging from the tree in the corner and a wooden shelf with a row of dumbbells. There was a rack with a bar set up at chest height, and stacks of rusted plates underneath it. Next to the fence was a big truck tyre and a sledgehammer.

Right in the middle of it all was a bench press. Steve was lying on it, adjusting his grip on the bar. He had white chalk on his palms. Dane was standing over the back of the bench. He wore a black tank top and rugby shorts.

Steve arched his back and pushed the bar upwards and then lowered it towards his chest. He grunted and his arms shook.

'Take it, take it, take it,' Steve said.

Dane leaned over and lifted the bar easily and set it back on the rail. I stared at how his muscles flexed as he did it.

Steve sat up. He shook his head and sweat sprayed off. His face was red. He was wearing a Bintang beer singlet and blue board shorts and thongs.

'Fuck sake,' he said. 'I'm not even lifting half of what I was before I did my back.'

'One day at a time, fella,' said Dane. 'I told you, just stick to the program I wrote you. Focus on your core work and your mobility, then worry about your compound lifts and rebuilding your strength.'

Steve was annoyed. He wiped his face with his singlet.

'It's too fucking hot. I need a drink.'

He walked past me and went inside. I stood and watched Dane sliding plates onto the bar on the rack. He ducked under and held the bar across his shoulderblades. He took a step back, then he crouched down and straightened up. He did it ten times before he set the bar back in its notch. Then he took a drink bottle out of his bag and shook it up. It looked creamy. He drank half of it, then he did another set with the barbell. As he finished, he noticed me watching. He wiped the sweat off his face and arms with a small towel.

'Hey mate.'

I walked under the tarpaulin and looked around. I could barely pick up the sledgehammer.

'We found all this shit on the verge for collection,' Dane said. 'Even had a rowing machine, but we couldn't fit it in the tray of the ute.'

'Can you teach me?'

'Teach you what?'

'How to do all this.'

'What do you wanna work on?'

'I don't know.'

Dane drank the rest of his bottle then looked me up and down.

'You want to put some size on? Or do you want better flexibility and lean muscle strength? You want to work on your legs or your chest or your whole body?'

I thought about it.

'How can I be like you?' I asked.

Dane laughed.

'Two words: practice and food. But if you actually want to learn and get stronger, we'll get you started on light weights and high reps and get your form right. But you gotta eat too. That's half the battle. We'll get you on some of this.'

Dane shook his empty bottle.

'What is it?'

'Whey protein and creatine. Tastes like shit.'

'Will it make me look like you?'

'Mate, you're skinny as a rake. Anything you can put in your body is gonna help. Come on, I'll run you through the basics.'

Dane took the plates off the bar. He showed me how to do deadlifts and squats and rows and the chest press and weighted bridges. He was patient with me. He made me practise in front of an old wardrobe mirror leaning against the fence so I could see my technique. I liked the way he moved my body around with his hands. He showed me shoulder raises and bicep curls and tricep extensions with the dumbbells, and he taught me body weight exercises, like lunges and chin-ups and pull-ups and planks and push-ups. He was really supportive. When I felt too tired and weak to lift the weight, he encouraged me so much that I could somehow do it.

Steve came out. He had showered and changed his clothes.

'Come on Dano. We're heading off.'

Dane gave me a slap on the back.

'Good job, buddy. Don't let this bloke here ruin your form, and don't let him stack on weight you're not ready for. You've already got better fundamentals than him.'

Then he left with Steve.

I stayed outside and spent hours doing exercises. I liked the way my muscles burned and ached, I liked the hot stabbing pain when I got so deep into a set that I dropped the weights.

My mum came outside to smoke a cigarette. She was sleepy and she scratched at her arms a lot. She talked about her plan to start an online clothing store. She said Steve wanted to rent a house near the beach in Rockingham, and I would have to enrol in a school down there. I was too focused on hitting the tyre with the sledgehammer to pay much attention.

Later, I stood under a cold shower until I started shivering. Then I went to the kitchen and made an omelette with six eggs and an old can of tuna that I had stolen for the cats.

In my room, I switched on the tablet. The wallpaper image was a photo of a man sitting on the same orange motorcycle that was under the carport. He must have owed Whippy money.

I reset the tablet then I searched for information about the bank robbery. My heart was beating really fast. There were lots of reports on news sites. They showed the security footage and had video of a bomb squad entering the bank. There were interviews with Gwen and Suzanne and the old lady on the scooter and the tradesman who had followed me.

There was a police sketch of my face without the sunglasses. It didn't look anything like me. They included the beauty mark above my top lip like the one I had drawn on for Fella Bitzgerald.

The police said they were looking for a Caucasian female in her early twenties. They said there was no reason to believe that the explosive device was connected to any terrorist organisation. They didn't mention anything about Vic or the Black Shadow. There was nothing about Aggie either.

I wondered how she was doing. I checked her Instagram page and there weren't any new posts. I scrolled through her pictures. I couldn't find the photo she took of the brownies I had made.

~

When I woke up the next morning I could barely move. My muscles were sore and my whole body ached. I tried to lift my leg and a shot of pain went up my side. I did it again. And again. I squeezed my fist and the same thing happened.

I crawled out of bed. It hurt to walk and I couldn't straighten my back. I shuffled to the shower and tried to stretch in the warm water. I dried off and got dressed and I made some coffee and eggs for breakfast and then I went straight to the backyard.

I spent the whole day outside lifting weights and doing exercises and hitting the tyre with the sledgehammer. In between sets I sat down because I was light-headed and I could feel my pulse beating against my temples.

In the afternoon, Steve came out with a can of beer and watched me doing squats.

'Arch your back and widen your stance, it'll give you better balance. You wanna have more kilos on that bar if you actually want to build any muscle.'

I ignored him. He finished his beer and crushed the can in his hand and went back inside.

~

I spent days out there. I had blisters and calluses on my palms. The skin of my shins were scraped away from doing deadlifts. I kept waiting for the police to turn up and arrest me, but they never came. I checked for updates on the internet every day, but there were no new reports.

After a couple of weeks I felt stronger but I wasn't getting bigger. Dane brought me a tub of protein powder and some flat gym shoes and a couple of his old tank tops to work out in. He said I was doing well, but I needed rest days to give my body time to recover. I told him I didn't want to stop, so he wrote me a program for a three-day cycle that focused on different muscle groups.

I did all three cycles every day. I liked feeling exhausted and I liked punishing my body. I imagined my muscles tearing apart. I wanted to rip myself up from the inside. I liked the feeling I got when I was so tired that my body wanted to shut down. My vision would get blurry and dark, and I would get taken over by an anger that I hadn't known I had in me. And it made me stronger.

The hair on my head was now long enough that you couldn't see how patchy it was. One night I got Steve's electric clippers from the cupboard in the bathroom and I shaved my head. I turned my head to the side. I could see the pink scar from my stitches.

I put on one of Dane's training tops, and I practised walking like him in front of the mirror. He had a way of rolling his shoulders back, and his feet were far apart. He always seemed to take up more space than he needed to. It was hard for me, because I had always tried to be small and invisible.

I tried my best to forget about Vic and the Meemedumas and Fella Bitzgerald and Edie and Julia Child and everything that had happened. If they came up in my thoughts I would shake my head quickly and pinch my skin. Sometimes I caved and checked Aggie's Instagram to see if she had posted anything new. I wanted to message her to tell her how sorry I was, but I knew it was best that I stayed away.

~

Mark showed me how to hit the heavy bag properly.

He taught me how to stand and how to rotate my hips to give my punches more power. He held up his hands and I did combinations of jabs and uppercuts and hooks. Then we did drills on how to dodge and weave and defend and how to counterpunch and read your opponent. After a few days of that, we started to spar. I felt awkward about trying to hit Mark, but he insisted.

'Come on, put your weight into it. It's okay.'

'Are you sure?'

'You won't hurt me. It's all good.'

'How many fights have you been in?'

He shrugged.

'Lost count.'

'Were you scared?'

'Of course.'

'What's it like to beat someone up?'

'Feels better than the alternative.'

'Have you lost many fights?'

'Had my arse kicked enough to know I don't ever want it to happen again. Now come on. Hit me.'

I was always tentative when we started sparring, but Mark had a way of riling me up. He wouldn't ever swing at me, but he would push me back with jabs which made me feel small and frustrated. When I threw nervous punches he would bat them away with his gloves and taunt me. And it worked. I got angry really easily. It was like a new part of me that sat under my skin all the time. When it took over I felt strong. I swung wild hooks at Mark. He never got upset or annoyed, even when my punches connected. He just spurred me on and reminded me about my footwork and my hips. I didn't listen, I just thrashed. Once I hit him in the face and he backed away. All my rage disappeared and I felt guilty and afraid, but Mark just blinked hard a couple of times, then he smiled.

'Nice cross matey!'

Sometimes we sat in the lounge room with my tablet and he pulled up famous boxing bouts and mixed martial arts title fights on YouTube. Then he showed me bar fights and street fights that people had recorded on their phones. Dane and Steve watched them too, and some of the fights made them laugh. Mark would pause the videos to tell me where the winner of the fight got their advantage and what the loser did wrong. He said I would learn more about real fighting by watching amateurs.

'Boxing and cage fighting are sports, but when people fight for real, there's no rules or refs. If you're in a pub or a cell block and it kicks off, you're not thinking about your footwork. You're trying to survive. You gotta be a fuckin' savage. Fight dirty. Scratch their eyes, snap their fingers, stomp on their ankles, punch them in the dick. If there's anything around you, pick it up and swing it hard as you can. It's you or them. Keep fighting until they can't get back up. But if you're out in the open and you're in a situation where you're outnumbered or you're outsized or they've got a weapon, it doesn't matter if you're a middleweight champion or a fuckin' black belt in jujitsu, my advice is always the same.'

'What's that?'

'Run.'

~

One night it was too hot to be inside the house, so I went out to the carport. Dane and Mark and Whippy were sitting on plastic chairs drinking cans of bourbon and cola. Steve was crouched down working on the orange motorcycle. He was covered in sweat and grease.

I slumped down on a chair and spread my legs the same as Dane. Steve dropped a socket and swore. He complained about having to sell his good set of tools when we left Scarborough, then he blamed Rosso for betraying him again and said he was going to get even one day.

'So do it,' said Mark. 'Stop fucking talking about it and let's go tax the cunt.'

'We should,' said Steve.

'I'm always up for a caper,' said Dane.

'What's wrong with the bike?' I asked.

'If I knew that I'd be sitting in that chair with a can in my hand,' Steve said.

'Won't start,' said Dane.

I nodded.

'How did you get it here?'

'Rode it,' said Steve. 'But it's decided to shit itself now that I've got someone coming to buy the fucking thing tomorrow.'

He wiped his forehead and spat on the driveway.

'Maybe the battery is flat,' I said.

'No, it's not.'

'Have you checked the spark plugs or the connectors?'

'Listen to this one!' said Whippy.

'Yes, I've checked the spark plugs.'

Steve sounded annoyed.

'Can I have a try?' I asked.

'Try what?'

'Fixing it.'

Steve laughed without smiling.

'I'm serious,' I said.

'You're not touching this bike.'

'But I might be able to get it running.'

'I doubt that.'

'I can do it.'

'The fuck do you know about motorbikes?'

Steve turned and stared at me. Everybody went quiet.

'If I can get it going, can I come with you guys when you do a collection?' I asked.

Mark and Dane laughed. Steve shook his head.

'No.'

'Jesus,' said Mark. 'Give the kid a crack at it.'

'He'll fuck the motor up,' said Steve.

'It's already fucked,' said Whippy.

'Come on mate,' said Dane. 'Sit down and have a drink.'

Steve slowly got to his feet.

'Alright. But I'm watching everything you do.'

I kneeled next to the bike. It was different to the Black Shadow, but I could recognise most of the parts.

I pushed the start button. The engine turned but it didn't catch.

'Tried that,' said Steve. He smirked and slapped a mosquito on his arm.

They were all watching me. I checked the spark plugs and tested each one against a head bolt. They worked fine. Vic had taught me that if the bike was firing okay, then it was usually a problem with the fuel. I looked over the engine, and then I saw the filter and I got excited. I had an idea about what might be wrong.

I removed the fuel filter housing and popped it open. It was really dirty. I took the filter out and it was almost black with grit. The tube it fed into was clogged too. I took it off and used a piece of wire to unplug it. Then I cleaned the filter and the casing using a rag soaked in petrol from the tank.

'Whoa, whoa, what are you doing?' Steve asked.

'I'm cleaning it. It needs replacing though.'

I refit the parts. They were still watching me. I was nervous when I pushed the start button. The motor whirred but it wouldn't turn over. I didn't want to flood it, so I stopped and waited.

'It's alright mate,' Dane said. 'It was a good try.'

Steve finished his beer and stood up.

'Come on, out of the way.'

'Wait.'

I tried the button again. After a few seconds, the engine fired. It was loud. I gave it a couple of big revs. I smiled.

Steve was shocked. Dane and Mark and Whippy threw their hands up and laughed. They were happy for me.

I cut the engine.

'Where did you learn that?' Steve asked.

I shrugged.

'So can I come out with you?'

'No.'

'Hey, you gave him your word,' Mark said.

'No I didn't. *You* did.'

'He's just saved your arse a lot of money,' said Whippy. 'Do I need to remind you what *you* were up to at his age?'

Steve looked at me.

'Don't tell your mother.'

'Don't tell me what?'

My mum opened the screen door and stepped out. She was wearing a short green kaftan and her hair was messy.

'Nothing,' Steve said. 'Go back inside.'

'But it's time,' she said.

'No it's not.'

'Yes it is.'

'No. You had it already this morning. Go inside, and don't ask me again.'

'I *didn't* have it!'

'Get inside!'

My mum went back in and Steve shook his head. I knew what she wanted. Steve had started locking the Fentanyl in the hallway storage cupboard and he kept the key with him all the time.

We heard loud bangs from inside the house.

'What the fuck?' Steve said. He got up and went in, slamming the screen door behind him. I followed.

My mum was trying to break the slide bolt on the cupboard door with a house brick we used as a doorstop.

'Sarah! Put that down!'

'Fuck you! Stop telling me what to do!'

Steve took the brick out of her hands and pushed her back and held her wrists. She struggled.

'I need it!' she said.

'No you don't.'

'I can make my own decisions!'

'Bullshit you can.'

'I've handled my whole life on my own. I don't need you!'

'You'd still be living in your car if it wasn't for me. Or you'd be in jail.'

'Fuck you! This is your fault! You started this shit. *You* started it! You knew what would happen. You knew!'

'*My* fault, eh? Never your fault, is it? I'm doing what's best for you. You can't be trusted. I'm trying to help you.'

'Bullshit! You just want to control me. That's what this is. When you lost everything because of your insurance bullshit, this is how you kept me on a leash. This is *worse* than fucking jail! I can't see my friends without your permission. I can't even go and get a TAFE certificate because you don't want me working.'

'I didn't hear you complaining when there was money coming in, when I was away for weeks busting my pick to keep you in bottles of fucking chardonnay! Didn't hear a peep then, did I? Didn't see you looking for work to make *my* life easier!'

'You think I want any of this?'

Steve pushed her onto the hallway floor and stood over her.

'So leave then. Fuck off. Try it. I'll have the DCS on you within a day. One drug test and you'll know what it's really like to lose everything. You don't know what rock bottom is. You're a spoiled rich girl who's allergic to work. And if I catch you trying to open this door again, you're gone. Is that clear?'

I didn't want to watch anymore. I went outside and sat down.

'Hey, chin up kid,' Dane said.

I pointed at the esky.

'Can I have one?'

Dane and Mark looked at each other. Mark shrugged. He threw me a can of bourbon and cola.

I opened it and took a long swallow. It tasted too sweet and it had a bitter aftertaste.

'Slow down, chief,' said Dane.

They kept arguing inside, but I blocked it out. After a while I heard a door slam. A few seconds later, Steve came outside. He slapped the can out of my hand and it rolled down the driveway. Then he pointed at Mark.

'We're going.'

'What, now?'

'Yes.'

'Who, the Thornlie guy?'

'Nah. Different one. I'll explain on the way. Dano?'

Dane stood up and rubbed his hands together.

'Let's crack some heads!'

Whippy stood up and said he had deliveries to make.

Steve opened the door to his car and looked at me.

'You coming or what?'

❧

Whippy had been recommending Steve to other independent dealers who needed help chasing up their debts. After a while, all sorts of people were asking Steve to retrieve things for them. Some had loaned money or possessions that they never got back, others had their stuff stolen.

A lady called Teneille had messaged Steve a few days ago, he explained as he drove. She had broken up with her boyfriend Brodie two months before, and they had agreed to share the custody of their one-year-old Rottweiler, Frank. But Teneille had since got a new partner, and now Brodie refused to give the dog back. He mistreated Frank because he knew it would upset her. Brodie had also taken six thousand dollars out of their shared savings account and used the money to buy a ute. Teneille wanted to take Brodie to court, but she couldn't afford it and it would take too long. So she had asked Steve to help get her dog and the money back. She gave him an address in Huntingdale where Brodie was staying with his friend Tyson. Tyson worked at a bar in the city, so he was out most nights.

After thirty minutes on the road, we turned onto Tyson's street. Steve drove slowly past the house. He parked fifty metres away and switched the car off. The lights were on inside. There was a blue ute in the driveway.

'What's that, a Falcon BF? XR6?' Mark asked.

'Get me those papers out of the glovebox,' Steve said to Mark.

'We good to go?' Dane asked. He rubbed the top of my shaved head. 'Come on kid.'

'Heads down,' said Steve. 'It's a shithole neighbourhood, but some of these houses still might have cameras.'

We got out and walked towards the house. Steve and Mark looked over the ute in the driveway. Then a dog started barking, and a security light came on. Through the slats in the side gate I saw Frank chained up in the backyard. He was so skinny I could see his ribs. It made me angry.

'It's okay, Frank,' I whispered. 'We're here to rescue you.'

The front door opened.

'Who the fuck are youse?'

Brodie looked like he was in his early twenties. He was thin and pale with greasy hair. He wore long black shorts and no shirt.

Steve smiled and pretended to be really friendly.

'Hey mate, I'm Tyson's cousin, Benny. How you doing?'

Steve shook his hand.

'Ty's at work.'

'Seriously?' Steve frowned and looked at Dane, who shrugged. 'Fuck, he said he'd be home. You staying here with him?'

'Yeah, just for a few weeks.'

'Hasn't got you paying rent has he?'

'Nah, yeah, I kick in a bit.'

Mark was crouching next to the car. He called out.

'This a 2007 model?'

'2008.'

'Many clicks on it?'

'Bit over two hundred thousand.'

Mark nodded.

'Custom rims eh? What these set you back?'

'I dunno. It was the previous owner.'

Brodie was starting to look concerned.

'Are you all Ty's cousins or what? He never mentioned you.'

'Fucking hot tonight, hey?' Steve smiled. 'Got a beer?'

Brodie hesitated, but he opened the door.

'Sure, come in.'

We walked in and stood in the lounge room while Brodie went to the kitchen. I could hear him rummaging around in the fridge.

'There's nothing cold,' he called. 'I think there's some warm cans in the laundry.'

'Don't worry about it, mate. We won't stay too long.'

Brodie came back into the lounge room and sat on the couch. We all stayed standing. I noticed Mark slip out of the room.

'Is that your dog out there?' Steve asked.

'Yeah.'

Dane stood close to Brodie with his hands behind his back.

'Is it your dog?' Steve asked again.

'Yeah. I just said that.'

Brodie frowned and looked up at Dane.

'You right there mate? Stop fuckin' starin' at me.'

Dane kept staring.

'It's not your dog though, is it?' Steve said.

'Yes, it's my fuckin' dog. Why do you keep asking me that? What the fuck is going on? Why don't you go see Ty at work or something?'

'Nah,' said Steve. 'I don't really know the bloke. And I don't really want to.'

Brodie was confused and suspicious. He tried to stand up, but Dane pushed him back down.

'Fuck you doin'?'

Mark came back into the room just as Steve cleared away an ashtray and a pizza box and sat on the coffee table facing Brodie.

'Well,' said Steve, 'the first thing we're doing is taking Frank back to his owner.'

'Who? Teneille? Get fucked. She got that dog for me.'

'That's none of my business, and I really don't care. I fucking hate dogs. But the other thing we're doing is getting the money you owe her. That *is* my business.'

'Fuck off! I don't owe her shit.'

'Yes you do, Brodie. You owe her the six grand you took from a shared savings account.'

'That's *my* fuckin money.'

'I have screenshots of the transaction history. You didn't make a single payment into that account. Teneille paid the breeder fifteen hundred dollars for that dog, plus the vet fees.'

Brodie shook his head.

'Get the fuck out of here. I'm not paying shit, and you're not taking my dog. I'm not scared of you, cunt.'

'You shouldn't be scared of me,' said Steve.

He pointed at Dane.

'But you should be scared of him.'

He pointed at Mark.

'And him.'

Then he pointed at me.

'And him.'

Brodie looked up and noticed me for the first time. I rolled my shoulders back the way Dane did and stared at him.

'Fuck you lookin' at?' he said. 'Huh?'

Dane suddenly grabbed Brodie's throat and squeezed. Brodie squirmed. He went red in the face and his eyes were wide. He tried to pull Dane's fingers back but he couldn't.

Steve kept his voice calm.

'We're not leaving until you transfer that money. Save yourself some pain and let's deal with it now.'

Dane let go of Brodie's throat. Brodie sucked in air.

'I don't have any fucking money. And I'm not paying shit to her, I told you. Fuck you.'

Dane lifted Brodie up easily. He pinned his arms behind his back. Mark kneeled and wrapped his legs up. He looked at me.

'Hit him.'

I froze. I took a step back and shook my head.

'Come on mate, you wanted to be here.'

Brodie struggled. He was sweating and full of fear and anger. Outside, I could hear Frank barking.

'Do it!' Mark shouted.

I stepped forwards and punched Brodie in the stomach.

'With your hips, like I told you,' Mark said. 'Fuckin' hit him! Come on.'

I changed my stance and I punched Brodie in the chest. It hurt my wrist.

'That's it. Again.'

Brodie wrestled and tried to tear himself free.

'You little cunt!' he said. He spat at me.

I got angry and I got mean. I stepped in and started swinging like he was the heavy bag. I wanted to hurt him. I looked at his skinny torso and it disgusted me and I wanted to ruin it. I focused on his ribs and his stomach and his flat chest. I could feel him tensing and flexing. I hit him with fast combinations. I imagined my fist going through his body. I hit him so hard that Dane had to brace himself.

Then I hit Brodie with a hard left cross and he went limp. He stopped struggling. Dane threw him back onto the couch. Mark stepped in and grabbed me and held me back. My hands were throbbing.

'You did good, you did good,' he whispered. I felt him put something in my pocket.

Steve tapped Brodie on the knee.

'You okay, mate? You listening now? Mate, we are not leaving until she gets her money.'

'I don't have it.'

'You got credit cards?

'No.'

'Then I have some bad news for you, Brodie.'

Brodie flinched and put his hands up.

'I'll pay her back, alright? I get paid next Thursday. I'll get some cash off my parents. I'll get it to her next week.'

'No you won't. I hear it every time. It's the same bullshit.'

'I will,' said Brodie. 'I promise I'll pay.'

'You're right. You will pay.'

Steve took a pen and the sheet of paper from the glovebox out of his back pocket.

'Just write your details on here and sign your name.'

'What's this?'

'Vehicle transfer papers.'

'My ute? What the fuck? It's worth like eight grand.'

'Probably closer to seven,' said Mark. He had the keys in his hand.

'You're not taking my ute,' said Brodie.

'Well that's up to you mate,' said Steve. 'I'm actually a very decent bloke. I know you don't believe that right now, but you'll come around when you have a chance to think about it, because I'm about to make you a reasonable offer. I'm giving you the chance to keep your ute. As you say, you're getting paid next week, and you might be able to scrape some other money together. If every cent you owe goes back into Teneille's account by Thursday, I'll bring your ute back and these papers will be torn up. If not, well, you're out a dog and seven grand.'

Brodie shook his head.

'You're a fucking cunt.'

'Don't hurt my feelings, Brodie. I didn't get you into this mess. Fill it out and sign it. If you don't, old mate here will snap each of your fingers until you do.'

Brodie took the pen. His hands were shaking. He started writing.

Steve kept talking in his calm voice.

'I know you're angry, and I know right now you're thinking about getting back at Teneille, so let me make this crystal clear: you're not going to contact her ever again. Not a text, not a call, not an email, nothing. If you come near her or you threaten her, if anything happens to her, it's us you'll be seeing. This isn't some bullshit VRO where maybe you'll get a court date and a fine. It'll be immediate, and it will be nasty. And if you even *think* about calling that ute in stolen, or claiming insurance, you'll be getting more than a few slaps from a welterweight. This man here *will* find you and he *will* take your eyes out. I'm not fucking with you. You don't want to know who we run with. Be humble and take the loss. Use your head. Tomorrow's a new day.'

Brodie signed his name and threw the paper at Steve.

Mark jangled the keys.

'We good?'

Steve stood and put the papers in his pocket. He kicked Brodie's foot.

'You hear what I just said?'

Brodie nodded. He was furious.

We went outside. Mark got in the ute and started it. Dane opened the side gate and I followed him down to the backyard. There was no grass, just brick paving and weeds. Frank barked and bared his teeth and pulled against the chain.

Dane stepped back.

'Jesus Christ. It's a fucking bear.'

Dane was afraid. But so was Frank.

'It's okay, Frank,' I said. I stepped forwards. 'It's okay. Shh. It's okay.'

Frank backed away and kept barking. I crept closer. Dane put his hand on my shoulder.

'Careful mate.'

I ignored him and kept talking to Frank.

'You're a good boy. You're a good boy. We're going to take you back home. Your mum's going to look after you. It's okay. It's okay.'

I squatted down and held my palms out. Frank whined and licked his lips. He bobbed his head down. Then he sniffed my hands.

'It's okay Frank,' I whispered. 'It's going to be okay.'

I sat down cross-legged. I knew Frank didn't want to hurt me. He growled and paced and then sniffed me again. I reached out and Frank flinched. I stroked his chest. His skin was loose and I could feel his bones. He calmed down. I kept patting him and saying nice things. Then his tail started to wag.

I unhooked him from the chain and held him by the collar and led him out to Steve's car. Dane got in the front with Steve and I sat in the back with Frank. Mark had already left in Brodie's ute. We drove off. Frank whined and sniffed at the gap in the window. I patted him and held him. At one point he yelped, and I saw that his paws were blistered from being chained outside on the hot bricks.

When we were a few streets away, Dane clapped his hands and laughed.

'I thought that little bastard was going to piss himself!' He turned and looked at me. 'And *you*! Hell of a kidney punch, kid. And I tell you what, you're braver than me. That was some real Crocodile Dundee shit back there. I thought this dog was going to bite your fucking hand off.'

I saw Steve watching me in the rear-view mirror.

'Don't let that thing drool on my upholstery.'

'He needs to go to a vet.'

'Not my problem,' Steve said.

Teneille was waiting outside her house when we arrived. Frank got excited when he saw her. He barked and clawed at the window. I let him out. He ran straight to Teneille and jumped on her. She hugged him and fell down on the lawn. She laughed and then she cried.

'Thank you so much. You have no idea what this means. Oh my God! I got my boy back. I got my boy. I'm not letting you go, ever again.'

She really loved Frank. It made me tear up. I looked away and pinched the skin on my arm so that I wouldn't cry in front of Steve or Dane.

On the way home, I remembered that Mark had put something in my pocket. I pulled it out. It was Brodie's wallet. There was a hundred and thirty dollars inside. I took out the cash and threw the wallet out the window.

Medicine

I trained in the backyard every day. My joints and my muscles ached all the time. I tried to eat as much as I could, but I still wasn't putting much weight on. I didn't look anything like Dane.

Everything was harder than ever. It was hard not to worry about Vic. It was hard not to send Aggie a message. It was hard not to watch clips of Julia Child. It was hard not to steal clothes and make-up and get dressed up at night. It was hardest to be what everyone wanted me to be.

One afternoon, I heard Whippy pull up out the front and I went outside to talk to him. He was still in his Kwik Traffik Courier Service van, messaging on his phone.

'Hey,' I said and waved.

He didn't notice me. I knocked on the window and startled him. He wound down the window.

'Jesus Christ, gave me a fuckin' heart attack.'

'Sorry,' I said.

Whippy kept texting and I waited. When he finished, he opened the door.

'What do you want, mate?'

I suddenly felt too nervous to tell him. Instead I blurted out a question.

'How come they call you Whippy?'

'Mr Whippy. It started as Mr Whippy.'

'Like the ice cream truck?'

He rubbed the door of the van.

'I bought this old girl off an old Serbian bloke when I was twenty-three. Bright pink it was.'

I looked at the van and saw how the panels had been repainted.

'You sold ice cream out of this?'

'Mr Whippy's Specialty Cones. I used to park her up and down the coast all summer. I sold soft serve and drinks and slushies and about five ounces of weed a week. Fucking crushed it. There were queues down to the water. That was the problem though.'

'What do you mean?'

'After a few summers, everyone knew I was dealing out of it.'

'So the police caught you?'

'Nah. Got robbed by a couple of French backpackers up at Trigg. Pricks hotwired it and drove off while I was halfway through a choc dip back there. Shit went everywhere. They parked behind a warehouse and beat the shit out of me. Took my stash and about three grand and said *au revoir*. They ditched the van back at the beach though, which was nice of them. But that was my last day serving ice cream. It's a shame. It was a solid set-up. Girls in bikinis, I could surf when the swell was good, and it was a fucking good laundry.'

'You washed clothes in there too?'

Whippy laughed.

'No, different kind of laundry. I make dirty money, which means I can't tell the government how I get it. So I need ways to disguise it. Whenever somebody bought a bag from me, I rang it up as ice cream or drinks or frozen bananas or whatever. That way the cash looks clean on paper.'

'Is that why you're a courier now?' I asked.

'Kind of. It's a registered business, and I do legit jobs so the fake invoices don't draw attention. But it's mostly good because I'm on the road all day doing other deliveries. Cops don't generally pull over couriers to do vehicle checks. Can't clean much money through it though.'

'How come?'

'You need a cash business. Service industries are best because you don't need to fuck around with stock orders and inventories and permits and inspections. So when I'm not driving around delivering parcels, I'm a very successful Kahuna massage therapist.'

'What's a Kahuna massage?'

'I have no fucking idea. But as far as the tax office is concerned, I've given thousands of them.'

'Oh, I get it. That's smart.'

Whippy seemed really proud of himself.

'Key to it all is just keeping your head down and staying ahead of the game. I swear, most of the dickheads around here carry on like they *want* to get caught. Anyway . . .'

He started to get out of the van.

'Wait,' I said.

'What?'

'I want to try something.'

'What do you mean?'

'I mean . . . I want to buy something off you. I have money.'

I showed him the hundred and thirty dollars from Brodie's wallet.

'Put that away,' Whippy said, then he looked over at the house. Once he was sure nobody was watching, he turned back to me.

'What do you want?'

'I don't know.'

'You don't know?'

'No.'

'Okay, well, how do you want to feel?'

'Um, I don't know. Like, I want to feel like not me . . . that probably doesn't make any sense. I want to be able to sleep better. I want my brain to stop. And to not have butterflies all the time. I just want to forget everything, I guess. I don't know. Sorry.'

Whippy looked at me hard. I thought I was in trouble. Then he went through his bag on the passenger seat. He held up two rolled cigarettes.

'Put these in your pocket. I'm trying out a new hydro guy. It's pretty smooth and it's a nice mellow high. No nightmares here, alright?'

I took them. They smelled spicy and musty.

'How much?'

'You can have those, but do me a favour and smoke them in one of these vacant houses or something. If you get caught, don't tell anyone shit, don't admit to anything, and you certainly didn't get it from me, understood?'

'Okay.'

'If you like it and you want more, come see me. But don't ever ask in front of Steve or Sarah. And if you want to try anything else, let me know.'

'Really?'

'You're gonna try it at some point, and I'd rather you had gear you can trust. I was selling and using at your age, and I've had no problems. You can do whatever the fuck you like. It's your body, nobody has the right to tell you what to do with it. Just don't smoke in your bedroom, alright?'

'Okay.'

'This your first joint?'

'Um, yeah.'

'You're gonna cough a lot, and you'll probably giggle like an idiot. You might see some stuff that isn't there. Just go with it. Don't panic. Just lie back and float outside your body.'

'That's what I want,' I said.

~

I waited until sunset, then I walked down the cul-de-sac to an empty beige brick house. All the doors were locked, but one of the windows around the back was broken. I pushed the rest of the glass out with a stick and climbed through.

It smelled bad. There was dust and rat droppings everywhere. I looked in all the empty rooms to make sure nobody was there, then I sat on the floor in the master bedroom and took out the two joints. I put one between my lips and lit it up. I breathed in. The smoke was hot and it tasted bad. I coughed a lot. My chest felt really tender.

When I could breathe again, I smoked some more. I kept coughing and smoking until the whole joint had burned out.

I was light-headed and my mouth was dry. The sun was down and the room was dark. I heard noises which made me worry, then I felt something brush against my leg. I slapped at my calf and stood up and backed away. I thought I saw a rat and I stamped my feet.

I quickly left the house the same way I came in. I stood in the middle of the street rubbing my legs and looking around to see if the rat was following me.

I knew I couldn't go back home for a while, so I walked a few blocks to a park. There was nobody else around. I sat on a swing in the playground and lifted my legs up so the rat couldn't get me.

I started to swing back and forth. I felt weightless, like I was flying. I leaned right back and looked up at the stars. My mouth was wide open. I let go of the chain and stretched my arms out and I fell off straight away. Sand went into my mouth. I spat it out and rolled onto my back. Then I started laughing, harder than I ever had. My stomach was sore and my eyes were wet.

I lay there for a long time. I made a sand angel by moving my arms and legs. I listened to crickets and cars going past.

A lady came walking through the park. She stopped and looked in my direction. I lay as still as possible so she wouldn't see me. Slowly, she came closer. She was older, in her fifties, and wearing a tracksuit.

'Hello? Are you alright? Hello?'

I kept lying as still as I could, staring at the sky. She kneeled down and shook me and I didn't respond. She gasped and started breathing fast. She got her phone out.

'Hello? Hello? Yes, I need an ambulance. I'm at the Henry Morley Reserve in Hamilton Hill. I've found a teenage boy here who is unresponsive. No, I don't know if there's a pulse. What? No, I don't know. Please hurry.'

I could see her face in the light of her phone. She was really worried. I realised that this was what would happen if I died. A stranger would find me and call someone who would come to pick me up and take me away and put me in the ground and that would be it. It made me sad, but it also made me feel relieved.

The lady held her fingers against my left wrist.

'I'm okay,' I said.

She shrieked and backed away.

'Sorry,' I said.

'Oh! You gave me such a fright! I thought you were dead!'

'I know. I'm not.'

'Are you okay? Did you pass out?'

'No.'

'Then what the bloody hell are you doing lying down here?'

I sat up and felt embarrassed. Her mood had changed and she was angry now.

'Don't you have a home to go to?'

'I don't know,' I said.

'What?'

I stood up and walked away. Behind me, I heard her apologising to emergency services on the phone. I started laughing again.

I shook all the sand out of my hair and my clothes before I got back to the house. Nobody had noticed I had gone. I was really hungry. I made four slices of French toast and ate them with strawberry jam in my room.

Then I laid on my bed and closed my eyes and when I opened them it was the next morning.

For the next couple of weeks I trained during the day and went to the vacant house in the evening. The only time I didn't go down there was when I helped with Steve's collections. Sometimes he dropped me off to do surveillance near somebody's house or work. If they were confronting someone, it was my job to go through the rest of the house to look for valuables and make sure nobody else was home. I didn't have to punch anybody again, and I made enough money to buy more bags of weed from Whippy. He gave me a little chrome pipe to smoke it with.

I spent hours down at the vacant house. I sat on an old plastic chair that I found on the side of the road and I lit some candles in the bedroom so I wouldn't get afraid in the dark. I started taking water and sandwiches with me because I knew I would get thirsty and hungry. I smoked until my body and my brain went numb, then I watched old movies on the tablet. When I came back home, my mum never asked where I had been. I wanted her to, but she never did.

She had changed so much. She was really thin and her skin was almost grey. Her hair was dry and flat. She smelled like cigarettes. She never put on nice clothes anymore. But it was who she was inside that was the most different. Even when she was right next to me, she had never felt so far away.

There were times when she came back to life. She would smile and she would be cheeky and funny and she would have some energy. But her mood would slip really quickly. She had fights with Steve almost every day, and it was always about the same thing.

I looked up Fentanyl on the tablet. I didn't understand a lot of what I read. It sounded like it made you feel really good, but it was addictive and dangerous because it was easy to overdose and die. Maybe Steve was doing the right thing by making sure she didn't take too much. But she was right to be angry too, because he had introduced her to it and now she couldn't quit.

There didn't seem to be an answer. Even if Steve was stopping her from having too much at once, she was killing small pieces of herself every day anyway. The more of it she had, the less of her there was.

~

One night when I was at the vacant house it started raining. I stood at the window and watched it pour down from the roof like a waterfall. It made me feel lonely, so I sat down to look at Aggie's Instagram.

There was a new post. It was a photo of a piece of paper that Aggie had written on.

It was a letter for me.

Sam,

I don't know if you'll ever read this, but I don't know how else to contact you. Vic was taken to the hospital in an ambulance today. I thought you should know.

Aggie x

I felt a horrible sick dread in my stomach. For a moment I couldn't swallow or breathe right.

I read the note again. It was only a few hours old. That meant Vic might still be at the hospital. I quickly hid the bag of weed and the tablet inside a roll of old carpet. Then I blew out the candles and I ran out into the rain. I stopped outside our house. Steve's car was gone. I didn't have any money for a bus or a taxi, and I couldn't ask my mum to help because she didn't want me to see Vic again. I started to panic. I didn't know what to do. I ran down the street and I didn't stop until I came to a main road. I waved down a car.

A lady with blonde highlights pulled over. I banged on the window and she wound it down.

'I need to get to the hospital.'

'Why? What's wrong?'

'Can you take me?'

I tried to open the door, but it was locked. The lady got angry.

'Get your hands off my bloody car!'

She drove off.

I was soaked through. I tried to flag down other cars but people kept slowing down and then driving away from me.

I started running again, but I didn't know where I was going. It was windy, and I was tired. The rain stung when it hit my face. My throat burned. My legs suddenly went rubbery and I collapsed next to a bus stop.

A car pulled up beside me and honked. A lady in the passenger side wound down her window.

'Are you okay?'

I looked up at her from the kerb.

'I need to go to the hospital.'

'Is it that bad? Have you hurt yourself?'

I stood up.

'No, my . . . my grandpa has been taken there. I need to see him.'

The lady looked at her husband, who was driving.

'Which hospital?' he asked. 'Murdoch?'

'I think so. Is that the closest one to here?'

'Get in,' he said. 'Come on.'

I got in the back seat. There was a toddler in a baby seat and a small boy who shuffled across to let me in.

'I'm really wet, I'm sorry.'

'It's alright, love,' said the woman. 'What's wrong with your grandpa?'

'I don't know. He coughs a lot. I would have gone with my parents but my mum is still at the office and my dad is out at sea. He's in the navy.'

'Oh yeah? My brother's RAN. What unit is your old man in?'

'I'm not allowed to say. I think it's classified. He doesn't talk about it much. He's pretty high up.'

The man and woman gave each other a strange look. They didn't ask me any more questions. My legs were bouncing up and down. I wanted to tell the man to drive faster. Their son kept staring at me then looking away.

We arrived at a big hospital and they dropped me off at the emergency entrance. I thanked them and jumped out and went through the doors. I ran up to the administration desk and told the receptionist I was looking for my friend. She told me to calm down. A security guard walked over and stood next to me. I told her Vic's name, and she typed it into her computer and stared at the screen for a long time. Then she made a phone call. I was worried he was at another hospital, or something worse had happened.

'Okay, he's in the respiratory ward,' she said.

'Is he alright?' I asked.

'I can't give you that information. He's in room twelve B. I'll show you how to get there.'

She wrote down directions on a piece of paper. Then I ran down the ward and I slipped over because I was so wet. Everybody in the lobby turned to stare and the security guard yelled at me to be careful. I took the elevator to the right floor, but I didn't know which way to go and I got lost. I found a cleaner at the end of a hall who didn't speak much English, but she led me all the way to 12B.

It was a private room and it was dark inside. The door was open. My lips trembled as I looked in. I could see Vic on the bed. He had a tube coming out of his arm and there was a monitor next to the bed.

I stepped in quietly and walked over. Vic was really still. I thought he might be dead, but then his chest slowly filled up and he breathed out.

I watched him for a few more breaths. Then I reached out and touched his arm and his eyes opened. Vic turned and looked at me.

'You're here,' he said. His voice was quiet and raspy.

'Vic, are you okay?'

'Fine fettle,' he whispered, and he tried to smile.

'What happened?'

'Your friend came round. The nurse. Found me in a bad way.'

'Did you do something to yourself?'

Vic shook his head.

'I'm very sick, mate.'

I didn't know what to say.

Vic took my hand.

'I don't want to die in here,' he said.

'You're going to be okay. You're in the hospital. You've got tubes in you and the doctors are here. You're going to get better.'

Vic shook his head again. He looked frightened.

'No. Sam, I don't want to die *here*. I want to go home.'

I realised what he meant and I started to cry.

'But I don't want you to die.'

'Hey, hey, it's alright. Sam, listen to me. Listen. I'm *tired*. And I'm in pain. My body hurts. My heart hurts. I have had my time. I'm not going to get any better.'

I shook my head and tears dripped off me.

'But they can fix you. They can give you medicine.'

'I don't want it. I don't want to kick the can down the road anymore.'

'What do you mean?'

'Every night I go to bed and I hope that when I fall asleep I'll just go in peace. That's all I want. Peace. I don't want to ache anymore. Don't be sad, mate. I've been lucky. I've had a blessed life. But it's my time. It's the right thing. I just don't want to be here anymore. You remember how you asked what I wanted? *That's* what I want. To leave. Will you help me? Help me get home. Help me go.'

I was squeezing his hand hard. I was crying so much I couldn't say anything. But I looked up and I nodded.

'Thank you,' Vic said, and he closed his eyes.

∾

I stood beside Vic for a long time while he slept. Every so often I started to cry again, but I tried to hold it in so I wouldn't wake him. I thought about how I was going to get him home. I remembered sneaking Steve out of the hospital when he hurt his back. I looked around the room for a wheelchair, but there wasn't one.

Then I heard somebody say my name. I turned around. There was a nurse standing in the doorway. He was tall and broad with neat brown hair.

'Sam,' he said softly. He stepped into the room and gave me a sympathetic smile. 'You don't recognise me, do you?'

I shook my head.

'I'm Peter. Fella Bitzgerald.'

I looked at him hard and saw it was true.

'Come on,' he whispered. 'Let's let him sleep for a bit.'

Peter led me out to the corridor and into an empty office. He closed the door. I sat down and he pulled a chair from behind a desk and sat close to me. He looked at the bumpy scar on the back of my head.

'Who took these stitches out?'

'Vic did.'

'What did he use, a hatchet? Why didn't you call me? I left my number.'

I shrugged.

We sat in silence for a while. All I could hear was the clock on the wall.

'How are you doing?' he asked.

I shrugged again.

'Vic told me you found him,' I said.

'I actually came to check on you. I knocked and knocked, then I tried the front door, and it wasn't locked. I found Vic on the floor in the garage. I don't know how long he had been there. He was severely dehydrated.'

The thought of Vic so alone and helpless made my chest go tight.

'He says he's really sick.'

Peter nodded.

'We're waiting on the results of a couple of tests, then we can make an assessment and look at treatment options.'

'Can he get better?'

Peter took a deep breath.

'I don't know, Sam. He's very ill. The tests will tell the story. For now, our focus is getting his fluids up and keeping him stabilised.'

'But what do you actually think?'

Peter looked at me. His eyes were sad.

'I don't know. I don't think he has very long.'

'He wants to go home.'

'I know.'

'He doesn't want to get better. He doesn't want any medicine.'

Peter looked at me for a long time.

'I know.'

'He just wants to go home.'

'I know.'

'I said I'd help him. I'm going to take him home. I'm going to take him now.'

'No, Sam.'

'But it's what Vic wants. He doesn't want to die here.'

'Sweetheart, I understand. But there are protocols. Vic needs to express his intentions to his doctor, and if he wants to act against medical advice he can sign a waiver and *then* he can leave.'

'You won't make him stay here?'

'Of course not. Sam, I understand what you're telling me. Let's give him tonight to rest and I'll speak with him in the morning. If it's still what he wants, and he's deemed fit to make that choice, then I can have him home by tomorrow afternoon. I'll speak to him about hospice care, and I'll arrange Silver Chain to bring him essentials. I'll visit too. But there is nothing you can do for him tonight.'

I nodded. Part of me had hoped that Peter was going to tell me Vic had to stay in hospital until he was better. I started to cry again.

'He's my friend. I only just met him and now he's going to leave.'

Peter leaned forwards and rubbed my back. He didn't say anything, he just let me cry. I was sniffing a lot. I wiped my nose on my sleeve. Peter squeezed my shoulder.

'I'm going to get you some tissues, okay? Stay here. When I get back, I want to talk about what's going on with you. Sam?'

He crouched down and looked at me. I lifted my head. I saw he had tears in his eyes too.

'I'm worried about you, and I care about you. Learning to talk is important. I know it's hard when we're not used to having people who listen. I'm here for you, I want you to know that. But I also have a friend called Diane. She's brilliant and she's lovely and she's wise, and listening is what she does for a living. I think you should talk to her too. Would you like that?'

'I don't know. Not really.'

Peter left. I turned and watched him go around a corner, then I stood up and walked out of the office and went the opposite way. I took an elevator to the ground floor and I walked out of the hospital.

It wasn't raining anymore. I didn't know where I was or how to get back to the house.

There was a taxi rank nearby. I got in the back seat of a cab and asked the driver if he could take me to Fremantle. He asked if I could pay, and I said I could. He started driving but he kept looking at me suspiciously in the rear-view mirror. After a few minutes, I heard a click. He had locked all the doors.

After a while I started to recognise the streets. When the driver stopped for a red light, I quickly wound the window down and I started to climb through it. The driver yelled at me and reached back and grabbed my ankle. I kicked my legs hard. My shoe came off and I felt my heel hit his face and he let me go. I crawled out of the car and got to my feet and ran as fast as I could. I turned down one street and then another and I hid behind a hedge outside a house. I waited there for twenty minutes, then I walked the rest of the way back to my street.

I went straight to the vacant house and I lit a candle and packed the pipe and smoked until my lungs hurt. I coughed a lot. I put my head against the window and watched the rain start falling again. I didn't feel any different.

I walked back home. Steve and my mum were asleep on the couch in front of the television. They didn't wake up when I came in.

I lay down on my bed and stared at the ceiling. I felt hopeless. I felt so much dread and anxiety that it was hard to breathe. I hated myself. I felt bad about kicking the taxi driver. I wasn't a good person. I stole things. I betrayed people who were nice to me. I was a burden to my mum. I had been born wrong and I couldn't be fixed. I was a bad person born in the wrong body and nothing would ever get better. It didn't matter what I did. I had nothing to look forward to. Every day would be harder and harder. I would suffer more and more as my body changed. The thought of it made me more afraid and panicked, and I rolled onto my side and curled into a ball. I was alone in the dark. I thought about Vic in the hospital, how he wanted to be at peace, how he didn't want to ache anymore. He wanted to close his eyes and go to sleep and never wake up. It's what I wanted too. I wanted to go with Vic. And I knew how I could do it.

The Soldier

I couldn't sleep.

I angled my watch so I could see the time in the moonlight. It was three in the morning. I got up and crept into the lounge room.

Steve and my mum were still asleep on the couch. The television was playing infomercials, and there was just enough light to find Steve's keys on the coffee table, next to his phone and his leather wallet.

I kneeled down and picked them up carefully so they wouldn't make a noise. Then I crept to the storage cupboard in the hallway. It was so dark that I had to put the keys into the padlock by feel. It took me six tries before I got the right one.

I opened it. I couldn't see the shelves properly, but I didn't want to risk turning on a light, so I used my hands to search around. I was rushing because I didn't want Steve to wake up and catch me. I felt the pistol and the shotgun, and then I found a small cardboard box. I thought it was what I was looking for, but when I picked it up it was heavy. I opened the box and it was full of bullets.

I put them down and kept searching. I couldn't find them anywhere. When I reached up to the top shelf, the padlock and the keys slipped out of my hand and hit the carpet. I stopped and listened, then I quickly picked them up and locked the door.

I crawled down the hallway and peeked around the corner. Steve had woken up and was sitting forwards rubbing his face. He fished the remote out from under his leg and turned the television off. Then he picked up his phone and stood up. He shook my mum awake and lifted her by the arm. She sounded annoyed. He led her to their bedroom. When I heard their door shut, I slipped out and put the keys back on the table.

The moment I let go, the door opened again and Steve saw me.

'Fuck are you doing?'

I froze. Then I reached out further and picked up the remote control.

'I can't sleep,' I said softly. 'I came out to watch TV.'

Steve snatched his wallet and keys from the coffee table.

'Go back to bed,' he said, and he walked away.

~

A few hours later, I heard the sound of metal plates clinking together. I opened my eyes. The sun was just coming up. I went out to the backyard and Dane was there training.

'Gym was too crowded,' he said. 'Wanna do some sets?'

I shook my head and sat on the bench and watched him do squats in the rack. In between he stretched. He was wearing a tank top with an Australian Defence Force logo.

'I have a friend who was in the army,' I told him. 'He said he was really scared.'

Dane nodded.

'Anyone who's been shot at and says different are either lying or dead.'

'Did you ever have to kill anyone?'

'Yes.'

'Do you feel bad about it?' I asked.

'I don't feel anything.'

'How come?'

'Because they kill that part of you first.'

'What do you mean?'

'That's what training is about. It's not about making you stronger; it's about breaking you down.'

'But you're so big.'

'I don't mean your body. I mean who you are. I'm talking about the twenty-two-year-old dickhead who knocked up his girlfriend out of high school, got married too young and couldn't support his wife and kid because he got fired from the last four jobs for fighting or drinking. *That* is the person they kill. The angry little smart-arse who thinks he knows better than everyone. And they replace that kid with a grunt who knows his place and does what he's told.'

Dane sat next to me on the bench.

'And then you head off and serve your tours. You do the right thing, pay off a chunk of the house, pay for your son's braces, and when you come back your wife complains that you're never there. But when you *are* home, she says you're a different bloke to the one she married. So you react badly and do some shit you regret, and she divorces you and shows the judge at the family court some stupid text messages and a video she secretly took of you punching a hole through a door, and just like that you can't see your kid anymore, and none of it meant anything.'

'I'm sorry.'

Dane shrugged.

'Thing is, in one respect, she's right. I'm not the same person she married. That person's gone. I can't fit back in here.'

'Maybe you should quit the army.'

'Nah.'

'Why not?'

'Because it's the best thing I ever did. I needed the discipline. I never had any before. If I hadn't joined when I did, I would have been sharing a cell with Mark or I'd be a fat bitter cunt like Steve. You know he's planning to run through the place of that old mate of his next week? The one he keeps talking about.'

'Rosso?'

'Got it all worked out apparently. Christmas Eve him and his missus are out at some Sailing Club function. Gonna do his dog in too. Some *Godfather* shit. Thinks he's a fucking mob boss these days.'

'Why would he hurt Rosso's dog?'

270

'Because he's a cruel prick. I had to talk him out of setting the place on fire.'

'Why are you still friends with him?'

'Steve? Mate, him and Mark and Whippy, they're more family to me than my own flesh and blood. Nobody gave a shit about any of us when we were growing up, so we had each other's backs. I'd still take a bullet for any of them. We're brothers. Back here, they're all I've got. When I'm on tour, I've got a clear purpose. Even when there's nothing to do, there's honour to it. I feel like I'm part of something out there. Closest I got to that back home was raising my son, but now that's gone.'

'Maybe when he's older you'll get to see him.'

Dane nodded, but he seemed lost in his thoughts.

'You know what? You're the only one who has ever asked me about any of this. You're a sensitive kid. You think your own thoughts. Don't ever lose that. Don't ever become a soldier. Don't go hard inside. Don't change who you are. I know you've been trying. But you don't fit in here either, and you never will, mate. That's a good thing. I know it seems like a long way off, but you're going to make it out of this shithole, and you're going to do better than any of us ever have.'

Dane slapped my back, then he got up and did another set.

⌇

I sent a text message to Whippy but I didn't hear anything back. I waited half an hour, then I texted again. He didn't respond to that either. After twenty minutes I called, but it went to his voicemail.

Steve left the house late in the morning. My mum was still in bed. I knocked on her door and said I needed to speak with her. She called out that she was sick and she needed to sleep.

I tried calling Whippy again, then I waited in my room. I was restless and anxious, so I made my bed and folded all my clothes and got everything neat and tidy. Then I deleted my search history from the tablet.

Finally I got a text from Whippy. He was in the city doing deliveries. I asked if I could meet him. He sent me the address of an apartment complex in East Perth and told me to be there within an hour.

I looked over my room one last time then I knocked on my mum's door again. She didn't answer, so I opened it and stepped in quietly. The room was a mess. There were clothes and towels and shoes and cigarette butts and cans and bottles all over the floor. It smelled awful.

I kneeled next to my mum. She was sweating, but her skin felt cold and she had goosebumps.

'Are you okay?' I asked.

'Leave me alone.'

She pulled her pillow over her face. She was lying at an awkward angle, but I gave her a hug.

'Stop it,' she said, then she groaned and rolled over.

'I love you,' I said. 'Goodbye.'

She didn't say anything back.

~

I caught the bus to the station and took the train to the city. Then I walked as fast as I could to the address Whippy had given me, checking the time on my watch. I was worried that he might have left already, but I found his van parked in a visitor bay. He was sitting inside it. I got in the passenger side.

'Hang on a sec,' he said. He finished typing a message on his phone, then he looked at me. 'Okay, what's so urgent?'

'I need something off you. It's really important.'

'I got that impression. What do you need?'

It was hard to say it. I took a deep breath.

'I need Fentanyl. A box of it.'

Whippy raised his eyebrows in surprise.

'It's not for me,' I said quickly.

'I know it's not for you. I'm not a fucking idiot.'

He shook his head and looked out the window with a strange smile. He seemed angry.

'You know, I thought this might happen,' he said. 'But I still can't fucking believe it.'

'Could you do it for me? I promise I'll never ask again.'

'Are you out of your mind? Do you have any idea how dangerous that shit can be for kids?'

'I told you, it's not for me.'

'I know that. I'm not talking about you. I'm talking about her fucking baby.'

'What do you mean? Whose baby?'

'Don't play dumb, Sam. You know who I mean.'

'I don't.'

'Sam, stop. I know Sarah has sent you out here. It's not happening.'

'No she hasn't. What do you mean about her baby?'

'I mean it can cause all sorts of problems. That's why Steve cut her off, mate. He doesn't want his kid born addicted to that shit, or with fucking defects. I'd do exactly the same thing. And I am sure as shit not going behind his back.'

It took a moment to take in what he was saying.

'She's pregnant?'

'Wait, they didn't tell you yet? Fuck, mate, I thought you knew. She found out a few weeks ago. Sorry.'

'What?'

'Yeah, you're gonna have a little brother or sister. Well, providing she can do the right fucking thing and stay off the drink and the pills. I warned them when Steve first did his back. I told them that shit is no joke, and now she's going through it. It's a nightmare. I never thought she'd actually send you out here, though. Jesus Christ.'

It was quiet in the van, but it was noisy in my head. Everything came at once. I was queasy and I was angry and I was shocked and I was jealous and I was devastated. I wanted to vomit. I was shaking. I was going to be replaced. There was no room for me in her life. They were going to be a family, and I would never be a part of it. She didn't love me. She didn't want me. She was ashamed of me. She regretted me. She was going to love this baby more than she ever loved me. I had lost her.

'You okay?'

I flinched, as though he had woken me up.

'It's not for her. It's for a friend.'

'Sam, I know that's bullshit, okay? Stop trying. And even if it was, I'm still not selling you that shit. I'm happy to sort you out with weed or whatever else, but this is fucking different.'

'You don't have to worry about me. I just need it. I don't have the money right now, but I'll pay whatever you want. Just tell me and I'll get it for you.'

'I'm not changing my mind.'

'I'll tell the police,' I said.

I hadn't planned to say it. It just came out. Whippy twisted in his seat to face me. He looked disgusted.

'What did you just fucking say?'

'I'll tell the police about what you do.'

'You don't want to do that.'

'I will. I'll do it. I'll tell them about everything, like all your other businesses and how you clean your money.'

I looked him straight in the eye.

We stared at each other for a moment, then he ran his tongue over his teeth and shook his head.

'Bullshit.'

'I will. I don't care.'

'Steve said you were a conniving little cunt. I never saw it, but I guess he's right.'

I was getting desperate. I took the watch off my wrist.

'I'll trade you this.'

He took it and inspected it.

'It's a fake.'

'It's not.'

He frowned and looked more closely.

'Where did you get this?'

'I found it.'

'Oh, I bet you did.'

He typed something on his phone and scrolled. He looked at the screen, then the watch, then the screen, then at me, then back to the screen. Then he put the watch in his pocket and got out of the van. I stayed in the front and waited.

A few seconds later he opened the back door and got inside. He rummaged around the stacks of parcels and boxes, then I heard him unzip a bag.

The back door slammed shut and he came back to the front and got into the driver's seat. He tossed a small box at me. It was Fentanyl.

'Thank you,' I said.

'That's it. No more. We don't speak again. I walk into a room, you leave it. And you tell your mother if she ever tries this shit again she had better think twice about swallowing anything I give her, because I don't give a fuck if that bitch lives or dies. And if you ever think about opening your mouth about me to anyone, I'll fuck you up worse than Steve ever did.'

'I'm not scared of you.'

'That's because we've never been properly introduced. I've been polite out of loyalty to my mate, but if you threaten me again, you'll find out what I'm about. Now get the fuck out of my van.'

I got out, and before I could close the door Whippy was revving the van loudly. He drove away fast. Once he was down the street, I ran in the other direction. I turned down an alley next to a Korean restaurant and hid behind a skip bin.

From my pocket I took out the wallet that I had stolen from his glovebox while he was in the back of the van. There was five hundred and eighty dollars in there. I took out the money and dropped the wallet in the bin.

Then I opened the box of pills. They were small and white and in two silver sheets. There were twelve in the pack.

It was enough for both of us.

～

I walked back to the main road and waved down a taxi. When I got in the back seat I showed the driver all the money I had. He drove me to the hospital.

I remembered the way to the respiratory ward. I checked the corridors in case I saw Peter. I found Vic's room and I went inside, but Vic wasn't in the bed. Instead there was an old lady eating jelly from a cup and watching television.

I backed out of the room. My chest started to tighten again. I worried that Vic had died here alone during the night and I had let him down. I checked every room in the ward, but I couldn't find him anywhere.

There was a lady sitting at a desk in front of the office I had sat in with Peter. I asked where Vic was and she opened a drawer and pulled out a file.

'He was discharged two hours ago.'

'How did he get home? Is he okay?'

'I'm not sure, I think . . . one moment, is your name Sam?'

'Why?'

'There's a note here addressed to Sam. Is it you?'

I nodded.

She gave me the sheet of paper. It was a handwritten letter.

Sam,

I came in early as I promised. Vic opted not to take the
advice of his doctor and requested to be discharged. He
has no next of kin, so I am taking him home. I'll get
him settled and I'll stay with him until my shift starts at
three. I'm sure he could do with a friend.

Peter x

I looked at my wrist to check the time, then I remembered I didn't have my watch anymore. I got my phone out, and the box of Fentanyl fell out of my pocket. I quickly squatted down to pick it up.

It was two-thirty. I stuffed the note and the box and my phone in my pocket and I left.

~

I took a taxi to Vic's house.

There was no car in the driveway. I looked around before I got out of the taxi to make sure nobody was watching.

The front door was unlocked.

It was dark inside the house. It smelled familiar.

'Vic? I'm here. Vic?'

I found him in the spare room. Two boxes of medication and a glass of water were on a chair near the bed. He was propped up on a couple of pillows and his legs were covered by a tartan fleece blanket. His breathing was raspy and his eyes were closed. The first time I had met him he was so big and powerful that he could lift me easily. He didn't look like the same person.

I rushed over and kneeled down beside him.

'Vic, I'm here.'

He opened his eyes, turned to me and smiled.

'Hello mate.'

He closed his eyes again. He didn't look afraid anymore.

I sat with him for a while, listening to him breathing.

'I think Peter left medicine for you,' I said.

Vic shook his head.

'I don't want it, mate.'

'Okay.'

I sat for a while longer. I was fighting with myself. I didn't want to say it, but at last I did.

'Vic,' I whispered, 'I have something.'

My hands were shaking. I took the box of Fentanyl out of my pocket and gave it to him.

'They give it to people who are in lots of pain, but if you have too much it kills you. I read about it. They say that it doesn't hurt. It's like going to sleep and never waking up. Like you wanted.'

He looked at me and he started to tear up.

'Is that true?'

'I think so. I read it.'

He held the box and squinted at it. Then he closed his eyes and breathed in as deep as he could.

'Vic? Is it really what you want?'

He opened his eyes and he nodded.

'Yes. I've wanted it for a very long time.'

'Are you sure?' I asked.

'I am.'

Vic opened the box. I put my hand over his.

'Wait, Vic. It shouldn't be in here.'

He thought about it. Then he nodded.

I helped him stand up and he clung to me. There was so much less of him.

'You got bigger,' he said.

I took the glass of water and Vic held the box. We shuffled out of the room and down the hallway. Vic opened the door to his bedroom. It was just as I left it. He stood in the doorway and looked around.

'Are you okay?' I asked.

Vic didn't answer. He stepped into the room without my help. He opened Edie's wardrobe and went through her clothes. Then he took one of her white nightgowns off a hanger. He held it to his face and he breathed it in.

Then he leaned over and laid it out flat on Edie's side of the bed. He handled the fabric delicately, like she was inside it. He sat on his side of the bed and he looked across to hers. There was a lump in my throat so big I couldn't swallow.

Vic looked up and beckoned me in. His eyes were wet.

I sat on the stool beside Edie's vanity table.

'Have you been alright?' he asked me.

I shrugged. It was hard to speak.

Vic smiled.

'I think you foxed those coppers,' he said.

'They didn't ask you about the bank either?'

'Not once.'

He laughed to himself, but it made him cough. It was awful to hear it.

'I know why you did it,' he said. 'You stuck your neck out for me like nobody ever did. But promise me you won't do anything that stupid again.'

'I fixed a motorbike all on my own,' I said.

'Oh yeah?'

'The air filter was blocked. I got it working. Like you showed me.'

He nodded and smiled, and I hoped he was proud.

Vic lay down. I pulled the stool closer to him and put the glass of water on the nightstand next to the white box. We were quiet for a long time.

'She's here,' he said quietly. 'Feels like she's here. She would have loved you.'

'Vic, I have to tell you something. I read Edie's diaries. I read all of them. I'm sorry.'

Vic closed his eyes and smiled.

'I didn't know you kept a diary.'

At first I thought he hadn't heard me properly, but then I realised he was talking to her out loud.

'Yes,' I said. 'For like, twenty years. You didn't know? They're all in suitcases in the wardrobe.'

'Last place I'd look. I hope you weren't too rough on me, love.'

It really did feel like she was here. There was a strange tingling on my neck, like someone was blowing on it. My mouth went tight.

'She loved you,' I whispered. 'She said you were her favourite person in the world. She said you were a rock of a man. She said that all the time. You were a rock. There wasn't a day in her life she didn't love you.'

Vic's eyes were still closed. He shook his head slowly.

'I should have told you more. I should have told you every day. I didn't put things into words as much as I should've. Tried to tell you in different ways, I suppose. But I know you wanted to hear it. And I'm sorry for that. You were more than love. You were my life. I wish I said it more.'

I held Vic's hand. He squeezed it back.

'She knew,' I said. 'She knew it.'

We sat together for a long time without talking.

Then Vic opened his eyes.

'I'm ready,' he said.

I felt dread when he said that. It got noisy in my head, but Vic was so calm. He took the two silver sheets out of the box and sat up a bit.

'How many?' he asked.

'I think six will be enough.'

He popped the pills out of one sheet and put them next to the water. His hands were steady. I picked up the other sheet.

'Vic, I want to go with you,' I whispered. 'I want to go together.'

He took the pills from my hand and he shook his head.

'No,' he said. 'No. No. Not you. Not you. I've lived my life. I have *lived* it. A lot of it was hard, especially the last ten years, but it was worth it, because it came to this. I was supposed to meet you. I was supposed to have you in my life. I never had money. I couldn't have kids. I never amounted to much. But I want to leave some hope for you. Don't give up. Don't give up, Sam. Sometimes it feels like there's no fixing it, but you got to give it a rip, mate. You got to give it a fighting chance. Find out who you are, and live that life.'

'I can't, Vic. I can't ever do it.'

He reached out and grabbed my shoulder firmly.

'You can. You can find a way. You *have to*. You have to.'

I had never seen him like this. I could see veins on his forehead and his eyes were wide. He was staring at me.

'You've got to make it,' he said. 'You've got to make it— for me.'

He pulled himself up further and starting speaking faster and louder.

'You don't understand, Sam. Listen to me now. Reuben Martin, the kid with the glasses, he stayed with the patrol. Glued to them, he was that frightened. It was me. It was me who came off the back. Just me. I was on my own mate. I was lost. I couldn't find a way out. I was on my own and I was terrified.

And I saw . . . I saw through the trees . . . Sam, I shot that poor girl. I killed her. *I* killed her. Just a girl. Just a girl your age. And I killed her. I tried to save her, but she was gone. I couldn't save her. And I ran. I didn't bury her. I ran away. Her blood all over me. The patrol heard the shot and they found me. I lied. I told them I killed a lookout. They gave me a medal. I threw it away. Nobody ever knew. Nobody ever knew.'

Vic put his hands over his face and he started to sob.

I reached out and hugged him and he gripped me and held me tight.

'Edie, I'm sorry. Edie, Edie, I'm sorry. It's my fault. It poisoned me. Edie, I'm sorry.'

I didn't know what to say.

Vic pulled back and held my face between his hands. His eyes were red.

'I met you for a reason. Sam, *please.* I couldn't save her. Help me go in peace. But not you. Promise me. Please. Promise me you'll make it.'

My lips were trembling and it was hard to talk.

'It's hard, Vic. It's so hard. You don't know. You don't know what it's like.'

'Promise you will try for me.'

'I'll try,' I said, because I wanted Vic to feel better. 'I promise.'

He looked at me, then he nodded and lay back down.

'Thank you. Thank you, Sam.'

I sat with him in silence again. The sun was setting outside. Orange light came into the room through the gap in the curtains.

'There's a pencil and a pad next to the phone,' Vic said. 'Can you get them for me?'

I went down the hall and got them and brought them back to Vic.

He flipped the pad to a fresh page. He wrote on it, then he tore the page loose and gave it to me.

I read it.

I am choosing to end my life.

It was signed and dated.

I put the sheet of paper on the nightstand, and I saw that the glass of water was empty and the pills next to it were gone. Then I saw that he had taken the pills from both silver sheets. He had swallowed them all.

I started to cry.

'It's alright, mate,' Vic said. 'It's alright.'

'I don't want you to die.'

'It's time. It's time.'

He reached out and took my hand.

'I'm scared,' I said.

He smiled. His eyes were bright again.

'Don't be scared,' he whispered to me. 'This is right. It's the right thing. It's what I want. You're a beautiful kid. You're going to have a big life. You're going to see the world. Be who you want to be. You'll see.'

'I'll try.'

'You saved me,' he said.

'I love you, Vic.'

'I love you too, mate.'

He grimaced and lay back. He closed his eyes. I squeezed his hand.

Vic put his other hand on Edie's nightgown.

'She's here,' he whispered. 'She's here. She's beautiful.'

I couldn't watch him. I put my head down and closed my eyes tight and held Vic's hand for a long time.

Then suddenly he tensed up and squeezed my hand hard. He made very small, fast gasps. Then he let out a long breath, but when he tried to breathe in again he couldn't. He twisted and his back arched, like he was being grabbed by the collar and lifted off the bed by his chest. His struggle seemed far away, like it wasn't happening in the room, like it was deep inside him. His eyes were closed. His expression didn't change. It looked like he was having a bad dream. He had Edie's white gown in his fist. He made small desperate gurgling sounds and there was a thin creamy foam coming from his mouth.

'Vic? Vic? *Vic?*'

But he couldn't hear me. I couldn't do anything but watch and hold his hand. I kneeled next to the bed and held him down, like I was keeping him here, like I was stopping him from being lifted up. He bucked and he thrashed and he made awful noises. I was frightened and I was sobbing. I bowed my head because I couldn't watch anymore.

I don't know how long it lasted, but it was the longest time of my life.

Then Vic went still. He settled onto the bed. I didn't want to look up. I squeezed Vic's hand, but he didn't squeeze back. He was gone but I wasn't ready to know it yet.

After a long time, I let him go.

I stood up. The room was almost dark now. I looked at Vic. His mouth was open. His eyes were closed. He didn't look peaceful. But he didn't look afraid, and he didn't look like he was in pain. He was just gone.

I wiped his mouth and his cheek with a tissue. I went around the other side of the bed and smoothed out Edie's nightgown. I took the empty white box and the silver sheets and I put them in my pocket.

I felt numb.

I didn't know what to do.

As I was putting the stool back under the vanity table I saw the piece of paper with Peter's number on it.

I felt like I was outside of my body again. I watched myself walk down the hallway and pick up the telephone. There was no dial tone. I realised I had never once heard it ring.

I didn't have a choice. I used my own phone to call Peter's number. It rang out and went to voicemail. I didn't leave a message.

I sat on the floor in the dark. After a while my phone rang. I watched myself answer it.

'Hello?' said Peter.

I didn't say anything.

'Hello, who is this?'

I couldn't talk.

'Sam? Is that you?'

'He died,' I said.

Then I hung up.

And I watched myself leave the house.

～

Nobody saw me walk down the street. I kept my head low and stayed in the dark.

My phone rang again. It was Peter. I switched it off.

I walked without any direction. I followed my own feet. When I reached a main road, an ambulance passed by with its lights flashing. I hid behind a bus stop. I wondered if they were going to Vic's house.

I felt like I was floating. I was weak and dizzy and tired. At one point I heard a car blaring its horn and I looked up and realised I was in the middle of the road. The driver swore at me then drove away.

After a long time I recognised where I was, and I knew where I was taking myself. A little while later I was standing on the Clayton Road overpass.

I stood where Vic had been that first night and I looked down over the rail to where he would have landed. I took the white box and the pill sheets out of my pocket and dropped them over the edge.

I saw a cigarette butt next to my foot. Then I looked across to where I had been standing before Vic saved me.

Vic had wanted to leave me with hope, but I couldn't feel any. Nothing was different, except now my friend was gone and the world felt emptier than ever. I wanted to cry, but there was nothing left in me. I had promised Vic I would try, but I didn't know how to do that. I didn't see how anything would ever get better.

I thought about Vic's secret, how killing that girl had haunted him for all those years. It must have hurt to carry it on his own for so long. Not even Edie had known about it. He had seemed so relieved when he told me, like a curse had been lifted.

I sat down and thought about that for a long time.

When I stood up, I knew where to go.

Tidings of Comfort and Joy

It was late when I came back to the street. I didn't see any police or paramedics outside Vic's place.

All the lights were off at the Meemeduma house. I hopped over the side gate and walked towards the backyard. I stopped outside Aggie's window. Her desk lamp was on, and I could see her studying through a gap in the blinds. I tapped lightly on the glass but she didn't hear me. I tapped a bit louder and startled her. She pulled back the blinds. When she saw me she put her hand to her mouth and opened the window.

'Sam?'

'It's me.'

'Sam, I'm so sorry.'

'What are you sorry for?'

'You don't know?'

'Know what?'

'Oh, Sam, I have really awful news. Vic died tonight. An

ambulance and the police were over there a few hours ago. My mum went to speak to them.'

'The police were there?'

'Yeah, I think they were talking to the neighbours about notifying next of kin and stuff like that.'

'Do they know how he died?'

'I think he was really sick. He must have just got back from hospital. Come around to the back door so I can let you in.'

'I don't want to wake anybody up.'

But Aggie had already left her room. She slid open the glass door at the back of the house and rushed outside and wrapped me up in her arms.

'I'm so sorry,' she said. 'I know he meant a lot to you.'

I hugged her back. We held each other for a while. When she pulled back to look at me she had tears in her eyes.

'Where is your *hair*? Look at your arms. You look like you've been kidnapped by neo-fascists.'

'I shaved it off.'

'You sure did. Maybe don't do that again. It really doesn't suit you. Come inside.'

Aggie took my hand and led me into her room. She sat down on her bed and crossed her legs, then she patted a spot beside her for me to do the same.

'It's so good to see you. Sam, I'm just . . . mortified. I said some unforgivable things to you, and I regret it so much. I was so shocked and overwhelmed. And I was angry. And when I get angry, I'm capable of being really hurtful and inconsiderate.

I mean, like, don't get me wrong, I'm still upset with you, but I know I overreacted. I'm so sorry.'

'Don't be sorry.'

'Too late, buddy. Anyway, where have you *been*? I've been trying to find you. Do you know how many Sam Watsons there are on the internet? There's a lot. It's like you vanished to another dimension. I honestly thought you were in jail. I even called remand centres pretending to represent a legal aid office to see if you were there. Like, I actually did that. But you weren't at any of them. What happened after you got arrested? Did they charge you?'

'No.'

'So what happened?'

'They let me go.'

'Seriously? So did your parents get you out? Do you have a team of lawyers or something?'

'No. It wasn't anything to do with the bank. And I don't come from a rich family. I don't have any money.'

'Sam, you don't have to play humble. I'm not envious, and it doesn't change my opinion of you.'

'It's the truth. I'm trying to tell you the truth.'

'Maybe we just have different definitions of wealth, but in my world people who can afford to wear a twenty-thousand-dollar luxury timepiece are pretty financially stable.'

'What?'

'Your watch. Well, you're not wearing it now, but the one you usually have on.'

'What about it?'

292

'I noticed it the first day you came over, because it's a fucking *Cartier* and you got brownie batter all over it and you didn't even care, and I was like, who *is* this guy? And so I googled the watch, because maybe it wasn't as expensive as I thought, right? Nope. Twenty-three thousand dollars. I thought maybe it was a fake or something, but then you told me about your parents and this big deluxe property in Sydney, and it all made sense.'

I put my hand over my wrist. I had been wearing twenty-three thousand dollars. I thought about what that money could have done. I could have given it to my mum. She could have left Steve and had enough for us to get by for a while.

'I don't have it anymore.'

Aggie shrugged.

'I don't like you because of your watch, Sam.'

'It *was* fake. I mean, everything was fake.'

'What do you mean?'

'I mean . . . you were so nice to me, and I've never really had a friend before, and I thought if you knew the truth about me you would stop liking me, so I lied to you.'

'About what?'

I took a deep breath.

Then I told her where I came from, and how I got here, and I only stopped because Aggie was so upset.

She gave me another hug.

'Oh my God, Sam. I had no idea. I really didn't. I couldn't see past any of my own petty bullshit to see that you were really hurting. I'm so sorry.'

'Stop saying sorry.'

'Sorry.'

We lay down on the bed and Aggie kept her arms around me.

I felt a bit better. I had told her a lot, but I hadn't told her the whole truth about who I was. I hadn't told her how I hated my body. I hadn't told her that I stole clothes and cosmetics and dressed up in them. I hadn't told her that I burned myself. I hadn't told her that I helped Vic die.

'I'm not going to stop being your friend,' she said.

'Really?'

'Nope. I'm stuck to you like a limpet, so lump it.'

'What's a limpet?'

'I actually have no idea. It's something my mother says sometimes.'

'Please don't tell her anything I told you.'

'What if she can help?'

'She can't.'

'But what are you going to do?'

'I don't know.'

Aggie sat up.

'You can stay here. Live with us.'

'I can't do that.'

'Sam, I'm serious. My parents can, like, informally adopt you or something. Or formally. They love you. We could do a direct trade for Dylan. Believe me, nobody would mind at all.'

'You can't do that.'

'Of course we can. I'm not being polite or making an empty promise. For all our faults, of which there are many, we're at least stable and very boring people. You could live here and go back to school and be safe. You've been through so much.'

'I can't.'

'Sam, surely you're not going to go back there.'

'I have to.'

'Why?'

'I can't leave my mum. I can't do it. I need to be there. I need to help her.'

'There are organisations and resources and facilities that can help her, Sam. You don't have to do it on your own.'

'We've always done it on our own.'

'So what are you going to do?'

'I don't know,' I said.

But I did have an idea. I just couldn't tell her.

~

When Aggie fell asleep, I got up from her bed. I wrote her a note with my number on it, then I left through the back door. I walked a few blocks and turned my phone back on to call a taxi. There were missed calls from Peter. He had left messages which I couldn't bring myself to listen to. He had written a text too.

We need to talk

I deleted it.

The sun was coming up when I got home. I curled up in my bed but I couldn't sleep. I kept thinking about Vic. I imagined the paramedics finding his body and reading the note and lifting him off the bed and wheeling him out. I wondered if they were doing tests on him. I wondered what happened when somebody died and they didn't have any family or friends to call. I wondered where Vic would be buried. I wondered if he would have a funeral, and if anyone would be there. It made me so sad that I started to cry again, and I buried my head under my pillow.

~

For the next few days, I tried to pretend everything was fine.

I bought groceries and pushed the full trolley all the way home. I cleaned the bathroom and the kitchen. I cooked my mum her favourite meals, like chicken Provençal and beef bourguignon, but she didn't eat much. I picked up her clothes and washed them. I waited for her to tell me that she was having a baby, but she never did. She was tired and irritable. She left the house a few times, but I didn't know where she went.

Peter kept calling me, but I wouldn't answer. I tried to keep myself busy. I trained in the backyard. Whippy came over a few times. As soon as I saw his van out the front, I left and went to the vacant house.

One night, when Steve and Dane and Mark were in the lounge room drinking, I overheard them talking about breaking into Rosso's house. I sat down in the hallway to listen.

They planned to steal an old van and go to Rosso's around nine o'clock on Christmas Eve. Steve would cut off the power and the phone lines, so there was less chance the alarm system could alert the security dispatch. To be safe, he said, they shouldn't spend longer than ten minutes inside.

Steve wanted to vandalise Rosso's house as much as steal from it. Mark was in charge of doing all the damage. He was going to slash open the upholstery on all the furniture and the beds, spray-paint the walls and the clothes in the wardrobes, and fill the drains and toilets with expanding foam and turn all the taps on. He would pour bleach over the carpets. It made Steve laugh. He called his brother the Minister for Mayhem.

Dane was going to take a couple of big bags in with him and fill them with jewellery and laptops and cash. Steve told him to make sure he stole their Christmas presents too.

The first thing Steve said he was going to do was go into the backyard with a bat and deal with the dog. It took everything I had not to go out there and plead with him not to hurt Snags, but I stayed quiet.

Steve was also going to search for a set of spare keys to steal one of the cars in the garage. Mark asked if they should bring me along, because that was something I could do. But Steve said he didn't want me there, and he didn't want me to know anything about it.

∼

The day before Christmas Eve, Steve and my mum were sitting on the couch sharing a cigarette. I stood in front of the television and asked if they wanted to go to the Carols by Candlelight in Fremantle the following night. I said I would make a picnic.

I knew Steve wouldn't agree, but I hoped my mum would. She didn't want to. I said we could have ice cream on Bathers Beach afterwards. She screwed up her face and shook her head.

I was surprised when Steve insisted that she go with me. They almost had a fight about it, but she gave in.

On the morning of Christmas Eve, I put my tablet and some clothes in a plastic bag and hid them in the vacant house. Then I went home and made shortbread biscuits and baguettes. We didn't have a picnic basket, so I packed them in an empty cardboard beer carton. For a rug, I packed a couple of old bathroom towels.

Steve drove us down to Fremantle just before sunset.

He was agitated. He honked the horn a lot and yelled at traffic. He dropped us off near South Beach and gave my mum fifty dollars for a taxi home. He said he was going Christmas shopping and would be out late. Then he drove away fast without saying goodbye. I watched until the car was out of sight.

It was a nice night. It had been a hot day, and there was a cool breeze. My mum was wearing a cotton floral dress, and she had put make-up on for the first time in a while.

We found a spot on the grass near the back of the crowd. There were families with young children, and lots of people had brought their dogs. I worried about Snags.

I laid out our towels and we sat down. I looked around. There was a woman behind us breastfeeding her baby and rocking gently back and forth. She caught me watching and smiled at me, and I blushed and turned around.

My mum looked bored.

'Do you want a baguette?' I asked. 'They're sliced pear, Jarlsberg and smoked chicken.'

'Not right now.'

I looked towards the stage. To one side, there was a group of small kids in matching reindeer costumes and a man in a Santa Claus outfit getting them ready to perform. I pointed them out to my mum.

'Look over there. Remember the honeybee?'

She nodded, but she seemed distracted. She was looking over the heads of the crowd.

'Is there a bar here?' she asked.

'I don't think so.'

'Can you get up and have a look?'

'Are you sure?'

'Yes.'

'But isn't it bad?'

'Excuse me?'

'I mean, because you're pregnant.'

That got her attention. She looked right at me.

'I told Steve not to tell you.'

'He didn't. I just suspected. And now I know.'

'I was going to tell you, but it's still early. Are you excited?'

'I don't know. Not really. I want to go back to how it was. When it was just us.'

'Well I don't. Ever.'

'But everything was better then.'

She looked annoyed.

'No it wasn't. You don't know how hard life has been for me. I had to do it all on my own. We had nothing. And why would you want to go back? You've got everything ahead of you. You're lucky. I worked hard to raise you so you could do things for yourself, so you could have all the opportunities I didn't have.'

'Like what?'

She laughed to herself, but she didn't find it funny.

'How much time you got?'

'Tell me.'

'Jesus, I don't know. Go to new places, see things, have adventures, all the stuff that girls want to do when they're young. I missed out on all that because I had to grow up so fast. Having a baby on your own is like being tied to an anchor. You can't go very far.'

'I'm sorry,' I said.

'You asked,' she said.

We were quiet for a while. She rubbed her bare arms.

'All I ever really wanted was to run a boutique with all my own designs. People would come in and try on stuff that I'd made and I'd make them feel pretty and stylish and they'd walk out feeling good about themselves.'

'Why didn't you?'

'Because I had to look after you. You don't get it, Sam. I never had enough money to save. There was never enough time to study. I could never have what I wanted.'

'Maybe you still can. Maybe I can help you. We don't need Steve. I can help with money. I can put in more effort. You don't need to worry about me at all. I can find us a place to stay in a nice neighbourhood, and I can help pay for it so you can study and do what you want.'

She shook her head. She was angry.

'I'm not leaving Steve.'

'But you were happier before.'

'No, I *wasn't*. I never was. And I'm not raising another kid on my own. Stop trying to sabotage my relationship. It's selfish. That's probably my fault too. Maybe I spoiled you. I gave you too much attention. You're not used to sharing. You need to grow up, Sam. You're not the only person in my life. You're going to have a little brother or sister soon who is going to need me. And it's all going to be different this time. Everything will be different.'

Just at that moment, everyone started applauding. A choir all dressed in white filed onto the stage and began to sing 'Silent Night'. When the carol finished, all the children dressed as reindeer were ushered onstage. They looked so small. They danced and sang 'Rudolph the Red-Nosed Reindeer'. Their parents took photos from the front row. When they were done, everybody clapped and cheered loudly and the kids bowed and waved and it just made me feel sad.

The sun went down and people lit candles. A performer came on to sing with the choir. I looked down and stopped listening. I was hurt by what my mum had said, and I was worried about what would happen tonight. Maybe I had made everything worse.

After a while, somebody tapped me on the shoulder. I looked to my right, and an old lady handed me a lit candle. I took it and thanked her and she gave me a smile.

The choir began another carol. It was a slow one. I didn't know what it was called, but it was sad and it was beautiful. There was a part where they sang *'Oh, tidings of comfort and joy*', which made the back of my neck tingle. I looked at the candle in my hands, and I thought about Vic. It felt like he was here. It felt like he was speaking to me. My throat swelled up and I turned my head away so my mum wouldn't see me trying not to cry. I closed my eyes as tight as I could. When I looked up, the song was over and the candle had blown out.

After a few more songs, my mum said she wanted to leave. I checked my phone. It wasn't quite nine o'clock yet. I asked if she wanted to get an ice cream first and sit on the beach. She didn't want to. I asked if she wanted to go to a movie, but she didn't want to do that either. So I suggested we walk into Fremantle and look for a taxi home and she agreed to that. I rolled up the towels and put them in the carton along with all the food I had prepared.

We didn't talk much as we walked. The wind came in stronger and messed up my mum's hair. I was trying to move as slowly as I could, but she told me to hurry up.

We reached the main street. It was really busy. My mum didn't want to get a coffee, and she didn't want to stop and listen to the buskers outside the markets. She said she was tired and she had a headache and she didn't like the crowds. She waved down a taxi. I looked at my phone. It was just after nine o'clock. My heart was pounding. I didn't want to go, but the cars were banking up behind us, so I slid into the back seat with her.

My mum got a message on her phone.

'Is that from Steve?'

'What? No. Mind your own business.'

I looked out the window and tried to breathe.

~

When we turned onto our street, the first thing I saw was red and blue lights flashing. My mum sat forwards and looked through the windscreen.

'What the fuck?'

There were two police cars parked out the front of our house. The door was open and all the lights were on. My mum got out of the taxi while it was still moving and ran into the house. The driver braked suddenly.

'Hey! You pay me!'

He locked the doors. I still had some money in my pocket, so I dropped some in his lap. I got out and left the food and towels in the back seat.

I walked slowly up the driveway. I could hear yelling. When I stepped inside, it looked like the house had been searched. The door to the storage cupboard had been broken open. My mum was screaming at a police officer in the lounge room. He was putting Steve's laptop into a paper bag, and she was trying to snatch it off him.

'Give it back! What the fuck is going on? What are you doing in my house? You don't have the right!'

The police officer was composed.

'Ma'am, I'm asking you to calm down, or I will detain you.'

'For what? For *what*? You're in my fucking house!'

Then Detective Buchanan stepped out of my mum's bedroom. He was wearing blue silicone gloves. He stopped when he saw my mum, and he was even more surprised to see me.

'What are you two doing here?'

'We fucking live here! What are *you* doing here?' my mum asked.

Detective Buchanan took his gloves off and looked at me thoughtfully. The other officers packed up around him.

'Sarah, I'm Detective Buchanan, we spoke a few weeks ago about Sam. Right now we're executing a warrant that authorises us to search these premises. Can I get you to take a seat? I'd like to ask you some questions.'

'I'm not answering shit! Get out of my house! I'm calling my partner.'

'Steven Pratt? Is that your partner?'

My mum didn't say anything. She let go of the laptop and sat on the couch.

'Sarah, Steve and his brother Mark were arrested this evening. They're presently being processed and detained at Fremantle lock-up.'

'Arrested for what?'

'At this stage it looks like breaking and entering, burglary, intent to commit property damage, vehicle theft, resisting arrest, assault of a police officer and what will likely be unlicensed and prohibited firearms charges. What do you know about these weapons stored in the hallway cupboard?'

'Breaking and entering? What the fuck are you talking about?'

'We apprehended your partner and two other men unlawfully entering the address of Mr Ben Ross. Do you know who that is?'

'No.'

'Is the dog okay?' I asked.

They both looked at me. Detective Buchanan narrowed his eyes, then he nodded once, like he had just worked something out.

'Following previous discussions with the owner, it's my understanding that the dog had been removed from the premises.'

Detective Buchanan turned to my mum.

'There was a third man who evaded arrest. Do you know who he might be?'

'No.'

'How about you, Sam? Got any ideas?'

I looked down.

'Don't speak to my son,' my mum shouted. 'This is all bullshit! You've got no right to come in here while we're not home. This is a set-up! Why is this happening? Why now? Why are you fucking up our lives?'

Detective Buchanan kneeled down.

'Sarah, I want to make it very clear that you're not in any trouble.'

'I know I'm not in any trouble! So why don't you leave us the fuck alone? Stop harassing us!'

'We're not in the business of harassment. We want to make your situation safer. I'm urging you to collect some things and come in with us and work with one of our community officers. We can get you sorted with crisis accommodation as early as tonight. How does that sound?'

'Get the fuck out of my house!'

I had never seen my mum look so furious.

Detective Buchanan sighed. He stood up and looked at me.

'How about you, Sam? Would you like to come with us?'

'He's not going anywhere!'

I came forwards a couple of steps.

'What if we leave?' I said to her. 'What if we go with them? They can help us find somewhere else to stay.'

'We're staying right here. Steve will make bail and he'll be home in a few days.'

I turned to Detective Buchanan. My hands started shaking. 'Is that true?'

'That will probably be for a magistrate to determine.'

I saw that my mum was staring at me. She had gone really still.

'What did you do?' She asked it quietly, but it felt loud.

'Nothing.'

'Sam? What did you do? What have you done?'

I looked at Detective Buchanan, then back at her.

'What? Nothing. What do you mean? I didn't do anything.'

She shook her head slowly but her breathing was getting faster. She was really angry.

'What did you do?'

I couldn't speak. She stood up.

'What did you do?' she yelled.

I took a step back. Then another. I remembered what Mark told me about what to do in a fight you could never win.

I ran.

Willpower

First I went to the vacant house and got my bag. Then I jumped the back fence and went through a yard and out onto the street. I ran until my throat was sore and my lungs burned and my legs were so rubbery it was like moving through water. I got to a main road and hid behind a bus stop to catch my breath and wait for a taxi to go past. I waved at two, but neither of them stopped.

When I saw the next taxi, I ran out onto the road in front of it. The driver braked just in time and honked the horn. I pulled the last of the money from my pocket and showed him. I said I would give him all of it if he took me to Vic's house. He agreed.

~

Vic's front door was locked, so I went around the back. I opened the bathroom window and threw my bag inside then I squeezed in after it.

I didn't turn on any lights. It was quiet. I went into the spare room and laid down on Vic's bed. It still smelled like him. I hugged my knees to my chest. I had lost everything.

After a while, I got my phone out of my pocket. It was on silent, and I saw I had ten missed calls from my mum. She had also sent a lot of texts.

> Answer your phone!!!

> Where did you go??

> Sam I need you to come back. We have to talk about this.

> Answer your phone!!

> What did you say to that detective? Did you know about Rosso's place?? Did you say something to the cops?

> Your not in trouble just come home I just want to talk.

> Answer your fucking phone! Where are you?

> You must have said something

> Why are you doing this??

I lay in the dark and I didn't move. Every now and then she would call again, or send another message.

> Sam please pick up.

> Come back I need to know exactly what you told them

> I can't believe this is real. I can't believe you would do this.

I felt sick and my chest was aching. Each new text made it harder to breathe, but I couldn't stop reading them. I stayed in the dark and closed my eyes, and then my phone would light up and they would all come at once.

> Steve just called me. Him and mark have been refused police bail. Has to go to court to get it. Have to find a lawyer for him.

> I won't see him for Christmas. Im on my own.

> He knows cops must have been tipped off. He wants to speak to you.

> If you did this I will never forgive you.

> Who else could have told them???

> You have fucked up our lives. This is a dog act even for you. I can't believe I raised someone so selfish and cruel.

I knew she was drinking and she was all alone and it was my fault. I wanted to write back and tell her how sorry I was. I wanted to tell her the truth. That I had called Detective Buchanan from a payphone on Farrington Street and said my name was Ricky Wragg. I had told him about the guns in the house and the robbery at Rosso's.

But I couldn't do it.

> You must hate me so much to do this to me.

> I am ashamed to call you my son. I hope my next child will be more loyal than you.

> I don't even want you to admit what you did. If Steve found out he would be just as angry with me. He would leave me and then I would have nothing and nobody which is what you wanted so well done.

> After everything I have done for you. You spat in my face. Theres no fixing it. You ruined everything.

With every new text I pinched the inside of my thigh hard and twisted it until all my pain went to that place.

Around midnight I got a message from Peter.

> Are you at Vic's house?

I knew he wanted to talk about how Vic died, and that I would be in trouble. I didn't want him to find me, so I lied.

> No

A couple of minutes later he texted back.

> Ok. Thanks for replying. I need to speak with you about Vic. It's really important. So please give me a call or let me know where you are. Or come visit me at the hospital, or at home. I'm working all of Christmas day. I'm worried about you. I know you're hurting. Please speak to me. xo

I didn't write back.

Everything went quiet for a couple of hours. Then I got more messages from my mum.

He might go away for years. Mark as well. Do you get that? He might not be here for the birth of his child!! Or to help me raise it!

You burned everything to the ground.

You don't know what you've done!!

Tell me you didn't do this to me Sam. Tell me you didn't put the only man who has ever given a shit about me in jail.

I can't believe I have to do all this on my own again.

You betrayed me. After everything I have done for you.

Why did you do this???

I wrote out a message saying that I was sorry and I had made a mistake and I didn't mean for any of this to happen. Then I deleted it.

I closed my eyes and tried to think about Julia Child. I was in the kitchen with her, and she was teaching me how to cook a Queen of Sheba cake for a champagne and coffee party. I had an apron on and I was melting chocolate in a bain-marie. She drank some of the rum that was meant for the cake and told me I was doing a good job.

I must have fallen asleep, because I woke up to someone knocking on Vic's front door. It was still dark in the room because the curtains were drawn. I looked at my phone. It was eight in the morning. I had another message. It was from a number I didn't know.

> Youre dead you fucking maggot

My hands were shaking. The knocking at the door continued. I quickly blocked the number and deleted the message. I stayed really still. The knocking stopped. I waited and listened. I thought I heard the side gate rattle. Maybe it was Dane. Or Whippy. Or Steve's cousin Gavin. Maybe Mark had got out already and knew where I was. I imagined all of them at the back of the house, looking around, finding the open window I had crawled through. I waited for them to rush in and get me. I was too afraid to move. I couldn't hide or run. I listened and watched the door. Every small noise from outside made me flinch.

My phone flashed with another message. I was too afraid to read it so I stuffed the phone under the pillow.

I waited for a long time, but no one came into the house.

I got the phone out and checked the message. It was from Aggie.

> Merry Christmas Samwise! Hope you're okay. My mum woke us all up this morning by setting off the smoke alarm trying to make Surprise Pancakes. All she managed to achieve was the Surprise. She is now banned from the kitchen. We are a Christmess without you.

While I was still reading Aggie's message I got one from my mum.

> Steve has bail hearing today. Cant find lawyer who will work Christmas so he has some lady from legal aid.

Then Aggie sent another one.

> Seriously though you're on my mind a lot today.
> Please say hi and tell me how things are with
> you. x

Then my mum sent more.

> Hearing is at 3 at Fremantle courthouse.

> I think you should come and show support
> because if your not there Steve will def suspect
> it was you and he might blame me and kick
> me out.

> You owe me this.

> Do the right thing for once.

> Hiding just makes you look guilty.

Aggie messaged again.

> Oh I got you a present too. It's only small. But
> hopefully I can give it to you soon.

I put the phone back under the pillow. Aggie was so close, but she seemed so far away. My mum was far away, but it felt like she was right there in the room with me. The air felt really thick and it was hard to breathe. My body felt heavy. Time went slow. I was thirsty and hungry but I couldn't move. I just lay there.

After a couple of hours I looked at my phone again. There was nothing from my mum. Aggie had sent more messages.

Ok so my mum bought Dylan the most GARISH shirt for Christmas and made him try it on. She proceeded to tell him that he is the spitting image of my dad at his age. So Dylan gets offended by that, and my mum gets offended that he's offended, and now they're legit arguing, and me and my dad are just looking at each other like wtf and sharing the proverbial popcorn. I'll keep you updated.

Btw what does 'spitting image' even mean? Like, why are we spitting and what does that have to do with looking the same?

Omg Dylan just threw his hands up in the air and literally just shouted the words 'Well I'm sorry I don't think my dad is sexy!' then got up and went to his room. Like that ACTUALLY just happened. My family is insane.

The Meemedumas are terrible at Christmas. Like, my dad is just mystified by it, so my mum tries to overcompensate so much that she burns out quickly and naps through most of the day. Then we typically reconvene in the evening with Chinese food to watch a shitty movie. Every. Single. Year.

Sorry I am texting so much.

Technically I am intoxicated by boredom. But also idk why but I have this intuition that tells me to poke you and try to cheer you up.

I tried to smile in the dark, but it was like I forgot how. I wrote back.

Thank you

Merry Christmas

I put the phone away again. My head was aching, but the pain felt distant. I was tired but I couldn't sleep. I was afraid of someone coming into the house, but I also didn't care if they did.

I barely moved all day. I just thought about how much I hated myself and how I got everything wrong all the time. Then I noticed it was completely dark in the room.

I looked at my phone. The brightness made me squint. It was eight in the evening. More messages had come in from my mum. I knew she would be angry at me.

> Meet you outside courthouse.

> Text me when your here.

> Where are you??

> It's almost 3 your not coming are you. I don't know why I expected anything different.

I almost stopped reading because it hurt so much. But I couldn't avoid the next message.

> Steve made bail! He is out.

> Being processed now. Mark still inside.

> Home now. House is a mess. Steve is in rage.

> He thinks it was you

> I am in bathroom

> You have fucked EVERYTHING

> He has thrown all your shit out the front

> He is making me choose between him and you but you already made that choice for me didn't you!??

> You can't come back here I can't protect you

> Wherever you are stay there. You cant live with us ever again

> You brought this on yourself

> Don't text me back either he checks my phone

> Goodbye

I had lost her.

And it was my fault.

It felt like someone was holding me down. My throat was so dry and swollen that I couldn't swallow. I had had no food or water all day and night. I didn't know how I was going to get out of this bed.

The phone lit up. I picked it up quickly, thinking it was my mum, hoping she didn't mean what she said. But it was from Aggie.

> Omg so for our Christmas movie this year we are watching ET the extra terrestrial because somehow it has eluded my father for his entire life. He is HATING it.

A few minutes later she texted again.

> He just paused it so he could rant to us He wants to know why this child is preventing scientists from studying the alien so they can learn the secrets of intergalactic travel and unlock the mysteries of the universe for the advancement of humankind. Tbh he has a point.

> He is now arguing with my mother, who just told him to calm down because it's not a documentary

> I wish you were here for this. He is actively cheering on the government agents. He hopes they arrest the kid. He is NOT going to like the ending.

Half an hour later there was another message.

> He did NOT like the ending.

I remembered watching that movie when me and my mum were living in an apartment that had a big old box television with dials and buttons that was already there when we moved in. She watched the whole thing under a blanket with me and it made us both cry. Thinking about it made me tear up.

I wrote back to Aggie.

> The boy wants to help ET get back to his family because his own family is broken and he can't fix it. That's more important to him than the universe.

Just after I pressed send, my phone ran out of battery.

≈

I lay in the dark for a long time worrying and regretting everything until my head started to throb and my mind went blank. My body ached. I had that feeling where I was floating outside of myself and I was looking down from the ceiling.

Then I heard a scratching sound.

I heard the front door open. I couldn't move. I listened hard. I heard footsteps coming down the hallway. Then a light was switched on and I saw a strip of yellow glowing through the gap under the door.

'Sam? . . . Sam?'

I hugged my knees tight against my chest.

The door opened.

'Oh, sweetheart.'

It was Peter, in his teal nurse's uniform. He kneeled down and put his hand on my forehead.

'I'm thirsty,' I whispered.

'Okay, let's get you up.'

He slipped his arms underneath me and lifted my body and I was so tired that I gave in. My shorts were soaked. I must have wet the bed during the night and hadn't even noticed.

Peter carried me to the bathroom and ran the shower. He helped me out of my clothes. I wasn't embarrassed about wetting myself, and I didn't even care that he could see all my scars or my naked body. I felt weak and dizzy, like I had a bad fever.

'I've got you. Don't worry, Honeybee. I've got you,' Peter said.

He helped me step into the shower and only let me go when he was sure I could stand on my own. The water was warm. I closed my eyes and opened my mouth and drank until it hurt my stomach. Then I lowered my head and felt the water wash over me and then I started to sob. I couldn't help it. I cried so much that I bent right over and collapsed onto my knees, like I was praying.

Peter didn't speak or comfort me, he just waited patiently. After a while he turned the water off and helped me up and wrapped me in a towel. When I was dry, he handed me some fresh clothes from the bag I had brought. I put them on and then he held me, and he was gentle. I could feel his big slow breaths in his chest and it calmed me down.

'Let's have a cup of tea,' he said.

∾

I sat at the table while Peter filled the kettle.

There was blue morning light coming through the kitchen window. Peter seemed to know where everything was. He put a mug in front of me and sat down.

'So it turns out I'm a pretty good stalker,' he said.

I kept my head down and looked at the table.

'I even hired a private eye. Well, not really. You know that lady a couple of houses down? Beverley? I was here a few days ago looking for you, and she appeared out of nowhere because she's a hopeless busybody. I explained who I was and everything that happened. She's a gossipy old queen, so we got on just fine. She's hilarious actually. By the way, you would *not* believe what happened to her ex-husband, totally scandalous, but I'll tell you another time. I asked her to keep an eye out and call me if anyone came to the house, which she did night before last.

That's why I asked if you were here. She knocked on the door, but I have a feeling you were hiding. Anyway, I'm here now.'

We were silent for a while. I could hear magpies outside. Peter shifted in his seat and rubbed his face.

'I got to know Vic a little bit. The night we met, after I stitched you up, we sat right here and talked for a while, mostly about you. I came back a few weeks later to check on you, but Vic explained that you had gone home. I urged him to see a GP. He knew he was very sick, but he didn't want to see a doctor. Nothing I said could convince him. I've dealt with enough stubborn buggers, so I arranged an outcall physician to come by, but Vic wouldn't let them in.'

Peter cleared his throat.

'Then a couple of weeks ago, we had an old girl leave us on the ward. Val. She was just . . . sunshine. Just delightful, you know? She had the kindest, youngest blue eyes. She was sassy and brave and funny, and she seemed to have an endless stream of children and cousins and nieces and grandchildren coming in to see her, and she introduced me to every one of them. But when she passed away, none of her family was there. She died on her own. I found her. And that one really hurt, Sam. That one hurt. I finished my shift, and I sat in my car, and I was a blubbering mess. And I thought about Vic, and I had a horrible premonition. It's hard to explain. But I drove straight here and I knocked but nobody answered. And I was still so upset and heartbroken that I just opened the door and walked straight in. I found Vic in a bad way and I called an ambulance. He wasn't happy about it.'

Peter sniffed and opened his bag and pulled a tissue out. He blew his nose and wiped his eyes.

'I know what he wanted, Sam. I read the note that he left. But I knew before that too. When I brought him back home after his overnight stay with us, he talked about his wife, and he talked about his life, and he talked about you. I'm glad you were here when he went. I'm glad he wasn't alone.'

Peter reached out and put his hand over mine.

'But before I left him that day, Vic asked me to look after you. He made me promise that I wouldn't give up, and that I would do whatever it took to see that you were okay. Then he told me something else.'

He slid Vic's keys across the table to me.

'These are yours.'

I shrugged.

'Okay.'

'You don't understand, sweetie. They're yours, because it's all yours.'

'What do you mean?'

'Vic left you everything he owned. This house, everything in it. It's yours. He had a few thousand left in his savings account too. That will be transferred to you.'

'It can't be.'

I didn't understand. Then Peter pulled a large envelope out of his bag and handed it to me.

'After you went home, Vic went to see a lawyer. He had them draw up his will and serve as the executor. He left it all to you, Sam. And Vic wanted me to make sure that you knew, and that you accepted it. That's why I've been trying to find you. He left you everything he ever worked for. He was a beautiful man. He loved you.'

I didn't know what to say.

'It's all yours, Honeybee. This is your home.'

I couldn't open the envelope. I didn't want it. It was too much. It didn't feel real. I wished Vic was here. I wished I could speak to him.

I looked up at Peter.

'Where is he?' I asked.

~

In the backyard I snapped off some bottlebrush and grevillea and picked a few chrysanthemums. I tied them into a bunch with string from the kitchen drawer.

Peter was waiting for me in his car. There was glitter everywhere. His back seat was stacked with dry-cleaned dresses and shoeboxes and wigs. I held the bouquet in my lap while he drove to Fremantle Cemetery. Peter had looked up the location of Vic's grave on their database.

We walked together up the main path, past old headstones and crosses and plinths. We didn't talk. The sun was coming up higher, and there was a little breeze.

Peter checked all the signs. I followed him up a long slope. After a while, Peter stopped and crouched in front of a marker, then we turned down a row. We walked until we found a mound of earth between a couple of graves.

'I think this is it,' Peter said.

There was no gravestone or plaque or cross. It was just dirt and sand and little rocks. I thought we must be at the wrong place, but then I looked at the name on the grave to the left.

It was Edie's.

I thought about how many times Vic had stood where I was.

Peter rubbed my back.

'Take your time,' he said. Then he left me alone.

I kneeled and put the flowers on the mound.

'I brought these from the backyard,' I said.

I didn't know what to do. It was strange to think that Vic was down there inside a coffin. I didn't like it.

I sat down and crossed my legs. I tried to imagine him standing next to me, like a ghost.

'I miss you,' I said, then I looked at Edie's grave. I tried to bring her to life in my mind too. 'I kind of miss both of you, I guess. Peter just told me what you did for me. I don't get it. I don't get why. I don't deserve it. You didn't have to. You didn't have to care about me at all.'

I plucked blades of grass and I teared up.

'It's too much. I don't know. It's like it's too nice. I don't know why you were always so nice to me. Even when you were hurting or when you were sick or when I did something wrong. You were always nice to me. I don't know what to say. It's like, saying thank you doesn't really mean enough. It doesn't do enough. It doesn't really show you how much it means to me. I wish I could have tried to tell you while you were still here.'

I cried for a while, then I wiped my nose on my sleeve and took some breaths.

'It's hard being here still. I did something stupid again, and I made everything even harder. If it wasn't for you . . . I don't know. I don't know what to do. I don't know how to make anything better. Maybe somebody else does. I think . . . I think I need some help, Vic. Because I can't do it on my own. I just mess stuff up.'

I stood up.

'I'll take really good care of your house. I'll keep it clean and look after it. I promised you I would try, but this time I mean it. As long as I can stand it, I'm going to try.'

Chaotic Good

That night Peter stayed for dinner.

I cooked Vic's Last Meal. Lamb roast and vegetables with trifle for dessert. When he took his first bite, Peter slammed his cutlery down and looked at me with wide eyes. I thought he was angry, but he just meant it was really delicious. He ate fast and had a huge appetite. He asked for seconds, which made me feel really good.

After we had the trifle, I poured the last of Vic and Edie's wedding anniversary brandy into two teacups. We clinked them together to toast Vic, then we drank.

When he finished the cup, Peter leaned back and scratched his chest and frowned at me.

'Listen,' he said. 'You didn't rob a bank, did you?'

I froze.

'What?'

Peter smiled.

'Didn't you hear about it? It was all over the news. Some girl tried to rob a bank with a bomb a few weeks ago, and when I saw the security footage I thought, *Oh my God, she looks just like our Honeybee!* It was seriously uncanny. I texted the girls, and they all said the same thing.'

I put my cup down and I looked at Peter.

'I did it.'

'What?'

'I did it. It was me.'

He went quiet and serious. Then he started to laugh.

'Oh, you're precious. You actually had me for a moment.'

∼

Peter stayed over. He slept on the couch and I went back to Vic's bed. I couldn't go into the main bedroom. I kept that door closed.

Peter took the next few days off work. He went with me to see Vic's solicitor. His name was Edward Denley and he must have been ten years older than Vic. He had white hairs growing out of his ears and he always closed his eyes and nodded to himself before he said anything. He didn't have a computer and he wrote everything down on a yellow pad.

Edward Denley explained the conditions of Vic's will. I didn't understand any of it. I was glad Peter was there. He asked questions about holding trusts and estate administration and age of maturity, and I felt really small and overwhelmed. I wanted to tell them that it must be a mistake, and I didn't deserve any of this. I wanted to give it all to my mum. Maybe she would forgive me and we could live at Vic's together.

'What if I don't take it?' I asked.

'Excuse me?' Peter said.

'What if I gave it to somebody else?'

Edward Denley closed his eyes and nodded.

'You can disclaim a bequest for many reasons—tax implications, for example, or if an inherited property is financially burdensome. Or a valuable asset might disrupt government benefits. Personal reasons too, of course. It's not a cumbersome process, you simply sign a statement of renunciation. However, you do not have the right to elect a beneficiary.'

'What does that mean?'

'It means you can't choose who gets it,' Peter said.

'Why can't I give it away to who I want?'

Edward Denley closed his eyes and nodded.

'You may, but not prior to receipt of the assets. And in your case there are additional restrictions. For example, the deceased requested that the property not be sold until after you turn thirty, which would mean you're not in a position to pass the title on.'

Peter touched my knee and spoke quietly.

'Sam, no. What are you doing?'

'I don't want it. It's too much. It's not right.'

'Having drafted the will, I can tell you the deceased was unequivocal in his wishes,' said Edward Denley.

'What does that mean?' I asked.

Peter squeezed my hands.

'It means it's what Vic wanted. It means it's yours. It means you deserve it. It means nobody else can take it from you. And it means we're not leaving here until you accept it.'

～

After a few days, Peter had to go back to work. I was relieved when he offered to keep staying at Vic's.

'Only if you want to,' I said.

Peter closed his eyes and nodded and did an impression of Edward Denley.

'I am unequivocal in my wishes.'

I liked Peter. At first I was suspicious because I didn't know why he was being so kind to me, but I was getting used to trusting him. He sang a lot, especially in the car, where he mostly listened to senior citizens radio. If a song came on that he liked he turned the volume right up and sang the whole thing, even if the windows were down and we were at a red light. Peter didn't care if people stared or laughed. He turned and looked right back and made *them* uncomfortable. Sometimes other cars honked or turned their radios up and joined in.

I liked his voice. It was loud.

～

I don't know how, but Edward Denley helped to get a copy of my birth certificate. Next to 'Father' it was blank. Peter said we could use it to get me a personal bank account.

On the way home from the lawyer's office, Peter turned onto Glenfield Road. As we approached the shopping plaza, he saw the sign for the Western Mutual Bank. He pulled into the car park.

'What are you doing?' I asked.

'There's a bank here. Let's just go in and set up your account now.'

'I don't want to.'

'It'll take five minutes.'

Peter started to get out of the car.

'No,' I said, 'let's just do it another—'

Peter gasped. He ducked his head back down.

'Holy shit!' he whispered. 'I think this is the same branch! You know, *the robbery*!'

I felt like I was going to vomit. Peter straightened and looked around the plaza.

'It *is*! Oh my God, now we *have* to go in. Come on!'

He was smiling and waving at me to hurry up. I didn't know what to do. If I said no, Peter might actually suspect something. But if I went into the bank, they would recognise me.

'Can't *you* just go in?'

'No, sweetie. They need a signature. Come on! It's easy.'

Maybe I deserved to get caught.

I got out of the car. I stayed close behind Peter and looked around nervously. When the automatic doors opened, I thought I might faint, but I pushed my shoulders back and I tried to walk like Dane. I tried to disguise myself as a boy.

We waited in the queue. I kept my head down. I didn't recognise any of the staff, but I felt like everybody was looking at me. It was like I was in a bad dream.

Peter had his hands on his hips. He was still smiling. He turned and winked at me.

We were called forward and my stomach dropped. Behind the counter was Suzanne. I hadn't recognised her at first because she had dyed her hair darker. She smiled.

'Welcome to Western Mutual, how can I help you?'

'Hello!' Peter was really cheerful. 'We're here to open a savings account. It's for my associate here.'

Suzanne looked at me, and hesitated for a moment.

'Oh, okay,' she said. 'Of course.'

Peter leaned forwards and spoke softly.

'I *have* to ask: is this the same bank where there was an attempted robbery a few weeks ago?'

Suzanne nodded and said yes. She looked at me again.

Peter puts his hands over his mouth, then he nudged me.

'I told you,' he said, then he gasped again. 'Oh, girl, was it you they interviewed on the news?'

'It was, yeah.'

'Did you change your hair?'

'I dyed it.'

'Oh, it looks gorgeous. Brings out those beautiful green eyes too.'

Suzanne blushed.

'Thank you.'

'God, you must have been terrified. Are you okay?'

'I was mostly in shock, you know?'

'Sorry,' I said.

I didn't think before I said it. She seemed so nice, and I felt awful about what I had done. She looked at me again. I expected her to realise and ring the alarm, but she just shrugged and turned back to Peter.

'It's okay. I'm totally fine. It was just really weird. It was like something out of a movie.'

'Did they find her?' Peter asked.

'We haven't heard anything.'

'Was it a real bomb? They never said.'

'I don't think so. They made us all evacuate the building. I think someone said it was just kitchen appliances and some wires.'

'At least you got the day off work,' Peter said.

'Yeah, but I left my keys in the break room and they wouldn't let me back in.'

'Oh, bloody hell. Disaster.'

'It's okay, my sister came to pick me up after I gave my statement and did all the interviews and we went and got drunk.'

'Good for you! God, you're so brave.'

'I wasn't really that scared. It happened so fast. We get a lot of randoms through here, but there's never been a robbery before. Anyway, it's a good story.'

I was glad she was okay.

Suzanne turned to me. She waved her finger in the air to gesture writing.

'So I'll get you a form and a pen to write down your details, okay?'

I imagined Vic beside me, laughing.

~

The next day, after Peter had left for work, I went to see Aggie.

When Mrs Meemeduma opened the door she acted like she hadn't seen me for years. She threw her arms around me and gave me a big hug. She was really soft and she smelled like mint and roses. Then she ushered me inside and called out for Aggie.

Aggie shuffled out of her room in her pyjamas. She looked grumpy because she had just woken up, but she brightened when she saw me.

'Sam! I've been texting you incessantly!'

'I'm sorry. My phone has no battery.'

She threw her head back.

'Ugh!'

In her room, Aggie gave me the Christmas present. It was wrapped in white tissue paper and it fit in my hand. It was so perfect and neat that I didn't want to open it. I just liked having a gift, I didn't care what it was.

'Open it!'

I carefully peeled the paper. It was a figurine of a woman with long brown hair in a fighting stance. She wore a leather skirt and bodice. She had a long tail and held a small sword.

'It's you!' Aggie said.

'Really?'

She laughed.

'Let me explain. I know it's technically female, but she's also a Tiefling, so we're suspending our disbelief anyway. I painted it myself!'

My hands were shaking. The figurine looked so fierce and brave.

'I love it. Thank you.'

Aggie went to her desk and got a sheet of paper from her top drawer. It was rolled up into a scroll.

'Okay, so this is the embarrassing part, because I'm an irredeemable nerd and I couldn't help myself. I made a character sheet for you. Do you want to see?'

'Yes!'

We sat on Aggie's bed. I unrolled the paper and saw lots of numbers and boxes and lists.

'I don't know what anything means.'

'Of course you don't. Okay, so your name is here—Sam, obviously—and next is your race. I chose Tiefling because they're outcast and misunderstood and they're also kinda secretive. For class I made you a rogue, which means you're stealthy and you keep to the shadows and you're a bit cunning. People underestimate you. Rogues are very talented thieves.'

That made me blush, but Aggie didn't notice.

'And under background I put urchin. So, like, maybe your character didn't grow up with many advantages or guidance or stability, which has made you super resourceful and independent and resilient. But you're also a bit distrustful and aloof. Urchins have certain skill proficiencies too, like stealth and sleight of hand, so you're known for pickpocketing and street-level scams. Is this, like, the most tedious thing in the world? Or is it too weird? Should I stop?'

I shook my head.

'No. It's really amazing.'

'Sure?'

'Yes.'

'Okay. So this section is your equipment list, which is pretty self-explanatory. First is typically your garment. Your character pretty much has negligible armour, which leaves you really vulnerable to attack. However, urchins are given a disguise kit, which helps them to commit crimes or escape dangerous situations. Does that remind you of anyone?'

'Maybe,' I said, and we both smiled.

'So for weapons I have given your character a set of knives. These have a dual purpose. Obviously they're for stabbing and slashing if you're faced with an unavoidable physical encounter, but your character is also a renowned chef. Tieflings are naturally proficient with fire, so it makes a lot of sense. Your character uses the knives, a copper cookpot and a high charisma score to forge unlikely alliances.'

'I like that.'

'Your last item is a trinket. I even painted it on, see?'

Aggie pointed to a yellow mark on the figurine's wrist.

'It's a Golden Enchanted Watch. You can use it to suspend time. Or whatever. I don't know. It's stupid.'

'It's not. It's really not. What does this part mean?'

I pointed to the top of the page.

'Oh, that's your alignment. Okay. So, this is actually the most important distinction because it speaks to the soul of your character. It's like the essence of who you are.'

'It says "chaotic good".'

334

'Right. Let me explain. Chaotic good means that you're governed by your own conscience above all other laws. You're benevolent and considerate and you'll take ridiculous risks and make stupid sacrifices if it means doing what you believe is right, even if it contravenes accepted practices or social orthodoxies. You're, like, a bit of a maverick. You're one in a million basically.'

It was so nice and thoughtful that I didn't know what to say. I hugged her, and she hugged me back.

'I feel bad,' I said. 'I didn't get you anything.'

'Of course you did. You're here. Oh, and *actually*, you got me the rarest gift of all.'

'What?'

'You outsmarted my dad.'

'What do you mean? How?'

'On Christmas night, I read him the text you sent about Elliott's broken family and why he was helping ET. He went super quiet and we were all just staring at him while he thought about it, because he actually looked a bit sad. And I've never seen my dad get upset in front of me, like, ever. He's very solitary when he processes things emotionally. Anyway, so my mum asks if he is okay, and he looks at her with, like, tears in his eyes and he says, "I forgot what it felt like to be young." It was so sweet and the whole movie suddenly made sense to him.'

There was a knock on Aggie's door. Mrs Meemeduma poked her head inside.

'Sam, would you like to stay for dinner? I promise you we won't cook, we'll order something in.'

I thought about it.

'Maybe not tonight. But I'd like to soon. I could cook something for you. I'm going to stay at Vic's house. Like, all the time. He said I could. It's in his will.'

'Really?' Aggie asked. She sounded excited.

I nodded. Mrs Meemeduma looked concerned.

'On your own? What about your family? Who's looking after you?'

'There's someone staying over for a little while. His name is Peter. He's a nurse. And a . . . performer. He knew Vic.'

Mrs Meemeduma frowned.

'And what's happening with the house? You'll need to pay council rates and water, and the utilities will have to be transferred into your name.'

'Ma!' said Aggie.

'I'm sorry Agnes, but it's true.'

I hadn't thought of any of that. I felt small and overwhelmed again and I was tempted to lie, but instead I looked up at Mrs Meemeduma.

'Will you help me?'

Brick by Brick

When I got home, I plugged my phone into an old charger that Aggie gave me. She had written me dozens of texts. There were none from my mum.

But there was one message from a new number.

> You're a dead cunt. I know where you are.

I deleted it and blocked the number. Then I turned off my phone and switched off all the lights. I sat on Vic's bed with my arms around my knees.

Around eight o'clock, I heard a key in the door. Peter called out to me and I got up. He was turning on all the lights.

'What are you, a bat? Why is it so dark?' he asked.

While Peter had a shower, I prepared dinner. I made croque monsieurs and a salad with a white balsamic vinaigrette. Peter sat in Vic's chair and ate really fast and told me I was spoiling him.

'I don't know how I'm going to go back to Lean Cuisine and packet ramen when I eventually return to my apartment.'

'You don't have to go back. You can just stay here,' I said.

'Don't tempt me.' He smiled. 'What's this?'

The figurine that Aggie gave me was on the table. I told him what it was, then I got the character sheet and explained what all the terms and numbers meant.

'She is so spot on! What an insightful girl.'

'You think?'

Peter put a big forkful of food in his mouth and nodded. I picked up the figurine and looked at it.

'I don't know,' I said. 'It's like she can see things that I can't. At first it was like she was talking about somebody else. Sometimes it's like she sees a whole other person to who I really am.'

Peter swallowed and shook his head slowly. He got serious.

'It's *you* who can't see what the rest of us can. I was the same until I started going to see Diane.'

'Who is Diane?'

'My friend, the one I was telling you about. It took me a while to hear what she was saying. I resisted her for the first few sessions. I'd been sent to a lot of counsellors when I was about your age, because praying the gay away hadn't been very successful, and all I learned from them was new ways to be ashamed of myself. So by the time I'd moved out and had a couple of breakdowns and a friend recommended that I see Diane, I was so entrenched in these cycles of self-sabotage and disgust that I couldn't accept that there was any other version of myself. But eventually she got through to me. It was like meeting myself for the first time. And she helped me understand how and why everything got dark and distorted, and who was actually responsible for that. I know it's strange that somebody else can teach you things about yourself, but she changed my life. I wouldn't be here if it wasn't for her.'

'Really?'

'*Really* really. Sweetheart, I've been down for the *count*. I had weeks where I couldn't get out of bed. Months where I drank myself stupid. Had a *lot* of bad sex with people I didn't like. I was lonely and scared of crowds and shy and quiet.'

'But you're so . . .'

'Obnoxious? Damn fucking straight. Because I know who I really am. Because I discovered drag and I have a real family now. Because I am worthy of love and I have a beautiful voice that deserves to be heard. Because I am ferocious and loyal and I am dedicated to healing myself and others. But even now I sometimes forget that, and I go under the covers and I lose my voice and I know that I need guidance and reassurance and redirection. And that's why I go to see Diane. And it helps. And you know what else?'

'What?'

'She wants to meet you.'

'How do you know?'

'I spoke with her on the phone today. She's on a break, but she said she can see you anytime this week.'

I looked down. I wasn't sure. Peter put his hand over mine.

'If you don't like it, you can just get up and leave.'

'But you'll be disappointed in me.'

'Of course I won't, Honeybee. Do you trust me?'

I nodded.

Peter looked at my plate. I had barely touched my croque monsieur.

'Now,' he said, 'more importantly, are you going to eat that?'

~

Diane worked from her home, which was a small red-brick house in Mount Lawley.

Peter drove me there and parked on the street. He kept the car running and said I should go in by myself.

'What if she doesn't like me?'

'You'll be fine. I'll be just around the corner having a coffee.'

I got out of the car and opened the garden gate and walked to the front door. I looked back and Peter gave me two thumbs-up.

I pressed the doorbell and waited. I heard footsteps on a wooden floor. The door opened.

Diane was tall and well dressed. She wore a pastel peach silk blouse and a tweed pencil skirt. She had bangs and tortoise-shell glasses. I thought she was going to be older, but she was probably under forty. She smiled.

'You must be Sam. I'm Diane. It's nice to meet you! Come on through.'

Her voice was soft and soothing. She looked over my shoulder and waved to Peter. I turned and saw him wave back and drive off.

I stepped inside. Her house was really tidy. She led me into the first room on the left.

There were two low armchairs facing each other on a round rug. Between them was a small table with a box of tissues on it. A greyhound came to the door and walked in like it was on tiptoes. Its ears were pinned down and it stood behind Diane.

'Oh, this is Brick. Is it okay if he joins us?'

I nodded. Diane brought her hands together.

'Now, I just boiled the kettle. Would you like some tea?'

'Um. No. It's okay.'

'Well I'm dying for some. Shall I bring a cup for you just in case?'

'Okay.'

'Take a seat, I'll be back in a minute.'

She left and I sat down. Brick and I nervously avoided looking at each other. I glanced around the room. One whole wall was a bookshelf. There were framed certificates hanging up behind a wooden desk. There was a lace curtain across the only window.

I could hear Diane in the kitchen and I could feel my pulse under my jawbone. I thought about getting up and walking out. I thought about stealing something on the way so she would never invite me back.

Then Brick came over and sniffed my feet. I held out my hand to pat him and he flinched.

'I'm sorry,' I said.

He smelled my hand carefully. Then he let me pat him. He was bony and his coat was smooth and shiny. He sat really close to me. He had big brown eyes and he made me feel calmer.

Diane came back carrying a tray with a teapot and two cups and put it on the table. She smiled when she saw Brick by my side.

'He's usually quite wary with people.'

'That's okay. He's nice.'

Diane sat down.

'He had a rough start to life. He was bred for racing but he was too timid to compete. He is *so* fast, but he was frightened of the crowds and the other dogs. His trainers tried to race him twice but he wouldn't even leave the gate, so they retired him to be a breeding male. They kept him in a pen on his own all day. He got an infection from flea bites on his back paw and no one bothered to treat it. Then he was rescued, and that's how he came to be my special buddy. And yours too, by the look of it. Can I pour you some tea? It's peppermint.'

'Okay. I mean, yes please.'

Diane poured out two cups.

'His racing name was Dynamighty Crackerjack. So alongside mending his paw and working on his socialisation and trust issues, I figured we had to find a new name for him too.'

'What made you choose Brick?'

Diane smiled. She was so peaceful and elegant. She spoke like she had all the time in the world.

'It was *his* choice, actually. The first week I got him he was very skittish. He'd just had his infection treated, so he had the bucket of doom around his collar. He hid under my bed or the table and peed on the floors and he was very unsure about me. I just gave him space, because you can't force a threatened animal to trust you. But one night I finished work late and I sat on the couch with a glass of wine and flicked around some channels until I settled on a movie, which was *Cat on a Hot Tin Roof*, because who doesn't like to wind down with a good tempestuous psychosexual melodrama, right?'

I smiled and nodded, though I didn't know what any of those words meant. I took a sip of tea. It was too hot.

'Anyway, within moments of Paul Newman appearing on the screen, he limped into the lounge room and sat right in front of my television and just stared. It was the strangest, funniest thing. He had no interest in any other characters, but when Paul Newman was in shot, he sat very still, like he was transfixed. That's when I knew that not only did my boy have outstanding taste in men, we were going to get along just fine. I asked if he had a thing for Brick, which is the name of the character that Paul Newman plays, and the moment I said it he turned around like it was *his* name, so it was decided.'

She took a careful sip of tea. Then she set it down.

'He was a different dog after that. There's great power in choosing your own name and taking ownership of your identity. It's like the title of a new chapter.'

I nodded again. I still didn't understand why he was called Brick, but I didn't want to sound stupid, so I didn't ask. Diane was a bit intimidating.

We sat quietly for a little while. It was uncomfortable.

'Tell me about you,' she said.

I blushed and shrugged. Diane's voice was soft and gentle.

'I understand you've lost somebody close to you recently.'

I shrugged again. I didn't know where to start. I hadn't just lost Vic, I had lost my mum too. I kept patting Brick, who tilted his head and looked straight at me.

Diane gave me a lot of time, but I felt like I must be disappointing her.

'You know, I spoke with Peter about you a number of times. He cares about you a great deal.'

'He's been nice to me.'

'He told me you're an amazing cook.'

I squirmed in the chair.

'I don't know. I like to cook.'

'What do you like about it?'

'Lots of things, I guess.'

'Like what?'

I scratched Brick behind the ears and thought about it.

'I like that there are so many things you can make even if you don't have many ingredients. If you just have flour and sugar and eggs and maybe butter and milk, you can still make anything, like pastry or biscuits or bread or custard or pudding or ice cream or cakes. And I like that everyone has their own way to cook. Even if two people follow the same recipe, what they make will taste a bit different. I like when I find an ingredient that I've never used before. I like that some people find cooking really hard, but I can do it. And I like it when people eat something I have made and they think it tastes nice. That makes me feel good about myself.'

'What else makes you feel good about yourself?'

I shrugged and didn't say anything.

'I'm impressed by how passionate you are. People can rarely articulate themselves so well about their interests. Who taught you how to cook?'

'Nobody.'

'Nobody? Someone must have shown you a few things.'

I took a deep breath.

'Do you know who Julia Child is?'

Diane gasped and spread her hands.

'Julia Child is *amazing*!'

After that we talked for a whole hour about how generous and loving and wise and funny Julia Child was. Diane even knew things about her that I didn't, like how she had worked at a spy agency and had invented a kind of shark repellent. I told Diane about the conversations I had with her while I watched episodes of *The French Chef*, like she was talking just to me. I told her that I liked to pretend she was my grandmother and how I thought about her when I felt anxious.

Then Diane asked about my real grandmother. I shrugged. She asked about my parents, and I shrugged again and looked away.

Everything went quiet for a long time. I patted Brick.

Diane checked her watch then put her hands on her knees.

'We're out of time for today, I think.'

I felt like I had let her down.

'Okay. I'm sorry. Do I need to give you money now? I don't know what to do.'

'No. Not at all.'

'Okay.'

There was a pause. Brick nuzzled my hand. He had sat with me the whole time. Diane stood up and led me to the front door.

'Listen, Sam. Would you like to come see me again tomorrow?'

~

I made Peter a leek and mushroom risotto for dinner. He had three bowls then leaned back and said he didn't leave mushroom for dessert. Afterwards, he sat on the couch while I looked through Edie's DVD collection. I found what I was looking for.

'Is that Paul Newman?' I asked.

'The one and only.'

'He's good-looking.'

'Don't *even* get me started. You know, I still can't believe that's how that dog got its name.'

'Diane never told you?'

'Nope. You're clearly her favourite already. And Brick's, by the sound of it. That dog does *not* like me. I've tried so hard, but he always backs away like I'm a rolled-up newspaper with legs.'

'He's friendly. I like Diane too.'

'Listen, you don't have to tell me anything that you discussed with her. That's between the two of you.'

'Okay.'

'And she won't ever share anything about you with me either. What you say to her is private and sanctified by her professional oath. Just so you know.'

'What do you mean?'

'I mean that, by law, anything you tell her can't be discussed outside that room.'

I thought about it.

'What about illegal things?'

'Child, have you never watched television? It doesn't matter if you confess to a spree of murders, Diane would only be duty bound to report something if you were in imminent danger, or if she considered you a threat to someone's safety.'

'Okay.'

'Are you a threat to anyone's safety?'

'No.'

'Are you in imminent danger?'

I thought about the messages on my phone. I thought about Steve getting bail. I changed the subject.

'Do you want to watch this with me?'

'Do I want to gaze at a sweaty, emotionally vulnerable Paul Newman for the next two hours? That would be a yes.'

I loaded *Cat on a Hot Tin Roof* into the DVD player and joined Peter on the couch.

'Oh Brick, you beautiful blue-eyed bastard,' Peter said. 'Come on out of that closet, I'll be your Big Daddy.'

Then he burped loudly and we both laughed.

∼

The next day Diane wore tailored navy blue trousers and a sleeveless linen blouse with a cherry blossom pattern. She stopped me before I could turn into her office.

'Let's do something different,' she said.

I followed her down the hallway. She had art on the walls that were just colourful painted shapes in a frame. We went into her kitchen. It had a marble-topped island bench and an induction stove and a big oven. On the counter, she had set out flour and butter and milk and sugar and eggs.

Diane sat on a high stool.

'I thought about what you said, about how just a few ingredients offered a great deal of potential, and I thought we might run with that theme today and pay homage to Julia. What do you think? Would you cook something for me? You can teach me as you go. I put out a few things for you, but take anything you need from the fridge or pantry.'

'I don't know. What would you like me to cook?'

'That's up to you.'

'Are you sure?'

'Am I sure about somebody cooking for me? You bet!'

I felt awkward searching through Diane's cupboards and shelves, but as soon as I found an electric mixer, I knew what I was going to bake for her. I pulled out the mixer and the attachments.

'I've always wanted to use one of these,' I said.

'Go for it! Please! It was a housewarming gift that I'm ashamed to say has never been used.'

I preheated the oven, then I measured out all my ingredients from memory. I poured water into a saucepan and brought it to a simmer on the stove. I placed a metal bowl over the saucepan to make a bain-marie, then I added eggs and sugar and beat them lightly.

'Okay Julia, so tell me what you're cooking.'

I held up the whisk and did my best impression.

'I've always said a party without cake is just a meeting, so get ready to soak up some flavour as we make a delicious Génoise sponge, today . . . on *The French Chef*!'

Diane laughed and clapped her hands together.

I poured the combined eggs and sugar into the mixer bowl.

'It's only three ingredients,' I said. 'But it's tricky because the only way you can get the cake to rise is by beating the eggs until they're really fluffy.'

After a few minutes, I carefully sifted the flour into the bowl and folded it into the mixture, then I poured the batter into a buttered cake tin and put it in the oven.

While the cake was baking, I opened a tin of pineapple rings I had found in the pantry. I used the juice to make a thick curd. Diane made me explain every step. Then in a frying pan, I caramelised the pineapple wedges with butter and sugar and a pinch of salt and cinnamon.

When the cake was done, I left it to cool on a rack. It didn't rise as much as I hoped, but Diane said it smelled amazing.

While I cleaned up, we talked about *Cat on a Hot Tin Roof*.

'I liked it,' I said, 'even though it was mostly just people talking. Maggie the Cat was my favourite.'

'Why is that?'

'She's so beautiful and kind, but I felt sorry for her too. She just wanted Brick to love her.'

'I like her too. She's cunning and she's loyal and she's also desperately lonely.'

'Would you say her alignment was chaotic good?'

Diane laughed.

'I would! You're so right.'

'I didn't like that Brick drank so much bourbon,' I said. 'And I cried at the part where Big Daddy said to Brick, *I've got the guts to die, what I want to know is if you've got the guts to live.*'

Diane watched me closely as I sliced the sponge in half and carefully lifted off one layer. Then I spread the curd and laid the chunks of pineapple. I put the top back on and dusted it with icing sugar.

'*Bon appétit!*' I said.

'Bravo!' Diane clapped. 'Look at that!'

Diane made a pot of tea and we sat down at her dining table. I cut her a slice of cake. My hands were shaking so much that I almost missed her plate. I sat and waited for her to taste it. She closed her eyes and shook her head.

'Sam, you are a *marvel.*'

I blushed. Diane had another bite.

'I mean it. This is incredible. I'm not just being kind. Aren't you going to have some?'

'I'm not hungry,' I said.

'Well I'm going to be rude and devour this in front of you.'

'It's not rude. I like that you like it,' I said. 'You have a really amazing kitchen. It's the nicest one I've ever cooked in.'

'Is that so?'

I nodded. I watched Diane take another bite. It made me like her more. And it made me feel safe.

'This one apartment we lived in, I opened the oven door and it came right off. There wasn't anything behind it. We didn't stay at that place very long anyway.'

'Did you move around a lot?'

'I guess.'

'With your mum and your dad?'

'Just my mum. I don't really know who my dad is.'

'That must have been hard.'

'We never had any money. Or any food.'

I paused for a moment. Then I took a risk.

'We used to steal things pretty often.'

I watched Diane carefully. I waited for her to judge me or ask me to leave. But she just took another bite of cake.

'Tell me more about that,' she said.

~

I saw Diane every afternoon for the next three days, and each time she asked me to cook something. I made crêpe dentelles with an orange and maple syrup glaze, and the next day I made vanilla panna cotta with a raspberry coulis. Then I made a carrot cake, because Diane said it was her favourite.

Each time, I told her a little bit more about myself.

On the third day, I told her how Vic saved me on the overpass.

Diane swallowed hard and put her fork down.

'What made you attempt to take your own life that night, Sam?'

'I don't know. I just wanted everything to be over.'

'Why?'

I shrugged.

'I don't like myself. I'm a mistake. It's just better for everyone if I'm gone.'

'Why do you describe yourself as a mistake?'

'Because I shouldn't be here. I was born wrong. And I do everything wrong.'

Diane looked at me really closely.

'Can you explain a bit further?'

'I don't know. I'm just *wrong*. And every day it's worse. There isn't any way out. There isn't any answer. Because I can't get better.'

'Why not?'

'Because it's already too late. I'll never get to—'

I stopped myself.

'Never get to what, Sam?'

I just shrugged and looked down. It was quiet for a while. Diane hadn't eaten any more of her carrot cake, and for some reason it made me so upset that I started to cry.

Diane gently pushed a box of tissues closer and waited. I covered my face with my hands because I was so embarrassed. It was a long time before I stopped.

'I'm sorry,' I said.

'You don't need to apologise.'

I blew my nose and wiped my face.

'Don't you like the cake?' I asked.

'It's delicious, Sam. But this is more important.'

'Maybe.'

'How long have you felt this way?' she asked.

'A long time, I suppose.'

'Was this your first attempt?'

I nodded.

'Do you still have thoughts about taking your life?'

'I guess.'

'How often?'

Every day, all the time. That was the true answer. But I stayed quiet and squirmed in my chair. My skin felt itchy and hot. I didn't know what would happen if I told her. She might have to refer me to a hospital or a facility. She might have to tell my mum, or the police.

'Not very often,' I said.

Diane nodded slowly.

'Okay. Sam, you've told me how you feel inside. I'd like to ask you about the outside. How do you feel about your body, your appearance?'

'I don't know. I hate it. It's ugly and disgusting.'

'Why do you say that? What don't you like about your body?'

I squirmed again and blushed. Everything got noisy. I tried to answer, but my chest had seized up like I was being squeezed and I couldn't breathe. I closed my eyes tight and I felt dizzy and I knew I had to leave. It was too much.

'I don't want to,' I said. 'I have to go. I'm sorry.'

I stood up and bumped the table and spilled Diane's tea and I ran down the hallway. Brick got up quickly and followed me. I got to the front door, but there were so many locks

I couldn't open it. I kept twisting and pulling. I could feel Brick's wet nose on my calves.

Diane was behind me.

'I can't breathe,' I said.

'It's alright. It's okay.'

She opened the door and I stepped out. I felt really stupid.

'I'm sorry,' I said. And I walked away.

'Sam?'

I turned around.

'I want to thank you for being so brave and so honest with me. Will you come back and see me on Monday?'

I didn't feel brave or honest.

'I don't know why you want to keep seeing me.'

'Because you're worth it,' she said.

Brake

The next day I was on my own. Peter was away for the whole weekend and the Meemedumas weren't home.

I wandered around the empty house. It didn't feel like I owned it. I went outside into the garden and watered everything and I watched the honeybees collect pollen from the bottlebrush. The lawn was getting long and the patch of dirt where Misty was buried had grown over.

I walked into the garage. It still smelled like oil and grease and dust. All the boxes were neatly packed and stacked and labelled. There was something pinned to the white sheet covering the Black Shadow. I walked over. It was a note from Vic.

Sam
Call this number. Ask for Len. He will know what to
do. It has all been sorted.
Vic

I read the note over and over. He had never mentioned anybody called Len before. I sat there for a long time, then I called the number at the bottom of the page.

'Yeah, hello?'

'Um, is this Len?'

'Speaking, yes. Who's this?'

He was loud and he sounded old.

'My name is Sam. I'm calling because of Vic.'

Len went quiet.

'Are you there?' I asked.

'Yeah. Sorry. Christ. Poor bastard. When did he go?'

'A few days ago.'

I heard Len sigh.

'He said he didn't have much left in the tank, but I didn't think it would be this soon, stubborn as he was.'

'Did you know him well?'

'We bumped into each other over the years. Every time I'd ask him the same question, and every time he'd say, *Over my dead body, Len.* I didn't realise he was making a promise.'

'Vic left me a note. I don't know what any of it means.'

'You're the kid. He said you'd be in touch.'

'About what?'

'About when I can come pick her up.'

'Who?'

'*Who?* The bike.'

'What bike?'

'The Black Shadow.'

'Oh.'

356

'I'm a collector. Len Oakes. Got a rare and vintage motor-cycle museum up in the hills near Roleystone. It's all been organised.'

The line was silent. I had no idea what he was talking about.

'Tell you what,' said Len. 'What are you up to this arvo?'

~

Len arrived two hours later. He drove a big four-wheel drive with a trailer attached. He was really short and he walked duck-footed. When he shook my hand his skin felt cold and papery.

I opened the garage door and led him over to the Black Shadow. He gently tugged at the white sheet, then stopped and turned to me.

'May I?'

I nodded.

He delicately removed the sheet and stepped back. He looked at it for a while.

'Bloody hell, she's beautiful. To someone like me, this is like . . . like buried treasure. It's the holy grail.'

He crouched down and his knees cracked. He ran his fingers over the chassis and the engine.

'Amazing. Not a spot of rust. It's in better nick than he said.'

'It still runs good too,' I said. 'I helped tune it.'

'Is that right? Can I start her up?'

'Sure.'

It was strange that he kept asking my permission. I had to remind myself that Vic had left all his possessions to me.

The bike started on the first kick. Len started to laugh and shake his head. He had big white false teeth.

'Listen to that!' he said.

He gave it a few revs, and he inspected the bike closely while it was running. Then he switched it off and put his hands on his hips and shook his head again.

'I've been trying to get a look at this bike for thirty years. First heard about it way back when Vic had the shop with Ray. He reconned some motors for a few boys in the bike club, and he happened to mention he had a fifty-three Black Shadow, but nobody ever saw him on it. He wasn't much for the group rides or the community aspect, old Vic. Kept to himself. Just his nature, I suppose. Very humble. Made sense he kept it under a dust sheet all these years. But me? I reckon a machine like this should be on display. Celebrated. I gave up hope of ever getting it, though. Then he gave me a call a couple weeks ago, from his lawyer's office. Told me he'd promised his old man that he would never get rid of the bike, not for love nor money, and he intended to honour that to the grave. But he said when his time was up, a young bloke would give me a call, and I should be the one to have it.'

'It's going to a museum?'

'Fancy name for a big shed full of bikes, but that's the gist of it. We get a few thousand coming through every year, from all over the world. As I say, for people who share the passion, it's like a pilgrimage.'

'You want to take it away now?'

'Well, if it's all the same to you. I'm a bit giddy, truth be told.'

I hooked my finger around the brake lever. I wasn't ready to let it go. It felt like losing Vic again.

'Listen,' said Len, 'why don't you come up and see the place? We'll take the bike with us, but if you're not happy to leave it with me, I'll bring it back and we can arrange another time. I know he was your mate.'

'Right now?'

'Yeah, it's only forty-odd minutes away in the hills. What do you reckon?'

~

I helped Len push the Black Shadow onto his trailer. He was careful about strapping it down. I liked that he was gentle with the bike. It made me feel a bit better. But when I locked up the house and the garage door and saw the Black Shadow on the trailer, it felt like we were taking Vic away in an ambulance again. I turned around and pinched my arm hard so that I didn't cry in front of Len.

Len talked most of the way. He used to be a mining engineer until he retired about fifteen years ago. He hated the cold, so every winter he travelled to the northern hemisphere and went on motorcycle expeditions. He had been to Africa and America and Asia and across Russia. He said he had been robbed and beat up and arrested, but the hardest part was leaving his bike behind at the end of every trip.

'Too expensive to freight them back, but it's tough to let them go. You get an attachment to them. They're more than machines. It's like losing a mate,' he said.

I mostly looked out the window. Len had been all over the world, but this was the first time I had ever seen the countryside. I stared up at the trees in the forest. We drove past orchards and vineyards and huge paddocks with horses and cows and sheep.

We turned off the highway after a while and went down some narrow roads. There were no other cars around. Finally we turned onto a long gravel driveway and parked outside a country house. There was a big shed to the side of it, with a painted sign that said VINTAGE MOTORCYCLE MUSEUM.

I helped Len unhook the Black Shadow and we rolled it towards the shed. He put a key into a padlock and slid the door open. Then he stepped in and disabled an alarm before switching on the lights.

There must have been a hundred old motorcycles in there, all clean and polished and standing in neat rows. It was impressive. I walked down the carpeted path. Each bike had a small sign with its make and model and year.

'What do you reckon?' Len asked.

'Where would the Black Shadow go?'

'Dunno. Why don't you pick a spot?'

I walked around for a while. I chose a space near the far wall that was well lit.

'Here,' I said.

Len wheeled the Black Shadow over. I told him about Vic's dad, and how he bought the bike after betting on a horse called Raconteur. I told him how angry Vic's mum was about it. I told him that Vic's dad took him for rides and showed him how the engine worked, and that's why Vic became a mechanic. Len liked the story so much that I had an idea.

'Would I be allowed to make a display about Vic and the Black Shadow? I have a photo of him and his dad next to the bike on the day he bought it, and a photo of Vic and Edie on the bike together. I could make it about Vic and his life and Edie's too. We could put it in a frame maybe and hang it up right here, so people can read about him when they visit.'

'That's a ripper idea. I'd be proud to.'

'I could give you Vic and Edie's helmets as well. Maybe we can put them next to the bike.'

Len smiled at me and nodded.

'Sure.'

I smiled back.

'Can I ask for one more thing?'

~

The helmet Len gave me didn't fit as snug as Edie's, and Len's waist was thicker than Vic's, so it didn't feel the same being on the back of the Black Shadow again, but I still liked it.

Len rode so fast that when I closed my eyes it felt like we were flying, like we had no weight at all. I held him tightly when we leaned into corners and felt protected from the wind. I pretended I was holding Vic and my throat swelled up and my eyes got blurry. When we went over the crests of hills my stomach jumped up to my chest. We were going really fast, but I wanted to go even faster. We climbed high enough in the hills to see the sun setting over the city in the distance.

I thought about tipping the bike. I thought about jumping off. I thought about grabbing the handlebars and pulling us into the cars coming the other way. It would be done. I wouldn't even feel it.

But I also thought about Vic's first ride on this bike with his dad, and I thought about his last-ever ride with me. I thought about Vic and Edie and how kind they were. I thought about Aggie and Peter and Diane, and I held on tighter to Len.

~

When we got back, Len took his helmet off and made a whooping noise.

'How about that, eh?'

He told me to wander around and look at the bikes while he went into his office, which was a small room inside the shed. Ten minutes later, he whistled and waved me over. I went in and sat down.

'So you're happy to leave the bike here with me?' he asked.

I nodded.

'Fantastic. So, first things first. I'm going to get you to sign this.'

He pushed a piece of paper across the desk. I wrote my name down where he tapped his finger.

Then he opened a small, thin pad. He wrote on it, and signed it, and tore off a piece of paper. He gave it to me.

'What's this?'

'It's a cheque.'

'What's a cheque?'

'What's a *cheque*?'

'Yeah.'

'You don't know what a . . . ? Never mind. It's a method of payment. It's yours. You take it to a bank, and they put that amount written there into your account.'

'Why are you giving it to me?'

'To purchase the Black Shadow. You just signed the bill of sale. Now, Vic and I both agreed on a figure, but the bike is in much better condition than he indicated. Out of respect to him and yourself, I've increased the purchase price by about fifteen per cent. I hope you see that as a gesture of good faith, and I hope you can see that the bike is going to be well housed under this roof.'

I looked down at the cheque. It had my name and a number written on it.

It was a hundred and thirty-five thousand dollars.

I stared at it.

'This can't be right.'

'Look, I believe it's a fair figure. But I'm prepared to suspend the sale and get the bike independently appraised at my cost.'

'I thought Vic was giving it to you.'

'No mate.'

'It's too much.'

'It's a very rare item. There aren't many around anymore. It's a lot of money. It can set you up for life, if you're smart with it. Make sure it goes towards something important.'

My heart was beating fast. It was hard to think. Len stood up.

'Put that in your pocket. Don't lose it. I'll give you a lift back home. And listen, anytime you want to come visit and see the bike or go out for a ride, you're always welcome, alright?'

I tried to say thank you but no sound came out.

~

It was dark when Len pulled into Vic's driveway. He shook my hand.

'It was nice to meet you, Sam. Give me a bell when you've got your display ready and I'll get it framed up for you.'

I got out and waved as he drove off.

Mrs Boyd's security lights came on as she walked outside. When I looked in her direction she called out to me.

'Sam! Sam?'

I ignored her and put my head down and walked towards the house. The cheque was in my pocket, and I was afraid she was going to take it off me. I thought she might accuse me of somehow tricking Vic into putting me in his will, and would call the police again.

I put the key in the door, but it was already unlocked.

I guessed Peter must have come home and let himself in, but when I switched the light on in the lounge room, I knew something was wrong. The house had been ransacked. All of Edie's collectables and framed photos had been thrown from the cabinets. The television had been pushed over.

I went into the kitchen. The drawers and cupboards were open, and plates and bowls had been smashed.

I walked slowly down the hall, turning on more lights as I went.

It was the same in Vic's spare room. His bed had been tipped over and my bag of clothes was ripped open.

The door to Vic and Edie's room was open, and I had a horrible feeling in my stomach. I didn't want to go in there, but I couldn't stop myself. I switched on the light and stepped inside.

Edie's wardrobe had been emptied out. Some dresses had been ripped. They were all over the floor and piled on the bed. The suitcases with her diaries had been opened and they were scattered everywhere. Her vanity table mirror was shattered. Her perfumes and cosmetics were all over the floor, and the drawers were removed.

The ruined gold flapper dress I wore to The Gavel was crumpled in front of me. I knelt down to pick it up. Then suddenly I was grabbed from behind and lifted off my feet and held in a headlock. I kicked my feet and struggled against the arm locked against my throat.

'So this is where you've been hiding with that old queen, hey? You suck his dick in here? Where is he now?'

It was Steve's voice.

He spun me around and pushed me down on the bed. He pulled my wrist back and the pain shot right up my arm and I screamed. He put his hand over my mouth. He was wearing latex gloves.

'Shut the *fuck* up. You have fucked up my *life*. First moment I met you I knew something wasn't right. You're a cancer that needs to get cut out.'

He took his hand off my mouth and pinned my shoulders down. He smelled like beer and sweat.

'What did you tell them? I need to know every fucking detail. Did you tell them about anything else? Do you understand who my cousin Gavin runs with? Who those guns belong to? Do you realise who you're fucking with? What did you tell them? And don't you fucking lie to me. I know it was you.'

'It wasn't.'

He slapped me.

'I said don't lie to me. What did you tell them? Did you talk about Whippy? You must have, because he's fucked off and nobody's heard from him. Did you rat on him too? Hey?'

'I didn't say anything to anyone.'

Steve put his hand around my throat and squeezed hard.

'You think anyone's going to fucking care that you're gone? You think anyone would even fucking notice? Except your old queen here. He'd be the only one. Let me tell you, Sarah would be fucking *relieved*. She doesn't want you. She never did. Your own mother. What do you say about that?'

He loosened his grip and I got a breath in.

'Do it,' I whispered. 'Do it. I hate you.'

He shook his head and tightened his grip again.

'You fucked my life. You fucked up my *life*.'

'Do it,' I mouthed at him.

There were bright sparks in my vision. And there was a thumping sound in my head. It was fast and loud. It went away for a few seconds, then it started again, even louder.

Steve let me go and stood up straight. He turned around. The banging in my head kept going. I sucked in air and it made me cough. Steve held his finger over his lips. He switched off the light. Then I realised the banging wasn't in my head. It was someone knocking on the front door.

'Help!' I tried to yell, but no sound came out. I tried to run past Steve. The room was spinning. He caught me in the hallway and held me down.

'No! *No!*' My voice was coming back.

The knocking kept going. Steve pushed my face down into the carpet.

I heard the doorhandle turn and the door creaked open. A woman's voice called out.

'Hello? Sam?'

I felt Steve let me go. When I looked up I couldn't see him anywhere.

'Sam?'

I got to my feet and made my way down the hallway with my hands on the wall to steady myself. I heard the back door sliding shut.

Standing in the front doorway was Mrs Boyd.

'Are you alright?'

I didn't answer. I just tried to stay upright.

'What's going on? Why is your face so red?'

I just shook my head.

She tried to look over my shoulder, then she focused back on me.

'Sorry to barge in. You should keep this door locked. We haven't met properly. I'm Beverley Boyd. I know who you are. And I've met your friend Peter. He's told me all about you. Look, I know I'm a bit of a busybody, but I like to keep an eye on things. So I wanted to let you know I've seen someone sniffing around the house here earlier. He came driving past a few times, then he got out and had a look around. Big fellow. I've got his licence plate, and I took some video on my phone. Anyway, I didn't want to scare you, I just wanted to make sure you were alright and not in any trouble, that's all.'

I let go of the wall. My legs were wobbly. I threw myself forwards and I hugged her.

It took her a few moments, but she hugged me back, and we stayed like that for a long time.

~

I was tempted to call Peter and ask him to come straight over, but I didn't want to bother him or frighten him or put him in any danger. I didn't want him to try to fix things or call the police either. I thought about going to Aggie's house and sleeping there, or even hiding in her backyard. Instead, I locked every door and turned on every light.

I spent the night cleaning up. I picked up the broken bowls and glasses and plates in the kitchen and swept the floors. I reorganised the drawers. I lifted the television back upright and returned things to the cabinets. I found some superglue and tried to repair Edie's bone china teacups.

It was late and I was tired, but I finally got to Vic and Edie's room. I couldn't leave it looking like that. I apologised to them both. I hung up Edie's clothes and arranged them by colour. I packed away her diaries in order, then I put everything back on her vanity table. I promised Edie I would fix the mirror. I folded Vic's clothes and put them back in the drawers. Lastly, I made the bed, then I took the cheque out of my pocket and hid it inside a pillow slip.

There was still a lot of cleaning and tidying to do, but I couldn't keep my eyes open anymore. I took the tartan blanket from Vic's bed and a sharp knife from the kitchen and I went into the garage. All the boxes had been pushed over and Vic's careful sorting had been ruined. At least the Black Shadow was safe. That made me feel a bit better.

I crawled into the back seat of the Kingswood and locked all the doors. It still smelled pretty bad in there. I curled up underneath the blanket and I thought about Julia Child until I fell asleep.

~

On Monday I caught the bus to see Diane.

I already knew what I was going to cook. I wanted to make her an apricot tarte Tatin, because I remembered her saying that she liked apricots and they were in season. I had a bag with all the ingredients.

But when I got to her house, Diane didn't take me to the kitchen. Instead we went into her office. I thought I had done something wrong, or she had just been polite about my cooking.

369

Then I worried that she was going to send me home because she couldn't help me, so when I sat down, I pinched the skin on my wrist and told myself that I didn't care.

She sat and smoothed her black skirt over her knees. She didn't ask if I wanted tea or water, and Brick didn't come in and sit beside me.

'Sam, I've done some thinking over the weekend. I know this has often been difficult, and you've done such a great job opening up to me.'

'But you don't want me to come over anymore?'

'Why would you think that?'

'Because we're in here today, and you're being really serious.'

Diane smiled.

'No. I'd very much like to continue seeing you. We're in the office today because I thought I might change the dynamic. I'd like to tell you a little bit about myself, about who I am and where I've come from. It's not something I often do, but I wonder if it might help us to understand each other better. Would that be okay?'

'Yes.'

'Okay, good.'

Diane took a deep breath.

'Well. My name is Diane, as you know. I grew up in the suburbs. My dad was an electrician and my mum was a part-time hairdresser. I'm the youngest of three kids. My two brothers were very rambunctious, so when I was little I spent most of my time with the twin girls who lived next door. As soon as I got to their house I would run into their bedroom and dress up in their clothes and put ribbons and barrettes in my hair. We choreographed dance routines and practised gymnastics and staged elaborate melodramas with their Barbies and plush toys. We indulged our obsession with *The Little Mermaid* by watching it on video every lunchtime. I refused to put my own clothes back on when I went home. Eventually both sets of parents just gave up and let me wear whatever I liked, and I wore their skirts and dresses every day. My mum wasn't precious. I was her third child, so she was beyond concern at that stage. However, it did become a problem when it was time to start school.'

'Why?'

Diane looked at me. She didn't say anything, and her expression didn't change. She let me work it out. I got a tingly feeling on the back of my neck. I had to put my hands together to stop them from shaking.

'You were in the wrong body,' I said.

She didn't nod, but she didn't shake her head either.

'School was very confusing and difficult. Suddenly I was under pressure to perform a role that wasn't natural for me. I was forever recalibrating, but failing over and over to make the adjustments that everyone else seemed to want me to make. I was bullied by boys, which further lessened my desire to be one. I gravitated towards the girls, but their parents often didn't approve, so it made me very wary of forming any relationships. I persistently reinvented myself, trying to find the right way to fit in. By the time I was your age, my identity was so scrambled, and my relationship with my own body was so full of disappointment and anguish and revulsion, that I had no idea who I was.

'However, I *did* make the choice to stop trying to accommodate everybody, and I went hard in the other direction. I became angry and contemptuous, and I deliberately provoked people. Sometimes this was an expression of my frustration, but subconsciously I was also stripping away the layers of lies that I had wrapped around my own truth. I went through a stage of questionable androgynous fashion, with lots of black clothing, ripped stockings, knee-high boots, goth make-up, big dyed hair, leather collars . . . you get the idea. I paired this with a brooding, snide cynicism and a resentment aimed at anyone who was happy and normal. I was on a strict diet of existential philosophers and very loud, very bad music. I was a smart kid, but I played dumb. I was mouthy and bitchy, so I ended up with nobody in my corner, which made me even more isolated and unhappy, and that just added fuel to my shame and self-loathing. By the time I staggered into my twenties, I was more hopeless and lost than ever. See, Sam, sometimes we don't quite know what's wrong, all we have are the feelings. We either lash out and express them in abstract ways, or we deny them or try to dull them. Either way, the root cause just swells inside us until it becomes unbearable. And that's what happened to me. I didn't see any way out.

'So almost ten years ago, on Christmas Day, which was always a complicated time for me, I swallowed a whole box of ibuprofen and half a bottle of crème de menthe. I woke up in a hospital feeling like my insides had been scraped out, which, in some respects, they had. When I was discharged, I was sent to a counsellor, and not for the first time. But this one was different.

She was firm and fair and intelligent and very perceptive. She guided me back in time, and she helped me to reconnect with the small child whose pure desire was to dance and wear pretty dresses and live as a girl. We unravelled my behaviours. All my disordered thinking, my self-medicating, my repression, my disgust. The way I had treated myself was completely demystified. Everything finally made *sense*. She helped me overcome my shame, and she helped me reunite with the person I had been forced to conceal. She encouraged me to let her out. It was as though I had permission to be myself.

'And from the very lowest rung, I began to rebuild. It wasn't easy. It was a slow, incremental process, and it took a lot of courage. There was a lot of falling and getting back up. But things got better, Sam. I began transitioning. I don't think it's correct to say my body is *wrong*, but hormone therapy and surgery has brought me closer to who I am. And as my body started to change, so did my opinion of it. I discarded the name that never represented me, and I chose one that fit. Best of all, I discovered all the other parts of who I am, like my vocational purpose. I wanted to dedicate myself to helping people who feel lost and trapped in their own dark place. I want to help them find their words, to find their strength, to find their value, and to help give themselves permission to live as who they really are.'

I sat on my hands. I looked at Diane for a long time. I was so stunned that I couldn't move. I couldn't believe where she had come from. There were so many parts of my story in hers. It made me feel less alone.

I opened my mouth and closed it again.

Then I told the truth.

'When I was little, I used to watch my mum get ready in front of the bathroom mirror. I remember exactly how she put her make-up on and how she styled her hair and how she chose earrings to go with her outfit. And it always felt normal for me to be just like her. I wore my hair really long. I used to dress up in her clothes all the time. I honestly thought that when I grew up I would look as beautiful as she did.'

That made Diane smile. I kept going.

'When I got older I wasn't allowed to dress up anymore, so I did it in secret. By then I knew I wasn't going to be anything like my mum when I was older. And it was really confusing, because it was still what I wanted. It was how I saw myself. Then, a couple of years ago, I found out why I felt so different to everybody else. And it was the best thing and the worst thing, because I finally knew what was wrong, and that I wasn't the only person in the world who was like this, but there was no way for me to fix it.'

'Why do you say that?'

'I have this nightmare, the same one every time. I'm on a train and I realise that it's going the wrong way. I stand up, and I'm panicking, but none of the other passengers will listen to me and the buttons won't work and there's no way I can get off. The train just goes faster and faster and gets further away from where I need to be.'

Diane leaned across and she put her hand on my knee.

'Sam, how about we stop the train?'

'We can't.'

'Yes we can. I'm here. I'm listening to you. And I can help.'

'You're really nice. But you can't help me.'

'I believe I can.'

'How?'

'Well, the first thing we might discuss is stage one treatment, which involves puberty blockers. This will inhibit the development of your body, and give you time to make determinations about your identity. There are further treatment options going ahead, but for now, we can try to prevent the nightmares.'

'You can do that?'

'Yes.'

'Right now?'

'Relatively soon, yes.'

I thought about it. My heart was beating fast.

'Okay. How do I get the blockers?'

'I will make an appointment for you to see an endocrinologist, and I'll refer you to a GP who I know very well.'

'Okay.'

'They will give you information about how the inhibitors work and what changes you can expect, so both you and your mother will better understand the process.'

My heart stopped.

'My mother?'

'That's right. Along with the necessary consultations, a precondition for receiving stage one treatment is the permission of your parent or a guardian.'

'Why?'

'Your mother will need to give her formal consent.'

'But it's for me. It's *my* body.'

'I know. But you're under eighteen, Sam.'

'Can't you just do it?'

'Do what?'

'Tell them I can have the blockers.'

'I'm afraid not. The pathway is quite rigid.'

'What happens if I don't get her permission?'

'If that's the case, then we'll petition a court for authorisation.'

'What do you mean? Like a judge?'

'That's right. A magistrate would review your case and make an assessment.'

I shook my head.

'But it's for *me*. I want to do it. Why do they get to decide?'

'It's how the law works, I'm afraid.'

'It isn't fair,' I said.

I was angry and frustrated. For some reason, I thought about Vic having to go to war. I thought about the Dungeon Master in Aggie's game, how the players couldn't decide the rules, they could only roll the dice.

But I couldn't even sit at the table. I had no chance. My mum never wanted to see me again. I couldn't invite her to see a doctor with me, I couldn't expect her to understand me the way Diane did.

The train was never going to stop. And I couldn't stay on it any longer.

Honeybee

S am Watson died four months later.

I missed Vic a lot. I had a headstone made for his grave, and I visited it every week. I brought fresh flowers from the garden and I sat and talked to him and Edie.

I missed my mum most of all. I thought about what I could do to make her forgive me. I made plans to give her all the money from the Black Shadow. I thought about how to give her Vic and Edie's house. But it wouldn't ever be enough. She was gone. She wasn't coming back, just like Vic wasn't coming back.

And that meant I wasn't going to get treatment.

Every day I found something new about my body that I dreaded. My shoulders looked wider. My jaw was too square. My eyebrows were too thick. There were hairs starting to grow on my face. There was a lump in my throat. My voice was changing. The longer I stared, the uglier and older I became. The man in the mirror was my enemy. And he was going to kill me.

Diane knew I was hurting.

'I wish I could, but I can't cure your sorrow,' she said. 'Grief is a beast that swallows us whole. All we can do is suffer and endure it until we're mercifully excreted out the back end. But it's important to remind ourselves that whether it's a bereavement or a break-up, we don't get to grieve without first having loved. It's the price we pay for our lives being blessed by something that mattered. The best we can hope for is that grief devastates us less and less over time, the same way we immunise our bodies against an illness. The next time we're exposed to it, the symptoms aren't as severe or as protracted. But we can't ever inoculate ourselves. Grief will always return, often when it's least convenient. All we can do in the meantime is address the things that we can control.'

'But I can't control anything,' I said.

I saw Diane almost every day. She had to fit me around her regular patient schedule, which meant I usually came over in the early evening. We went back to the kitchen and talked while I cooked her dinner. It was just how I always imagined being with Julia Child, except I was preparing the food and showing Diane how to cook.

Diane was really good at listening, and she always seemed interested in what I had to say. I was comfortable around her now. She told me I should feel welcome to wear whatever I liked when I saw her. The next day I brought over a plastic bag with a sleeveless navy A-line dress of Edie's and some white plimsolls.

I got changed in her office, and when I came out, Diane didn't make a fuss or treat me any differently, she just spoke to me like it was a normal thing to do.

I started dressing up at home again. Peter still came to stay a few nights a week, and he *did* make a fuss. He helped me with my make-up and showed me how to be more subtle with my contouring and layering. He brought over a couple of wigs, and I wore them in the house until my hair was long enough to style with a comb again.

Diane challenged me to face my fears about being seen. Together, we took Brick for walks around her neighbourhood after dinner. At first I walked behind her, but soon I was stepping side by side. We went up and down the main street of Mount Lawley together, then one night we went into a cafe. It was loud and busy, and I got spooked. I grabbed Diane's arm and asked if we could leave. Diane wasn't disappointed in me, but I wanted to make her proud, so we tried again the next day. We sat in the cafe and shared a pot of rose tea.

I built up the courage to go outside on my own. One evening I took the bins out to the kerb wearing a peach wraparound dress. Then, after midnight, I went back outside and walked around the block. I carried the figurine that Aggie gave me in my left hand. I was still scared, but it was exhilarating. When I got back inside, I immediately wanted to go out again.

Then one Sunday at twilight I put on a cute blue floral sun dress and a pair of sandals and I combed a side part into my hair and I walked down the street. A neighbour across the road was washing his car. He stared at me, but I didn't stop.

I knocked on the door of the Meemeduma house. I was shaking as I waited.

Dylan answered. He looked disappointed.

'Oh, hey. I thought you were the pizza guy.'

Then he walked away and left the door open.

I found Aggie in the lounge room watching *Game of Thrones*. She looked at me and frowned, then she stood up and ran on the spot and screamed with her hands pressed to her cheeks.

'You are fucking *adorable*! Oh my *God*!'

She came over and hugged me. Then she took my hand.

'Okay, so we *need* to talk about this.'

She led me quickly through the house, past her parents, who were playing backgammon on the dining room table, and into her room. She closed the door.

I told her everything. I told her about dressing up, I told her about stealing clothes, I told her about my body and how I felt about it, I told her about how confused and sad I had been. I told her about Diane and how she was helping me.

I told her who I really was.

When I was finished, Aggie was quiet for the longest period of time since I had met her. I started to worry.

'What's wrong?' I asked.

She shook her head.

'It's just, like, suddenly you make so much sense to me. Everything fits. Like, if I look at you through this paradigm, it's all just so clear to me. It's all in focus. Like, I *know* who you are now.'

'Is that good?'

'Of *course* it's good. I've always wanted a sister! The only problem is you're going to need to eat a fucking tonne of brownies if you want to borrow my clothes.'

I smiled. Aggie clapped her hands together like she had an idea.

'Oh! And the best part is that you qualify for the all-girl D&D league I just started.'

'Really?'

'Yeah, I think we can fit you in.'

'How many of you are there?'

'Technically? Two. But we've literally just doubled our membership in the last minute, so we're growing pretty fast.'

∽

Peter took me into the city to shop for new clothes. He told me Edie's clothes were beautiful, but I should explore my personal style and have clothes of my own.

Aggie came along too. I wore blue jeans and a white t-shirt with the sleeves rolled up and I tied one of Vic's red handkerchiefs into a headscarf. I had a little bit of foundation on too.

The first store we went into was called Valourie, and it was a high-end boutique. I followed Peter and Aggie. We were the only customers in there. I was shy and nervous. Compared to all the times I had entered shops to steal clothes, it was more frightening to go in with money to buy them.

The girl behind the counter had angled bangs and heavy rust eyeshadow and she gave us a snobby look. She sounded bored when she asked if Aggie wanted any help.

'Not unless you stock cheap oversized black t-shirts for short chubby brown girls,' Aggie said.

Peter put his hand on my shoulder.

'Actually, we're shopping for this young lady here. But you look really busy, sweetie. We'll give you a shout if we need you.'

The girl gave us a strange look, and I blushed and looked away. I was glad Peter and Aggie were with me. It felt like Fella Bitzgerald was there too. Peter was loud and funny. He quickly pulled dresses and tops and skirts off the shelves and piled them into my arms and tried to make me laugh.

I went into the change room. I took off my clothes and looked at my body in the mirror and felt really disheartened. I tried on a black baby-doll dress. It was beautiful and it fit nicely, but I still hated looking at myself. I could hear Aggie and Peter talking while they waited for me. They seemed to like each other. They were speaking really fast about jazz and big band and swing music. Aggie told Peter that she played the euphonium.

'The what?'

'Euphonium.'

'What in gracious is that? It sounds like a Russian nerve agent.'

'It's a brass instrument.'

I don't know where it came from, but I called out from behind the curtain.

'It's naht a tuba! It's *naht*!'

Aggie started laughing and snorting so loudly that the shop assistant came over.

'Okay, so, like, I'm actually going to have to ask you all to leave, because you're being super disrespectful right now. So, like, yeah.'

Everything went quiet, then I heard Aggie whisper.

'Oh my *God*! Sam! I just got us kicked out. I'm so sorry.'

I opened the curtain. Peter and Aggie saw me and they both stood up and screamed.

'You are giving me *life*!' Peter said. 'Give me a twirl, girl!'

I blushed and shook my head and closed the curtain because I was embarrassed, and I heard the shop assistant asking us to leave again.

I smiled at myself in the mirror before I took the dress off.

We went to a dozen different stores, and every time I stepped out of the change room, Peter and Aggie were really nice and supportive.

When I got home I laid out all the clothes I had bought on the bed. It cost over four hundred dollars. I had never spent that much money in my life, and it made me feel a bit queasy. I didn't regret it, though. It was exciting to have my own pretty clothes that I didn't have to hide in a bag or feel guilty about.

∽

The next afternoon, I put on my new Breton striped t-shirt dress and cinched the waist with a brown leather belt, and I went out to shop for groceries on my own. I carried a small handbag of Edie's. I wore a big pair of sunglasses and lots of make-up.

At the store I grabbed a basket and glanced around to see if anyone was staring or laughing, but nobody seemed to notice me. I quickly went up and down the aisles, and after a while I could breathe. I took off the sunglasses so I could see what I was shopping for. I filled the basket and carried it to the checkout and I paid with my new bank card. I was shocked at how normal it felt.

I carried the bags back to Aggie's house and she let me in. We were surprising her dad with a Sri Lankan meal, and Aggie wanted to help me prepare it. I got her to peel the potatoes. It took her a long time.

We talked about Peter, and how caring and kind he had been to me. I told her about his beautiful voice, and how fearless he was when he performed. Aggie said she wished her school band performed with a vocalist.

I stopped what I was doing. I had been trying to think of something nice I could do for him, and I had an idea.

'What if you did perform with him?' I asked.

'With Peter?'

'Yeah. Maybe not like a concert. But what if it was in a studio? He could perform as Fella Bitzgerald, and your band could play, and they could record it.'

Aggie's face lit up.

'That would be *amazing*. I don't know about the whole band, like, it's pretty big, but I know at least six of us would find that so fun. I don't know about a studio, though. They're super expensive.'

'That's okay. I'll pay for it.'

'Seriously?'

'Yeah.'

'Oh my goodness, that's so exciting! We'll rehearse some old jazz standards and we can surprise him.'

'Do you think we could really do that?' I asked.

'Totally!'

I smiled and sautéed some onions and garlic with some dry spices while Aggie kept peeling. Then I browned some chicken, and I added some stock and some coconut milk and turned the heat down.

When I turned around, Aggie had stopped peeling.

'Hey,' she said. 'So, since we're on the topic of clandestine acts of benevolence, I kinda have to tell you something.'

'What?'

'You know that school starts soon, right?'

I didn't, but I nodded anyway.

'So, like, what are your plans? I know that school has historically been pretty unpleasant for you.'

'I don't know,' I said.

'Okay. So, look, I should preface this by assuring you that there is zero obligation for you to action this at all, and, you know, something like this should probably have been done with your consultation, but you're aware by now that my parents are complete maniacs, and so they just went ahead and did it.'

'Did what?'

'My mum wants to tell you tonight, but I think it's probably best if I forewarn you, especially if it's not something you're interested in.'

I was suddenly nervous.

'What are you talking about?'

Aggie took a deep breath.

'Okay, so by now you should be well aware that my parents love you vastly more than either of their biological spawn, for very good reason, but sadly that means you are now burdened by them being concerned for your future, which is frankly a considerable weight lifted off *my* shoulders, so thanks. Anyway, my point is, they may have gone ahead and enrolled you at the Perth Culinary Institute and, you know, paid for your tuition and stuff. It's like a technical college where you train to be a certified chef. I think the course is three years, and it's a pretty well-regarded qualification. Also, they may have inadvertently lied on your application and said you were sixteen. I told them that's how old you were, because I knew that was the minimum age to study there.'

I was stunned. I couldn't believe they would do that for me.

'I don't know what to say.'

'I mean, obviously I think you should be teaching there, not studying, but my frame of reference for cooking is pretty narrow. Like, the fact that you can make anything edible from these weird-arse ingredients is a kind of arcane wizardry that I'll never comprehend. And look, if you do go and you hate it, you don't have to stay or anything.'

I turned back to the stove. I felt really overwhelmed.

'Oh, and there's one more thing,' Aggie said. 'It starts like next week.'

~

Diane was excited for me.

'This is brilliant, Sam.'

'It's not.'

'Really? I can so easily imagine you being a chef. Wouldn't you like to have your own restaurant one day?'

I shrugged and felt tingles on my neck.

'I guess.'

'Tell me about it.'

I shook my head. It was the thing I had hoped for my whole life. I couldn't bring myself to say it out loud. I was worried that sharing it might make it more fragile. Like how telling someone your wish after you blew out the candles of a birthday cake meant it wouldn't come true.

'Humour me,' Diane said. 'Let's say you could design your own fantasy restaurant. What would it be like?'

Diane waited patiently while I thought about it. I closed my eyes and put myself there. My restaurant was so different to how I used to imagine it.

'It would be small,' I said.

'Okay, what else?'

'And really cosy. With nice soft lighting and long tables where everybody had to sit together. And it would be called Raconteur.'

'Interesting name.'

I opened my eyes.

'It's after a horse that won at Ascot.'

'I didn't know you liked horseracing.'

'I don't. It's a long story,' I said. 'The menu would be French cuisine. But my signature dish would be lamb roast and vegetables, with a trifle for dessert. And the people who are special to me, like you and Peter and Aggie, could all come and eat for free. And my mum would visit all the time and tell the customers how proud she is.'

'That's very kind of you,' Diane said and smiled.

'And it would have an open kitchen, so I could look out and see all my customers enjoying my food, and they could all see me cooking.'

'I think that's a wonderful and achievable dream.'

I shook my head.

'A dream is all it is.'

'Why do you say that?' she asked.

'Because it won't ever happen.'

'Why not?'

'I can't go to the institute.'

'Why not?'

I started to get frustrated and annoyed. I hated how Diane always made me say what was in my head.

'Because I'm not good enough to be there. They'll kick me out and Mr and Mrs Meemeduma will have wasted all that money and I will have just let them down.'

'Sam, I'm sure that won't—'

I interrupted her.

'No, you can't be sure. You know as much about cooking as they do. I won't be good enough. I won't be able to do it right. I can't go there. Everyone will hate me. It will be just like school again. And I can't go work in a kitchen. Nobody will ever hire me. Nobody will want to work with me. I can't have a restaurant of my own. Strangers won't want to eat my food. Nobody wants to see me cooking in a kitchen. They'll think it's disgusting. And my mum won't ever visit and she definitely won't tell anyone she's proud of me. Forget it. It doesn't matter. I shouldn't have told you about it. Nothing matters. I won't be able to finish the course. I won't be there at the end anyway.'

My fists were balled up so tight my knuckles were white.

'Why do you say that?'

'Why do you keep asking me why? *Why why why*, all the time. Because I'm not good enough, that's why. I already told you. You don't know how hard it is, okay? Nobody knows how hard this is.'

Diane looked at me. She was quiet and thoughtful for a while. She held her hands together like she was praying and pressed them against her lips. I was really embarrassed. I had never spoken to anybody like that, but I was too upset to apologise.

Then Diane shifted forwards in her chair and cleared her throat.

'When we don't think we're worth much, we find ways to make our world small. We don't allow ourselves to hope, because we've already accepted failure. And this pattern of thinking often determines the outcome of our most important choices. But, Sam, I have to tell you that doubt and confidence are *both* acts of faith. They're both predictions of our capabilities. We either tell ourselves that we can or that we can't. And these beliefs are a self-fulfilling prophecy, because we validate our doubts by giving up just as much as we embolden ourselves by refusing to give in. The only way you can break this cycle is to be brave. You have to ignore your doubts and risk failure. You have to try to achieve something that seemed unachievable. This is the best recipe for confidence. And confidence is how we start giving ourselves permission to take up more space in the world, to want more for ourselves, and to feel as though we deserve it. Sam, *I* know that you're a very talented cook, just as I know you will perform brilliantly at the Culinary Institute, but *you* won't know it until you put your fears aside and prove it to yourself.'

It felt like Vic was in the room with us. I thought about what he said just before he died. He told me not to give up, even if I couldn't fix things. I thought about what he had done for me, and I remembered the promise I made to him.

'Okay,' I said. 'I'll go.'

~

I was really nervous on the first day.

The workroom was a large kitchen with rows of island benches, and a long bench up the front with a whiteboard behind it. There were thirty students. I was the youngest by far.

I wore high-waisted blue jeans with a yellow sleeveless t-shirt and a pair of red Converse high-tops. I applied a light foundation and a nude matt lipstick. I had one white hairclip pinning my fringe back. I stood behind the bench right up the back. I tried to be invisible, but I got some strange looks from the older students.

Our teacher was called Chef Bob. He was old and chubby and short and he had red cheeks. He liked to tell bad jokes. The first thing we did was bake a cake. As soon as I started cooking, I knew I would be alright.

I liked the course. Chef Bob taught us food science and history and methods and techniques and how commercial kitchens operated. He did a lot of demonstrations for us on his bench. But my favourite part was when we got to cook.

When we finished a dish, Chef Bob would walk around the room and assess us. He commented on our plating, and then he tasted our food and gave us his opinion. He was hard on people. It seemed like there was always something wrong, except when he came to my bench. He was always complimentary. He spoke loudly and drew attention to me. I wished he wouldn't, because I didn't want the other students to hate me. I made an asparagus soup in the third week, and he made every other student bring a spoon to my bench and taste it. It made me really embarrassed. I was tempted to ruin my meals on purpose, but I couldn't bring myself to waste the ingredients.

I wasn't very good at the written tests or the assignments. All I wanted to do was watch Chef Bob cook and then do it myself.

At the end of the fifth week, Chef Bob made me stay back after everybody had left. He asked me to come over to his bench. He sounded serious, and I thought I was in trouble.

'I want you to make me some scrambled eggs,' he said.

'Now?'

He nodded.

I went into the pantry and collected the ingredients. I whisked two eggs with some cream, then I melted butter in a pan and I stirred the eggs lightly on a low heat. When they were done, I seasoned and plated them and garnished with fresh chives.

Chef Bob looked over the plate, then he tasted the eggs. He took another bite. He took a deep breath and sighed. He looked disappointed. He stared at me for so long that it made me uncomfortable.

'You shouldn't be here,' he said.

It was what I had been waiting for him to say since I had started.

'Is it over-seasoned?' I asked.

He shook his head.

'Let me ask you a question, and I want you to be honest with me. Are you really sixteen years old?'

'No,' I whispered.

'How old are you?'

'Almost fifteen.'

'That's what I thought. Sam, I'm afraid this means you're ineligible to continue studying at the institute. It's a legal and liability issue. If you were to injure yourself on the premises, it would not be good. Rest assured your tuition will be fully refunded, I'll see to that. And there will always be the opportunity for you to further your training . . .'

I didn't hear the rest because my face got hot and my head got noisy. I apologised and quickly walked out of the workroom.

I felt stupid and embarrassed. I knew I shouldn't have got my hopes up. I shouldn't have believed I could be good enough.

Chef Bob called out my name, but I pulled my apron over my head and dropped it and ran so he couldn't see how upset I was.

~

The day after I left the Culinary Institute I started getting calls from numbers I didn't know again. I blocked them straight away. After Steve broke in I had new deadbolts installed on all the doors, and I knew Mrs Boyd would tell me if she saw anyone hanging around, but I was still afraid all the time.

I lay on the couch and watched old movies by myself. I couldn't bring myself to see Aggie and tell her about what happened at the institute. Her parents would be so disappointed. I wished I had never gone. Whenever it seemed things were getting better, it didn't work out and then I felt worse than before.

I slept in the Kingswood whenever Peter wasn't there. I woke up if I heard noises or voices or cars going past, and then I couldn't get back to sleep.

Three days after I left the institute, I was in the kitchen when I saw the shadow of a man pass across the window. I grabbed a knife from the drawer and crouched down. My phone was in another room. I was trapped.

There was a knock on the door. I pressed myself against the wall and I waited. It was quiet for a moment. Then the knocking started again, louder.

I held the knife tight and stayed silent.

'Sam? Hello? Sam?'

I recognised the voice.

I didn't know how he had found me, or why he was here. I hesitated, not sure what to do.

When the knocking didn't stop, I got up and slowly walked down the hall. I took a breath, and opened the front door.

Chef Bob smiled at me.

'There you are! The elusive Sam Watson. Good to see you're still in the kitchen.' He pointed at my hand. I was still holding the knife.

'Oh. Yes,' I said.

'Sorry to arrive unannounced, but I've been trying to call you and couldn't get through.'

'Yeah, my, um, my phone broke.'

'I see. You left quite abruptly the other day, and I had more to say to you.'

'Do I need to give you money?' I asked. 'For the course, I mean.'

'No, no, that's not it.' Chef Bob shook his head. He looked serious.

'Sam, have you heard of Jean-Philippe Vollard?'

'No.'

'He is the owner and head chef at The Blue Goose, one of the finest restaurants in the country. Jean-Philippe is an alumnus of Le Cordon Bleu, and he's worked kitchens in Paris and London and New York. A decade ago, he fell in love with a Western Australian woman and followed her back home, and we've been celebrating his cuisine here ever since. You know, Jean-Philippe came from a very humble background, and just like you he was impatient to start his career. Occasionally he visits us at the institute and runs workshops. He's passionate about inspiring the next generation. He once told me that if I ever had a student with extraordinary potential whom I felt would benefit by learning in a more rigorous atmosphere, he would commit to training them in his restaurant. Sam, I am very impressed by your talent. I've had hundreds of students come through my kitchen, a lot of them very fine cooks, but I see something special in you. What I was going to tell you the other day is that I have recommended you to Jean-Philippe, so you can have the opportunity to learn under him at The Blue Goose. It will be hard work in the beginning, lots of food preparation and general duties, but if you stick with it, the skills and experience you'll gain will be much more valuable than what we offer at the institute. So, what do you say?'

I was shocked. I was having trouble taking it in.

'I don't know,' I said. 'What if he doesn't like me?'

'He will like you just fine, Sam. But it will require maturity and commitment on your part. It's a high honour to be a member of his kitchen staff. Hundreds apply every year.'

'But . . . why me?'

'Because you're a natural talent, and if you want it, you will go far.'

He smiled and handed me a business card.

'Get yourself a new phone, and call this number. I'll be checking in with you too. Good luck!'

I watched him leave. Then I read Jean-Philippe Vollard's business card. It had gold writing and a picture of a blue goose. I scrunched it up in my fist and tossed it into the garden.

~

'Sam, I want you to know that you're doing really well. And I know how hard you're fighting.'

I had been speaking to Diane for over three months. One night, I was really upset and I didn't want to talk. I just sat on the floor with Brick. Diane was sitting across from me with her legs crossed. I knew what she was going to ask, and I dreaded it.

'You missed your appointment again with Dr Russo,' she said gently.

I didn't say anything.

'Do you want to talk about it?'

'Not really.'

'What's been on your mind?'

The Clayton Road overpass had been on my mind. Every time I closed my eyes I imagined myself back there. Standing in the dark. Looking down. It was quiet and I was alone, but then I would hear voices. Peter and Aggie and Diane and Vic. They were searching for me. Calling my name. I felt so guilty and ashamed for letting them down that I didn't want them to find me. So as much as I wanted to climb back over the rail for them, I stayed where I was.

I would hear them getting closer, and this made me so dizzy and anxious that I let go of the rail and leaned forwards. For an instant I had no weight. I was falling. But then somebody grabbed me. I kicked my legs and I was really scared and I looked up and it was my mum holding onto me. I needed her to pull me up. I needed her to save my life. But she didn't. She told me it was time to stop. And then she let me go.

'Sam?'

I shook my head.

'Nothing,' I said.

'Would you like me to schedule another appointment for you?'

'I don't know.'

'Are you having second thoughts about the inhibitors?'

'No. I really want them.'

'Is there a problem with your mum's availability?'

'No. That's not it. It's my fault.'

'Are you sure?'

I nodded.

'You don't like to talk about her.'

I shrugged.

'Are things strained between the two of you?'

'No.'

'Is she aware of the issues you're struggling with?'

'Kind of.'

'Have you talked to her about Dr Russo and your treatment options?'

I shrugged.

'Are you worried she won't support you taking this medication?'

I shrugged again and squirmed.

'When was the last time you spoke with your mother, Sam?'

'I don't know.'

'Was it recently?'

'I don't *know*.'

'Does she know how unhappy you are? What is it you're not telling me, Sam?'

My face was getting hot. I closed my eyes and shook my head. I wouldn't talk about her. It wasn't loyal. I had already betrayed my mum once, and I had lost her. She didn't love me anymore. I was breathing fast. Diane must have sensed that I was getting upset.

'Hey, it's okay,' she said. 'It's okay.'

My hands were shaking. Diane reached out and held them. We sat like that for a long time without talking.

Then she asked a question I had never been asked before.

'Sam, what's your happiest memory?'

~

When I was seven, my school was doing a performance for Environment Week called 'Wonders of Nature'.

Each year group had to do a separate act. My class had been learning about pollination, so our section of the play was a honeybee visiting flowers and collecting nectar and pollen while 'Flight of the Bumblebee' played. One of us would be the honeybee and the rest of the class would dress up as flowers.

Our teacher, Mrs Grayson, asked who would like to be the honeybee. Everyone put their hand up except me.

Mrs Grayson wrote all our names on post-it notes and folded them up and put them into an empty tissue box. Then she shook it and pulled out a name. It was mine.

Everybody groaned and looked at me. They were disappointed and angry. I wanted to tell Mrs Grayson to give the part to somebody else, but I had never won anything before and I wanted to tell my mum.

We were all responsible for our own costumes. Most of the class made theirs at home with their parents on the first night. I asked my mum if she would help me make the honeybee outfit, and she promised she would. But every night that week she went out and left me at home by myself.

We did a dress rehearsal on the day before the performance, and I was the only one without a costume ready. Mrs Grayson was stressed and annoyed, and she told me that if I didn't have an outfit by the next day, the whole class would miss out.

That night, I laid out some of my clothes on the table, along with some scissors and supplies that I had stolen from the art room, ready for my mum to help me. I sat and waited patiently while she talked on the phone in her room. When she came out she was wearing a pretty black dress and said she was leaving for a little while to see a friend. She promised she would help me when she got home.

I started to cry. I knew she wouldn't be home in time. I was angry with her. She didn't understand how important it was, or how much my classmates and their parents were going to hate me if we couldn't perform our act because of me.

She looked at me. I thought she was going to yell, but instead she put her bag down and took off her shoes and she hugged me. She told me she was sorry.

Then she took my measurements. I told her about the play, and what I had to do, and we looked at pictures of bees together. She sketched the costume on the back of an envelope. Her phone rang a few times, and she didn't even answer it.

She went to her room to get her sewing kit. She also went through her wardrobe and collected clothes that were black or yellow.

I gasped when she cut into one of her dresses, but she just smiled. She told me her parents had been really strict about what she wore, so she would go shopping with her mum and buy sensible outfits and then she would secretly alter them later. That's how she learned to sew.

She was really good at it. She worked for hours, but I was still worried that we wouldn't make it in time. I tried to stay awake, but at some point I must have fallen asleep at the table. My mum woke me up the next morning. I was in her bed, and she was holding my costume. She had worked all night to finish it. It looked amazing.

It had a stuffed stinger tail with black velvet and yellow satin stripes. She shaped wings out of wire coathangers and stretched pantyhose over them. There was fur on the shoulders, and a tight black cap covered my head and my neck, with two antennae that stood straight up. There was also a pair of her black wool socks that I could stretch all the way up my legs.

I tried it on. It fit me perfectly.

She was really proud of it. She clapped and took lots of photos of me. Best of all, she promised to come to the performance.

When I got to school, I couldn't wait to show everyone what she had done. Mrs Grayson was impressed and relieved. The other kids were envious.

The performance was held in the school theatre that after-noon. Backstage was busy and loud. Teachers were getting their classes into lines and making last-minute adjustments. I peeked out at the audience and saw my mum finding her seat right up the back. I wanted to wave to her, but Mrs Grayson came to get me.

I was nervous when it was our turn to go on stage. All the flowers went out first and got into position. My job was to quickly run around to each one. They would hand me a furry ball of pollen which I placed in a basket, then I stuck a different-coloured ball of pollen onto their petals.

The music started and I ran out on stage. I had to move really fast in time with the music. I tripped and dropped a couple of balls of pollen, and when I bent to pick them up, the rest rolled out of the basket and I had to pick those up too. I could hear the audience laughing, and I worried they were making fun of me, which made me go even faster. The crowd kept laughing. The whole act took less than three minutes, but it felt like time had stopped. When it was over, everyone cheered really loudly.

I turned around to look for my mum, but the lights were too bright. I waved anyway, and the crowd cheered again. I kept waving. I didn't realise I was the only one left on the stage until Mrs Grayson came to get me. Offstage, she smiled and gave me a big hug and told me I did a good job.

Everybody else got changed, but I kept my costume on. I loved being the Honeybee. People treated me differently. I felt like I could be myself.

After the performance, I found my mum in the car park. She was really happy. She gave me a hug and said I was a star. A few parents came over and said nice things too. I told everybody that my mum had made my costume.

We drove to a shopping centre. I followed my mum into a liquor store, and the lady behind the counter said I looked adorable. I showed her how I had run around collecting pollen, and it made her laugh. When my mum got her change, she gave me the coins. Then she walked me to a doughnut shop and told me to choose whatever I wanted.

I had never had money of my own to spend before. I walked up and down the glass display cabinet, but I was so overwhelmed that I couldn't choose. My mum apologised to the man behind the counter because I was taking so long. I started to panic, worried that I was going to run out of time and miss out.

Then the man smiled at me and held up his finger. I watched him take a plain round jam doughnut out of the display. He put it on the bench behind him and turned his back to us. I looked up at my mum, but she just shrugged.

After a couple of minutes, the man showed me what he had done. He had decorated the doughnut with stripes of caramel and chocolate icing and made it look like a bee. He had even drawn wings with vanilla icing, and stuck on two candy eyes. He put it in a small white box and gave it to me.

'Little friend for you,' he said.

I tried to give him my coins, but he waved me away. I looked at my mum again before I took the box.

'What do you say?'

'Thank you,' I whispered.

I held the box carefully. I was confused. I didn't understand what had just happened. The man nodded and smiled. My mum put her hand on my back.

'Come on, Honeybee,' she said.

The moment she called me that, I started to tear up. I stood at the counter and I couldn't move. Everything had been so nice.

'What's the matter?' my mum asked. 'Why are you upset?'

But I couldn't say.

I stayed in the costume when I got home. I opened the box with the doughnut, but I didn't touch it. I just looked at it.

'Aren't you going to eat it?'

I shook my head.

I buzzed around being the Honeybee, picking up shoes and cushions and pens and keys and putting them down somewhere else while my mum drank wine.

When it got dark, she started to get dressed up. I watched her put on her make-up in the bathroom. I wanted her to stay home with me. She said she would only be an hour or so, but I knew it would be longer.

Her phone rang.

'That's my ride.'

Then she turned her face from side to side and winked at the mirror.

'That'll have to do, kid,' she said.

She slipped into her shoes, picked up her bag and went to the door.

'Wait,' I said. 'Don't go. Stay with me.'

'I won't be long. Couple of hours.'

'Wait.'

'What?'

'Call me Honeybee again.'

'What?'

'I like it when you call me Honeybee. Say, *Goodnight, Honeybee!*'

She smiled and rolled her eyes.

'Say it!'

'Goodnight, Honeybee.'

Then she walked out the door and she didn't come home until the sun was up.

I put on the costume every day after school. I didn't want to stop being the Honeybee. I wanted to wear it to school, but my mum wouldn't allow it. I never ate the doughnut. I just liked opening the box and looking at it. It went bad after a week. When my mum threw it out, I stopped wearing the costume.

It didn't feel as special anymore. We put it in a black plastic bag and my mum kept it in her wardrobe. But she still called me Honeybee, and it always gave me a tingly feeling on my neck.

Then there was the day we had to leave our apartment in a hurry, and my mum left the costume behind. I wanted to go back for it, but she refused. It was gone. And that was when everything started to go really wrong. We moved in with Steve, and she stopped calling me Honeybee.

'Why does this memory mean so much to you?' Diane asked.

'When I was the Honeybee, I felt like she really cared about me and she was proud of me and I was important to her. The first time she called me Honeybee, what I heard was that she loved me.'

～

A week later, I was on my way home from seeing Diane when I got a message.

> Sam I need to talk to you

It was from my mum. My hand shook as the texts came through.

> I know it wasn't you

> I need to see you. I said so many bad things and I regret it.

> I have to see you. I miss you. I need you to forgive me. I'm so sorry.

I felt queasy. I put the phone face down and closed my eyes. It vibrated again. I looked at the screen.

> I thought it was you but I know it wasn't.

> Please text me back.

> I need to make things right with us I miss you so much.

It was so unexpected that I was suspicious. I thought it might be Steve trying to trick me. I wrote back.

> Is this real?

A few seconds later my phone rang. It was her. I silenced the call and waited for it to ring out. Then I messaged.

> I can't talk. I'm on the bus

I waited.

> Ok. Will you come see me?

I started to type a reply, then deleted everything and tried again.

> I don't want to see Steve

She replied straight away.

> Steve isn't here

> He is in jail

> He got 6 months

> I'm on my own again. Its just me here.

> Will you come see me? I will explain everything.
> I miss you. Your my son. I need you in my life

> Please.

I turned my phone off and looked out the window. My heart was beating fast and I was so anxious I wanted to throw up.

When I got home I wandered through all the rooms. I imagined my mum here with me. I imagined giving her the keys. I could have her back and we could be a family and we wouldn't have to move out. I thought about where the baby would sleep, and how I might help to raise it so my mum could live her life and never worry about money.

I turned my phone on.

> I will come see you tomorrow

~

I caught the train there. She wasn't living at the house in Hamilton Hill anymore. She gave me the address of a one-bedroom apartment in Kingsley.

I was nervous. I was wearing a yellow summer dress cinched with a thin black leather belt. I wore some clip-on earrings and I took Edie's big black leather handbag. I had applied some liquid foundation and done some light contouring. I chose a cherry red lipstick.

I didn't feel comfortable. I had changed back into boy clothes ten times before I made myself leave in my new dress.

Before I did, I stared at myself in the mirror.

'Come on, Honeybee.'

∾

I needed to show my mum who I was. I needed to tell her the truth. And I wanted to tell her about all the things I had to look forward to.

I wanted to tell her about my friend Peter. Tonight Aggie and I were surprising him at the recording studio. Aggie had been practising old jazz and swing standards with her bandmates for weeks.

I wanted to tell her about Jean-Philippe Vollard. A week ago I had dug out his business card from the front garden and called him. His accent was hard to understand, but he invited me to work and train at The Blue Goose. I would begin with food preparation during the day, and when I was good enough he would put me on his service team. I would have my first day at the restaurant tomorrow.

I wanted to tell her about Vic and Edie and what they had done for me. Next weekend, Len Oakes was putting on a barbecue for all his club friends to unveil the Black Shadow. There would be over two hundred people there. I had finished writing about Vic and Edie for the wall display, and I was going to read it out for everyone there. It would be the funeral that Vic never had.

I wanted to tell her about Diane. How she grew up and what she went through and the person she was now. I wanted to tell her how similar we were, and how much she meant to me.

Then I had to ask my mum for two things.

～

I stood up when we approached Greenwood Station. The train slowed down and stopped. I pushed the button and the doors opened.

I stepped onto the platform and walked up the ramp and across the railway bridge. Halfway over I stopped to look over the rail at the tracks below.

Then I kept going.

My mum's apartment was on the ground floor of the block. The lock on the security door was broken and the wire mesh was ripped.

I knocked and waited. I looked around.

It was a clear, hot April day.

It was the day that Sam Watson died.

～

My mum opened the door.

She was wearing one of Steve's old grey t-shirts. Her middle was round, like she had a basketball under there. Her hair was oily and flat, and her skin was puffy and blotchy. She had bags under her eyes. She didn't look beautiful anymore.

We stared at each other for a moment.

'I didn't even recognise you,' she said.

'It's me,' I said.

She kept staring. I felt awkward. Then she half smiled and shook her head.

'Sorry, come in.'

I followed her inside. It was dark. There were beach towels covering the windows. The linoleum floor was sticky. It was really hot and hard to breathe. The air seemed thicker somehow.

It was like walking into a dream. I felt like I had been here before. I had grown up in this apartment.

She didn't have any furniture other than a round plastic table and two chairs. There was an ashtray with cigarette butts in it. We sat down. The door to the single bedroom was closed. I don't know why, but it made me uncomfortable.

'If you want a tea or a coffee you got to heat the water in the microwave because the gas isn't connected.'

'It's okay,' I said.

'So you're wearing this stuff all the time now?'

'Yes.'

'It's a pretty dress,' she said. 'Looks expensive.'

'I bought it.'

'You been living with that old man again?'

'No.'

'Good.'

I was starting to sweat.

'Are you here by yourself?' I asked.

'Yeah, I'm on my own again. But there's only one person to blame for that.'

She looked down and picked at her nails. Then she looked up again.

'Sam, I'm sorry. I made a mistake. I said some horrible things. I should have believed you. But I know it wasn't you who tipped off the cops.'

I wanted to feel relieved, but I still wasn't sure.

'Who was it?'

'Whippy.'

My heart was beating really fast. I pretended to be surprised.

'Really?'

She nodded.

'Steve was going to fight his charges in court, so before the trial they sent him the police facts sheet. In the statement it said they acted on information provided by Ricky Wragg. That's Whippy's real name. He was the one. Not you. Steve reckons he must have got picked up and he tried to cut a deal by giving people up.'

'Steve is sure it was him?'

'Yeah. The night Steve got arrested, Dane went straight to Whippy's place to hide out. When he explained what happened, Whippy said it must have been you. He said you threatened to rat on him once. Dane said he was acting really paranoid. Then the day after, Whippy disappeared. Just packed up and cut off his phone and left. At the time, Steve thought he was just being careful, but now he knows why. He's devastated. Whippy was like a brother to him. Steve knew he had no choice but to plead guilty. They gave him six months. Could be out in less though. Mark got eighteen months because he took the gun charge and had prior history.'

'What happened to Dane?'

'They never arrested him. Steve and Mark wouldn't give him up.'

'Where is he now?'

'He's working private security somewhere up north I think. I haven't heard from him.'

'What about Whippy?'

'Dunno.'

That made me uneasy. I remembered how he had threatened me.

'You really don't know?' I asked.

'Wherever he is, he's not stupid enough to come back here.'

'Why?'

'Because he'll get what he's owed.'

'Okay.'

'So now it's just me. I don't have anyone. Except you. Like it always was. Gavin kicked me out of his place, so I'm staying here until Steve gets out. He's got twelve weeks left.'

'Twelve weeks? I thought you said he was in for six months.'

'He went in start of January.'

'Wait. So how long ago did you get the facts sheet?'

She shrugged.

'Couple of months now, I guess.'

The air went out of me and my stomach knotted up. All those weeks I was hurting, I could have had her back.

'Why did it take you so long to tell me?'

She didn't answer.

'You said you didn't want me in your life anymore. I thought I was never going to see you again. I've been on my own. Why did you wait? Why didn't you tell me as soon as you knew?'

She shook her head and looked away. Then she started to cry.

'I'm ashamed, Sam. I'm so sorry. I missed you so much, but I didn't want to face what I said to you. I didn't mean those things. When Steve got locked up I was just afraid of losing everything and I put it all on you. Oh God, I did it to you again: I left you on your own. I've been such a terrible mother.'

'Please don't say that. You always did your best. I made it hard for you. You did a good job.'

'You have to understand, I was so young and I was on my own. People wanted to help me, but I pushed them all away because they made me feel ashamed for having you, and I thought I could do it all by myself. I was a stupid, stubborn kid. I didn't know how hard it would be. I knew it was too much for me. I just wanted to run away from everything. But you can't run away when you have a baby. You can't do it. I tried.'

She gasped and covered her face with her hands.

'Sam, I did some horrible things. I did some horrible things to you.'

'Don't say that. You were always there. Even when we had nothing, we had each other.'

She shook her head. I was just making her cry more.

'You don't get it, Sam, okay? It's not just that I couldn't provide for you. I went to some dark places. I almost killed you. I almost killed my little baby.'

'No you didn't. Don't say that. It's not true.'

I reached across and rubbed her back. She was crying so hard now it made my heart hurt.

'It is. It *is* true! It *is*.'

She tried to suck in air. She couldn't look at me.

'It was so hard. You wouldn't stop crying. You were just a little baby. You would *not* stop. Nothing worked. There was nothing I could do. I didn't know what I was doing wrong. I didn't know what you wanted. Every night, you cried and cried. I tried to comfort you and feed you and soothe you, but you wouldn't *stop*. And I knew I couldn't do it. I just felt all this regret and all this dread. I was out of my depth and I was all on my own. And I hated you. I *hated* you. I thought about giving you up, but then everybody would know I'd failed. Then one night I just snapped. I couldn't do it anymore. Sam, you have to understand, I was young and scared and I was so tired. I was so stressed out. I can't . . .'

She took a deep breath. Then she kept going. She spoke so softly I could hardly hear.

'I got a plastic bag. One of those big green ones. And I put you inside it. I thought I could tell people it was a cot death, you know? I tied it up and I walked out of the apartment and down the stairs and I kept walking. I made it about a block away and suddenly it was so quiet. I couldn't hear you anymore and I realised what I had done. And I turned around and

HONEYBEE

I ran. I ran as fast as I have ever run. I ran even though I knew it was too late. I ran back into the apartment and you weren't crying anymore. And I felt the most awful kind of sickness, I can't even tell you.

'I ran to your cot and I saw that you had torn a little hole in the bag with those tiny fingers. That's how much you wanted to survive. You were so strong. I ripped the bag open and I picked you up and I begged you to be okay. All I wanted was to hear you cry again. I felt your little heart beating. You were alive. But you barely ever made a sound after that. And I always worried that it damaged you somehow, that it did something bad to you. I'm sorry. I'm so sorry. It's my fault. Everything is my fault.'

She put her head down and I watched her sob.

I didn't comfort her. I didn't defend her.

I saw who she was, not who I wanted her to be.

My mum looked up.

'I almost lost you then, but I got you back. And now I almost lost you again. I don't deserve to have you back this time, I know, but I hope you can forgive me. Sam, you're the best thing in my life. You're the only thing I've ever been proud of. Sometimes, when I'm really down, I think to myself that there must be *some* good in me, because I made you. You're a part of me. But you're better. You're *better* than me. You always have been. You should hate me, but you don't. I don't deserve to be loved by you. I've never done enough for you. The way you are, the person you're going to be. You're a miracle. You don't need me anymore. You've outgrown me. But this baby

415

will need me. And I'm going to do better this time. I'm going to *be* better. It's going to be different.'

I looked around. It didn't feel different. It seemed like she was trying to convince herself. She wanted to believe it so badly.

And so did I.

I reached across the table and took her arm.

I didn't let go.

I was hanging over the edge of the rail, and I needed her to save me.

'I *do* need you,' I said. 'I still need you. I need you to be my mum right now. It's important.'

'Really? You still want that?'

She sounded hopeful and grateful.

'Of course I do. You've been my whole world. I always wanted to grow up to be just like you. Did you know that? You were so beautiful and stylish. I wore your clothes all the time.'

'I know. You loved to play dress-ups.'

'But that wasn't dress-ups for me. When I went to school or I had to go outside, *that's* when I was playing dress-ups. That's when I was pretending to be somebody else.'

She leaned back and stared at me. I held onto her. I had to make myself keep going.

'This is hard to say. I'm not . . . comfortable in myself. It's been really confusing and hard and I have hated myself for a really long time and I didn't know why. I'm not happy in my body. I never have been. It isn't who I am inside. And it's getting worse. And I can't do it. I can't be the person that you want me to be. I have to be who I am.'

'What do you mean?'

'I've been talking to somebody, a counsellor. Her name's Diane. There's medicine I can take to stop my body going in the wrong direction. Then later I can take hormones that will help me to live as who I really am and look the way I'd like to look. But I'm not allowed to choose that for myself. I'm too young. You have to come with me to talk to the doctors and say it's okay. And I need to hear you say it too.'

She thought about it for a long time.

'What are you saying? I have a daughter now?'

'No. You *always* did,' I said.

'Are you sure about this? How can you know?'

'Because it's me.' I pointed at my chest. 'This is me.'

She frowned.

'It must be something I did wrong.'

'It has nothing to do with you. And I'm not *wrong*, I'm me. And I don't want to be invisible anymore. I want people to see who I am.'

'Sam, I don't know. I need to think about it.'

'There's no time. If you won't help me, I have to go to a court and ask them.'

And as soon as I said it, I knew that I would. I knew I had the strength to fight for myself. I let her arm go.

'A court?'

'Yes.'

'Fuck that. Fuck them. You're my child.'

'So will you do this for me?' I asked.

She looked at me for a long time. Then she nodded.

'Do you promise?'

She reached over and put her hand over mine.

'Yes. I want you to be who you are.'

'Thank you.'

She smiled and shook her head.

'You're growing up. You're changing. And if this is part of it, then I want to help. You know, I always had this fantasy of going back in time so I could pull myself aside and tell myself not to fuck my life up. You're the closest I get to that. Seeing you, knowing you're not going to make any of the mistakes I made. It's like a second chance.'

I picked up my handbag and put it on my lap.

'There's something else I need to ask you.'

I pulled out a document. And a pen. My hands were shaking.

'I need you to sign this.'

'What is it?'

'It's a form. To register a change of name.'

'You want to change your name?'

'Yes.'

'Change it to what?'

I pointed.

'It's here on the form.'

She read it out.

'Victoria Edith Watson.'

Hearing it out loud made me blush and tear up. It made my back straighten.

'That's me,' I said. 'That's my name.'

'Victoria. It sounds very proper.'

She picked up the pen. But she didn't sign.

'It makes me sad,' she said. 'Can't you still be Sam?'

'No.'

'Why not?'

'Because this is *my* second chance.'

She read the form. I could barely breathe. Then she bent down, and she signed it.

And just like that, Sam Watson was dead.

I had killed him.

'Victoria,' she said. 'Why Victoria?'

'It's a name I want to live up to.'

'*Victoria*. I'll get used to it, I guess.'

'It's still me,' I said. 'It fits me better. It's who I am. And soon I'm going to look like me too.'

She went quiet again.

I got a message. I dug into my bag and checked my phone. It was from Aggie. She was asking about tonight. The band was getting there early to set up and rehearse. I had so much to do. I still had to cook appetisers and a chocolate cherry cake for everyone. I had told Peter to dress up and be ready by seven o'clock, but he didn't know why. I had hired a limousine to collect Fella Bitzgerald and take her to the studio. I couldn't wait to surprise her. I couldn't wait to tell her my name. I felt light-headed. There were electric tingles going down my back.

I stood up and put the form in my bag.

'I have to go.'

'You're leaving already?'

'Yes.'

'Wait. Don't go. Stay with me.'

'I'll come back,' I said.

'I thought you might want to live here too. There's room.'

I shook my head. She grabbed my arm.

'Wait. Don't go yet. I'm on my own. I don't have anyone. I don't have anything.'

She sounded so desperate. It hurt me to hear.

'I'll come around again soon. And I'm going to bring you food and make sure you're eating and help you clean up. I'll get you some furniture and some curtains and a proper bed. I'll get everything delivered. And I'll get your gas connected. I'll get a cot and clothes and all the things you need for the baby too.'

'How? Do you have money?' she asked.

'Don't worry about that. I'll take care of it.'

'You can just give the money to me and I can get all that stuff.'

I knew what she was really saying. I looked down at my mum. She looked so small. I felt sorry for her. And I knew I had to be the strong one.

'No. I'll arrange everything.'

'Okay.'

She nodded and looked down.

'Are you having all your check-ups and scans and all that? I have a friend who is a nurse. He can help.'

'I've delivered a child before.'

'I know. But you don't have to do it all by yourself.'

She started to cry again.

'Don't go. Don't go yet.'

'I have to go meet my friends. But I'll be back again soon.'

I walked towards the door.

'Sam?'

I turned around fast.

'No,' I said. '*Victoria.*'

'Sorry, Victoria. Victoria. Wait. Wait there a second.'

She got to her feet and shuffled slowly towards the bedroom. She opened the door, and I took a step back. But there was nothing in there except a mattress and her clothes. I heard her rummaging through some plastic bags. Then she came back out.

'Look what I found! It turned up when I was unpacking.'

She was holding the honeybee costume.

It looked so small. It was hard to believe I ever fit inside it.

'See?' she said. 'I had it all this time. You thought I left it behind, remember? You loved it so much.'

'I remember.'

She stuffed it back into the plastic bag.

'Here.'

She held it out for me to take, but I shook my head.

'It's okay,' I said. 'You keep it.'

Acknowledgements

Writing is a solitary pursuit, but crafting a novel requires a team. I've been blessed with the assistance and support of many remarkable people:

Firstly, a lifetime of gratitude to my mother, Chris, as strong, kind and considerate a lady as you'll ever encounter.

To Clare, a reliable sounding board for good and bad material; a Captain's compass. Your belief in me will always ring out louder than my doubts.

To the Gang and to the Boys—Sammy Swish, Szabo, Dizzy, Kettle, Ed, Marko, Rizz. To Johnboy and Wan and Foreman Frank. And, of course, to Mac. Frankly, you should all be thanking me, but before you do, you're welcome.

To my biggest fan, Brooke Davis, who is paying $1100 for this acknowledgement. Also you're very talented and beloved, but I didn't say that out loud.

A crisp, clear hoot across the seas to Ali J. Bowden.

Admiration and awe for the glittering firecracker that is Kate Mulvany. Thank you for seeing something in this story when it was an awful play.

Thank you to Johnny Schnitzel. Thank you to my favourite social assassin Genevieve Hegney, and to Matthew F. Moore. You couldn't be closer to my heart.

To Benython—Obrigado, Merci, Danke.

To the astoundingly generous Clare Drysdale and Brad Johnson, who gobbled me at gammon and kept me warm in their Eagle's Nest through the power of puns. I'll never forget your kindness and I miss you both dearly.

Thank you to Willy Vlautin. And to Lesley Thorne: here's to new adventures.

To the infinite graciousness of a man called Clancy, universally admired and adored for very good reason. You're a wise counsellor, an all-weather friend, and a reminder to write boldly, lad, and never fear the spills.

To the incomparable Frances O'Brien, formerly Bald E. Frontbum. Thank you for your guidance, your judgement, your inscrutable eyebrows and your fearsome backhand.

I do not care to speculate on where I would be without Jane Palfreyman. Thank you for your conviction, your courage, your vision, your strength, your wit, your passion, your intelligence, your friendship and your belief. I'm deeply indebted to you.

To the shit-hot Ali Lavau—you're a genius, and you made this novel shine. Thank you for your judicious advice, and above all for your care. I appreciate it so much.

To Christa Munns, Aziza Kuypers, Peri Wilson and my extended family at Allen & Unwin. Thank you to the immeasurably talented Lisa White. Thank you to Dan Grant. Thank you to Lee Tiger Halley.

To Wendy, as always.

To the generosity of Rachel Perkins, may our bickering never cease. Thank you for believing in me, and for making me a better storyteller.

A very special thank you to the incisive, forthright and formidably wise Charlie Murphy of Trans Action Warrang. To the illuminating, genuine, and dazzlingly talented Veronica Jean Jones. To the articulate and insightful Lauren Butcher. To the brilliant Lu Bradshaw. To the poised, determined and inspirational Alyce Schotte of TransFolk of WA.

Thank you to the totemic, towering Skye Scraper for leading me through the depths of drag. Thank you to the Queens of The Court.

And while I'm here, my deepest gratitude to every crew and cast member whose efforts brought my work to life on stage and screen. Thank you to every teacher who has introduced my writing to the classroom, every librarian and every bookseller who has been an advocate for my stories. To every reader who has given me the honour of their time. It is sincerely appreciated.

And lastly, to Renée Senogles, one of the most wonderful, vivacious, kind-hearted and adventurous people I ever had the privilege to call a friend.